PRAISE FOR
THE WOMAN WITH A PURPLE HEART

"*The Woman with a Purple Heart* is historical fiction at its finest! With its indomitable heroine and harrowing, real-life events, this story captured my heart and never let go. Vivid, nuanced, and inspiring, it's a book I'd recommend to all my friends—nurses and non-nurses alike!"

—Amanda Skenandore, author of *The Second Life of Mirielle West* and *The Nurse's Secret*

"*The Woman with a Purple Heart* vividly portrays a little-known story in a well-known time on a day that will live in infamy. The actions of Army nurse Annie Fox—the first woman to win the Purple Heart for her incredible courage and leadership following the attack at Pearl Harbor and Hickam Field—reveal the kind of staggering bravery that both captivates and inspires. A stirring read!"

—Erika Robuck, bestselling author of *The Invisible Woman*

"A wonderful tribute to a true American hero. Equal parts touching and heartbreaking, *The Woman with a Purple Heart* paints a vivid picture of what it was like at ground zero in the attack on Pearl Harbor. Historical fiction lovers, put this on your list!"

—Sara Ackerman, *USA Today* bestselling author of *Radar Girls* and *The Codebreaker's Secret*

"Fast-paced and immersive, *The Woman with a Purple Heart* captures the bravery and dedication of U.S. Army nurses in Oahu during World War II. Not only does this gripping story spotlight Annie Fox, a hero who's been overlooked for far too long, but it delves into Hawaii's complicated wartime racial and political dynamics. This is the kind of story that sticks with you long after turning the final page."

—Elise Hooper, author of *Angels of the Pacific*

"In *The Woman with a Purple Heart*, Diane Hanks brings to vivid life the story of the chief nurse of Hickam Hospital, Lieutenant Annie Fox, who responds to the call to serve her country without hesitation—until she's provoked on a profoundly personal level by the duplicity and injustices of politics and war. Immersive and intense with brilliant characterization, elegant and pacey writing, and riveting drama, Hanks takes us deep in the heart of Annie as she struggles to reconcile her professionalism, patriotism, and conscience. It's enthralling, poignant, and an absolute treat."

—Penny Haw, author of *The Invincible Miss Cust* and *The Woman at the Wheel*

"A complex and delicious morality tale. In *The Woman with a Purple Heart*, Diane Hanks walks with Army nurse Annie Fox through the fires and the fighting as she faces the reality of war at the tip of the spear. When the Japanese attack Pearl Harbor, Annie's challenges as chief nurse at Hickam Field go beyond the drama of duty and the shock of massive death. Annie's journey to the Purple Heart is one marked by courage, the drive to stand up to injustice, and the heartbreak of daily life and death decisions in war. We can't help but pull for her every step of the way."

—Mari K. Eder, Maj. Gen. (U.S. Army, Retired), author of *The Girls Who Stepped Out of Line*

"A meticulously researched, moving tale that will stay with readers long after they turn the final page. Based on the true story of Annie Fox, this novel recounts her incredible bravery and courage, and also depicts what life was like for Japanese Americans in the aftermath of the Pearl Harbor attack."

—Soraya M. Lane, Amazon Charts bestselling author
of *The Girls of Pearl Harbor* and *The London Girls*

"Annie Fox and her heroic Army nurses take center stage in Diane Hanks's *The Woman with a Purple Heart*. This bold, compelling, page-turner of a novel doesn't flinch from exploring both the courage of those caught in the attack on Pearl Harbor as well as the injustices that followed one of the most tragic moments in America's history."

—Alix Rickloff, author of *The Girls in Navy Blue*

THE WOMAN

— WITH A —

PURPLE HEART

Based on True Events

DIANE HANKS

Please be advised:

This story contains war-related themes, including violence and trauma, as well as racism and racial slurs that could trigger certain audiences.

Published by Sourcebooks Landmark, an imprint of Sourcebooks
P.O. Box 4410, Naperville, Illinois 60567-4410
(630) 961-3900
sourcebooks.com

Cataloging-in-Publication Data is on file with the Library of Congress.

Printed and bound in the United States of America.
LSC 10 9 8 7 6 5 4 3 2 1

For the nurses.
And the men and women who served at
Hickam Field on December 7, 1941.

As a member of the Pearl Harbor Survivors Association, I am often asked what ship I was on. When I reply that I wasn't on a ship but was stationed at Hickam Field, I am usually asked, "Where is Hickam Field?"... The Japanese certainly knew!

Former Master Sergeant Thomas J. Pillion
400th Signal Company, Hickam Field

ONE

November 3, 1941

After more than a year, First Lieutenant Annie Fox had grown used to the relatively high altitude at the John Hay Air Station in the Philippines. The mosquitos had also acclimated to the altitude, and she swatted several away as she strode past the U.S. Army Hospital and quickened her pace toward Lieutenant Colonel Horan's office, assuming he wanted to discuss the latest outbreak of malaria. A week ago, every hospital bed was occupied with a soldier stricken by the disease. Before the outbreak, Annie and the other nurses had done what they could; they'd handed out antimalarial pills and had given talks about how important it was to stick to the regimen they laid out. But telling healthy young men that a mosquito bite might cause more harm than an enemy combatant was something they'd shrugged off as well-meaning but useless advice. One young soldier had even compared Annie to his overprotective mother. Granted, at forty-eight, she was old enough to be his mother, but she still outranked him.

At the thought of that encounter, her adrenaline spiked. Just as well given that Annie was about to meet with the commander, whose disregard for her input on anything but how to rid himself of hemorrhoids was beyond irritating.

When she entered his office, he was sitting behind his polished desk. She'd told him he should try to stand as much as possible, but he'd ignored her advice in favor of sitting on a large pillow his wife had sewn for him. She'd even embroidered an eagle on the pillow with an oak leaf to signify his rank. Not that anyone could see the eagle or the leaf.

Annie saluted the commander and his pillow and stood before his desk, where he made her wait while he signed a few documents before saying, "At ease, Lieutenant."

"Thank you, sir. If you'd like me to report on the number of men still occupying beds, I'm afraid it's about the same. The course of malaria can be long."

"That's not why you're here."

"Nevertheless, it's something we should discuss. If Japan continues to expand into Indonesia, many of our troops won't be combat ready."

"My troops aren't your concern anymore. You're being transferred to Hickam Field."

Annie was stunned. "I didn't request a transfer." In fact, she'd never even mentioned a transfer. Nor had she ever complained, and as far as she knew, no one had complained about her. Not in twenty-three years of service.

"Sorry you weren't consulted," said Horan sarcastically, holding out the document he'd signed.

Annie didn't reach for it. "With all due respect, I didn't ask—"

"Would you prefer to finish your career at Walter Reed?"

"*Finish* my career?"

"Neither of us is getting any younger. Dismissed, Lieutenant."

He wasn't just dismissing her from his office. He was dismissing her entire adult life, which she'd dedicated to the U.S. Army.

Suddenly feeling as worn down as an old boot, Annie took her transfer papers, saluted, and left his office like a good soldier. It was all she knew how to be.

Boarding the Lockheed 12 Electra Junior—a six-passenger transport plane that would take Annie to her new duty station—she wondered if being a good soldier for the past few decades had earned her much more than a steady paycheck. Of course, that was one of the reasons she'd left Pubnico, Nova Scotia, to join the U.S. Army.

Having an abundance of natural beauty, Pubnico was unfortunately bereft of opportunities for young women outside marriage. Several young men had asked Annie's father for her hand—not because they were in love with her, but because there were so few women from whom to choose. And Annie was considered a good catch not only because she was pretty but because she was athletic and daring. She'd never turned down a challenge and could outrun and outswim any other girl in the province. She would have made an ideal farmer or fisherman's wife. But Annie wanted to be a doctor, like her father. Until World War I broke out.

Canada was part of the British Empire, so when Great Britain declared war on Germany in the summer of 1914, Canada was also officially at war. Annie had wanted to serve, but her father asked her to stay back. In return, he'd offered to have her accompany him on house calls. But she'd been doing that for years and wasn't tempted to stay, so he'd sweetened the pot by allowing her to perform some of the simpler procedures. Thus, Annie had agreed to give some of the young men in Pubnico an opportunity to impress.

By 1918, Annie had not found a man who impressed her enough to give up her freedom, and her father reluctantly let her go, resigned to the fact that his twenty-five-year-old daughter was an old maid. His only consolation had been knowing she had sufficient medical knowledge to make a difference. "You'll make a damn fine field nurse," he'd told her, thinking Annie would represent Canada well. She hadn't told him she wanted a bigger life, nor had she told him the confidence he'd instilled in her over her four-year apprenticeship had given her the courage she'd needed to make the bold move of joining the U.S. Army, after which she was transferred to the frontlines of the Great War. Annie hadn't wanted her father to blame himself if the worst happened.

Three days after she'd left the Philippines, Annie glanced around the transport plane that would take her from San Francisco, where she'd stopped at the Presidio Army Base to visit a few friends, to Hickam Field, which was on the island of Oahu, adjacent to Pearl Harbor. Annie gazed out the window and could just make out the island. It looked like an emerald on a sea of shimmering blue and nearly took her breath away.

"It's beautiful," she said.

"Say again, ma'am?"

She turned to the young man in the seat beside her. "I said, the island is beautiful."

"Yes, ma'am," he said, glancing at a young nurse sitting across the aisle. "We sure did get lucky."

Wishing she felt lucky, Annie gazed out the window at the sapphire waves, watching them change to turquoise before rushing over pristine pale-pink sand. The beaches stretched for miles, all the way to the immovable gray of battleships and destroyers that slumbered in Pearl Harbor. Practically next door was Hickam Field, where she could see the gray runways of the biggest Army airfield in the Hawaiian Islands—home to more than two hundred heavy bombers, mostly the Boeing B-17 Flying Fortress. Hickam was also home to nearly seven thousand enlisted men and almost eight hundred officers, all potential patients. And behind the flight line for the B-17s, she finally saw the red cross on the roof of her new duty station—Hickam Hospital.

TWO

November 5, 1941

The wood inside the women's barracks, located behind Hickam Hospital, was so new it still smelled freshly cut. Set in neat double rows were utilitarian bureaus, lockers, and half a dozen twin beds. However, only five women, all in their early twenties, sat on their respective beds, gossiping like girls at summer camp rather than Army nurses at a new duty station.

"I was so glad they transferred me to Hickam," said Sara Entrikin, strategically placing another bobby pin to hold a twist of dark hair near her temple.

"No kidding. Do you know the ratio of men to women is twenty to one?" asked Monica Conter in a subtle Southern drawl as she applied pale-pink polish to neatly trimmed fingernails.

"I wasn't referring to men," said Sara. "My twin sister, Helen, is a nurse at Pearl Harbor, so we're right next door to each other."

"You'll have to compare notes and see if the best-looking men are Navy or Army," Winnie Mallett added as she scanned articles listed on the cover of the November 1941 issue of *Woman* magazine: "Women Talk Too Much," "Diamonds on a Budget," and "The Sergeant's Wife Speaks Up." The others shouted "Army!" with enthusiastic loyalty.

"What difference does it really make when we're not allowed to marry?" asked Kathy Coberly, who was busy painting her toes. She'd searched for weeks before her transfer to Hickam to find the same crimson polish Rita Hayworth had worn in *Blood and Sand*.

"Well, we're allowed to have fun," said Monica. "When I got my transfer notice, my supervisor told me to pack three things—my uniform, a swimsuit, and my evening clothes."

"Waikiki is the best beach if you're looking for men. But if you want waves, Waimea Bay is the best spot." Irene Boyd had been on base the longest—two weeks—and had spent her time off scouting for places to surf.

"How long have you been surfing?" asked Sara.

"Since I was a kid," said Irene. "I'll teach you. If you're not going to have sex, you'll need something to do when you're off duty."

"Who said I'm not going to have sex?" asked Sara.

They all giggled until Kathy whispered, "Ten-hut!"

Annie entered, wearing her robe, as she'd just come from the shower. Grabbing a novel from her bureau, she laid it on her bed while she fluffed her pillows. The cover of *This Above All* depicted an air and sea battle set during the Battle of Dunkirk, and she was confident that the novel would help compensate for the island paradise. Not that there was anything wrong with paradise. She just wanted something to make her feel more…alive.

She got into bed and leaned back against her pillows. "I wouldn't mind learning to surf," she said from behind the book. A half smile on her lips, she waited for an invitation, but her nurses remained silent. Not a surprise. After all, she was their superior and twice their age. She could be their mentor, teacher, and mother but never their friend.

Wondering if she was the oldest woman on base, Annie wanted to pull the blanket up over her face. Instead, she focused on the opening chapter and tried to ignore the girl talk.

The next morning, Annie left the women's barracks, one of several that surrounded the large, grassy parade ground. Wearing her uniform— jacket, skirt, white shirt, black tie, and service cap—she walked down "Main Street," passing the post exchange, where she could buy anything from soda pop to soap powder, and the theatre, where a sign read "Coming Soon—*How Green Was My Valley*." A golden cross on the steeple of the chapel shimmered in the morning sun, and Annie crossed herself as she passed before pausing to watch children line up near the front door of the schoolhouse, where several military wives stood nearby waving goodbye. Feeling a twinge of regret over not having her own children, Annie purposefully strode toward her new hospital.

Hickam's hospital had just opened and was set next to headquarters and only three blocks from the flight line, where the bombers and other aircraft were parked and serviced. Built of reinforced concrete, the hospital was three stories high with wide screened porches on three sides. Being a small hospital, it only had forty beds. Seriously ill patients were often sent to the U.S. Army's Tripler General Hospital, which was nearly ten miles away but much larger.

On Hickam Hospital's porch, Annie stood and gazed toward Pearl Harbor, where U.S. Navy planes were practicing maneuvers over the Pacific. She thought being this close to the ocean might remind her of home, but the Atlantic was so different and always changing—from blue to gray, calm to stormy. In contrast, the Pacific appeared serene, as if it never lost its temper.

The first floor of the hospital was home to the administrative offices, while the second floor housed the operating theatre and clinic, with the patient ward on the third floor. The hospital also had an elevator for transporting patients, which Annie appreciated as she got off it to inspect the patient ward.

The hospital's iron-framed beds nearly shone against the white walls. Only two of the beds were occupied by young men who were stable and appeared to be asleep. Quietly checking the beds with mattresses to make sure the sheet corners were tight, she noted that fifteen beds were without mattresses, which would need to be rectified.

No doubt, Lieutenant Colonel Horan transferred her to Hickam Field because he'd considered her too old to handle a larger patient ward. Since he'd informed her of the transfer, she'd felt trapped between insult and self-doubt; seeing the small ward did nothing to help.

Moving on to the operating theatre on the second floor, Annie inspected the equipment. She checked for dust on the large lights suspended over the operating table, then ran a finger around the steel washbasin on a table that would hold surgical instruments. Putting an empty glass IV holder up to the light, she saw that it was crystal clear. On her way out, she examined the oxygen tanks standing at attention against the wall and smiled her approval.

After informing him about the missing mattresses, Annie stood at ease before her new superior, Major David Lance, who had been blessed with good looks. Over her lifetime, she'd known several men who'd let a handsome face take them as far as it could, whether ●be to a wife with a sizable fortune or an embassy post that required more charm than political expertise. In most instances, there was little behind the face but greed and ambition. She didn't think that would be the case with Major Lance, who seemed to have an intensity of purpose in his eyes as he folded his hands over the list of items she felt they needed.

"I'm aware that we don't have enough mattresses, Lieutenant Fox," he said.

"Not by nearly half, Major."

"We only have two patients."

"For now," she said, crossing her arms. "But what if we—"

"Get an outbreak of sunburn?"

Annie raised a brow. Maybe he was just another handsome face.

"I don't mean to be flippant," he said with an apology in his tone. "It's just that most of our men are young and healthy."

"I'd still like to request that my ward…our ward…"

"It's all right. You are chief nurse."

She returned his smile. "Your chief nurse respectfully requests fifteen new mattresses."

"Duly noted," he said. "Anything else?"

"New hospital. Healthy soldiers. Blue skies. Can't complain." Yet given the chance, she'd argue for a new posting.

"Paradise can take some getting used to. Take the afternoon off and try."

Annie nodded, seeing an understanding in his eyes that she could get lost in. "Thank you, sir." She saluted, more to remind herself of the chain of command, and left his office. Besides, she was too old to have a crush.

Annie stopped outside the nurses' quarters to take off her cap and unbutton her jacket when she heard voices from the main room.

"Who's coming?" asked Irene.

"I don't have a surfboard," moaned Winnie.

"You can rent one," said Irene.

"Then I'm in," said Winnie in a much cheerier tone.

"Me too," said Monica.

"Okay, grab your swimsuits," said Irene.

Annie nearly entered the room, ready to join them, when—

"What about the chief?" asked Monica.

Annie stood frozen.

"She did say she wanted to learn," said Irene.

"She's old enough to be my mother," said Winnie. "I'd never let her near a board. She'd…break something."

"I'll take responsibility for her," offered Monica.

"Then I can blame you for making me spend my day off with our boss," said Winnie.

"She probably has other things she'd rather do," said Irene. "My mother loves her knitting circle and bridge club."

"It's settled then," said Winnie. "We'll leave the chief to things that older women like to do."

Annie felt both anger and self-pity—two emotions she had little tolerance for in anyone, especially herself. She remained hidden until they left.

Strolling down a street in Honolulu, Annie wore a civilian dress that made her look as soft as the hair that brushed her shoulders. She could pass for a housewife out window-shopping, which was what she was trying to do. Nearly every woman she'd ever known liked to window-shop.

Walking past several shops, her eyes settled on three cocktail dresses in a store window. The red dress had too many sequins and the blue one too much lace. But the black one had just the right mix of modesty and sexiness. She tried to imagine herself wearing the black dress and dancing with Major Lance at the officer's club but couldn't quite get there.

Feeling as if she lacked some essential feminine attribute necessary for romantic daydreams, she was walking away from the store with the perfect black dress when another sign caught her eye: Nurses Wanted.

Entering the Japanese American Community Center, Annie saw that a meeting was taking place. She quickly made her way to the back of the room, sitting in a chair at one of the only empty tables. Most tables were filled with Japanese American women between the ages of twenty and seventy. In doing her homework before coming to the island, Annie had learned that more than one-third of the population of Oahu was Japanese.

Annie turned her attention to the woman who stood on a small stage that was unadorned except for an American flag. Introducing herself as Kay Kimura—the nurse who ran the center—she appeared to be in her midthirties and was very poised. Like she was used to speaking in front of a crowd or was simply comfortable in this particular setting.

"I realize there's growing fear in our community," said Kay. "But there's growing fear everywhere as Germany and Japan become more aggressive."

"Japan is not the same as Germany!" said an older Japanese gentleman whose wife pulled him back into his chair.

Ignoring the outburst, Kay continued calmly. "Because our country may go to war with Japan, some people will see us as—"

"Aliens! That's what they call us. That and worse!" The older man remained seated, looking at his wife as if daring her to disagree. She did not.

A tall Hawaiian man in his late thirties stood and faced the audience. "My name is Makani Hale. Many of you call me Mak and know I'm a nurse and a liaison between your people and mine, so this might not be the first time you've heard me say that everyone on this island who isn't a descendant of Wākea, our Sky Father, or Papahānaumoku, our Earth Mother, is an alien. Including the Chinese, Filipinos, and the American military."

The room seemed to grumble at the mention of the American military, and Annie straightened like she'd put her uniform back on.

"Oahu is a U.S. territory," said Kay. "They have the right to—"

The older Japanese man stood. "Turn the island into a military base?!"

"I understand your frustration, Mr. Taketa," said Kay, "but the military is here to stay, so we must learn to live together."

Mr. Taketa remained standing.

Looking past his frown, Kay said, "I think we would all feel better if we just accept—"

"American rules and regulations?" asked Mak.

Annie could no longer stay silent and stood. "They are in place for a reason."

Everyone turned to her, most appearing surprised at her presence if not dismayed.

"Have you ever considered the fact that having such a large military presence here keeps everyone safe?" said Annie.

"From everyone but them," said Mak.

Annie looked around the room and saw nearly everyone nodding in agreement. But not Kay, who appeared conflicted and concerned.

Nearly two hours later, as Annie helped gather paper cups from the tables, she saw Kay say goodbye to Mr. Taketa, who took a small white envelope from his jacket pocket and gave it to her. She kissed him on the cheek and slipped the envelope into the pocket of her dress as she closed the door behind the older couple.

Annie placed the paper cups in the trash and approached Kay. "Mrs. Kimura…"

Startled, Kay turned to her. "Thank you for helping, Mrs.…?"

"Miss Fox," said Annie. "And you don't need to thank me. I stayed because I'd like to talk to you about volunteering." She pointed to the Nurses Wanted sign in the window.

Annie stood at relaxed attention while Major Lance studied her from the chair behind his desk as if she were an interesting specimen under a microscope. "Why do you want a second job? And why did you tell her you worked at the civilian hospital?" He gestured to the chair next to her like he was sure it would take a while to explain.

Sitting, Annie wondered if she should be truthful. She had never lied to a superior, but telling him she was already bored with his small hospital might not be wise. "I want to help at the center because I think we should try to improve our relations with the community. During their meeting, it became very clear that they resent our presence on the island. Not just the Japanese but the native islanders as well."

"So we're the enemy," he said. "That's why you told them you work at Queen's Hospital?"

"Yes, sir." Queen's Hospital was the largest civilian hospital on the island.

"Okay," he said after a moment. "You can try working at the community center on a trial basis, for the sake of building better relations with the civilian population. But if it interferes with your duties here, it ends."

"Understood, sir. One more thing?"

He nodded permission.

"I was invited to a tea ceremony on Tuesday. I shouldn't be gone long, and I'll meet more people than I would during several house calls."

"Fine," said Major Lance. "But keep me informed, and I'm not just talking about an outbreak of measles."

Annie knew, as everyone did, that the relationship between the United States and Japan was on shaky ground. If things fell apart, many wondered which country the Japanese American community would support. "Is insurrection an actual concern?"

"We can't rule it out," he said. "But if you're not comfortable with…"

She could see he was having trouble finding the right words. "Spying on my patients?"

"You are an Army nurse, Lieutenant. However, if you're not up for it, I'll understand."

Annie had been through a world war and knew intelligence could make the difference between winning and losing. She'd just never envied those who'd had to do it; there was too much deceit involved. "I'll report anything of importance." Standing, she saluted, certain that helping the people she'd met at the center would lead to nothing she'd need to share.

THREE

November 12, 1941

At the tea ceremony, back in civilian clothes, Annie kept her ears open to the gossip, at least what was in English, as she made her way to the kitchen where Kay, wearing a kimono, was arranging sweet buns and dumplings on silver trays.

"Sweets before tea?" asked Annie.

"It's tradition," said Kay.

"I take it having someone like me as a guest isn't traditional?" She glanced into the main room where women at several nearby tables eyed her with a mix of suspicion and curiosity.

"Not yet." Kay took one of the trays, Annie following with extra napkins, and set it down at the table where Mrs. Taketa sat. "How is Mr. Taketa?"

"Opinionated and stubborn," said Mrs. Taketa.

"Then nothing out of the ordinary." Kay bent down to give her a hug, slipping a small envelope into the older woman's open purse. Mrs. Taketa had been ready.

Pulling her eyes away from the transaction, Annie went back to the kitchen to answer the phone. "Community Center. May I help you?" She listened as Kay returned and then held the receiver out to her. "For you."

Kay took the phone. "Nurse Kimura speaking. How may I—" As she listened, her eyes went to her medical bag, sitting on a nearby shelf. "I'll leave right away, Chie." She hung up the phone and turned to Annie. "Can you start a little sooner than we'd planned?"

"Of course."

"Good. I'll go to the ladies' room and change, and we'll be on our way. While I do that, could you ask Amai to take over the tea ceremony?" She pointed to a young nurse who'd just sat at the table with Mrs. Taketa.

"Will do," said Annie, catching her military-speak. "I'm happy to ask. It'll give me a chance to introduce myself."

Smile in place, Annie walked toward Amai, who looked at her like Mak did—with eyes full of wariness. "Amai?" said Annie, holding out her hand. "My name is Annie Fox."

"Pleased to meet you, Mrs. Fox," said Amai.

"Miss Fox," said Annie, who was used to people assuming she was married at her age. "Kay asked me to let you know that she has to make an urgent house call, and she'd like you to take over hosting the tea ceremony. I'd help, but she asked me to go with her." Annie thought she noted some relief cross over Amai's face.

"Thank you for letting me know, Miss Fox."

"Please, call me Annie."

"I should get back to our guests," said Amai, with a barely there smile.

Annie was sure that she would need to win over both Mak and Amai, if that was possible. However, gaining Kay's trust would go a long way with them.

Kay led Annie into her first-floor apartment, leaving her shoes next to a few pairs already neatly lined against the wall. As she watched Annie do the same, Kay thought about the fact that she'd never had a white person in her home before. It hadn't been intentional; she'd just never had the opportunity, which was just as well, at least while her husband had been living there. She'd come to learn that he believed other races were inferior and could imagine his expression if he were watching Annie enter his domain.

Pushing her husband out of her thoughts, Kay saw Annie glance at the small Buddhist altar on the wooden table. She assumed there weren't many white people with an understanding of the Buddha's teachings, but Annie's expression reflected more curiosity than judgment before her attention turned to the pregnant woman on Kay's couch, her hands running soothing circles over her belly.

"I'm sorry, Kay," said the young woman, pointing to another room. "My water broke in the bathroom. I was going to clean it up but—" A pain-filled moan escaped.

Kay took her hand. "Squeeze. I won't break." As the woman squeezed, Kay made introductions. "Chie, this is Nurse Annie Fox. She's helping out at the community center. Annie, Chie Ikeda is one of my neighbors. She watches my children after school on the days I'm going to be late. Don't know what I'd do without her."

"Rely on your mother?" Chie said, looking at Kay with exaggerated horror.

Normally, Kay would have laughed, because her mother was never her first choice as babysitter. Not because she wasn't more than capable of taking care of her grandchildren; there was no one Kay trusted more. The only reason Kay didn't like leaving her mother with the children was because of her penchant for snooping. Her mother believed it made no difference that her daughter was a grown woman with children of her own; she still had every right to know everything that was going on in Kay's life, just as she did when Kay was a child. If that meant searching through drawers and reading Kay's mail, then so be it. This was the main reason Kay had never kept a diary when she was a girl. Even if locked, her mother would've found a way in. And now Kay had even more secrets to hide.

"Happy to meet you, Mrs. Ikeda," said Annie.

Chie smiled but kept her eyes on Kay. "Do you think the baby's turned?"

"Only one way to find out, but I need to wash before I examine you." Kay waited until the contraction passed, watching for Chie to relax. Every woman was different. Some would moan with every contraction, starting off low, coming to a crescendo, and fading to a whisper in relief as it passed. But with some, it was all about the breath. She watched Chie's chest rise with a deep breath and then hold as she waited for the contraction to pass. She would need to remind her patient to breathe on the way to the hospital. "We'll be right back, Chie. In the meantime, try to relax with a few deep, slow breaths."

In the bathroom, Kay washed her hands while Annie took a towel from the rack and placed it over a small pool of amniotic fluid on the floor.

"You're a midwife too?" asked Annie.

Kay thought she heard a little envy in Annie's voice, which was normal. Most nurses who weren't also midwives thought delivering babies was the best thing about being a nurse. And Kay could say that nothing compared to handing a mother her healthy newborn. There was also nothing that compared to telling a mother her child was stillborn or would die soon because of a tragic birth defect. Having to tell Chie such a thing was unthinkable. "I examined Chie two days ago, and the baby hadn't turned. If that's still the case, I'll need to take her to the hospital. She and her husband can't afford an ambulance."

"Is there anything I can do?"

Kay hesitated. If her mother ever learned that a woman Kay barely knew had watched over her grandchildren, she would never speak to Kay again. But if Chie had a difficult time, Kay could be at the hospital for hours, giving her mother plenty of time to find what Kay should have destroyed by now. "My kids will be home from school soon. How do you feel about babysitting?"

"Whenever my father had to take a patient to the hospital, I'd care for the children in the household if there was no one else," Annie replied. "Between that and babysitting my younger siblings, I've had plenty of experience. I'm fine with staying until your husband gets home."

"My husband is away," said Kay, relieved to hear Chie moan with another contraction so she didn't need to say more.

Having cleaned up the amniotic fluid and deposited the towel in the hamper, Annie turned to see a boy and a girl, young enough to fit side by side in the bathroom doorway.

"Who are you?" asked the boy, who was nearly as tall as his sister but looked younger.

"That's rude, Tommy," said the girl.

"In your brother's defense, I am a stranger standing in your bathroom. Let's fix that." Smiling, Annie extended her hand to Tommy. "My name is Annie Fox."

"Fox like the animal?" Hesitating, Tommy shook her hand.

"Yes, like the animal."

"Where's Mrs. Ikeda?" asked the girl, taking her brother's other hand like she was ready to run should Annie's answer give her cause for concern.

"Her baby was coming feetfirst, so your mom gave her a ride to the hospital so they can help turn the baby around before she delivers." She could tell Kay's daughter appreciated the details of Chie's condition. "I was with your mom, so she asked me to stay with you until she gets back."

"When will she be home?" asked the girl.

"It might take a few hours if she stays until Mrs. Ikeda gives birth. But she didn't say whether she planned to stay for sure."

Tommy turned to his sister. "You need to clean my back before Mom gets home."

Sighing, the girl extended her hand to Annie. "I'm Beth. I'm nine. Tommy has something on his back that we need to get off. Can you help us?"

Annie took Beth's hand. "Pleased to meet you, Beth. And it's good to know you're old enough to assist me while I take care of whatever's on your brother's back."

A few minutes later, Tommy placed the Captain America comic

book he held on top of the hamper with care and stood with his back to Annie, who sat on the edge of the tub.

"Are you sure this will work?" asked Beth, handing her a bottle of baby oil.

"I think so." Annie took the bottle. "Do you have cotton balls?"

Beth stood on tiptoes to reach back into the medicine cabinet. Taking down a glass jar of cotton balls, she took out a few and brought them to Annie.

"Thank you, Beth. You're a big help."

"She is not," said Tommy. "This was her fault in the first place."

"He's only six," said Beth. "He doesn't know anything."

"I do too!"

"Tell me what happened, Tommy," suggested Annie as she began to gently rub his back with baby oil.

"They took Beth's jump rope. The one Dad made. It has special red, white, and blue handles. Like Captain America's shield." Tommy pointed to the cover of his comic book. "That's why Bobby took it."

"Bobby Larkin took it for his sister," interjected Beth. "She wanted to trade paper dolls for my jump rope, but I said no."

"I would've said no too. Never liked dolls as much as jump rope." Annie threw the used cotton ball into a nearby trash basket and soaked a new one with baby oil.

"When Bobby took the jump rope, Beth cried," said Tommy.

"Maybe a little. But I didn't ask you to fight him."

"Same thing," he said.

Beth rolled her eyes but didn't disagree.

"Bobby's friends held me down, and he drew something on my back, and they all laughed. But Beth won't tell me what it is."

"Because it's just a big blob. You squirmed and foiled their plan." Beth looked plaintively at Annie.

"Your sister's right, Tommy," said Annie, realizing Beth was struggling to keep the hurt inside so her brother wouldn't see it. "You foiled their plan. Just like Captain America does with the bad guys." She saw Tommy grin and went back to work, tenderly wiping away the word *JAP* until it resembled nothing but a faded bruise.

It was late by the time Annie returned to the women's barracks, and the first thing she did, as always, was check on her nurses. All slept under a sheet and a sheen of sweat, except for one whose cover was pulled all the way up. Knowing what she'd find, Annie lifted one foot and kicked what should have been Winnie Mallett's behind. Instead, a pillow fell off the other side of the bed.

Annie parked herself on the back stoop of the barracks, where she would have come in if she were Winnie. Yawning, she checked her watch and tried to remember the last time she'd pulled such a stunt. Fort Mason in San Francisco? No. It had been when she was stationed at Fort Sam Houston in San Antonio. She's still been in her twenties. It seemed like yesterday and a million years ago at the same time. She was trying to remember the name of the young man who'd kept her out past curfew when she heard the click of heels.

Peering into the darkness, Annie saw a frozen shadow about a yard away. "Come forward, Mallett."

Winnie stepped out of the darkness and into the dim light over the back door. She smoothed her hair and stood up straight. "I was just—"

"Whatever you're about to say, the truth will be easier for both of us."

Winnie took a deep breath. "I was with a man."

"Army or Navy?"

"Army pilot. B-17 Flying Fortress," Winnie responded with pride.

"Good for you," said Annie without sarcasm. "Just make sure Flyboy's worth what you'll lose if you have to marry him. Speaking of which, please tell me he used a condom."

A blush spread across Winnie's cheeks as she took herself out of the glaring light and sat on the stoop near Annie. "I'm not sure. It was all kind of…fast."

"Doesn't sound worth the risk."

Winnie appeared unsure as to whether she should argue the point.

"If you stay out with Flyboy after curfew again, you'll be on bedpan duty for a month."

"Yes, ma'am."

"And let me know when you get your period."

"Yes, ma'am."

Opening the door to go inside, Annie glanced back at the anxiety in Winnie's face with empathy. Like every woman on a military base where there were twenty men for every one woman, Winnie would have to learn to take care of herself when it came to the opposite sex.

The exam room was pristine but also spare. Annie thought clutter led to distraction from patient care, which she wouldn't allow. Therefore, exam rooms contained only what was essential: one cabinet for supplies, one stool, one chair, and one exam table.

Corporal Jeremy Tig, who'd been next to Annie on the transport plane to Oahu, sat on the exam table as she studied a large bruise. The contusion spread from his back to his left side like a flower blooming just under his skin.

"How did you get this, Corporal?"

Silence.

"Whatever you tell me is confidential, just as it would be if you were speaking to a doctor. Unless you got this during a bank robbery, in which case I'd have to report you."

"No, ma'am. I didn't rob a bank." Jeremy managed a crooked smile.

"Then how did it happen? I need to know if it was a fist or a blunt instrument."

"Me and my friends were in a bar, and we got into a disagreement with some Japs."

"Rephrase, Corporal," said Annie sharply.

"We got into a fight."

"Fist or blunt instrument?" she asked again.

"It was a hand that felt like a blunt instrument." He held his hand out straight, awkwardly mimicking a sideways motion. "Couldn't hardly breathe after that, which didn't exactly make for a fair fight. They have some sneaky moves."

"I suppose your opponent would have called it clever rather than underhanded. No pun intended, Corporal."

"He wasn't clever enough to avoid my right hook. Got a couple in before he pulled that goddamn magic trick. Pardon my language, ma'am."

"Until you figure out the magic in the trick, I suggest you stay away from that particular bar," she said, gently probing the skin surrounding the bruise to check for swelling.

A knock and Kathy entered. "Major Lance would like to see you, Chief. Stat."

Annie took an elastic bandage out of a drawer. "Please finish checking for any swelling before you wrap him up, Nurse Coberly." She handed the bandage to Kathy and turned to Jeremy. "Keep yourself safe, Corporal. Your body needs time to heal."

"Yes, ma'am," said Jeremy, his attention focused solely on the young nurse.

Annie had always appreciated the fact that both of the surgeons sitting across from Dr. Lance—Captains Carl Metcalfe and Dennis Doyle—exuded self-confidence and a certain detachment. Dr. Doyle, the younger of the two, also had a healthy dose of cocky, but Annie had never seen him make a bad decision regarding a patient because of it. On the other hand, Dr. Metcalfe tended to play it too safe. Once he made a cut, he was myopic about his surgical mission. Last week, Annie had assisted him during an appendectomy. The patient was a fifty-year-old plane mechanic and otherwise healthy. Once Dr. Metcalfe removed the appendix, Annie had spotted a growth the size of a grape in the patient's small intestine. She'd pointed it out and assumed he would excise it or at least take a biopsy. He'd done neither. And now the mechanic was waiting to heal only to be cut open again to find out if he had cancer. Waiting had been to no one's benefit except Dr. Metcalfe's, because the major had more experience with abdominal surgery and would perform the excision. If the patient died, it would be listed under his mortality count. Annie assumed this was why she'd been summoned but didn't know why Dr. Doyle was there.

Closing the door behind her, she saw that both captains appeared unpleasantly surprised by her presence. The major noticed it too. "I said senior staff would be read in," he said, moving a chair from the opposite wall closer to his desk, where he motioned Annie to sit.

Ignoring her, Dr. Doyle addressed only the men. "Opinions are split, as far as I can tell."

"I agree," said Dr. Metcalfe. "One day, I hear rumors about Japan attacking the Panama Canal, and the next day, it's Singapore. I'm not sure we can take any of it too seriously."

"What I take seriously is the fact that our diplomatic relationship with Japan isn't getting any better," said Major Lance.

"You think they'll attack?" asked Annie.

"I think the alert level might be raised. Sooner rather than later."

"So we should prepare for an attack?" she asked calmly.

"Don't worry, Annie," said Dr. Doyle, his voice dripping with condescension. "There's no country on earth that would dare attack our Pacific Fleet, including Japan."

Dr. Metcalfe spoke up with serious self-importance. "I played golf with General Short yesterday, and his main concern is sabotage from the Japanese who already live on the island."

"Sabotage?" said Annie.

"There's no need to speculate until we receive further information. I just want you to be ready when...*if* our alert status changes. I'll keep you informed of any updates," said Major Lance. "Dismissed."

Dr. Metcalfe started out of the office. Right behind him, Dr. Doyle asked, "I heard General Short's handicap is eight. Is that true?"

Annie waited until they were gone before speaking as if it pained her to say the words. "I have to agree with Dr. Doyle. Japan wouldn't attack us here. It would be suicide."

"You're probably right," Major Lance said unconvincingly.

"If we're attacked, we only have fifteen beds with mattresses. Is there any way to speed up the request process?"

"I'll see what I can do," he said. "Tell me how it's going at the community center."

"Are you wondering if I've heard anyone plotting to invade Pearl Harbor?" she asked with a half smile. "Besides, I'm sure we have experienced spies on the ground. I don't have any training in collecting intelligence."

"You don't have to be Mata Hari. Just pay attention to what people do and say, and report back to me if there's anything you think I should know. If everyone at the community center is on the up-and-up, then nothing lost, nothing gained."

"Okay," she said. "I'll keep you posted."

"Thank you, Lieutenant."

"Yes, sir," said Annie, like she'd said it a thousand times before to countless superior officers over her career. But never with such a sick feeling in her stomach.

FOUR

November 15, 1941

Annie stood in the kitchen at the community center, arms folded in frustration. "I really don't think Mak will ever warm up to me. Or any other American."

"Oh, I don't know," said Kay, pouring them both a cup of coffee. "He seems to have warmed up to me. Lukewarm most days, but still."

"I'm sorry. I didn't mean…"

Kay held out one of the cups. "It's all right, Annie."

"No, it's not," said Annie, taking the cup. "I know you're as American as anyone else who was born here. I'm just not used to…" She wanted to say that she wasn't used to thinking outside her military family. But she had to keep that secret. "Being around Japanese Americans. My fault, not yours."

"Agreed. Whatever happened, it's your fault, Annie." Mak entered the kitchen with a box of *malasadas*—or, as Annie called them, Hawaiian doughnuts—and set them on the counter.

The kitchen had a stove and refrigerator and lots of counter space.

The counters were neatly stacked with items that included evaporated milk to make baby formula, petroleum jelly—used to treat everything from diaper rash to burns—and cigarettes. The last was Mak's idea. If someone ran out of cigarettes or the money to buy them and came into the community center for a pack, Mak or Kay might be able to talk them into having their blood pressure taken.

Mak checked his watch as he poured himself a cup of coffee. "New mothers will be here in fifteen."

"What can I do to help?" asked Annie. "I've never been a mother, but I know the basics of caring for a newborn."

"What I really need is someone to help Mak with any walk-ins this morning," said Kay, "and you can answer the phone until one of the other nurses comes in."

"What if the person calling only speaks Japanese?"

"Holler for me," said Mak. "I know enough to get by."

"Okay, thanks," said Annie, attempting a smile as she tried to recall the last time the most important part of her job was answering the telephone. She really was getting old.

An hour later, Kay was telling the young mothers how to take care of diaper rash as Annie listened from the kitchen, waiting for the phone to ring. Maybe she should retire and apply for a job as a telephone operator. No one would see her, so no one would know her age. She could work until she had white hair and walked with a cane.

The phone rang, and Annie tested out her operator's voice. "You've reached the Japanese American Community Center. This is Nurse Fox. How may I help you?" Annie listened to the woman and knew by her tone that there was an emergency somewhere. But the words were Japanese, and she couldn't tell where one word ended and another began. "Hold on, please," she said, hoping the woman understood, and rushed to get Mak.

Annie sat shotgun as Mak drove Kay's car past what seemed like endless acres of sugarcane—tall, woody green stalks that barely moved with the breeze. When Mak said they needed to make a house call at a plantation, she'd assumed that a worker had had some kind of accident or that someone had fallen victim to heat exhaustion. She had not expected they would be tending to the manager of the plantation. For what, she had no idea. Mak wasn't able to get the woman on the other end of the phone to calm down long enough to find out.

"Do you know the person who's taken ill?" Annie asked. Mak had barely said a word since they'd left the center, and she was beginning to take it personally.

"I know enough," he said. "A while back, Japanese organizers brought together the Filipino, Chinese, Spanish, and Portuguese workers. They wanted higher wages and safer conditions, so they formed the Hawaii Laborers' Association."

"A union?"

"That was the plan. But when Billy Lardner found out his workers joined the union, he fired every last one of them."

"Isn't that against the law? You can't be fired for joining a union."

"Not now, but in 1920, you could be. And that was what he did. Billy fired everybody who worked at the plantation first thing Monday morning. And by that afternoon, he'd replaced every last one of us with men who'd never join a union."

"Us?" asked Annie.

"I was fourteen years old. It was my first job. Billy Lardner was a real son of a bitch, but there wasn't anybody on the island who didn't respect you if you'd managed to work for him for more than a week. I'd worked under his thumb for seven months. I had no trouble getting a job at another plantation."

"It must have been incredibly hard work for a child," said Annie. Mak shrugged and turned off the main road.

The dirt road they followed finally led them to the manager's quarters—a well-kept white bungalow with a long porch where a young Japanese woman paced. As soon as she heard the car, she flew down the porch steps shouting, "*Tasukete! Tasukete!*"

"That means help me," said Mak, parking the car close to the house. "'*Tasukete*' was the first Japanese word I learned. Make it yours too."

Annie grabbed her own medical bag and opened her door. Being on a plantation, she was glad she'd dressed in comfortable slacks and loafers like her favorite movie star, Katharine Hepburn. The young woman on the porch looked back and forth between the slacks and Annie's face as if trying to discern her gender before directing them inside the plantation manager's home.

Billy Lardner was half sitting and half lying on a well-worn leather couch, his hand reaching for a whiskey bottle on a side table.

"That won't help unless you've got an open wound." Mak grabbed the bottle and put it out of reach. "And I don't see one you need sterilized."

"Asshole," said Billy, pushing his graying hair out of his face. He wore work clothes. The cowboy hat, stained with what appeared to be months if not years of sweat, lay on the floor nearby as though it had fallen off as he fell onto the couch.

"Can you tell me what happened, Mr. Lardner?" Mak sat on the leather chair across from him.

"My maid called you against my wishes is what happened," Billy said, trying to sit up. "That goddamned center was the only place she knew how to call."

"Why did she feel the need to call for help?" asked Annie. "Are you in pain?"

"Who the hell are you?" asked Billy.

"My name is Annie Fox. I'm a nurse." She came forward and held out her hand. Over her career, she'd found that people responded to touch. If you could shake their hand with warmth and just the right amount of authority—firm enough to let them know you're confident without being overpowering—they usually felt more at ease.

"Billy Lardner," he said, squeezing her hand hard enough to let her know he still had a good amount of strength. "I run this planation."

"Did you have some kind of accident while you were working?" she asked. "Or did you suddenly feel ill?"

Billy looked past her at Mak. "You can leave."

Mak looked at Annie, who said, "I'll call for you if I need help."

"You'll do no such thing," said Billy. "I don't allow them in my home."

"But we can work the plantation," said Mak.

"You won't see your kind on this plantation. I learned my lesson. You people don't know the meaning of hard work. Now get the hell out of my—"

"It's not your house, Mr. Lardner. Never will be. It belongs to the plantation, just like you do." Mak looked at Annie and gestured to the maid. "Send her if you need me."

By the color rising in her patient's face, she thought that might be soon. "Mr. Lardner," she said calmly, setting her medical bag on the coffee table, "please tell me what happened."

"Nothing." He glanced at the whiskey bottle again. "I was out riding—checking on the workers, like usual. You need to let them see you. Otherwise, they'll take advantage."

Annie had seen a horse tied up near the porch, a shotgun still in the saddle scabbard. "How did you feel when you were checking on your workers?"

"Same as always. Annoyed. A few of 'em are still too"—he glanced at her slacks and apparently assumed it was okay to continue— "fucking slow."

"May I take your pulse?" asked Annie.

Hesitating, he nodded.

"Thank you," she said, taking his wrist. "Then what happened?"

"I kept riding, trying to figure out where we'd give up the land."

She felt his pulse quicken. "Give up the land?"

"They're expecting a war. They want us to set aside land to plant vegetables. They asked seventeen plantations to sacrifice acres of rich soil because they think this country's going to run out of food." He rolled his eyes at the ludicrous thought. "They want us to give up three hundred and fifteen fucking acres!"

His pulse raced. Annie needed to calm him down quickly, and there was only one way other than giving him an injection of pentobarbital, which she suspected he'd protest. She poured him a finger's width of whiskey, handing it to him with a smile. He drank, and as she'd hoped, his pulse began to slow, if only temporarily.

"Do you feel any pain in your chest?"

He shook his head, eyeing the bottle of whiskey for more.

"How about your arms?"

"Left arm. From here to here." He ran a finger from under his collarbone to the tip of his index finger. "And I had a little trouble catching my breath."

Annie sat in the chair next to him. "Mr. Lardner, I believe you've suffered a heart attack."

He laughed. "I'm as healthy as my fucking horse. Always have been."

"You're also sixty-two years old." It was a guess, but she'd been guessing men's ages for almost a quarter century. Many soldiers she'd tended to in the Great War were unconscious when she first made their acquaintance.

"Sixty-one," corrected Billy, obviously insulted.

"You still need to be examined by a doctor."

"I'm not going to the hospital." Sitting up as if suddenly better, he poured himself another drink.

"That's your choice, Mr. Lardner." Annie knew it was time to implement her chief nurse demeanor. "But you should let your boss know. That way, if you don't come back from the field, where I suspect you'll certainly die, he can send someone to find your body. You might also want to let him know which acres you think he should give up. Unless you don't mind someone else making that decision."

"Fine," he spat out between gritted teeth. "I'll drive myself to Queen's."

"You may not drive yourself, Mr. Lardner. If you have another heart attack, you could get into an accident. Hurting yourself is your decision to make, but I can't allow you to hurt someone else. We'll take you."

"I won't get in a car with you and that—"

"If you have your own car, I can drive you to the hospital."

"You drive?" he asked suspiciously.

"Since I was old enough to reach the pedals."

Billy Lardner almost smiled.

Annie's demeanor was rarely grim when her patient was still alive and talking, but Mak had insisted on following them to Queen's Hospital. And if he followed them inside, he might find out she didn't work there.

Parking near the ambulance entrance, Annie got out of the car and went around to help her patient, but he was already out and on his way inside. She started to follow, hoping Mak would let her take the lead and wait outside.

Annie caught up with her patient and walked with him into the waiting room, which, thankfully, was nearly empty. "Have a seat and rest, Mr. Lardner. I'll go speak with a nurse."

Annie approached the nurses' station, where the nurse on duty lifted her head with a cool professionalism. "There are a few people ahead of you. If you'll take a seat with your husband." She glanced at Billy. "I'll take your information soon."

"I'm not his wife. I'm his nurse," said Annie. "I was making a house call, and I think Mr. Lardner may have had a heart attack."

"Symptoms?"

"Pain radiating down his left arm, shortness of breath, and tachycardia."

"Let's get him into an exam room." The nurse came out from behind the long desk and started for a wheelchair.

"I doubt he'll get into that." Annie had known too many soldiers who'd refused a wheelchair unless ordered, and she didn't outrank Billy Lardner.

"We'll see," said the nurse, taking the wheelchair with her.

Annie walked behind the nurse and the wheelchair toward Billy.

"I can walk, for Christ's sake!" said Billy, glaring first at the wheelchair.

"It's hospital policy, Mr. Lardner," said the nurse.

"Which is just one reason why I've never been here before."

"I understand if you're afraid," said Annie. "I had my tonsils out when I was seven, and I remember being terrified." In fact, she'd wanted to stay awake and watch. "Would it help if I held your hand?"

"I'm not a child!" Billy swatted her away.

"Then quit acting like one," said Annie. "Cooperate and stop wasting everyone's time, or call a taxi to take you back to the plantation."

Like a petulant child, Billy got into the wheelchair, folded his arms across his chest with a pout, and let the nurse wheel him toward an examination room.

With a sigh of relief, Annie started toward the exit, only to meet Mak on his way inside.

"Sorry you had to come back to the hospital on your day off," said Mak. "But would you mind giving me a tour? I'd love to see an operating room if there's an empty one. Not that I wouldn't appreciate observing a surgery."

"Do you mind taking a rain check? I've got a migraine coming. Too much time with Mr. Lardner, I think." Annie saw his disappointment and added, "I'll see if I can get you a ringside seat on a surgery soon. Brain or belly?"

"Brain," he said without hesitation.

"Good choice." Annie returned his smile as they left the hospital. Neurosurgery wasn't common. She could put him off for several weeks. By then, she'd be able to tell him and Kay who she really was, because Annie had confidence that the United States would soon learn the new steps in her diplomatic dance with Japan.

FIVE

November 17, 1941

It was another gorgeous day in paradise, and Annie and Major Lance were having their daily update outside. They'd met on the parade grounds and had walked along Hangar Avenue, which started at Hickam's main entrance and ended at the huge Hawaii Air Depot building that housed the volunteer corps, a civilian paramilitary unit whose personnel helped with routine operations at the airfield, including repairs and maintenance.

Just beyond Hangar Avenue was the pride of Hickam Field—the newly finished and completely modern barracks for enlisted men, which had cost more than a million dollars to build. No more tent city that had been erected near the hangar line. Now the enlisted men lived in a multi-wing, three-story, concrete building with a hub that boasted barber and tailor shops and a mess hall that could feed three thousand soldiers, many of whom flew or fixed the heavy bombers Hickam Field was built to accommodate.

The Boeing B-17 Flying Fortress—a four-engine heavy bomber—was the gem in Hickam's fleet, in addition to the twenty-one B-17Ds that had arrived in May. The Fourth Recon Squadron of the Fifth Bombardment Group that occupied the new barracks were all anxious for their first mission. Annie had heard the men talking about it when she went to their mess hall to compare their breakfast to the one served in Hickam Hospital's much smaller dining hall. The breakfast at the new facility won hands down, and she had vowed to start her day there more often.

"How soon is soon?" asked Annie.

"Your guess is as good as mine," said Major Lance. "The request for fifteen mattresses has been filed. Now we wait. You know how it goes."

"Maybe I should go buy fifteen sleeping bags just in case." She was only half kidding.

"Your last commander didn't tell me about your sparkling sense of humor, Lieutenant."

"Sorry. I just don't like being unprepared."

"Neither do I," he said.

"Are we prepared?" she asked, hearing the rumble of a B-17 as it taxied down one of the runways in the distance.

"To be honest, I'm not sure."

"Do you think war with Japan is inevitable?"

"What I think doesn't matter. I have as much control over the situation as you do. Let's just be grateful we only have…how many patients?"

"Two. One recovering from pneumonia and the other from hernia repair, both improving." Annie tried to sound pleased rather than bored.

"Have you heard anything of interest at the community center?" he asked, shielding his eyes to watch a B-18 bomber take off for a practice run.

"No, sir," said Annie. "We don't discuss much beyond the patients."

"You need to be in a more relaxed setting to loosen their tongues."

Annie had often wondered what Major Lance did in more relaxed settings. Surely someone like him was seeing someone. Because she hadn't heard the girls gossiping, she'd assumed it was a woman who lived off base. Annie had let herself imagine his girlfriend several times and had even named her—Peggy. Lovely, gracious, and sophisticated, Peggy was also a very good cook and could speak French and Italian fluently. How could any man ever leave twenty-seven-year-old Perfect Peggy for forty-eight-year-old Annie?

"How about asking them to join you for drinks? After work?" he suggested.

Annie considered the prospect. "Kay has her kids to get back to after work, and I'm not sure Mak would accept an invitation from me."

"Make it a special occasion so they can't say no. Tell them it's your birthday."

"But my birthday isn't until—"

"August. I know. But they don't."

Annie could not remember the last time she'd celebrated her birthday. Yet she suddenly felt like she had reason to celebrate even if it was on the wrong day in the wrong month. She looked away so the major couldn't see her grin, knowing it was silly to be happy simply because he'd remembered her birthday.

For her very premature birthday celebration, Annie had chosen a bar in Honolulu that was quiet enough to have a conversation but loud enough not to be overheard. She also appreciated the fact that the bar was only lit by tiki torches, which were kind to older women. Having a fake birthday made her feel like she was already forty-nine, which was a hairsbreadth from fifty. Annie's mother had died at the age of fifty-five, making Annie assume, whether it made scientific sense or not, that she was already on the exit ramp.

Wearing a civilian dress that flattered her figure, Annie sat in a back booth away from the native Hawaiians who filled the bar. Suddenly, the smell of jasmine filled her as a lei of flowers fell over her head and settled like a colorful, fragrant necklace. The lei had small seashells between orchids, jasmine, carnations, and plumerias. She couldn't remember the last time someone had given her flowers.

Looking up, Annie saw Mak. "Thank you," she said, wondering if he heard the unexpected tremor in her voice.

"You're very welcome."

"Happy birthday, Annie!" said Kay, sliding into the booth next to her.

"Thank you both for coming," said Annie. "I really need to get drunk so I can forget how old I am." *At least that wasn't a lie,* she thought.

"Hold that thought," said Mak, disappearing.

"I hope your husband doesn't mind you going out tonight," said Annie, who'd never heard Kay speak about him except to say he was away.

"My husband isn't… We're not together. My mother is with the kids," said Kay. "She likes babysitting because after they're asleep, she gets to snoop."

"That can be dangerous. My sister, Maria, found my diary when I was eleven and shared it with our four sisters. Luckily, my two brothers weren't interested in my crush on the boy who delivered our milk."

"You had seven siblings?" said Kay.

Before Annie could answer, Mak set down a large wooden mug and poured three glasses, handing Annie hers first. "This is your birthday drink."

Smiling, Annie took a gulp before Mak could stop her and then coughed until the tears ran down her cheeks. "What the hell is that?"

"Okolehao," said Mak.

"Okay, what?" asked Annie.

"It's Hawaiian moonshine," said Kay.

In all her travels, Annie had never tried moonshine. Grinning, she raised her glass to him and took another drink, sipping this time.

An hour later, Annie had wandered into the "thrill" stage of drunk—thrilled that she was still conscious and coherent. Mak poured her another drink, and she held up her hand, which he ignored as he continued his story. "I stood there looking down at this black pool, and I thought I was either going to earn my older brother's respect or die trying."

"His respect was worth dying for?" asked Kay.

"Of course," said Mak earnestly. "I had to prove myself before he would let me help support the family."

"Didn't your father have a say?" asked Annie.

"He'd died the year before, which left my brother as head of the family."

"I'm sorry," said Annie.

Mak waved away her sympathy. "It was a long time ago."

"Well, I understand why you had to jump off that cliff," said Annie. "Sometimes you have to do something extreme to be taken seriously. Because you're too young or too inexperienced or...too fucking old."

Kay and Mak paused mid-drink.

"My grandmother told me that age sneaks up on you like a wolf in a dark forest. She said, 'One day, you're Little Red Riding Hood, but before you know it, you're the grandmother stuck inside the wolf.' She told me to enjoy being young—to take advantage of every day—because once you go gray…" Annie absently brushed back the few gray strands of hair at her temples. "You're invisible. Men won't look and no one will listen, because a woman with gray hair has lost the ability to think about anything more complicated than preparing Sunday supper. And I don't cook, so I'm pretty much fucked."

"Agreed," said Mak.

"Mak!" said Kay. "I'm sure you don't mean that."

"It's not what I believe," he said. "It's how white people think. They only like things that are shiny and new."

"Never thought I'd say this," said Annie, "but you're absolutely right, Mak."

Suddenly, drunken laughter rolled in like high tide, and they all turned to see three sailors in white swagger to the bar.

Noting Mak's disdain, Annie leaned forward and spoke more harshly than she meant to. "They deserve your respect."

"For what? Maintaining military rule over lands that aren't theirs?"

"Do you really see us…Americans as your enemy, Mak?"

"What do you think?" he said, poker face in place.

"I think that if you could, you'd put every sailor and soldier on a huge ship back to the mainland and tell them never to darken Oahu's door again."

"I sure as hell would," he admitted.

"What about Japanese Americans?" asked Kay.

"You can stay." He winked at her.

"Even though some are rumored to be plotting against the military?" asked Annie.

"You don't really believe that, do you, Annie?" asked Kay.

"I'm not sure," said Annie. "But if there is some kind of sabotage in the works, I don't think you're part of it, Kay."

"What a relief," said Mak with sarcasm.

Kay shot him a look, but before she could say anything, a cheer erupted from the bar. They all looked at the young sailor with a buzz cut as he stood on top of the bar and shouted, "Navy's gonna win again this year! Hope you're prepared to lose, Army!" Expecting no one to respond because they could only see locals, his buddies laughed.

However, Annie could not let it stand. She stood on her chair and raised her glass. "Our luck's about to change, Navy! Don't bet against us!"

"Your husband must be Army!" said the blond sailor. "Sorry!"

"I'm not married. And you can address me as First Lieutenant Annie Fox!" Annie shouted with pride, lifting her glass toward the sailors.

"Good luck, Army!" he shouted back. "Your team will need it!"

"We'll see, Navy!" Suddenly realizing what she'd done, Annie lowered her glass and looked at Mak and Kay. Both appeared dumbfounded.

"Mak, please make sure *Lieutenant* Fox gets home safely," Kay said. "I believe Hickam Field is the only Army base on this island with a hospital." Taking her purse, she walked out of the bar before Annie could think of anything to say in her own defense.

They turned off Kamehameha Highway, which ran north and south from Pearl Harbor to Honolulu, and were on the short road that led to Hickam. Annie had kept her head near the open window for miles but still felt woozy from the Hawaiian moonshine. Knowing there wasn't much time left, she pulled her head back inside the car. "I really did want to help at the center."

"You did. You're a good nurse," said Mak. "You're just a lousy friend."

He hadn't raised his voice, but Annie felt as if she'd been slapped and was glad to see the guard shack and gate. "You can stop here."

He pulled up to the guard shack. "Don't come back to the community center, Annie. I don't know what your agenda is, but I know it's not in our best interest, because nothing the military does ever is."

Not trusting herself to speak without inflaming the situation, she got out of the car and tried to stay dry-eyed and straight-backed as she showed her ID to the guard.

Hoping she might sober up a little before she entered the women's barracks, Annie took her time walking back, wondering about her ability for friendship. Since she'd left Nova Scotia, she had usually outranked the women she served with, and men didn't see her as a friend; she was either a subordinate or a threat. It had been different with Kay, who seemed to see her as an equal, though Annie had likely ruined their friendship.

After a few hours of trying to walk off her disappointment, she felt the blisters on the backs of her ankles rubbing raw and stopped. She looked to the east where the sun was just beginning its rise over the foothills of the Koolau Range. There had been rumors that hundreds of Japanese soldiers had parachuted somewhere along the thirty-seven miles of mountains with plans to recruit young Japanese American men waiting to join them in an attack on Pearl Harbor. Some thought they would sneak onto the ships and plant bombs, causing chaos, while others rushed in to slit the throats of servicemen while they slept.

"Get off the damn runway!" boomed a voice as if God had spoken.

Startled, Annie turned and saw what seemed to be a very small man waving at her from the air traffic control tower, where she could just make out the glowing end of his cigarette. She stood at attention, saluted, and limped off the runway in heels she wasn't used to walking in.

She made her way back to Hangar Avenue, close to the women's barracks. The pain in her feet had sobered her enough that when she saw Major Lance jogging toward her, wearing sweats, she didn't panic but tried to appear as if she'd just come out to watch the sunrise. "Good morning, Major Lance," she said with as much enthusiasm as she could muster as he took in her appearance, wilting lei and all.

"I take it you went out for drinks last night," he said.

"Yes, sir. As we'd discussed."

"I don't remember discussing you getting drunk," he said with disapproval.

"In my defense, I'm not used to okae…Hawaiian moonshine."

"Which I assume your new friends from the community center gave you?"

"I don't think they're still friends. I accidently admitted my military rank. Apparently, I'm unable to control my enthusiasm for Army versus Navy when inebriated," she said.

"It happens." He shrugged with a sardonic smile.

"Not to real spies."

"You're not a real spy. You're my chief nurse, who's on duty in"—he checked his watch—"two hours. Enough time to sober up if you shower and get some—"

"Please don't say food, sir. I'll have coffee. Lots of it."

"Good. Afterward, stop by my office. We need to talk."

"If it's about my ex-friends, I'm sure they're good, loyal citizens. I never heard anything that made me suspicious."

"It's not about them," he said. "We're on full alert until further notice. The official announcement will be made at 1000 hours. You and I should talk about how best to tell your nurses so they're not taken by surprise. But first, sober up."

"Yes, sir," she said, part of her wishing she was still in the bar with Kay and Mak, drinking moonshine, laughing over childhood stories. Just an ordinary woman.

Annie had decided on an operating room for the talk rather than the women's barracks. She wanted her nurses to be in an environment where they were in uniform and on duty rather than in their pajamas with a pillow close by that they could cry into. Despite the setting, Sara still seemed close to tears.

"Any questions?" asked Annie, eyes on Sara even though all of them had their hands raised like they were in a classroom.

"If we're on full alert and can't leave the base," said Sara, "does that mean we can't visit Pearl Harbor? Because it's just next door, and we're both military bases."

"We're Army and part of the Hawaiian Air Force. Pearl Harbor, as you know, is Navy. So unless you're asked by me or Dr.

Lance to go to Pearl Harbor for a specific reason, you'll stay on base." She knew Sara's concern was related to her twin, but there was nothing to be done for it. "No days off until the alert is lifted unless you're ill."

"No days off means no surfing," said Irene.

"No dancing at the Halekai Club," said Monica, exchanging sad glances with Kathy.

"No men," said Winnie with a deep sigh.

"Chins up, ladies. It's not like you're stationed in the backwoods." Annie had been and knew the difference. In comparison, Hickam was a small city, with a gym, theatre, tennis courts, swimming pools, and baseball fields. It even had its own public school and fire department. Married officers lived with their families in spacious stucco homes surrounded by manicured grounds. All in all, not a bad place to be sequestered. "Any other questions?" asked Annie.

"Yes, ma'am," said Monica. "Why are we on full alert?"

Annie knew Monica would be the one to ask. She was thoughtful, organized, and a good planner. Annie had hopes of Monica replacing her as chief nurse in a few years. "Admiral Kimmel and General Short received a warning from Washington about a possible attack on an American target in the Pacific."

"What about the Philippines?" asked Kathy.

"Or Guam?" said Winnie.

"Or Hong Kong?" said Irene. "Japan is no fan of the British."

"Well, they won't attack Pearl Harbor," said Sara with confidence. "Their fleet is too strong, in addition to all the bombers we have at Hickam."

"There's no point in speculating," said Annie, redirecting their focus. "In the morning, we'll clean every inch of the hospital, and we'll take an inventory of all our supplies. If we need anything, I want to know by end of day tomorrow."

A collective moan. But better they be annoyed with their assignment than thinking about where Japan might attack the United States.

SIX

Having sent her nurses off to clean and take inventory, Annie entered the hospital ward to find Major Lance directing the placement of fifteen new mattresses with several young soldiers, including Jeremy, who were moving them onto the iron beds.

"Thank you, Major Lance." Annie moved closer to him and spoke so no one could overhear. "Does this mean we'll be needing the beds soon?"

"We're still listed as a potential target, but so are the West Coast and the Panama Canal. Japan doesn't have the capacity to hit everything at once. If you ask me, they'll hit the Philippines. But let's make sure we're ready, just in case."

"Yes, sir. In progress."

"Good, then I'll leave you to supervise the moving of the mattresses. I've got a meeting with General Short. I'll let you know if I learn anything new."

She watched him leave, hoping he'd get more clarity from the general, then turned to her movers, noting that Jeremy was favoring his bruised side as he lifted a mattress. "Corporal Tig?"

He turned to her with his usual smile. Jeremy was one of those people who was born in a good mood and seemed to stay that way no matter what.

"Please take over coordinating the placement of the mattresses while I get bed linens," she said, wanting him to take it easier without appearing weak in front of his peers.

"Yes, ma'am," he said with a hint of relief.

"When I get back, we'll see which one of you young men can show me the best hospital corners." A groan from the men followed Annie out of the ward, but she saw Jeremy smile as if he welcomed any competition, even one that involved making beds. She'd noticed that about American men—how most thrived when competing, even when they were injured and confined to a bed. During the Great War, she'd set up tables between beds and passed out games: cards, checkers, chess, and any kind of board game she could get her hands on. If an American patient didn't perk up when playing and lost without so much as a "goddamn," she knew she had a very sick man on her hands.

Annie wondered if they had any games in the hospital and put it on her list of to-dos.

The supply closet had been neatly organized before they'd started taking inventory, so Annie and Monica were making fast work of it. Annie counted supplies while Monica jotted the numbers down on a clipboard. Next to "games" was a zero.

"Fourteen bottles of Mercurochrome," said Annie, straightening the rows. Monica wrote it down, and Annie moved on to rubbing alcohol. "I know this isn't an exciting part of the job. It's not like assisting in the OR."

"I'd rather be here than in the OR," said Monica. "My father's the surgeon, not me."

"You don't want to follow in his footsteps?"

Monica shook her head. "I wanted to be an actress."

Annie could see that Monica was pretty enough to be an actress. They were even using her photograph in the "Uncle Sam Needs Nurses" campaign. But she was still surprised. "You really wanted to go to Hollywood and be on the big screen?"

"As far back as I can remember," Monica said wistfully. "But my parents felt that I needed a real job. And if I became a nurse, I could meet an eligible doctor. They're very keen on me getting married, because both my aunts are spinsters. Apparently, there's nothing worse than… Sorry, I didn't mean… Of course, I don't think that way. I think—"

"Stop digging that particular hole, Monica." Annie smiled. "Just tell me how your search for a husband is coming along."

"I have been seeing someone special," Monica said, her eyes lighting up. "He's an airman at Pearl Harbor, but Barney and I haven't discussed marriage."

"Before he asks, think about what you want. You don't have to give up being a nurse to be married or to have children. At least not outside the Army."

"When I have children, I won't work," said Monica as if she'd made up her mind about this long ago. "While I'm good at my job, I haven't ever felt as though it's my calling."

Annie couldn't hide her disappointment.

"I'm sorry," said Monica. "I've never said that out loud. But I think it's true."

Turning the disappointment in her protégé to a shelf lined with an assortment of wound dressings, Annie began to sort. She couldn't fault Monica for having her own dreams.

President Roosevelt had officially declared the third Thursday in November as Thanksgiving Day, and Hickam Field was still on full alert. While the mess hall in the new enlisted men's barracks was large enough to accommodate every soldier on base, they ate Thanksgiving dinner in shifts so every post would remain filled.

Military wives and their children had decorated the mess hall. Tables were anointed with vases of poinsettia or hibiscus and ginger plants, while pilgrims, pumpkins, and turkeys—cut out of construction paper and colored with crayons—hung on strings or were taped to windows. The mess hall looked like a cross between a grandmother's dining room and a public school.

When Annie and three of her six nurses—Irene, Kathy, and Sara—came in for dinner, they sat behind several rows of enlisted men and apart from the officers and their families. Given the day, most parents allowed their children to be as loud as they liked; some of the younger ones were even playing tag in an open space near the back of the hall.

When they first sat down with their plates full of turkey, mashed potatoes, carrots, and all the trimmings, Annie and her nurses watched the children play. They were so carefree and full of joy, it was difficult to pay attention to anything else. But when dessert came—ice cream and pineapple upside-down cake—the children ran back to their tables and settled into their sweets.

Annie's nurses fell silent. It was difficult to imagine that you could be both bored and anxious at the same time, but that was where they were. They needed a respite, even if it lasted only as long as dessert.

Annie thought of something that might help. Not quite a game, but close enough.

"Irene, if you could relive one moment of your life, what would it be?" asked Annie.

"Excuse me, ma'am?" Irene looked up at Annie while stirring her ice cream into a soup.

"If you could relive any single moment from your life up to now, what would it be?"

It took Irene only a moment to answer. "My nineteenth birthday. Surfing at Rincon Point, California. Even before my best friend and I got out of the car, everything felt right. The first wave I caught that day was one I'll never forget. I felt like I was part of it. Like the ocean was telling me I was welcome. If that makes sense."

"It sounds wonderful," said Annie. "What about you, Kathy? What moment would you relive?"

Kathy took a sip of her eggnog as though pondering a very serious question. "I'd like to relive my tenth birthday. Specifically, making a chocolate-cherry cake with my grandmother."

"It must've been some cake," said Sara.

"It was," said Kathy. "But it was more about my grandmother. Spending time with her was so easy. I felt completely safe and loved. And that's how I feel every time I eat a chocolate-cherry cake. Which may cause some problems as I get older." Smiling, she patted her full but still fairly flat stomach.

"You were very lucky to have her," said Annie. "Your turn, Sara."

"I would like to relive my night at the Snake Ranch beer garden."

"Where?" asked Annie.

"It's part of the enlisted men's main barracks," said Sara. "There's a small garden area outside where the men gather after especially grueling lectures or tests to have a few drinks. One night, I happened to walk by, and one of the officers asked me if I wanted a beer. I almost said no because my twin, Helen, wasn't with me. She's much more comfortable in social situations than I am, especially if men are present."

"Tell me you got comfortable," said Irene, pushing her dessert away.

Sara smiled. "After a few beers, I talked to a fellow who was sitting by himself, looking kind of lonely. Come to find out, he was from Eastport, Maine. I told him I was from Camden, which is just down the coast. We spent hours talking about home and how different things are here. It was really nice."

Annie saw Sara's blush spread up her neck to her face and wondered if she would lose her to the young man from the Snake Ranch.

"You haven't told us what moment you'd like to relive, Chief," said Kathy.

Unsure, Annie poked at her pineapple cake. "It was late September 1918. I was in the Forest of Argonne in France taking care of men in the First Army, who were under constant assault. It was the beginning of the third day of battle. I had a canteen in my hand and was giving water to the wounded when a man reached out to me. He didn't want water. He just wanted to thank me for taking care of him the night before. I honestly didn't remember him; there had been so many wounded. But I'd done something right, because he held my hand and thanked me for saving his life. Up to the moment, I'd wondered if I'd done the right thing—leaving home and joining another country's Army. I'd had no idea what I was getting myself into. After that night, I never questioned my decision again."

A glass shattered. A few women shrieked and many jumped. It was only one of the children who'd dropped a glass of milk. But the spell had broken.

Annie and her nurses picked up their trays and silently brought them to the front of the mess hall, each glancing one more time at the pilgrims, pumpkins, and turkeys—and at the children playing—before they went back to full alert status.

Other than the fact that she wore a surgical mask and gloves, Annie looked more like a housekeeper than chief nurse as she dipped a sponge in a bucket of water and cleaned the operating table. The door opened and Annie looked up to see Irene, also wearing a mask, enter with a fresh pail of ammonia and water. Leaving it near Annie, Irene picked up the bucket with the old dirty water. "Need anything else, Chief?"

"Surfing lessons," said Annie, unsure the words had come out of her own mouth.

Irene appeared just as unsure.

"Obviously not now," said Annie. "When the alert lifts. Unless you don't think someone my age can learn."

"I've seen lots of older women surf."

"It's a date then," said Annie. "Just start me off on a beach where the waves aren't too big. If I can get the hang of it on a rented board, maybe I'll buy my own."

"Sounds like we have a plan," said Irene as she left.

Dipping her sponge back in the water, Annie tried to imagine getting to her feet on a surfboard, but Kay and Mak kept getting in the way.

She'd thought of them often over the past few days, wondering if they were still angry with her for not being truthful about being a military nurse. Rehearsing an apology over and over while she carried out her duties had only made her feel slightly better about lying to them. Even in her imagined apology, she was cheap with the truth, leaving out the part about her awkward attempt at spying.

As she gathered her cleaning supplies, ready to move on to another operating room, she promised herself that the first place she would go when the alert was lifted was the Japanese American Community Center. She would be almost completely honest about what she'd done and why, and she would ask them for another chance. She would also not ask questions about the mysterious envelopes going back and forth between Kay and the Taketas, though she was very curious. Could be they contained payments for Kay's house calls to treat Mr. Taketa's gout. But if that was all they were, why be so secretive?

Annie pushed the question out of her mind. If she was going to make amends with Kay and Mak, she needed to put any suspicions away, because they were completely unfounded. She wouldn't let herself become paranoid about every Japanese American on the island.

★

The Japanese American Community Center was relatively quiet. Amai was tending to the victim of a roller-skating collision who might require a few stitches while Kay and Mak folded clean diapers on a corner table to restock their supply.

Mak glanced up at Kay, who pensively studied the diaper in her hands. "You're thinking about Annie again."

"Actually, I was thinking about the Red Cross."

"Why?"

"They've been moving a lot of supplies into a building downtown." Kay placed her folded diaper on a neat pile and picked up another. "Sam Fukuda helped unload the trucks. He said they were filled with medical equipment and supplies, but that was all he knew so I called a friend who works with the local Red Cross."

"And?"

Kay spoke softly. "She told me they're putting together twelve fifty-bed Red Cross first aid stations in Honolulu. They're also recruiting doctors, nurses, and first aid personnel. Obviously, they expect some kind of catastrophe, and they don't want to alarm the public."

"If a volcano was about to erupt," said Mak, "we'd be having tremors."

"I think war is about to erupt. That could be why we haven't seen Annie. Maybe the Red Cross isn't the only one preparing for casualties."

"I didn't think you wanted to see her."

"I just thought she might try to apologize."

"Would an apology be enough?"

Kay shrugged. "Let's focus on getting ready for whatever the Red

Cross is expecting." She took one of the diapers and ripped it in half. "Bandages?"

"Good idea." Mak took a pair of scissors out of a drawer and began trimming the diaper she'd torn in half. "Do we tell the others?"

"There's no point in alarming anyone until we know for sure."

"We'll be the last to find out. They're too suspicious of your people, and they don't give a shit about mine." Mak picked up another diaper and began cutting it into strips.

Kay couldn't disagree. "I'll go tell Amai we're doing a diaper inventory so she doesn't come looking for us unless there's an emergency."

Heading into the main room, smile in place, Kay would act as if nothing was out of the ordinary. She was getting very good at it, having had lots of practice since her husband left. She put on a show every day—in front of her children, her mother, her patients, and her friends. Only the Taketas knew the truth, and they pretended, as she did, that everything was fine.

SEVEN

December 6, 1941

Annie was in the backyard of the hospital pulling weeds when she saw Major Lance strolling toward her while lighting a cigarette. "My mother likes to pluck crabgrass," he said, taking a long drag. "She told me it's therapeutic."

Yanking a weed out, Annie threw it in the bucket, stood, and brushed off her trousers. "First, I'm not old enough to be your mother. Second, I'm doing this because mowing doesn't kill the crabgrass. You have to pull it out by the roots."

"Evidently." He gazed at her fingernails, covered with dirt. "Maybe you could do something about those nails before the dance."

"Dance?" She put her hands in her pockets.

"The alert's been lifted. We seem to be out of danger. To celebrate, there's a dance in the officers' club tonight. Word is that a wealthy Japanese banker is putting the party on. Must be a sign that our countries are back on semisolid ground." Grinning, he walked away.

Annie felt her fifteen-year-old self emerge as if the last thirty-three years never happened.

Did he just ask me to the dance? Or was he only being polite and letting me know there is a dance? He'd have to tell the officers so we can tell our staff. But he smiled. Which doesn't have to mean anything, because he smiles a lot. And he didn't ask me to the dance. But he clearly wants me to go. With him?

"For Christ's sake, get a hold of yourself." Annie picked up her bucket and trowel. She would go, but she would not let herself get excited. No expectations led to no disappointment.

Annie's nurses were in high spirits. Irene and Sara had volunteered for night duty at the hospital because they'd both gone off base as soon as the full alert was lifted. Irene had gone surfing, and Sara had gone to Pearl Harbor to spend time with her sister. Monica spent the afternoon choosing which evening dress she would wear. Having received a note from her airman, she left early in the evening to meet him. Winnie and Kathy, who'd spent the entire afternoon primping for the dance, got picked up by a friend who drove them to the club.

Not wanting to leave for the dance at the officers' club until after her nurses had left for the night, Annie took her time getting ready, paying particular attention to her nails, making sure not a trace of dirt remained. After her nails were painted a pale pink, she'd waited at the barracks until well after eight o'clock because she hoped Major Lance might pick her up. He hadn't. But he'd never said he would come for her, so she left on her own.

Annie was in a festive mood as she entered the officers' club, which was new and featured a dining room, bar, fully equipped game room, and a ballroom. Officers had to wear dress whites or a white formal jacket, and women wore their finest dresses. Annie wore the black dress she'd seen in the shop window by the community center. Before the alert, the officers' club held dances nearly every week, and she'd bought the dress with the hope that she would be asked to one of those dances. It was like having a weekly prom, and tonight would be Annie's first.

When she entered the ballroom, the sight that most surprised her was what the waitresses were wearing—colorful Japanese kimonos. She supposed it had something to do with the founder of the feast, so to speak. Or perhaps it was a show of goodwill that would somehow find its way to the negotiation table. Whatever it was meant to be, the kimonos didn't fit with the decor, which was decidedly American.

Red, white, and blue balloons and streamers decorated the stage where a band of off-duty soldiers played as dapper officers and their dressed-to-the-nines wives or girlfriends danced the Lindy Hop on a floor polished to a shine. Annie watched with admiration. She couldn't recall the last time she'd danced, at least not in public.

As she made her way to one of three punch bowls, she watched a distinguished-looking man take a flask out of his jacket pocket and spike the punch. He turned to her like a kid caught with his hand in the cookie jar, but she only smiled and asked, "Vodka or rum?"

"Rum." Grinning, he slid the flask back into his pocket.

Filling her glass, Annie decided to drink before searching for Major Lance, giving herself time to rehearse what she would say. *How nice to see you, Major.* Wouldn't make sense; she'd seen him earlier that day. *Shall we dance, David?* Too forward. She'd also never called him David. *Do my nails look better?* She could hold out her hands, which might prompt him to remember telling her about the dance. Or she could be painfully honest and say, *I feel very awkward because I don't know if this is a date or not, so please take the lead.* At which point he would take her hand and gently pull her toward the dance floor.

She emptied her glass and began searching for the major. Skirting the edge of the dance floor, she saw Winnie and Kathy with their respective partners doing the swing dance. Her nurses looked so full of joy and energy, as if dancing was as simple as breathing. Just watching them made Annie feel tired, but at the same time, it filled her with a strong desire to join in.

Annie's foot tapped to the music as she scanned the room, spotting his dark hair standing head and shoulders above his dance partner—a blond. Moving closer, Annie saw that the woman was in her mid to late twenties and probably from Pearl Harbor. There were so few women serving at Hickam that Annie was familiar with nearly all of them and didn't recognize her.

Annie watched the grace with which they danced, as if they didn't have to think about how their bodies were moving. The major and "Peggy" seemed completely natural together.

Pulling her eyes away, Annie went back to the spiked punch bowl and filled another glass, very grateful for the rum that might dull the blade she felt had been thrust into her heart. How foolish she had been to even entertain the hope that he'd invited her as his date.

"Care to dance, Lieutenant?"

She turned to see Jeremy, who looked like a high schooler attending his senior prom.

He held out his hand. "Let's show 'em how it's done."

"I'm afraid you'll have to show me how it's done first, Corporal."

If nothing else, at least she could say someone had asked her to dance. She set down her drink.

Jeremy grinned, took her hand, and pulled her to the dance floor. At first, she was clumsy and awkward as he tried to teach her the foxtrot. Then he pointed to her heels. Hesitating because she had always been self-conscious about what she believed were her big feet, she kicked off her heels. No longer afraid of falling because the worst thing had already happened—the major and Peggy were dancing again—she finally caught on.

As Jeremy whirled her around, Annie saw Winnie and Kathy watching, wide-eyed, as she and her partner finished the foxtrot with a flourish. Annie knew she must look as exhilarated as a child who had just ridden her first bicycle without training wheels.

Clapping for the band, Annie turned to Jeremy to thank him for teaching her, but his attention was elsewhere, specifically on a young woman on the other side of the dance floor.

"Thanks for the dance, Annie!"

"You're welcome, Jeremy," she said, watching him hurry toward the young woman.

The band began a waltz, and suddenly Annie was standing alone in the middle of a crowded dance floor with no partner. After searching for her shoes as inconspicuously as she could manage, she followed several older male officers, cigars in hand, as they went outside where they formed a smoking circle, which she circumvented and continued on her way through the base.

Annie walked until her nylons were shredded at the soles, needing to expend the energy she'd worked up during that one glorious dance. Without a specific destination, she found herself at the base of Hickam's landmark—a beautiful concrete tower of Moorish design that enclosed a five-hundred-thousand-gallon steel tank that held an emergency water reserve. At the base of the tower was a nursery where thousands of tree seedlings and shrubs were nurtured to help beautify the base. How the Army had managed to buy seedlings instead of mattresses for the hospital was something she'd like to bring up with the powers that be. Her eyes traveled to the top of the tower where she was sure the view was spectacular.

She thought the door at the base of the tower would be locked, but it opened easily. Leaving her heels by the door, she climbed the steep spiral staircase to the room with the view above the tank. Various rumors had circulated about what was inside the room. Some said it only contained Christmas lights that would transform the tower into the largest holiday display on the island on Christmas Eve, while others said it housed an advanced radar system.

Halfway up the 171-foot octagonal tower, Annie felt winded, but the thought of the young woman dancing in the major's embrace gave her the will to ignore her aching thighs. Finally at the top, she put her hand on the doorknob and turned. The door was unlocked, but instead of seeing boxes of Christmas lights, she saw radio equipment.

"Who are you?"

Startled, Annie turned and saw a young man. As always when she met someone new, she took in his appearance as it might relate to his overall health. Everything about the young man was pale—hair, skin, and eyes. And he was thin. It looked like the uniform he wore was the smallest size the Army had to offer. "Who are you?"

"Private First Class Samuel Baker."

"I'm First Lieutenant Annie Fox, chief nurse at the hospital."

"What are you doing here, ma'am?"

"Just curious. I was out walking, and I looked up and wondered what the view was like. How about you? What do you do here?"

"Radio operator."

"So no advanced radar systems?" she asked, surveying the room.

"Hickam has an SCR-270, but it's not here."

"Sorry. I know nothing about radar systems."

"An SCR-270 operates at one hundred and six megahertz with one hundred kilowatts of pulsed power. It allows us to detect enemy aircraft or ships up to two hundred and forty miles off our coast. That way, we can send bombers out to meet them before they get close enough to do damage."

"You know your radar, Private Baker."

"I helped set it up. I start training on it tomorrow." He smiled with pride.

"Good for you, Private," said Annie. "I'm sure you'll be very good at your new job, and we'll all be safer."

"Between radar and the Pacific Fleet, you couldn't be safer."

"Don't forget our boys and their Flying Fortresses."

"No, ma'am. They're the best."

She looked out the window. The tower was near the residential area, and she could see Christmas lights strewn on houses and trees where officers and their families lived. Looking in another direction, she saw an ocean of lights in Honolulu, which was less than ten miles away. After her shift was over tomorrow, she would drive into town and make her apologies to Kay and Mak. It was the least she could do for even entertaining the notion that either one would hide secrets that could endanger their country.

Kay had been sitting at her kitchen table for what felt like hours, staring at the new note Mrs. Taketa had slipped to her earlier that day. After the children had gone to bed, she'd taken the envelope out of her coat pocket and laid it on the counter. She always approached the notes from her husband in steps, giving herself time to prepare, and she always read them at night after the children were sound asleep because the notes made her cry—or want to scream in frustration. Once, she'd barely reached the living room to grab a pillow to hold over her face before she shouted a string of words she'd never say in front of Beth and Tommy.

The pillow was on the kitchen table next to the note and a glass of sake. She'd already drunk one glass and was sipping her second, yet she still hadn't been able to read the note. Her husband, Daiji, had a knack for using only a few words to communicate a lot. It was one of the things that had attracted her to him. She'd thought it meant he was a man who gave things a lot of thought before he spoke and therefore didn't have to convince others before convincing himself. But now she understood it had only meant he was stubbornly opinionated and didn't want to invite a debate. His decisions weren't open to discussion; they were to be accepted as fact, especially by his wife and children.

Picking up the note, Kay told herself she should be used to this by now. Letters had begun arriving every few weeks after Daiji left.

Dissatisfied with menial labor on a sugarcane plantation, he'd tried to find a position teaching at a university or a high school. But as when he'd first arrived in Oahu ten years ago, no white person took a Japanese degree in engineering from Kyoto University seriously.

After working on the plantation for nearly a decade, he'd told Kay he must return to Japan where he would get the respect that he'd earned. She'd understood, and they'd planned to reunite the family as soon as he was established. Though she and their children had never lived anywhere but Oahu, Kay was willing to start a new life in Japan. Keeping her family together was her primary goal.

At first Daiji's letters were dedicated to his longing for her and the children. He had never been overtly expressive with his emotions, but it was clear that he missed them more and more. After a few months, he wrote of other things, like how he'd been remiss in understanding the importance of what the Emperor, better known to Americans as Hirohito, wanted for his people—domination over China and Southeast Asia. This had not alarmed Kay too much because tensions between Japan and other Asian countries had been going on for a very long time. It was when Daiji wrote that he'd stopped seeking a teaching position in order to devote himself exclusively to the Emperor's goals that made her wonder what that meant for him—and what it would mean for his family. After her response to that revelation, which was less than supportive, his fairly lengthy letters became cryptic notes.

Taking one more sip of sake, Kay slowly unfolded the note that had traveled from Tokyo to Mr. and Mrs. Taketa and finally to her. The briefest note she'd ever received from him made her tremble. Reacting on pure instinct, she went to the telephone and called the only person she could trust with the information—the only person she trusted enough to give her advice. Because she would need to decide whether to do what her husband had asked—leave Oahu immediately.

Kay was pacing by the living room door when she heard a soft knock. Unlocking the door, she let Mak inside and handed him the note. "It's from my husband." She gestured for him to read it.

"You know I can't read Japanese," said Mak.

"You don't need to; it's in English. Daiji made sure he could speak and write it perfectly before he came here. He thought it would help him get a position at the college."

Unfolding the note, Mak read aloud. "Bring the children to the mainland. Do not stay on the island beyond 6 December. You must do as I say. For our children's sake, not mine."

"What could he mean?" asked Kay.

He glanced at the wall clock. "It's past midnight, so I guess we'll find out."

She heard his calm and knew she'd been right to call him. But he didn't know the whole story. "I'll be right back." Moments later, she returned with a shoebox full of her husband's notes, which she'd kept hidden from the children. "These are all from Daiji. I need someone to read them and tell me if he's…lost his way."

"I can't read what he wrote to you, Kay. That's between a husband and wife."

"Please, Mak." She set the box on the coffee table in front of him. "I'll go make tea."

When she returned with the tea tray, she set it down and let him finish reading. Other than raising a brow every now and then, Kay couldn't tell what he was thinking. After what seemed like hours, Mak read the last note.

"Do you think he's suffering from schizophrenia?" Kay asked. "Because I really can't think of anything else that would explain the change in him from the first letter to the last note."

Mak shook his head. "I think Daiji is as sane as any man can be who believes his political leader is right in wanting to take over a large part of the world."

"But he never thought about politics before, not seriously."

"I'm not sure it's about politics. I think he sees himself as…" He picked up one of the discarded notes and read, "'An instrument to be used by the Emperor for the greater good.' But the only thing that's clear is that he wants you and the kids in Japan."

"If we leave, we won't come back. Everything would change." She looked at him, unable to imagine never seeing him again.

"You need to do what's best for your family, Kay."

"But if Japan goes to war with the United States… The children and I would be at war with our own country."

"Then you need to decide whether to stay loyal to your husband or to your country."

He was right, but it was a choice she dreaded. Kay knew she would be up all night, the pros and cons going back and forth in her mind like Ping-Pong balls.

The dance was over, and the curfew had passed, so the first thing Annie did when she returned to the barracks was check on her nurses.

All were in bed asleep except for Monica. Someone had placed pillows under the blanket on Monica's bed, but a breeze from the windows had blown it back. Annie took a shower and set her uniform out for the next morning. Monica's bed still empty, she put her robe on and went out to sit on the front stoop.

It was a beautiful night. The sky was clear and there seemed to be a million stars overhead. But she was tired. Leaning back against the barracks and closing her eyes, she heard footsteps on the path, followed by the soft voices of Monica and a man. She didn't want to eavesdrop, but she also didn't want to embarrass Monica by making her presence known.

"I have the a.m. shift," said Monica. "But I can be ready by two o'clock."

"How about we go for a swim at Waikiki, then drinks and dinner at Trader Vic's?"

"Sounds wonderful, Barney. I'll see you tomorrow."

Annie saw a taller shadow, which had to be Barney the airman, lean down to kiss Monica, and she turned away to give them privacy. A few moments later, Monica's face—her expression still dreamy from the kiss—came into the outside light of the barracks.

"Oh, shit," said Monica, who saw Annie at the last moment and nearly stepped on her.

"Agreed," said Annie. "Stepping on me wouldn't have made the situation any better."

"I'm late."

"I know."

"I was with Barney."

"I know."

"We hadn't seen each other in two weeks, and we…lost track of time."

"Allow me to catch you up. You and I are on duty in"—Annie looked at her watch—"four hours and fifty-seven minutes."

"Yes, ma'am. I won't be late."

"But you will be tired, and so will I."

"I'm sorry."

"Did you have a good time?"

Monica looked at her like it was a trick question and hesitated before she said, "Yes."

"Then I suppose it was worth it. But don't do it again. We have a curfew for a reason."

"Yes, ma'am. I mean, no. I won't be out past curfew again."

Annie got up and held the back door open for Monica, making sure the last nurse in her care was safely inside before closing it.

EIGHT

December 7, 1941

The parade ground was nearly empty, most men still asleep on this early Sunday morning after the party at the officers' club. If they hadn't attended the dance, those who weren't on duty had gone somewhere off base to celebrate the end of full-alert status. It had been a late night for almost everyone who hadn't been on duty.

Back in uniform and sensible shoes, Annie was on her way back from the large mess hall at the new enlisted men's barracks. She hadn't woken with a big appetite, but she hadn't wanted to run into Major Lance at the smaller dining hall at the hospital. It wouldn't be awkward for him, but it would be for her. At least for a few days.

She couldn't remember having had a crush like this on anyone else—one in which her breath caught every time she saw him. She'd thought of other women who described feeling this way as suffering from some type of romantic insanity because they couldn't seem to focus on anything but their feelings for a particular man. Annie had been certain it would never happen to her. She was too practical, too tethered to reality. Therefore, she would nip it in the bud before she began acting like a schoolgirl rather than just thinking like one.

Gazing up at the clear blue sky, she smiled as a sea breeze gently lifted the wisps of hair at the nape of her neck, and she knew what she would think about instead of the dashing major: surfing. Looking toward the ocean, she searched for the surfers who, like Irene, were out there nearly every morning. Instead, she saw planes flying in low formation.

"Navy must be practicing dive-bombing again," said a man from behind.

She turned to see a private in uniform, who kept pace with her as they crossed the parade grounds.

"Don't tell anybody I said this, but Navy has all the fun." He winked at her before gazing back at the planes that continued to come in at a very low altitude. And then they both turned toward the booming sounds coming from Pearl Harbor. "Bombing practice," he said. "Like I said, they have all the fun."

"Does bombing practice account for the smoke?" Annie pointed at the black swirling up toward a cloudless sky.

He shrugged. "Could be one of the tanks they use to store oil had a leak and—poof."

The sound of a loud engine came closer. They stopped walking to watch the planes approach, descending so low they could see the pilot as well as the rear gunner. Annie and the private both raised their hands to wave, but the pilot beat them to it.

Then he tipped the wing so that the rising sun insignia—the mark of a Japanese long-range fighter aircraft called a Zero—was visible.

"Japs!" shouted the private. "They're attacking!"

Stunned, Annie watched the pilot pull the Zero up before strafing the parade ground. Bullets ricocheted off anything they didn't penetrate.

Several soldiers ran out of their barracks moments later. Awakened by gunfire, most only wore underwear. A few held .45-caliber pistols and began shooting at the planes overheard.

Hearing a brief whistling sound, Annie turned to see one of their B-17s go up in flames. The bombers had been parked wingtip to wingtip to deter sabotage, and the fire was spreading rapidly from one plane to the next.

Another whistle followed by a huge blast and Hangars 7 and 11 were in flames. She knew Hangar 11 housed the Eleventh Bombardment Group's armament and the aircraft maintenance technicians. Hoping there were survivors, she started to run toward Hangar 11 when she saw the private who'd been standing next to her sprint toward two soldiers trying to set up a Thompson submachine gun at the end of the parade area. Another soldier, kneeling in some bushes nearby, shot at the attacking planes with a bolt-action Springfield rifle.

Halfway to the submachine gun, the private she'd been talking to was gunned down by another low-flying Zero. Annie had almost reached him when she saw a soldier she knew. Hair still tousled from sleep and wearing only the bottom of his sweats, Jeremy was sprinting toward the submachine gun. "No, Corporal! It's too far!" she yelled.

"I'm fast!" he shouted back.

He was fast. Like a deer with a hunter at his back.

Jeremy had nearly reached the submachine gun when Annie got

to the private, who was beyond help. Looking back up to check on Jeremy, she saw red bloom on his back at the center of his fading bruise as if it were a bull's-eye. Nevertheless, he kept running for a few moments before he stumbled and fell.

As Annie ran toward him, more men in various stages of dress entered the parade ground. Using pistols or rifles, they shot at the Zeros until another large explosion made them all turn toward the million-dollar men's barracks in time to see a cloud of fiery concrete rise into the air.

Kneeling beside Jeremy, Annie thought about the building she'd just left. The entire barracks centered around the mess hall, with all nine wings connected to it by a series of hallways in which Annie had gotten lost. The sailor who'd helped her find the mess hall had said, "It's so big, you could fit six regulation-size basketball courts in there. You'll spot it just down that hallway to your left, ma'am." Was he still alive? Were the hundreds of men she'd just left, smothering pancakes and waffles with syrup like they were little boys, still alive?

Hearing another Zero approach, she shielded Jeremy as best she could as the strafing began again. Head down, she felt for a pulse in his neck. It was there, and she felt a whisper of relief before another big blast. A loud crack and then the sound of something splintering, like a giant tree being blown apart.

She lifted her head and saw the men who'd tried to set up the machine gun lying on the ground. Knowing their bullet-ridden bodies were beyond help, she tried to help Jeremy to his feet. "We're going to the hospital. You're going to be okay, Jeremy," she said with a confidence she wasn't sure was her own. He moaned in response. She struggled to lift him upright, trying to use one hand to stanch the bleeding from his wound at the same time.

Suddenly, Jeremy was lifted away and over the shoulder of a burly middle-aged sergeant who carried him toward the hospital as if he weighed no more than a sack of potatoes. "Movin' out, ma'am!"

Annie followed like he was her very own platoon sergeant. Crossing the pandemonium of the parade ground, he sidestepped bodies mutilated by bullets or splintered by shards of wood torn from the surrounding buildings. Except for the most obvious instances—where lifeless eyes stared back at her or the damage was too grievous—Annie stopped to check for a pulse on the neck, wrist, or ankle, wherever she found skin that was undamaged. She only found one soldier with a pulse, but he was unconscious and too big for her to lift. Taking off her jacket, she covered his bare chest and arms, hoping to delay shock. Catching up with the sergeant, she made him glance back at the young soldier and promise he'd come back to get him.

Annie followed the sergeant inside the hospital and took a quick survey. Several soldiers already sat in chairs with various wounds that didn't appear to be life-threatening, but one patient had a large wooden splinter sticking out of his thigh.

"Two gurneys!" she shouted, wondering who would answer. Her mind raced, trying to determine where her nurses would be.

Monica and Irene were on the a.m. shift so should be at the hospital. But where were Kathy, Winnie, and Sara? Had they gone to the enlisted men's mess hall? It was so big, she could've missed seeing them. Or had they gone out for an early morning walk? Had Sara gone to see her sister at Pearl Harbor? They often went to a service together on Sunday mornings. But she and her sister had attended the Battle of the Music semifinals together at Pearl Harbor last night to see who would face off against the bands from the USS *Arizona* and the Marine Corps barracks. Sara had returned just before curfew, jubilant that the USS *Pennsylvania* had made it to the finals. Hopefully, she'd slept in.

Irene appeared with a gurney, and the sergeant laid Jeremy down gently, then turned to leave as another explosion rang in Annie's ears. She grabbed the sergeant by his shirtsleeve. "Wait just a moment, and I'll go with you."

"No, you won't, ma'am. You've got your job to do, and I've got mine. I need to bring more boys in here so you can fix 'em up."

She knew he was right. They were all inside a war zone now. With difficulty, she let go of him. "Thank you, Sergeant…?"

"Drummer, Ma'am. Stanley Drummer." He gave her a "no big deal" smile, like he was going outside for a smoke.

Annie turned to Irene. "Where's Dr. Lance?"

"In his office," she said, quickly scooping her hair into a ponytail. "He wants to see you."

"My other nurses?"

"Monica went for bandages. Kathy, Winnie, and Sara have the day off, but I'm sure they'll be here as soon as—"

Another boom so close that the wall behind them cracked. They watched the plaster spider itself across the newly painted wall. When the cracking stopped, Annie saw the panic rise in Irene as her natural fight, freeze, or flight instincts kicked in. Annie couldn't let her do any of those things. "Nurse Boyd, please get our patient prepped for surgery."

Irene looked at Annie as if she'd lost her mind.

"Our patient needs to go to the OR," said Annie as calmly as she could.

"Yes…ma'am," said Irene, her voice trembling.

Annie looked down at Jeremy, whose eyes were dazed and half-closed. "You're at the hospital, and we're going to take very good care of you." She thought she saw him try to smile as Irene wheeled him toward the elevator that would take them to the operating theatre on the second floor. How long the elevators would keep working was anyone's guess.

The bombing was constant as Annie made her way to the major's office. The building shook with the closer blasts, and she expected it to cave in at any moment. But she had to put one foot in front of the other, and quickly, until it did. She would stay focused on her job. That was all she could do, and it beat hiding under a desk. Though that was tempting.

When she got to the major's office, she knocked. When he didn't respond, she opened the door. Half expecting to find him unconscious from falling debris, her heart skipped a beat. Instead, he was on the phone, clearly frustrated.

"This is *not* a false alarm," he said, standing at his desk. As if on cue, Hickam Field's siren began to blare, and he held the phone out to pick it up as well as the sounds of plane engines, bombs, machine guns, rifles, and pistols firing before bringing the phone back to his ear. "Those bastards are bombing the hell out of us! If they take out the hospital…" He glanced at Annie, a look of relief on his face, and motioned her inside. "Even if they don't," he said into the phone, "we'll have more casualties than we can handle. We need ambulances to transfer patients to Tripler General. And we could use gas masks and helmets."

"Major," interrupted Annie, "we'll need bandages, blood, and morphine too."

He spoke louder to be heard over the ceaseless gunfire. "We also need…" He hung up the phone. "Goddamned line's dead!"

"There's a soldier on his way to the OR that'll be the same if we don't get going."

"Are you all right?" Standing before her, he put his hands on her shoulders and looked her up and down, head to toe.

"I'm fine. But our patient won't be if we don't move fast."

"Let's go," he said. "I can't do anything more from here."

Major Lance, Annie, and Monica each wore a white gown over their clothes and a surgical mask. Annie controlled the flow of oxygen and anesthesia while Major Lance worked on Jeremy, his abdomen open so the bullet that had entered through his back could be removed. Monica stood beside the major within easy reach of a surgical tray holding instruments.

"He got lucky," said Major Lance. "The bullet didn't hit the liver."

A knock on the door, and the major shouted, "Come!" to be heard over the continuing and seemingly endless shelling.

Annie silently thanked God when she saw Winnie enter.

"They're beginning to stack up outside," said Winnie from behind her mask.

Another blast. In unison, everyone ducked under the operating table but Annie, who leaned over Jeremy. When the building stopped shaking and the plaster stopped falling off the walls, they rose and resumed their work as if nothing had happened.

"How many in the queue?" asked the major.

"Eight emergent and four that can wait if it's not too long," said Winnie.

"Drs. Doyle and Metcalfe?"

"Dr. Doyle's in OR two, and Dr. Metcalfe's doing triage."

"How's our patient, Annie?"

"BP's low. How much time do you need, Dr. Lance?" While in the OR, everyone was referred to as either Nurse or Doctor. It had been Major Lance's rule to leave rank and ego outside the operating theatre. It was one of the things Annie most admired about his management style.

"Just a few more minutes," he said.

"You've got it," said Annie. "This young man is strong."

"When we're done here, you'll relieve Dr. Metcalfe so he can get to OR three."

"Yes, Doctor," said Annie, who was grateful she could see Jeremy through surgery before she turned to triage, which would need to be fast and impersonal.

Dr. Lance removed the bullet and dropped it into the metal bowl Monica held out for him. "Is there another nurse who can handle anesthesia?"

"I've been training Nurse Coberly," said Annie. "But I'm not sure she's here."

"Kathy's here, ma'am," said Winnie.

"And Sara?"

Winnie nodded, and Annie sighed with relief behind her mask.

"Tell them we'll have a quick meeting in twenty minutes. Supply room on the second floor. All my nurses except Kathy. Let her know she'll be taking over for me in the OR."

"Yes, ma'am."

Annie moved her focus back to Jeremy, willing the color to return to his cheeks as Dr. Lance began to suture the wound.

Annie nearly ran to the supply room. She stood in the middle of a semicircle surrounded by her nurses, except for Kathy, who were already spattered with blood. Still under fire, Annie had to speak loud enough to be heard over the bombs, machine guns, and antiaircraft blasts.

"We can't waste a second," said Annie, catching her breath, smelling the gas and sulfur from outside. "While I talk, fill your pockets with bandages, morphine, and ten-cc syringes. You won't have time to change needles very often."

They efficiently gathered supplies, no one reaching for the same thing at the same time. But Sara stood still, gazing down at the pajamas she'd been wearing when the bombing had started. She had no pockets.

"Grab an apron, Sara," said Annie.

Shell-shocked, Sara didn't move.

"Nurse Entrikin," said Annie firmly, "put an apron on over your pajamas and fill up those pockets. No time to waste."

Sara looked at Annie's steady gaze, as if this were just another day, and snapped out of it. She grabbed a nurse's apron from the hook on the wall and went to the shelf that held bandages, filling one pocket.

Taking small bottles of Mercurochrome, Annie slipped a bottle into each nurse's apron as she spoke. "Our main goal is to stabilize the critical patients so they can be transported to Tripler General or Queen's Hospital."

"They won't all go to Tripler General?" asked Winnie as another explosion shook their own hospital.

"I'm sure the overflow will go to civilian hospitals, and Queen's is the largest," said Annie. "In addition to stabilizing patients for transport, what you'll be doing more than anything else is passing out morphine for pain and dressing wounds. Supplies need to last, so don't be too generous with the morphine. But I don't want patients to suffer needlessly either. Use the Mercurochrome to note the time of the dose on their foreheads. And use your watches. The clocks have stopped."

They all glanced at the clock on the wall, which had stopped at 7:55 a.m., as had every other clock on the base, immortalizing the time the attack had begun.

"We don't want to risk giving a patient too much morphine and depressing their respiratory system," cautioned Annie. "Especially if they're going into surgery."

"How about plasma?" asked Winnie.

"Good question," said Annie. "We can't be too generous with that either. Save it for patients clearly in shock. Otherwise, we'll need it in the operating theatre."

A nearby explosion shook the hospital more violently than before. The nurses stopped what they were doing and turned panicked eyes on Annie, who returned their gaze with an unshakable stillness, as though the plaster wasn't falling from above their heads like snowflakes. Finally, the hospital stopped quaking and they resumed gathering supplies.

"We don't know when the attack will end," continued Annie. "We can't waste time worrying about things that are out of our control. Instead of thinking about what's going on out there, we focus on our patients. We need to do everything we can for them."

"It doesn't feel like there's much we can do," said Winnie.

"If all you can do is hold their hand and let them know they're not alone, it will be enough. But most of the time, we can do more. We can tend their wounds to slow bleeding and help prevent infection. For the severely wounded, stabilize them as best you can, and get them to the second floor. We want them ready for surgery when there's an available OR. When the shelling stops, we'll transfer some of the patients to Tripler General and Queen's." Annie pulled a small box from a shelf and ripped it open to reveal prescription pads, then she opened a box of pens. "Take a pad and pen, because the dying might want to send a message home. Write down their name and serial number first, followed by who they're sending the message to and what they want to say. Try not to let them dictate a novella. We can't spend more than a few minutes with each patient."

One of Annie's biggest regrets from the Great War was that she hadn't been prepared to take notes for the dying. She'd tried to remember what they said but had forgotten too much. After that initial failure, she'd never gone near a battlefield without a pad and pencil.

"And blankets." She tucked a pad and pen in her own pocket. "We need a stack in every room on every floor. Shock will be a constant problem. Do I have a volunteer for blankets?"

"I'll take care of it, Chief," said Irene.

"Thank you." Annie was glad she'd offered. Because Irene surfed regularly, she likely had more physical stamina than the others. She would need it. "Use the back stairwell to deliver the blankets. No one ties up the elevator unless you're transporting a patient."

They all nodded.

"Any questions?"

"What if the elevator stops working?" asked Sara.

"Then we put our patient on a gurney and take him up the stairs. But ask one of the orderlies to help."

"I haven't seen the orderlies yet," said Winnie.

"They'll be here," said Annie, praying she was right.

"What if we need a surgical consult?" asked Monica.

"If you can't find me, you'll need to make the call yourselves. I expect the operating theatre will be backed up all day, depending on how many patients we transfer elsewhere. But if you think your patient's life depends on a surgeon's skill, get him in the queue. Anything else?"

"What do we do with the dead?" asked Sara softly.

"Until we can set up a proper morgue, we'll use the backyard." Annie was glad she'd spent all that time out there. At least they would rest on well-tended ground. "First, make sure your patient has passed. I've seen men who suffered egregious injuries on the battlefield be left for dead only to make a full recovery. If you can't take a pulse, check their breathing and their pupils as well as bowel and bladder release. If you still can't tell whether your patient is hanging on to life, err on the side of caution, and leave him where he is until you can get a second opinion. If you're sure he's passed, use the Mercurochrome to place an X on his forehead. And *do not* try to move a body to the backyard without help. Anything else?"

"No, ma'am," they answered in unison.

"Then let's get back to our patients." Annie watched with pride as her nurses rushed back into the fray, not missing a step as another explosion fractured the ceiling into lacework.

On the first floor, Annie enlisted the help of men who weren't too badly hurt to clear all the desks in the administrative offices so they could hold the wounded. They also moved chairs and coatracks to make more room on the floors. She taped signs on doors, designating the different offices: Critical—Hickam OR; Critical—Tripler General or Queen's; Stable; and Backyard. She'd left Major Lance's office alone, thinking they would need a war room. That done, she went back to triaging patients.

Two soldiers wearing blood-spattered T-shirts and sweats carried a man in on a door that had been blown off whatever building it once belonged to. The man's skin was still smoking, like he'd just been taken off a spit over a fire.

"This way." Annie led them to the room with critical patients who would need to be transferred to Tripler General or Queen's. There was nothing they could do for burn victims at Hickam except pass out morphine and apply tannic acid jelly—until they ran out.

As they walked toward the office, one of the men carrying the door spoke to Annie with a slow southern drawl that sounded much like Monica's accent. Annie had always found the dialect soothing but couldn't reconcile the accent with what he was telling her. "Damnedest thing, ma'am. We were on the apron in front of the hangars, shootin' at the Japs, when we saw this guy." He gestured with his chin toward the man lying on the door. "He climbed into a B-18 and mounted a .30-caliber machine gun on the nose of the plane. He don't look big enough to pick up the machine gun, never mind get it on the plane, but he damn well did. He braced it against his shoulder and shot a stream of fire at those sons of bitches until a Zero flew low and set the B-18 on fire. We all wondered how the hell that boy was gonna get outta the burnin' plane, but he didn't even try. He just kept on firin', even when the flames…" He glanced down at the charred body and shook his head. "Damnedest thing I ever saw."

Annie looked at the soldier carrying the other end of the door, who nodded, eyes filled with tears. She directed them to place the door and the patient on top of the desk.

"Can you help him?" asked the soldier with the southern drawl.

"We'll do everything we can," said Annie.

"Thank you, ma'am."

"How bad is it?" she asked. "I haven't been outside in a while."

"It's pretty bad," he said. "They even hit the baseball field. Two guys set up a machine gun between home plate and some trees along the edge of the field. The bastards killed 'em both."

"Take care of each other" was all she could think to say as she watched them leave. Annie took a deep breath before turning to her new patient, reconciling herself to the smell of burning flesh.

The only thing that wasn't scorched was a few strands of pale blond hair and the blue eyes that opened to her. She couldn't take his hand because she was afraid the skin would fall away. Instead, she reached into her pocket for the syringe and leaned down to speak to him. "I'm going to give you something that will take away the pain."

"I'm not in pain, Lieutenant Fox."

Startled, though not by the comment, because fire destroys nerve endings, Annie looked at him more closely and saw a small patch of nearly translucent skin near his hip. "Private Baker?"

"Yes, ma'am."

He'd been so excited about being trained to use the radar equipment, so enthusiastic about what the Army and life had to offer. Why… She stopped herself. She knew better than to ask a question that had no answer. But his burns were so extensive, there was no question about his prognosis. She reached for her pad and pen. "Sam, is there anyone you'd like to send a message to?"

"My father. Samuel Baker. Cleveland, Ohio. 225 Jefferson Road."

She wrote it down. "What would you like to say?"

"Please tell him I was learning about radar. I was with the base commander in the control tower. He was waiting on a dozen new B-17s from California. Lieutenant Colonel Bertholf was there too. He's with the Hawaiian Air Force."

Annie took notes, wanting to catch every word.

"Radar picked up a bunch of planes coming in from about ten thousand feet, but the lieutenant colonel thought it was Navy planes taking off from Ford Island for Pearl Harbor. And Colonel Farthing thought it was the B-17s coming in. And then we saw the first bomb drop on Pearl Harbor. The lieutenant colonel, he rushed right down the tower to sound the alarm, and the colonel left too. I thought I should do something, because I knew they'd come for us. We have all the bombers. So I got a machine gun, and I…"

Annie looked up from her notepad, watched his eyes close, and knew they wouldn't open again. Her eyes traveled to the blood that had seeped from his bullet wounds into a puddle on the door. She wasn't sure if he had died from the burns or the bullets but wrote down "gunshot wounds" as the cause of death because it would be easier for his father to live with than imagining what the fire had done to his son. She didn't need to write down anything else. She would not forget the very pale and very brave Sam Baker if she lived to be one hundred. Which was in doubt as the biggest blast yet rocked the building.

She left the office to get a sheet to cover him and saw patients hurrying to the porch. Joining them, she saw what everyone was silently staring at, mouths agape. A crater took up most of the front lawn. She turned to the person standing closest to her, like her a lieutenant, according to his stripes, who had a wooden splinter impaled in the meat of his right arm. Noted in Mercurochrome on his forehead, his last dose of morphine was administered at 8:22 a.m., which would give him relief until they could remove the splinter and suture his wound.

"It's about forty feet around," he said, gesturing at the crater. "Don't think anything less than a five-hundred-pound bomb could make a hole that big."

"Thank God they missed."

"They missed on purpose. They just wanted to let us know."

"Know what?"

"That they could take out the hospital if they wanted to. They still might. Don't think they're done yet." His tone was resigned. "If I were them, I'd finish us off and hit the West Coast. It's the only thing that makes sense."

Annie knew his matter-of-fact demeanor was probably due to the morphine, which didn't make it any less plausible. "May I take you to the waiting room?"

"Sure," he said.

Annie was leading the lieutenant to a room for noncritical patients when a young soldier stumbled past her. His eyes were unfocused, and he appeared confused about where to go and what to do with the severed lower half of his left arm, which was cradled between what was left of that arm and his right arm.

Pointing the impaled lieutenant in the right direction, Annie hurried across the hospital lobby to the young soldier, making sure she didn't slip on the blood that was already so deep it nearly covered the soles of her shoes. The sheet to cover Sam would have to wait.

Annie opened the door of the supply closet to look for a mop and bucket and instead found her neatly ordered supplies in disarray. Winnie was making even more of a mess in a somewhat frantic search. "What are you looking for?"

Winnie turned to her chief, her eyes leaking tears.

"If you need a minute—"

"I just need Kotex," sniffled Winnie.

Even in the disarray, Annie knew right where it was and handed her the box. But Winnie still wept.

"Weren't you relieved to get your period?" Annie asked.

"Yes," said Winnie. "Because why would I want to bring a child into a world where this kind of cowardly butchery is possible?"

"Because things will get better. Eventually," said Annie. "All we can do for now is—"

"Pass out painkillers. Only I'd rather get a gun and kill every one of those bastards!"

"We're all angry."

"You could've fooled me," said Winnie without rancor. "I swear you've got ice water in your veins. How can you act like nothing's happened, even while it's still happening?"

"Because that's my only option."

"No, it's not. You could…" Winnie appeared stumped.

"Run and hide? Except I don't think there's a safe place on base.

At least not at the moment." Annie gave her a tilted smile and then put a finger to her lips. "Listen."

Winnie listened—to the silence. She wiped her eyes, waiting. "Do you think it's over?"

"Maybe, for now. But not for us." Annie glanced at the box of Kotex. "After you've taken care of yourself, grab more morphine instead of a gun. That's an order, Nurse Mallett." Annie winked before grabbing a mop and bucket. If only the blood they mopped from the floor could be put back into their patients, because they were running out.

NINE

They'd heard the first bombs drop just before eight o'clock. Kay had left her children with Chie while Chie's husband and Kay went up to the roof of their apartment building. They weren't alone in thinking that would give them the best view of what was going on. Several others from their building had also gathered to watch the smoke rise over Pearl Harbor and Hickam Field.

As they all stared in stunned silence, Eddie Endo joined them. Eddie was a fishmonger and up at dawn to collect the morning catch and deliver it to his biggest customer—the U.S. Navy. Stumbling over his words in his hurry to get them out, he shouted his message in English and then in Japanese to make sure even the older men on the roof understood the gravity of the situation. Eddie told them the USS *Arizona*, which had been docked near the USS *Nevada* at Pearl Harbor, where he'd just dropped off a one-hundred-pound tuna, was likely on the ocean floor by now.

"The Navy got caught with its pants down!" he shouted over an explosion in the distance. "I lost count of how many enemy planes I saw. There must have been hundreds! We can't count on anyone coming to our rescue because *they* need to be rescued. All we can do is get inside and pray those planes don't come our way."

Everyone followed Eddie back into the building. Fear was evident in their eyes, particularly the older and wiser, likely wondering what would happen if Japan took control of their island. Would they kill everyone who didn't look like them? Or would they build prisons? Kay had read an article in the local newspaper about a place called Dachau, where Hitler was keeping hundreds of Jews and others he thought were less than the superior race he envisioned. Would the Emperor believe Japanese Americans were inferior because they'd been born in Hawaii and put them in prison too? Or would he take them back to Japan? Perhaps to be subservient to the "true" Japanese born in Japan. Perhaps to serve as soldiers so they might prove their loyalty to him.

Running down the stairwell with Chie's husband, Kay heard another explosion—this one closer—and considered staying with them, but they only had one kitchen table to hide beneath. Besides, Chie's newborn had been crying since the bombing began, likely picking up on his mother's distress, which was also making Tommy and Beth more anxious. She would take her children home. Being in their own surroundings might help calm them.

Back in their own apartment, under the kitchen table where their breakfast had grown cold, Kay tried to explain what was going on. She wanted to be truthful without causing panic.

"The explosions are happening at Pearl Harbor and Hickam Field." She wouldn't tell them she thought they might also be a target. "Japan has sent airplanes to fight against the United States."

"Why?" asked Tommy.

"The reasons are complicated," said Kay.

"That's what you always say when you think we won't under-stand," said Beth. "Or when you don't want to tell us."

There was another explosion that sent a small tremor through the floor beneath them. Kay wondered if the Japanese pilots had orders to bomb the entire island and pulled her children closer while trying not to appear too frightened.

"All I can tell you is what I've read in the papers. Japan wants to expand…" She saw Tommy's bewilderment and rephrased. "Japan wants more land than it has. Like when your friend Joey wanted all the marbles at recess—more than his fair share. I think Japan thought our country would stop them from taking more marbles, so the Emperor of Japan thought he would show President Roosevelt who's boss."

"But President Roosevelt is the boss," said Beth. "Isn't he?"

"Yes," said Kay. "And I'm sure he'll let the Emperor know. Soon."

Another explosion shook the house. Kay realized someone's home or business must've been hit and wondered if their building would be next. She couldn't remember ever being more afraid in her life, and there was nothing she could do but cower under the table. She could never have imagined feeling this powerless when her children were in danger.

"Is Annie okay?" asked Tommy as he tugged on a piece of the tablecloth like it could hide him from the enemy.

"You mean Miss Fox," said Beth.

"She said we could call her Annie," said Tommy defensively.

"She's an adult," said Kay. "Call her Miss Fox. And I'm sure she's fine." Though she wasn't at all sure. How would those stationed at Pearl Harbor or Hickam Field survive this onslaught? She imagined thousands of casualties, especially if ships had actually sunk as Eddie had said.

"Why are our ancestors trying to kill Miss Fox?" asked Tommy.

Kay suspected who had planted the seed for this concern. Her mother, who the children called Sobo—Japanese for grandma—kept an altar that held a tablet on which were inscribed the names of their ancestors. As soon as Beth was old enough to understand, Sobo would bring the tablet to the couch and sit with her granddaughter. She would read the names of the dead and talk about each one like she was reading a book of fairy tales. Then she and Beth would prepare rice as an offering. Beth had started to do this when she was three years old; Tommy had begun when he was four.

While Kay wanted her children to learn about relatives who had passed, she wanted them to be more invested in and obligated to the living—in their own country. However, their grandmother was adamant that no person could live to their full potential without accessing the strength and wisdom of their family tree, which was firmly rooted in Japan.

Another explosion came from somewhere to the south. Holding her children tightly, Kay waited a moment so she could speak without her voice trembling. "Why would you think our ancestors want to harm Miss Fox?" she asked.

"Because Sobo said they protect us from evil," said Tommy.

Kay was still unclear and looked to Beth for clarification.

"Sobo said the battleships were made to do evil," said Beth. "And that she wished our ancestors would push them all off the edge of the ocean."

"First of all, ships can't fall off the ocean because our planet is round. Second, the battleships were made to protect us," said Kay, reminding herself to keep it simple. "Anyway, Annie…Miss Fox doesn't work on a battleship."

She sometimes wished her children were old enough to understand the dichotomy that existed within their grandmother. On the one hand, her mother was very grateful that the United States had accepted her and her husband after they'd fled Japan for speaking out against the regime. Thus, she very much valued the U.S. constitution and the freedoms it provided. On the other hand, she believed any war machine was built to kill, and the United States had built the biggest machines. Hence, she both loved and feared her new country. Kay would not let her pass that fear on to her grandchildren.

"Do the bad guys have battleships?" asked Tommy.

"What if they have more than we do?" asked Beth.

Kay struggled to find a way to explain this without making them more afraid and do it without lying. "You know how sometimes when we listen to *The Lone Ranger*, we get really scared that he and Tonto won't make it out of whatever jam they're in?"

The Lone Ranger was their favorite radio show. They'd sit together and listen, holding hands during the harrowing parts.

"Sometimes it seems as if the bad guys are going to win," said Kay. "But somehow, the Lone Ranger and Tonto always defeat their enemies."

"Because they're the good guys," said Beth matter-of-factly.

"Like Captain America." Tommy held up his Captain America comic book as evidence. It was the only thing he'd grabbed to take with him under the table.

"Exactly," said Kay. "Even when it seems like good won't triumph, it does."

"Will Uncle Kenji kill the bad guys with his sword?" said Tommy.

Again, Kay looked at Beth for help.

"Sobo said our *great*-uncle Kenji was a samurai," explained Beth, "and he defeated many enemies with his sword."

"We gave him rice last week," said Tommy. "If he liked it, maybe he'll take care of the bad guys for us. And maybe he'll protect Miss Fox because she's one of the good guys."

"Maybe he will," said Kay. Whatever helped her children get through this was welcome, even the ghost of Great-Uncle Kenji.

They had been huddled together under their kitchen table for almost two hours. The hardest thing, other than the fact that they could be blown apart any minute, was that Kay was used to having options. Even when there were no more effective treatments for a patient with a terminal illness, she could offer palliative care to make them comfortable. Under her kitchen table, she had no options. If a bomb hit her apartment building, all she could do to protect her children was shield them with her body. Her flesh might act like a large sandbag, though it would be less effective. On the other hand, sand could not console or comfort, which made her wonder who was comforting her own mother.

Kay also thought about her nurses. Two were married and likely with their husbands, and one still lived with her parents. Amai had just gotten an apartment of her own—her first—and she'd been so excited. Kay hoped her mother and Amai weren't alone and had taken shelter with neighbors. Mak also lived alone, but she couldn't imagine him being afraid under any circumstances. She could, however, imagine him boiling over with rage at the enemy for causing even more damage to his beloved island.

It surprised her that the last person whose safety she thought about was her husband. Maybe that made sense. After all, he wasn't on the island. But had Daiji somehow been part of this attack? Why would he have told her to take the children away before today if he hadn't known something horrible was about to happen? If she'd opened his note sooner and listened to him, her children would be safe. Unless Japan had also attacked the mainland. There was no way of knowing.

After what felt like days, Kay and the children crawled out from under the kitchen table, took a deep breath, and stretched. She saw the relief in Beth and Tommy and knew they believed the worst was over. She would let them believe it. She told them to pack a few things because they were going to spend the night at Sobo's house. She didn't tell them it was because their grandmother's home was farther away from Pearl Harbor and Hickam Field. She didn't tell them she wasn't sure the attack was over. All she said was that their grandmother was alone and frightened and needed them but that Sobo would never admit it, so they would tell her they needed her.

On their way out of the apartment building, they saw many of their neighbors doing the same, carrying overnight bags to their cars. Kay was about to get into the driver's side of her own car when she heard someone calling her name. Assuming someone needed medical attention, she nearly didn't turn because she was so desperate to get Beth and Tommy to a safer neighborhood. But it wasn't a patient; it was her neighbor and friend.

Ivy Watanabe had lived next door for as long as Kay could

remember. A good neighbor who was there when you needed her but didn't make a nuisance of herself when you didn't, Ivy worked at the Iolani Palace downtown as Governor Poindexter's secretary. By the look on Ivy's face, which was typically cheerful, Kay wondered if the palace had been hit, which would be a shame. The palace had housed every ruler of the kingdom of Hawaii.

"Ivy, are you all right?" asked Kay, staying by the car in case they heard the sound of planes coming.

"I'm fine," said Ivy, smoothing her dress as she'd just gotten out of her own car, which she'd parked behind Kay's. Ivy was always dressed impeccably out of respect for the governor's office. "But I need to tell you something that you must keep to yourself. I'm not allowed to repeat anything I hear while I'm at work."

"Of course."

Ivy smiled at the children and gave them a little wave through the car window. Keeping her smile in place, she spoke softly. "A bomb dropped in the street in front of the governor's home this morning."

"Is he all right?" asked Kay.

"Yes, but another man was killed. Someone who just happened to be crossing the street. And there are two craters in the ground just outside the palace, near the veranda where the governor sometimes has his coffee."

"Then they're not just targeting the military," said Kay.

"We can't be sure if they're hitting civilian targets on purpose. It could be that Honolulu was hit by antiaircraft fire. Either way, you need to be prepared for what you might see. For what the children might see."

"Thank you for warning me." Kay started to reach for the door handle.

"There's something else." Ivy moved closer to her. "General Short—"

"General Short?"

"He's the man in charge of all the military installations in Hawaii. He had a meeting with the governor this morning, and they talked about there not being enough police if the Filipinos and Chinese turn against us."

"Why would they turn against us?"

"I'm sure you've heard rumors that some Japanese Americans have been helping the enemy and that some are planning an insurrection. The Filipinos and Chinese might blame us for the attack."

"That's ridiculous." Even as she said it, Kay wondered if her husband had written to any of his friends on the island about such a plan. If not her husband, maybe other disillusioned men who'd returned to Japan.

"After what's happened, Governor Poindexter said he couldn't take any chances. He doesn't think the local police could handle an insurrection or the people who might rise up in protest against one. He's going to impose martial law. It goes into effect at 3:30. Today."

"What does that mean?"

"It means that all of us will be under military rule," said Ivy somberly. "General Short plans to institute a curfew and a blackout that will begin tonight. From now on, the military will be in charge of everything— from how food is distributed to how traffic is routed. The hospitals and emergency facilities will all be under the Army's control."

"Even my community center?"

"Yes. People may already be there. We've heard reports of injuries in addition to civilian fatalities."

"What about Pearl Harbor and Hickam Field? How bad is it?"

"We fear there have been thousands of casualties," Ivy whispered. "At least two ships have sunk, and hundreds of planes are still burning."

Kay suddenly had an image of Annie drinking okolehao and laughing. She filled with grief but pushed it back down. Her children needed her. "Will the Japanese planes come back?" Kay asked.

"They can't be sure," said Ivy. "But I think you should prepare for the worst. I only came home to check on my husband and collect a few things. The governor needs me to stay at the palace for the next few days; we'll be working around the clock. Whether or not the Japanese planes come back, he expects the president to declare war."

Kay covered her mouth with her hand and, at the same time, wondered how she could be shocked. Of course they were at war with Japan. President Roosevelt had no choice. But her husband had, and he'd chosen Japan. He would be expecting her to do the same.

"One more thing," said Ivy. "Like me, you were born here and are considered a citizen of the United States. And like me, your parents were born in Japan, so Japan considers you to be one of its citizens."

"Are you asking where my loyalty lies?" Kay and Ivy had talked for too many hours over sake about how loyal they were to the country in which they were born. There was a cumbersome process in which a U.S. citizen of parents born in Japan could legally be untangled from automatic Japanese citizenship, but it had never dawned on Kay or Ivy to go to the trouble.

"Of course not, Kay" said Ivy gently. "I only want to remind you in case Japan takes the islands. If that happens—and I'm not saying it will—you might have to make a decision based on what's best for your children."

They embraced, and Kay knew every decision she would make that day would be for her children.

Taking as many back roads to her mother's home as she could, Kay was relieved that Beth and Tommy had not witnessed anything more disconcerting than empty streets. People were still too afraid to come outside unless they were trying to get to another part of the island.

Kay found her mother kneeling at the family altar, praying for the strength to deal with whatever happened next. Kay waited until she'd finished praying and then explained that she needed to go to her community center to help the injured and would return as soon as possible. Her mother wasn't happy but understood, and not for the first time, Kay was grateful for her. While she was never satisfied unless she knew everything about Kay's life, she could always be counted on not to add to an already difficult situation. Even when Daiji left, she hadn't said a word against him. He was the father of her grandchildren and deserved respect.

Before Kay left for the center, her mother handed her an *omamori*—a small silk brocade bag. Inside was a prayer written on a folded piece of paper. She had been saving it as a New Year's gift, but because it was considered a protective talisman or good-luck charm, she gave it to her daughter now. Kay had to promise that she wouldn't open it to read the prayer, which was bad luck.

Tucking the small red bag into her pocket, she kissed her mother goodbye, wondering if it would be the last time, and whether she would see her children again. Because if there was one thing she believed with near certainty, it was that the Japanese bombers would return. It wasn't in their nature to leave a job unfinished.

On her way to the community center, Kay thought about how she and her family used to spend their Sundays. She and Daiji would take the children to the beach, where they would have lunch and swim. Along the way, he would drive through neighborhoods where people were having cookouts, talking with neighbors, or playing with kids in the yard. Sundays were happy days. But today, even the birds seemed to be hiding.

When Kay got to the center, she saw a long line of people waiting to get inside. An older man slowly made his way toward the entrance, and she rushed over to help him. He'd been in his backyard tending to a rosebush when he heard what sounded like loud gunfire right before his backside was impaled by a piece of his garage. He'd pulled the stick out, stuck several dish towels down the back of his pants to stanch the bleeding, and started walking toward the community center.

When they got inside, Mak led their new patient to an examination room, while Kay took a mother whose ten-year-old's head had been cut by broken glass. Amai, who had arrived soon after Mak, was treating a victim who needed stitches in another exam room while two of Kay's other nurses manned the phone and door, respectively.

While picking bits of glass out of the young girl's scalp, Kay was surprised that her hands were steady. She also felt relatively calm for the first time since she'd heard the initial bombing. Maybe it was because she was doing her job, which made it feel more like a normal day. Or maybe it was because the community center was undamaged. She hadn't realized she'd been worried about the building being bombed until she had time to sit and think.

The building had been the first laundromat on the island, but the space proved to be too small for the demand. When Aloha Dirty

& Dingy moved to a bigger space, Kay took out a one-year lease on the building and recruited friends and family to create the Japanese American Community Center. By 1941, Kay was on her fourth one-year lease.

For the rest of the morning, patients came in with various injuries. People also came in for reassurance, particularly the elderly. Whoever wasn't tending to a patient was offering words of comfort along with tea and rice crackers to soothe nervous stomachs. A few hours passed before Kay had a chance to speak to Mak alone about something other than a patient. When they were finally in the kitchen at the same time, she gave him a quick hug.

"Thank you for coming in today." She'd been so happy to see him when she'd first arrived. Mak was like one of the mountains—solid and somehow everlasting.

"Where else would I be?" he asked.

"With your family."

"My brother and his family are with my mother. They're safe. The kids?"

"They're with my mother."

He nodded his approval. "Her house is a good distance from Pearl Harbor and Hickam Field. They should be safe too."

"If we're not attacked again."

"They attacked the military," said Mak, "not us."

"Tell that to our patients."

"I didn't see any Japanese planes over Honolulu. The injuries might be a result of U.S. antiaircraft fire."

"That's what Ivy said."

"What else did she say?"

"The governor will impose martial law at 3:30."

"Jesus Christ, that means the military's taking over."

"That might not be a bad thing, considering."

"Considering the fact that we wouldn't have been attacked if not for—"

"Don't start, Mak. We have enough to worry about." She reached for her cup of tea, her hand trembling again.

"What's wrong?" he asked.

"Other than the fact that those Japanese planes could come back any minute? Or that we're at war with the country all my ancestors are from?"

"Are you worried about Daiji?" he asked, unfazed by her sarcasm.

"No," she said flatly. "Leaving was his decision. And if he's chosen to fight for Japan, he's chosen never to return."

"Unless he believes Hawaii will become part of Japan."

"Don't count us out yet," she said.

"I'd never count you out, Kay."

She wanted him to hold her and tell her everything would be all right. It would be difficult not to believe it in his arms. But he wasn't her husband, and she had no right to his strength. "Do you think Hickam Field was hit as hard as Pearl Harbor?"

"The bombing went on for more than an hour. And the Japanese are...precise."

For the first time that day, Kay wanted to weep. Instead, she filled the kettle to make another pot of tea. More people would need a cup of warm comfort.

TEN

After designating a small crew to mop duty, Annie made it up to the third floor to check on her ward and found Sara grappling with Sergeant Drummer, who had carried Jeremy in from the parade ground. "What's going on?"

"The sergeant wants to leave," said Sara. "Against my advice."

"Are you injured, Sergeant?"

"A bomb hit close enough to send me flyin', and I bumped my noggin. Told the master sergeant I was okay, but he ordered me to get checked out. So here I am. But like I told your nurse, I feel fine."

"Nurse Entrikin?" asked Annie. Sara wouldn't have advised him to stay—not with the hundreds of patients they already had—if she didn't think it was necessary.

"I suspect he has a concussion," said Sara. "Perhaps a hematoma. There's bruising on the back of his head, and he's exhibited some confusion."

"Is there anybody who's not confused right about now?" he asked.

"I doubt it," admitted Annie. "But do me a favor and stay put, Sergeant Drummer."

"Don't see any reason why I should," he said.

"Maybe because my lieutenant asked you to," said Sara, "and she outranks you."

A soldier first, the sergeant appeared reluctantly resigned.

"Just sit down for a little while, Sergeant," said Annie. "You've earned a break. But don't fall asleep. And if you feel any worse in any way, tell one of us. That's an order."

"Yes, ma'am."

Annie led Sara away from the patients. "Is there anything you need?"

"Besides a dozen more nurses and more of everything but patients?"

"Yes, other than that." Annie returned her half smile.

"I need to know what's happened to my sister. I need to know if she's okay. They bombed the hell out of…" Her chin quivering, Sara couldn't continue.

"I wish I could tell you how bad it is at Pearl Harbor, but we've got no communication with anyone who doesn't come through our doors. Just keep in mind that they bombed the hell out of us too, and we're still here." Annie gave Sara an awkward hug, which took them both off guard. Nevertheless, Sara hung on even after Annie let go. Not knowing what to do, Annie stayed still, letting Sara pull away when she was ready.

Annie stood in the major's office, holding out a ham and cheese sandwich wrapped in waxed paper. Hickam's kitchen was intact, and a few of the military wives who didn't have children had come to make food. Having passed out sandwiches to her nurses, the major was last on Annie's list.

"No time to eat." He wore a blood-spattered surgical gown and was rifling through a cabinet. "I just came to see if I have building schematics. On top of everything else, we have a break in the water main, and they need to know exactly where the pipes are located."

Annie put his sandwich on the desk. "I'll look. You eat."

"Have you eaten?" he asked.

"I'm fine. I had a big breakfast." Not for the first time, she wondered if the hundreds of men she'd had breakfast with were still alive. "But if you don't eat, your hands might shake. A surgeon's hands can't shake."

He picked up the sandwich and took a resentful bite, seeming to swallow without bothering to chew. "Hickam's fire department got hit, so we put in a call to the Honolulu Fire Department. They're sending engines from Palama and Kalihi, but I doubt it'll be enough. Our water main got hit by a bomb that left a huge goddamned crater that's filling with water, so none of the hydrants are working."

"Let someone else focus on the fires outside the hospital," said Annie as she searched through a file cabinet for the schematics. "You've got enough to deal with right here."

He took another bite of his sandwich.

"Do you think the Naval hospital at Pearl Harbor is still standing?" she asked.

"They left us alone, so I'm assuming they respected the big red cross on top of the Naval hospital as well. They've only got two hundred and fifty beds, which won't be enough. They're building a new hospital off base, but it's nowhere near ready for patients. If the hospital ship *Solace* is undamaged, they'll send men there. But we're bound to get some of the overflow, at least until the Navy can get patients to Tripler and Queen's."

"Even without their overflow, we need more nurses," said Annie, continuing her search.

"We also need the seriously wounded out of harm's way, but we don't have enough vehicles for transport. I need to go to Queen's; it's the biggest hospital on the island. I'll ask them to send ambulances, along with nurses, supplies, and blood."

She pulled out the building plans and handed them to him. "Ambulances, nurses, supplies, and blood. Got it. I'll leave now."

"I said I'm going."

"You can't. Who knows how many more men you'll need to operate on before they're stable enough to be transported."

"Point taken. Send one of your nurses."

"I won't ask any of them to go. For all we know, the enemy could be setting up headquarters in Honolulu as we speak."

"Which is why you're not going."

"Well, we can't send any of our doctors or any man able to lift the wounded or the dead. And we need to send someone to Queen's who knows what they're talking about."

"Agreed. Which of your nurses is the best driver?"

"I am," she said, making sure to use her most determined tone. "And I know my way around Honolulu from going to the community center."

"Then write down directions. I won't lose you, Annie."

Despite what her head knew about their relationship, her heart skipped a beat.

As if he'd heard it and needed to make a course correction, he said, "You're my chief nurse."

"I'm going to Queen's Hospital," she responded resolutely.

Unlocking a desk drawer, he pulled out a .45-caliber pistol and held it out to her. "In case the rumors are true."

She took the pistol and put it in her pocket, next to the ham and cheese sandwich she was saving for whenever she had a chance—and the appetite—to eat it.

"Change into civvies before you leave," he said. "You'll have a target on your back otherwise."

"Will do."

"And report to me as soon as you get back."

"Yes, sir."

He pulled a set of keys out of his pocket. "Take my Jeep. First gear's a little sticky, but she'll get you where you need to go, and she's got a full tank of gas."

Annie put the keys in her pocket.

"I expect my car to be returned without a scratch," he added.

"I'll do my best." Forcing a smile, she wanted to embrace him, as Sara had embraced her, and hang on until night fell. But it was early yet, and there was so much more to do.

Without running water and not wanting to use rubbing alcohol or anything else the patients might need, Annie had a difficult time cleaning the blood off her hands and face with only a rag. She'd quickly changed into civilian clothes and put the gun and sandwich in her purse. Rather than walking over the bodies lying in the backyard, she left through the front door, which meant passing many patients who needed help. Yet for her, it was better than walking past patients who were beyond help.

The huge crater in the front yard was still smoking. The flagpole holding the American flag had snapped in two, the flag lost down the black hole. Annie had an impulse to hang over the edge and reach in to see if she could pull it back up, but she knew that was foolish. Of all the sights she'd seen that morning, she wasn't sure why this bothered her so much.

"Hey, Army," came a voice from behind her on the porch.

Turning, Annie saw one of the young sailors who had cheered from the bar for the Navy football team. The night she'd gone out drinking with Kay and Mak seemed so long ago, but it had only been a few weeks. She knelt by the sailor, whose white uniform was covered with black oil. Both of his hands were burned, and the fingertips of his right hand looked like sticks of charcoal one might use for sketching.

"My ship… The *Oklahoma* went down."

It was incomprehensible. She felt as if she'd slipped into another world where nothing made sense. "Navy always comes back to win," she said like they were back at the bar.

He managed a smile that trembled before it disappeared, and he began shaking. Surveying the porch, she spotted a diminishing pile of blankets.

"Be right back," she told him before gingerly walking over and around other patients to grab a blanket and bring it back, gently covering him. "I have to go get more supplies, but I'm going to send my best nurse to take care of you."

"The best *Army* nurse." He winked as she rose to leave him.

Navigating her way around more injured soldiers, she went to the back side of the porch where Monica was triaging patients. "I'm leaving the base to get supplies. If I'm lucky, I'll bring back nurses and blood too."

"Chief, it's not safe. You can't—"

"You're in charge while I'm gone, Nurse Conter. If something comes up that you can't handle, consult Major Lance. He'll be in OR one. And there's a patient on the other side of the porch, a young sailor covered in oil with burnt fingers. He's going into shock. I gave him a blanket, but he needs IV plasma and saline with five percent glucose. I told him I was sending my best nurse. Don't make a liar out of me."

Smiling sadly, Monica nodded. "Be careful, Chief. And please don't be gone too long."

"That's the plan." Annie turned to step off the porch and saw the horror that was their backyard. Bodies were stacked side by side, some burned, some covered in oil, some limbless, while others appeared untouched, likely having died from brain trauma or internal injuries.

Two soldiers waited by the next body while Irene checked for a pulse. There was no obvious damage other than minor abrasions, so Irene felt for a pulse at the throat, wrist, and ankle. She nodded, and the two soldiers picked up the body.

Annie bowed her head in silence as they carefully placed Sergeant Drummer on the ground next to the others. Sara had likely been right; he'd had an intracranial hematoma from the bomb blast, which probably would have been fatal even with surgery. Before he died, the sergeant had carried several injured men to the hospital. Jeremy was still alive because of him, and Annie vowed he would stay that way.

Enveloped in smoke, dust, heat, and the overwhelming smell of fuel, Annie stopped at the parade ground as she made her way to the parking area and looked toward Pearl Harbor. All she could see was a mass of smoke and flames. Hickam's airfield was the same; many of the bombers were still burning. The enlisted men's barracks had suffered heavy damage, and she wondered how many men had died without having a chance to get out of bed. The fire station and chapel were also in ruins, and the theatre looked like a pile of matchsticks; the only thing left was a half-buried sign with the words "Coming Soon" still visible.

Seeing what was left of Hickam made her wonder when the Zeros would be back. In the next ten minutes? In an hour? Or would they wait until dark? No matter when it happened, she was sure they would be back to finish the job. Unless the Japanese had offered to curtail another attack in exchange for Hawaii. Perhaps President Roosevelt was negotiating terms of surrender. Annie's heart hammered at the thought of abandoning the island and its people.

By the time she reached the parking lot, she'd tamped down her own panic, but there was more than enough on display as mothers and crying children deserted Hickam's residential areas and ran toward civilian cars that would take them away from the madness. She couldn't blame them for leaving but knew the only road off the base would be backed up because of it.

Major Lance's Jeep did have a sticky first gear, and it didn't help that Annie had to shift gears every other minute as she inched her way onto the Kamehameha Highway, where at least the cars were moving. Cajoling the shift into third gear, Annie made good progress until the traffic stopped again. "Goddamn it to hell!" She hit the steering wheel with her hands until she saw what had been holding things up.

A Ford sedan was parked on the side of the highway. Smoke

seeped through what appeared to be hundreds of bullet holes as paint peeled from the driver's door like sunburned skin. The driver's clothes had burned off, and black skin outlined a face no longer recognizable. In the seat beside him, the passenger was bent forward, still holding a Thompson submachine gun. Whoever they had been—locals or off-duty servicemen—they'd been coming to help.

Annie gripped the wheel tight and kept her focus forward. As if channeling Annie's intent, the mother driving the car in front of her was pointing forward in a directive to her children—two boys who appeared to be around eight and eleven. The younger boy obeyed his mom and looked away from the atrocity on the side of the road, but the older boy kept staring, as if trying to understand what had happened.

Annie wondered if anyone would ever understand.

Annie got off the highway and drove down the empty residential streets toward Queen's Hospital. She assumed civilians had been warned to stay inside due to the attacks on Pearl Harbor and Hickam Field, but then she saw the first house that had been split in half— and then another. Had these homes been hit by the Japanese or by misfired U.S. antiaircraft shells? There was no way of knowing for sure until there was an investigation.

Driving more slowly, as if passing a cemetery, Annie saw several homes that had been obliterated, like a tornado had touched down, choosing its victims at random. And then she saw Mr. Taketa sitting on a curb in front of a house that appeared untouched. She pulled over to the curb, got out of the Jeep, and approached him. "Mr. Taketa, are you hurt?"

Slowly, he peered up but didn't seem to recognize her. He was in his stocking feet, as though he hadn't had time to put his shoes on when the bombing began and had run out to see what was happening.

"I'm Annie Fox...from the community center."

He still looked bewildered, and she wondered if he understood what she was saying. She'd heard him speak English, but not very much of it and not very often.

"I'm a nurse, like Kay," she said more loudly, in case he had trouble hearing.

He understood something she'd said because he rose and took her hand, pulling her toward his bungalow-style home with urgency. When they got inside, the living room also appeared untouched by the day's destruction. Everything was uncluttered and neat, like the two pairs of shoes aligned by the door.

Annie slipped off her shoes and followed him into the dining room where a typical Japanese breakfast for two—steamed rice and fish—was set on the table. Mr. Taketa's part of the local newspaper was on the floor, where it must have fallen when he stood. His wife's part of the paper lay by the side of her breakfast plate, which Mrs. Taketa was slumped over, a thin line of blood trailing down her face. Annie didn't need to feel for a pulse but did so to satisfy Mr. Taketa, who watched her every move. Glancing at a small hole in the window, Annie imagined that was where a bullet or some other projectile had come through before penetrating Mrs. Taketa's temple.

Annie turned to Mr. Taketa. She'd seen the look on his face a hundred times before—hope hanging by a frail thread that she was about to break. "There's not much blood." She took his hand. "That means your wife died almost instantly. No pain."

Still dazed, he looked at his wife and then back at Annie.

"Do you understand?" she asked.

Hesitating, he said, "No pain."

Annie watched the grief settle into the lines of his face, where she thought it would reside permanently. People who'd been married as long as they had didn't get over the death of a spouse. Often, they couldn't even accept it. She remembered a couple who her father had treated. In their eighties, they had been healthy for the most part until one morning when Louise woke to find that her husband of sixty-two years had died in his sleep while lying right beside her. From that point, Louise always referred to his death as "that awful dream."

Annie helped Mr. Taketa move his wife to the couch, where they covered her with a blanket. Before she left, Annie saw him pick up a book from the coffee table, sit in a chair beside her, and begin to read aloud. Maybe Kay would be able to help him accept his wife's death. Maybe he wouldn't live in a dreamworld as Louise had done. Until then, it would hurt no one if he believed his wife was only sleeping.

As she drove along a deserted street, Annie counted seven stores that were damaged to some extent, including a drugstore that might have supplies they needed. If she could find the owner, she would ask permission. If no one was there, she would leave a note saying the U.S. Army was grateful and would be happy to reimburse them after the war was over. She was certain they were at war. A surprise attack on the Pacific Fleet could result in nothing else. And war gave her license to take what she needed for the sake of keeping the troops in fighting shape.

She parked the Jeep near the drugstore, got out, and tucked

Major Lance's gun inside her waistband before walking by odd pieces of wreckage scattered on the ground. Half-burned Christmas cards—on one, "Joy to the World" was still visible. A twin-size mattress that would have been a great find if it hadn't been burned. An array of canned food—contents unknown because of the blackened labels, though it looked like the red and white of Campbell's soup. A twisted child's tricycle. And right in front of the drugstore, a metal Pinocchio lunch box that was unscathed.

Annie picked up the lunch box and took it with her into the drugstore. The walls were charred and rippled, appearing ready to cave in at any moment. She started toward the pharmacy section when she heard something crunch under her foot. A package of scorched bonbons. Ignoring the ruined treats, she picked through bottles of pain medications, searching for anything with morphine, and put what drugs and burn ointments might be useful in the lunch box. She quickly scanned shelves for soap that would help clean the black oil off the skin of patients and their nurses. As she put bars of Lava soap in the lunch box, she nearly dropped it as something crashed behind her.

It was a display of Coca-Cola, the brown fizzy liquid running toward the worn shoes of a teenager filling a white pillowcase with sandwiches. The drugstore had prepared an assortment for their Sunday shoppers, and he was taking a few of each: chicken salad, egg salad, toasted pimento cheese, and BLTs. He began to add several bonbons that hadn't fallen on the floor to his pillowcase when he spotted Annie.

Trapped and scared, he no longer looked like a teenager but a looter who was nearly six feet tall and capable of doing harm. Annie thought about taking the gun out of her waistband but knew she wouldn't be able to live with herself if she shot him. He was some-one's son. Instead, she held up the lunch box and shook it gently so he could hear the click-clack of her own loot. Then she backed up. Slowly. And so did he. Détente.

On her way out of the store, she passed the soda fountain, where there was a half-eaten chocolate sundae on the counter. *Why would someone let their child eat a sundae for breakfast?* In the next moment, she thought herself ridiculous for judging anyone's parenting skills on such a day. She hurried toward the Jeep and placed the lunch box on the passenger seat. Glancing at Pinocchio as she started the car, Annie knew it had also been absurd to think a lunch box full of medication would be of much help in treating the hundreds of patients waiting for relief at Hickam Hospital. She pulled back onto the empty street, shifting past the sticky gear as she accelerated, and counted on a much bigger take from Queen's Hospital.

Annie took a deep breath in relief when she saw the unblemished facade of Queen's Hospital, which had originally been built because so many Hawaiians were threatened by diseases brought by outsiders, particularly smallpox. Evidenced by the line of ambulances outside the emergency department, the hospital was currently coping with another onslaught brought by outsiders.

At least two dozen patients with various injuries filled the seats of the emergency department's waiting room. Not as serious as the wounds she'd seen at Hickam, but bad enough to require medical attention. Quelling an urge to triage, she walked past them toward the nurses' station where a dozen more patients stood in front of her. Unable to wait, she repeated "pardon me" as she made her way to the head of the line. Most were too dazed to care, but one woman who held a young child with a break in her forearm was outraged. "Who do you think you are?"

"I'm so sorry. I have an emergency."

The woman looked Annie up and down. "Where?"

"Not me." Annie turned to the triage nurse, who was in her thirties. "I'm from Hickam Field."

Hearing this, the woman with the child didn't step back, but she was quiet as Annie addressed the nurse.

"We need help," said Annie, willing her voice not to shake. "May I speak to the doctor in charge, please?"

"When he's not busy," said the nurse.

"I can't wait. Hickam is—"

"Right next to Pearl Harbor," the woman with the child told the nurse. "My cousin's stationed there." She turned to Annie. Her child groaned with the shift in position, and the woman gently stroked her back, keeping her tone even, like they were discussing the weather. "Did they hit the ships?"

Annie wanted to lie. She wanted to say she was sure many had survived the carnage. But she couldn't. "Yes. I'm afraid some were hit," she said, turning back to the nurse.

"Follow me." The nurse gestured for another woman to take her place and led Annie through the double doors.

Doctors and nurses entered and exited various exam rooms, letting the beeps and buzzes of machines, the moans of adult patients, and the cries of children escape into the hallway. Annie waited impatiently outside one of the exam rooms. Her stomach growled and she was tempted to reach for the ham and cheese sandwich but didn't want to speak to the doctor with a mouthful of food. Finally, the doctor came out.

"Lieutenant Annie Fox, chief nurse at Hickam Hospital." Annie held out her hand.

"Theodore Thomas, chief of staff. I'm not usually in the ED, but we need every pair of hands." He gestured to a quiet alcove, and Annie and the nurse followed. "How bad is it out there?"

Annie had to be careful. If people knew Pearl Harbor and Hickam Field had been decimated, it would only spread panic. On the other hand, she needed his help and couldn't sugarcoat it. "There are many casualties and communications are down, which is why I've come to you for help. We don't have enough ambulances to transport patients to Tripler or here. We could also use more doctors, nurses, and supplies. Not to mention blood."

"I can send ambulances and supplies, but I can't give you blood or personnel."

"Queen's is the biggest hospital on the island. Surely you can spare—"

"If you hadn't noticed, Honolulu got hit too. I have no idea how extensive the damage is or how many patients we'll get. And I don't think anyone knows when the enemy will be back. We have to be prepared to take care of many more patients."

"I understand. But there are so many soldiers who might die if—"

"We're happy to take care of all servicemen who come here, and I'll send a few ambulances out to Hickam Field." He turned to the nurse. "Nurse Kekoa, please give Lieutenant Fox whatever supplies you think we can spare, given our own uncertainty."

Before Annie could say another word, he strode into an examination room.

Twenty minutes later, Annie, Nurse Kekoa, and an orderly carried several boxes down a long hallway. Hickam Hospital still needed blood, nurses, and doctors, but at least she would return with more medication. She was especially grateful for the morphine.

"Thank you for the supplies," said Annie.

"I wish we could do more," said Nurse Kekoa.

"You could come with me. Even one person could make a difference. If you saw—"

"Maybe you need to see." She stopped and put the box she carried on the floor. "Please come with me."

Reluctantly, Annie followed Nurse Kekoa into the hospital morgue. They were quiet, like they were in a church. Staying near the door, the nurse motioned her forward. The first thing Annie noticed was the cold. She couldn't remember the last time she'd been in a morgue. It must have been in nursing school, but she couldn't grab hold of the memory. Holding her sweater close instead, she saw burned bodies lying on slabs in whatever grotesque position they had died. Fear equally contorted the final expression of every ethnicity on the island, their clothes a bluish-black from incendiary bombs.

Annie involuntarily backed up and nearly tripped. Steadying herself, she saw another slab. Lying on it was a little girl, her feet and legs badly burned. Her red sweater was singed along the edges. The handle of a jump rope seemed to have melted into her right hand. Streaked with ash, the handle was red, white, and blue. Like Captain America's shield. Annie didn't think it could be the same girl Beth had spoken of, but her eyes still pooled for the girl who had wanted to trade paper dolls for a jump rope.

In the parking lot, they loaded the back of the Jeep with boxes.

"Do you think a smaller civilian hospital would give me blood?" asked Annie.

"I doubt it," said Nurse Kekoa. "Everyone's expecting another attack. But if you're open-minded, I know where you might be able to get donors."

Annie nodded, and the nurse whispered in her ear. Annie didn't think anything else could have shocked her that day, but she was wrong.

ELEVEN

Even though many homes and schools had been damaged or destroyed, Hotel Street had been spared. As Annie had suspected from her time in the Great War, there was no rhyme or reason to where the darts landed on life's big bull's-eye. Whoever was throwing those darts was either blind or didn't care who or what got hit.

Despite the street having been spared, it was difficult to imagine that the women who lived in these second- and third-rate hotels would consider coming with her to Hickam Field to donate blood. Hickam had been one of the two main targets that morning, and there were military police on base. The last thing a prostitute wanted to see was a policeman, unless he was paying for her services. Nevertheless, Annie had run out of options. She'd quickly stopped at two smaller civilian hospitals who'd also refused to give her blood, though she had added a few boxes of tannic acid to her supplies. With all the burns they would treat, those pit stops had been worth the extra time.

She pulled up to the "best" of the hotels, which wasn't saying much. As she got out of the Jeep, a woman in her late twenties came out the front door. She wore a low-cut dress, and her hair and makeup had been done to imitate Rita Hayworth. "We're closed," she said. "On account of the attack. But even if we were open, there aren't many of us who entertain women."

"No," said Annie. "I'm not here for… One of the nurses at Queen's Hospital told me the women who work here might be willing to give blood. For the soldiers."

The woman took a silver cigarette case out of her dress pocket. "One of my girls went to Queen's this morning and tried to give blood. She was told they didn't need our help." She took a cigarette out of the case with long red nails, lit it, and took a drag.

"I've come from Hickam Hospital, and we'd be very grateful for your help."

The woman took a measure of Annie and her sincerity and seemed satisfied. "We do have a lot of regulars from Hickam Field. How many of us do you need?"

"As many healthy women as you can spare who won't faint at the sight of blood."

"The bombs seemed to drop for fucking hours. To be honest, I'm surprised there's anyone left who needs us."

Annie would also be honest. Despite the fact that her patients desperately needed blood, she wouldn't trick someone into coming with her. "Hundreds were wounded. And hundreds, if not more, were killed. We're also not sure whether the Japanese will come back, so I can't promise you'll be safe."

"Is anyone safe on this island?" The woman peered past Annie toward the Jeep, the back filled with boxes. "Looks like we'll need a couple of cars. I've got one and so does Carole."

"You'll come?"

"I will. And I'll check with my girls to see who else is willing to join in the fun."

"Thank you, Miss…?" Annie held out her hand.

"I'm Rita," she said, giving her a quick handshake.

"Annie." She checked her watch. She'd been gone for nearly two hours, but it wouldn't take long to get back. All the traffic would be going out, not coming in. No matter. She had one last hope for more help. "I just need to make one quick stop on the way to Hickam."

Fifty folding tables and chairs were randomly set up as though done in haste. Some of the wounded sat in chairs, while others lay on tables. Most appeared to be suffering from broken bones and/or contusions. Several nurses, including Kay's right hand, Amai, tended to them. All wore white uniforms covered by white aprons that hadn't, at least not yet, been spattered with blood.

Kay and Mak each tended to their own patient near the door so they could triage when necessary. Annie walked in as Mak finished bandaging a gash on a boy's leg. He got up and headed toward the door, slowing when he saw who it was. "If you're here to help, there are bandages on the back table." His tone was clipped, like Annie was a total stranger—or someone he knew couldn't be trusted.

"I saw Mr. Taketa on my way here." Annie said it loud enough for Kay to overhear and then walked several feet away from the patients.

"Is he all right?" asked Kay, joining her and Mak.

"Physically, yes. But his wife was killed during the attack. I'm sorry, Kay."

Instinctively, Mak put his hand on Kay's shoulder in comfort and support.

"I think Mr. Taketa is in shock," said Annie. "He shouldn't be alone."

"I'll go to him," said Kay. "He doesn't have anyone else."

"Our patients need you here," said Mak. "If he's not hurt, he'll have to wait."

"Not hurt? He lost his wife. And we've already sent those with serious injuries to Queen's. You and the others can handle the rest now that Annie's here."

"Actually, I came for your help," said Annie as a car horn blared.

Kay and Mak peered past her to see one late-model car with Rita at the wheel as well as the junk car driven by Carole, who took pride in being made up like her idol, Carole Lombard. Both cars were filled with prostitutes. Mak continued to stare while Kay looked at Annie with both surprise and amusement. "Are they—"

"Yes," said Mak before Annie could answer. "I know one of them."

Kay raised a brow at Mak.

"Never pretended to be a monk," said Mak.

"They've volunteered to give blood," said Annie. "But we need more than blood. We need nurses."

"You expect us to help you?" asked Mak.

"I hope you will at least listen to what I have to say. If you say no, I'll leave."

Kay hesitated, then nodded. Annie stepped away to climb onto the stage, which was half filled with bandaged children. "If I could have your attention, please!"

Nurses and patients alike turned their attention to Annie, and the bewildered state they'd been in since the bombs dropped didn't ease with the appearance of a white woman.

"As you know, the island was attacked this morning. The targets included every military installation, but Pearl Harbor and Hickam Field took the brunt of the attack."

"Good!" shouted someone from the back of the room.

"I know some of you resent us being here, and you might blame us for what happened this morning. But I think you'll have a much more serious problem if Japan takes ownership of this island."

A young man in the back of the room stood. "Maybe we'll be better off with our own kind." Some applauded the notion.

"Whether it was your parents or grandparents who left Japan, they left for a good reason. However, I don't have time for political debate. This morning, Japanese pilots attacked without warning. They murdered defenseless men and women as they slept and countless soldiers and sailors who fought back to defend your country. If that's your idea of honor, then there's nothing I can say to change your minds." She paused to clear the anger from her throat. "At Hickam Hospital, there aren't enough people to count the dead, never mind treat the wounded. We need volunteers who don't care about anything but relieving someone else's pain. Because that's what this is about. It's not about who's right or wrong or who owns this island." Annie glanced at Mak. "It's only about relieving suffering and saving lives. If that's important to you, then please come with me."

Everyone in the room exchanged looks of anger, sorrow, and fear.

Amai stepped forward. "They won't want our help."

"She's right," said Mak. "The last thing those men will want to see is a foreign face, especially someone who's Japanese. And what if you're attacked again? You said Pearl Harbor and Hickam Field were the main targets. Why should anyone risk their lives to save—"

"People who are dying because they chose to serve their country? *Your* country?" Annie interjected. "Whether you like it or not, Hawaii is part of the United States. As citizens, you enjoy the privilege of—"

"The war you brought to us?" Mak opened his arms to the wounded.

Annie glanced at the children, and it was only the fear in their faces that kept her calm enough to answer without expletives, but her fists still clenched. "I can assure you the planes that flew over Pearl Harbor and Hickam Field this morning were not there at our invitation." Shifting her focus to the nurses, now gathered closer to Kay and Amai, she unclenched her fists. This was her last chance. "As nurses... As human beings, we have an obligation to alleviate suffering. Please come with me and do what you can. Even if you only dole out pain medication and apply dressings, you'll make a huge difference."

"How will you protect us?" asked Amai.

"With whatever we've got left. But I'm not sure it will be enough. The only thing I know for certain is that if I don't bring help, many will die who might live." Annie looked at Kay, knowing others would follow her lead. "Each man is someone's son or brother. Many are fathers with children of their own. And there are young women who haven't even had the chance to begin their lives beyond military service."

Kay approached Annie and spoke to the room. "Mak's right. Pearl Harbor and Hickam Field were the targets of an attack that might not be over. And as Amai said, the injured might not want our help."

Clearly feeling vindicated, Mak glanced at Annie, who was as close to tears as she had been all morning.

"However, it will be their choice to refuse our help," said Kay.

"It is my choice to go with Nurse Fox and do what I can in honor of those who have died—for all of us."

For a few moments, no one moved. Then Amai came closer to Kay, followed by four other nurses. And finally, Mak joined them.

"Are you sure?" asked Kay.

"I won't let you or the others go alone," said Mak. "Some of those soldiers might do more than refuse your help."

"Help you don't want to give," said Kay.

"Have I ever given a patient less than my best?"

"No," said Kay. "But you've never treated American soldiers before."

The color rose in his face. "I'll ride with Carole."

"Fine. Maybe you can get reacquainted along the way."

At any other time, Annie might've been happy to watch Mak squirm. But this was not that time. "Please bring your medical bags. We're running low on everything." Annie would wait patiently while they gathered what they needed because she was going back with supplies, blood donors, and nurses. For the first time since 7:55 a.m., she felt hopeful.

The gate to Hickam Field was twisted like a pretzel, and the guardhouse looked like a pile of toothpicks, but four heavily armed guards stood across the road as the three cars approached and stopped. Annie got out of the Jeep, telling the others to stay put.

Taking out her ID, she approached the soldier who appeared to be the oldest and had the stripes of a higher rank, assuming he would be less apt to overreact. "Lieutenant Fox," she said, holding up her ID. "I've brought supplies and nurses."

He looked at Rita and her girls and back at Annie. "Those women are nurses?"

"No, they came to give blood. There's a nurse in my car and more in the last car."

Walking closer, the corporal got a better look at the faces in the car Mak was driving and put his hand on his holster.

"They're nurses, Corporal," said Annie firmly. "And they're all Americans."

"You've got permission to bring them on base, ma'am?" he asked skeptically.

"I do," said Annie. "If you'd like to drive to the hospital to verify that with Major Lance, we'll wait here until you get back. He's likely in surgery, though, and won't appreciate the fact that you'll be wasting time that could be used to help our soldiers. Every second counts today, as you can imagine."

"Fine, but I'll have to conduct a search," he said.

"Excuse me?"

"I'm in charge of who passes through this entry point. And every person who doesn't belong here is getting searched for weapons."

"I'll take responsibility for—"

"With all due respect, this is my responsibility."

"Then make sure the search is conducted with due respect, Corporal."

"Yes, ma'am."

Annie quickly explained the situation, and in short order, though reluctantly, Kay and her nurses were standing in a line near the ruined gate. Mak stood by Kay while Annie stood next to Amai, watching the corporal's every move. The nurses took off their sweaters and nursing aprons and laid any purses and medical bags on the ground.

"Search those," the corporal told two of his privates.

The corporal approached Kay for a more personal search. Like the others, she wore only her white uniform.

"Anything in your pockets?" he asked.

"Peppermint Chiclets," said Kay. "They're in my right pocket. The peppermint soothes my stomach."

The corporal stepped forward to check for the gum.

Mak followed. "Look at her pockets," said Mak. "Do you see the bulge of a gun or the outline of a knife?"

"Your name, sir?"

"Makani Hale." Mak stood several inches above the corporal and moved a little closer to emphasize his height. "And if you touch her, I will break every finger—"

Annie stepped between the two men. "Mak, please back up."

He only took half a step back, but the concession was enough to defuse the anger in the corporal's face, at least somewhat.

"Corporal," began Annie, "as you can see, these nurses are hiding nothing, including their love of country. Why else would they come to the second biggest target on the island? So unless you see something I don't, please return their belongings and let us pass. Every minute we're delayed is one that could be used saving a soldier's life. And I assure you, that's not an overstatement."

The corporal walked to the end of the line and carefully checked each nurse—front and back—but only with his eyes. At the end of the line, he stood before Mak. "You'll need to be searched. Step away from the others and spread your arms and legs, sir."

"He's also a nurse," said Annie.

"And I'm not Japanese," said Mak. "Some people can't tell the difference. If we're not white, we're alien. But my people have been on this island a helluva lot longer than the U.S. Army."

"I don't care, Mr. Hale," said the corporal. "If you want access to this base, you'll be searched. Otherwise, you're free to leave."

Glancing at Kay, who appeared alarmed at the thought of his leaving, Mak stepped away from her and spread his arms and legs. Eyes forward, he showed no emotion while the corporal searched him.

Finished with his search, the corporal addressed Annie. "You may all get back in your cars and continue through the checkpoint."

"Thank you, Corporal." Annie and the others gathered their belongings.

Stepping aside so the cars could pass, the corporal motioned his men to do the same. As the three cars drove by, the soldiers kept their eyes on Kay and her nurses, who all looked in the other direction— away from the suspicion and contempt.

Annie drove the Jeep straight to the hospital where several civilian trucks—from milk wagons to mail trucks—as well as a few ambulances from Tripler General formed a line of rescue vehicles. A soldier with a clipboard stood near the driveway, ticking off patient names as they left.

As she'd done at the gate, Annie pulled over, gesturing for Rita and Mak to do the same. She got out of the Jeep and walked toward the soldier with the clipboard, who was yelling at the driver of the truck in the lead, which appeared stalled. "Move out!" The truck didn't budge.

"I'll take care of it!" Annie was closer to the truck and walked to the driver's door, where the driver's head rested on his arms, his hands loose around the steering wheel. She hated to wake the gray-haired gentleman; mental and physical exhaustion could overcome anyone that day. Yet he had to move the truck forward. "Wake up, sir. It's time to leave." He didn't, so she nudged him. "You'll need to leave now." Still nothing.

A cowboy hat sat on the passenger seat, giving Annie an idea about the man's identity as she gently pulled his shoulder back so she could see his face. It was Billy Lardner. His eyes were closed, his lips tinged with blue. She checked for a pulse and found none, then let his body rest back against the seat.

Annie walked to the soldier with the clipboard. "You need another driver. He's dead."

"What the hell?"

"Looks like he suffered a heart attack," said Annie. "His name is…was Billy Lardner. He managed a sugarcane plantation on the north side of the island."

"I'll make a note. Not sure when we'll have time to let them know though." He grabbed a private who was passing by. "Get somebody to help you take the driver of that ambulance over to the…"

"Hospital. Backyard," said Annie. "It's been set up as a temporary morgue."

The private started for the truck, grabbing another soldier on the way.

"I need a driver!" the soldier with the clipboard shouted.

"I'll be pulling around the line to get to the hospital," Annie said and held up her ID. "I've brought supplies and more nurses."

He glanced at her ID. "Okay, Lieutenant, just make it fast. As soon as I have a driver, that truck is moving out."

Annie hurried back to the Jeep. She wanted to get them all past the man with the clipboard while he was preoccupied with finding another driver. There was only one checkpoint left—the major.

Even though she was alone, Annie stood at attention. Anxious to get her nurses where they needed to be, she glanced at the door every few seconds until Major Lance strode in. He was clearly relieved to see Annie and gave her a weary smile. "At ease."

She tried but couldn't. She was too apprehensive about how he would respond to who she'd brought back.

"Were you able to get supplies?" he asked.

"Yes, some." She took the gun he'd given her out of her pocket and put it on his desk. "They're being unloaded."

"What about blood?" He put the gun in the side drawer of his desk but didn't lock it, clearly knowing he might need it on a moment's notice should the base be invaded.

"Queen's couldn't spare any. Honolulu got hit too."

"Jesus Christ. How bad?"

"Not like here, but civilians were injured and killed. Including children. I don't think anyone knows how many yet."

He rubbed his hands over his face like he could wipe away the reality of the day. "I have men waiting for surgery who'll die without a transfusion. And they're too weak to be transferred to Tripler or Queen's, even if we had enough vehicles."

"I brought blood donors. Not as many as I would've liked, but it'll help."

"Then why do you have that look on your face?"

"What look?"

"The one you get in the OR when my patient's vitals are about to tank. What's wrong?"

"Nothing. The donors are just…"

"Needle phobic? Come on. I need to get back to the OR."

"They work…on Hotel Street. But they appear to be in very good health."

"Fine."

"Fine?"

"It's not like I've got a choice."

"I agree," said Annie. "In fact, Monica's already taken them to start with transfusions."

"What about nurses?"

"I brought six."

"Thank God. Use them to relieve your nurses. They need a break. We can't give them long, but… You've got that look again. I assume the nurses you brought aren't also ladies of the night?"

"No, sir. But you might wish they were."

She watched him sit behind his desk with the heaviness he'd carried with him from the OR and wished to God she didn't have to add to it.

TWELVE

Annie had left Kay and the nurses in the supply closet to familiarize themselves with what they had and where things were kept. She had also asked them to reload the shelves with the supplies she'd gotten from Tripler General. Annie had entrusted Kay with the Pinocchio lunch box because it held the opiates from the abandoned drugstore in Honolulu. Opiates would need to be carefully doled out depending on the level of an individual patient's pain. "These will be like gold in a few hours," Annie had said, handing her the lunch box. "We still don't have nearly enough for the patients who need them."

Kay had taken the lunch box, thinking about how they would decide which patients received the strongest pain medication. Then she remembered that it wouldn't be her decision to make. Annie would give them guidelines to follow. For once, Kay was glad she wasn't the nurse in charge.

Looking at her own nurses, she could tell they were afraid to touch anything without permission. It was like being invited into a stranger's home and not understanding what was proper and what would be considered an insult.

"Please set your supplies down and gather around," said Kay.

As Mak turned to set his box down, she saw the butt of a gun sticking out of his waistband. It was in his nature to be protective, so seeing the gun didn't surprise her. But getting it past the guards did.

"How did you get that in here?" she whispered. "The guard searched you."

"I left it in the car with Carole. She put it under her dress, between her legs."

"Someplace a soldier wouldn't dare put his hands while on duty." Kay admired the strategy, if not his accomplice. Taking a deep breath to excise the thought of what else he and Carole had done together, Kay turned to her nurses. "I know this is difficult for all of you. It took courage to come here today," she said. "I also realize that everything happened very fast, so if anyone has second thoughts after seeing the gravity of the situation, feel free to leave. You could get a ride in one of the ambulances back to Queen's Hospital, where I'm sure they'd welcome your help today. If the enemy returns to take the island, it will be safer for you to be nursing civilians than soldiers."

If Japan took control of the island, they might give Japanese Americans a chance to surrender in gratitude. The Emperor might look favorably on those who would thank him for setting them free from America's tyranny. However, those caught helping and healing American soldiers would likely be treated with more contempt than white people descended from the original Pilgrims.

Waiting a moment, Kay expected at least a few of her nurses to opt for a ride to Queen's. When no one did—to her surprise—she continued with the business at hand. "Does anyone have any questions before we begin our work?"

"How long are we staying?" asked Mak.

Kay nearly chuckled. Sometimes he reminded her of a boy who didn't want to be at school and needed to know exactly when the bell would ring to let him out. "We'll stay as long as we can do some good. However, no one's under house arrest. If anyone wants to leave—at any time—just let me know."

"Do we take orders from the Army nurses?" asked Amai.

"We're not in the Army, so no," said Kay. "But if one of the Army nurses or doctors asks us to do something, we should comply. Unless you think it's medically questionable. In which case, please check with me or Mak."

"We should discuss the severity of the injuries," suggested Mak.

Kay agreed. The patients they were about to care for would have injuries unlike anything they had seen before. "Working here today will be very different, and not just because we're on a military base. We won't be treating people for bronchitis or diabetes or gout. We'll see patients who have been hit by bullets or shrapnel, and I'm sure there will be many burn victims. You'll likely see parts of the anatomy you never thought you would unless you attended autopsies as part of your training." She waited a moment and saw only two of her nurses nod. "No matter what you see today, the most important thing you can do is remain calm and professional. No matter how grievous the injury, no matter how shocking. The patients will take their cue from you. If you look at them and show panic, they'll panic."

"What should we do if we feel that we can't cope with a situation?" asked Amai.

"If you feel overwhelmed, get someone to relieve you and take a break," said Kay. "We'll need to work quickly because of the number of patients and the severity of their injuries. But I have the utmost confidence in your ability to do your job well, especially if you ask for help when you need it and take a break when necessary. And believe me, each and every one of us will need to take a break at some point."

"What if a soldier refuses our help because we look like the enemy?" asked the youngest and most inexperienced of Kay's nurses.

"Then we will politely tell him that we'll get another nurse," said Kay. "An Army nurse."

"What if there isn't time?" asked Amai.

"Then be honest," said Mak. "Tell him he doesn't have time to wait. But if he'd rather die than be treated by—"

"Nurse Hale," said Kay sternly, "our patients have not only been injured, they've been traumatized. Think of how it must have felt to be here this morning. We've only seen a fraction of what they endured."

"Which is why they should accept whatever help is being offered," he said.

"We're only one generation removed from Japan," said Kay. "After what's happened, can you blame them for being suspicious?"

"Yes," said Amai. "For months, there's been talk about everyone with a drop of Japanese blood being traitors. I'm tired of feeling guilty for something I haven't done, and so is everyone else. I won't be made to feel guilty after coming here to help."

Kay watched the others murmur in agreement, but she was prepared for their resentment. Thanks to her husband.

They had been lying in bed after making love. Daiji had sat up, as he always did, and leaned against his pillow to smoke a cigarette. Kay often thought that was the part he enjoyed most. It was as if he had done his duty, performed well, and could now relax.

Most of the time, Kay would let him enjoy his cigarette. She would quietly get out of bed, clean herself in the bathroom, slip back between the covers, and go to sleep. She had also done her duty.

More than once, she had tried to remember when making love with her husband had become nothing more than an obligation. Lately, she wondered if it had ever been more. It wasn't that she did not love him, because there was much to love about Daiji. While not handsome in the classical sense, he was attractive in the way he always carried himself with such dignity. Whether the act of copulation had produced inner fireworks for her or not, it had produced two children she could not love more. And Daiji was a very good father. Unlike Kay's father, Daiji did not hold back his affection. If they cried, he held them. If they were sick, he sat by their bed and read them stories. He didn't play with them because play was not in his nature, but he provided love, protection, and comfort when needed.

When American company after company turned him down because they didn't value an engineering degree from Kyoto University, he still held on to his pride. Even after working ten-hour days cutting sugarcane, he never came home with his head down and shoulders slumped.

As far as Kay was concerned, his most impressive feat was maintaining his composure when he was put on rat duty. Rats were a huge problem for every sugarcane field. Daiji chose to look at it from a scientific perspective on his first day as the rat catcher and killer. As Kay cleaned several rat bites on his feet and ankles, he explained the situation as if she were sitting in his very own lecture hall, telling her all about the three species of rats that plagued most sugarcane fields.

She admired his ability not to be resentful. As he described both chasing and being chased by rats—or so it had felt to him—his voice never rose above its normal tenor. Though she hadn't always appreciated such self-control.

Kay would often count the blessings of her marriage as she smelled his Chesterfield cigarette burning down after lovemaking. She had nearly counted her way to sleep this particular night when Daiji did something he had never done before after sex. He spoke.

"I'm thinking about going to Japan," he said. "To get a better job."

Despite the adrenaline that shot through her body, Kay was tempted to pretend she was asleep. If they had this conversation now, she would be up all night.

"I want to do what I was meant to do," he said, obviously intent on discussing it. "I know I can get work as an engineer in Kyoto or Osaka. If we settle in Osaka, we'll be close to my parents. I'm sure my mother would watch the children if you'd still like to work, though you wouldn't need to. I'd be making enough for you to stay home."

"No." She said it without thinking but immediately recognized it was because she could not leave Oahu or the community center or her friends. Or Mak, which made her feel guilty enough to soften her resolve. She sat up, glancing at the glow of his cigarette. "The children are Americans. Their lives are here."

"They're more Japanese than they are American. All their ancestors are Japanese. Every one of their relatives was born in Japan. Except for you."

She'd always suspected that he was slightly ashamed of marrying a woman who had not been born in Japan. "When we married, you agreed we would raise them here so they could take advantage of the opportunities of being an American citizen."

"This is the only opportunity America has offered me." He held out his arms, scratched by rats as much as sugarcanes. "I won't let my children end up in the fields."

"They won't. They'll go to an American college. They'll—"

"Still be Japanese in the eyes of every white person. They'll hear the word 'no' many more times than they will 'yes.' They'll always be looked down on. They'll always have to work harder than everyone else."

"What makes you think they'll have a better life in Japan? People have been leaving there for decades. Wages are low. Jobs are scarce."

"Our children won't be farmers or day laborers in Japan. They'll be well educated."

"An American education will be better for them, Daiji. By the time they graduate from college, things will be different here."

"Things will be different. When we get to Japan," he said calmly. "I'll go first. Once I'm settled, I'll send for you and the children." Lying down, he turned his face toward the breeze coming through the window. In a short time, his usual light snoring began.

A few weeks later, one night after the children were asleep, he packed his suitcase and left. He'd said it would be better if she told the children in the morning. He'd told her to explain to them that he was going to Japan to find work as a college professor and that he would send for them soon. Daiji also told her to tell them many stories about how beautiful Japan was and how their grandparents would spoil them. He left without ever asking if she would actually come. As always, he assumed she would follow his direction.

Kay wondered why she'd let him believe his family would be reunited. Maybe she was simply too cowardly to tell him to his face. Or maybe she feared that if she told him she and the children might not be coming, he would stay.

Kay had often looked at his empty side of the bed at night, and rather than cry because she missed him, she stretched her arms out wide and enjoyed the extra space. She did not miss having to pretend to be aroused by his touch. This, of course, had made her feel like the worst of all wives—and mothers. The children missed him. She told them they would discuss joining him after he'd begun his new job and was certain he really liked it.

The children hadn't been any more enthused about the possibility of living in Japan than their mother, but they did miss their father. At first, they would ask Kay about when they were leaving at least once a day. However, as time went on, the children seemed less and less curious about when they would go to Japan. Though they still enjoyed hearing Kay read their father's letters aloud, at least the parts meant for the children, which was what Kay read to them.

In the parts of his letters meant only for Kay, she noticed a change. He no longer wrote about teaching; instead, he wrote about what he had learned about Japan's conflict with the United States. In his last letter to her, he'd railed against the embargo on iron and petroleum, saying her country had no right to stop all trade with Japan because of the Emperor's ambitions in Indochina. He wrote that the embargoes would do nothing but strengthen Japan's resolve to take Malaya, which had half the world's tin and a third of its rubber, as well as the Dutch East Indies, which was rich in oil. Daiji made the potential invasion of another country seem like a sound business decision.

When relations between Japan and the United States took a turn for the worse, Daiji's letters stopped coming. For several weeks, Kay heard nothing. Until Mrs. Taketa passed her the first secret note from her husband. With each subsequent note, Daiji became more and more bold in his criticism of Kay's country and more strident in defense of Japan. There was no longer any pretense that Daiji had adopted the United States as his own. In his notes, he often referred to Japan as "home." Except that it wasn't Kay's home, and she didn't think it ever could be, despite the fact that nearly all her ancestors had been born and had died there.

And then she'd met Annie, whose passion for nursing had been like looking in a mirror, and Kay knew she couldn't go to Japan because Daiji would make her give it up. Putting it off for as long as she could, Kay finally wrote to tell him. She'd written that while she loved him, she could not bring herself to leave the country she also loved. Nor could she take her children from the only home they'd ever known. She didn't even mention leaving her mother, who she knew would never go back to Japan.

Over the following few weeks, she'd imagined every kind of scenario. Mr. and Mrs. Taketa begging Kay to reconsider on his behalf. Her own mother begging her to reconsider, despite never having liked Daiji all that much, because keeping the children from him would be worse. She'd even imagined Daiji coming back for his children. But Kay had never imagined her husband writing one last note telling her to get her children off the island before December 7.

★

The supply closet shook. Kay and everyone else froze, all cocking their heads slightly to see if they could hear the whine of an engine overhead. Instead, they heard the rumblings of an explosion in the distance.

Glancing at Mak, she felt as though they would need to set a good example. They couldn't show fear to the others. Though she didn't say a word, he seemed to understand.

"Not a bomb," said Mak, his voice smooth and steady. "Probably a fuel tank."

Everyone seemed to take a breath in relief. Then the door opened, startling all of them.

An Army nurse entered, her hand pausing near her face where a damp tendril hung over her right eye. Staring at the women and Mak, her cheeks blanched as she tried to find her voice.

Kay stepped forward, hand extended. "My name is Kay Kimura. Lieutenant Fox brought us here. She asked us to get familiar with the supplies and to put what we were able to bring with us on the shelves until she got back. She went to speak with your major."

Smiling, the nurse shook Kay's hand. "Nurse Irene Boyd."

"Makani Hale," said Mak. "Can you tell me where you keep your IV solutions? I've got lactated Ringer's and dextrose."

The back-to-business question appeared to snap Irene out of her disbelief, and she pointed to the shelf behind him. "Lactated Ringer's is kept on the second shelf, dextrose on the third, and saline on the first shelf."

"Thanks," said Mak.

As it did with most women, his smile appeared to bring some color back to Irene's cheeks. "Thank you all for coming. I was just looking for the chief to tell her something."

Kay could see that whatever the something was, it was more serious than finding them in her supply closet. "Is it that they're coming back? The Japanese planes?"

Irene hesitated.

"If Hickam is about to be attacked again, we have a right to know," said Mak.

"I don't know anything for sure," said Irene. "It's likely just a rumor."

"Please tell us, Nurse Boyd," said Kay. "We'll take the source into consideration."

"The source is a patient…was a patient. Before he died, he told me Japanese troops had parachuted onto the north shore. He said they wore blue overalls with red emblems. But he'd been badly injured inside Hangar 7 and was likely in shock. He may have been at the north shore the day before and seen men working in blue overalls, and the red emblems might have been their company's logo. Or he might have been at a bar last night and heard people gossiping. Rumors have spread like wildfire these past few weeks." Irene looked at them like she was a witness and they were a skeptical jury.

"You should tell Annie," said Mak. "No one can be too careful. Not today."

"I will," said Irene. "After I help you put things away. Everyone has their own system, and ours might be confusing at first. And before you get to work, I should tell you there's no time to switch needles between patients. We're putting ten doses of morphine in each syringe. When you've distributed those doses, you can change the needle. After we administer a dose, we write the time on the patient's forehead with Mercurochrome. Please take a bottle and keep it in your pocket."

"But reusing needles risks passing infection or disease between patients," said Amai as she reached for a bottle of Mercurochrome.

"There are too many patients in severe pain to follow proper protocol," said Irene. "Did you bring any tannic acid jelly from Queen's?"

"We have one box of tannic," said Mak. "It's pretty heavy. If you need it on the ward, I can move it for you."

"Thanks," said Irene, "but I'll get an orderly. We have three who ran through a hail of bombs and machine-gun fire to get here this morning. I'll introduce you. They've been a godsend, especially when we have to transport patients to the OR. And they'll help get the dead to the backyard, where we've had to put them temporarily. One of the orderlies, Maguleno—we call him Mags—he says a prayer over each body. It takes a little extra time, but it seems to help those of us on backyard duty. We need to make sure the patient is deceased before the body's placed there. The backyard's already getting crowded."

"Can you give us a quick lay of the land?" asked Kay, wanting to get everyone's mind off what was happening outside the hospital and its temporary morgue.

"Sure," said Irene. "Our administrative offices are on the first floor. Except for Major Lance's office, they've all been turned into holding rooms for the OR or transport to Tripler and Queen's. The operating theatre is on the second floor. We try to send patients up there *only* if we think they won't tolerate transport to another hospital, because we only have three surgeons. Our patient ward is on the third floor, and our forty beds are full. The orderlies are pulling mattresses from the closest barracks that are still intact to lay on the floors."

"Thank you, Irene. That's very helpful." Kay returned her smile, but she knew Annie's nurse wouldn't leave anyone who looked like the enemy with all the supplies they had left. It didn't matter that the chief had done it; Irene was going to be more careful. Kay could hardly blame her. It was difficult to know who to trust.

They had finished doing what they could in the supply closet when Mak suggested Irene take them to where they might do some good. She hesitated, glancing at the door several times, no doubt hoping Annie would return.

Kay and her nurses followed Irene to the busiest place in the hospital other than the OR and the backyard—the lobby. No sooner had they arrived when one of the orderlies pulled Irene toward a patient, and all three hurried toward the elevator.

Kay surveyed the reception area, which was lined with wounded soldiers. Those who weren't unconscious stared at her and her nurses. Arms crossed and chin up like a bodyguard, Mak stepped in front of them. Part of her wanted to stay hidden behind him, but she'd already seen too much.

Stepping away from Mak, she approached the soldier closest to her. He sat on the floor, his leg broken, the bone protruding from his calf. Kay squatted down beside him and set her medical bag on the floor. "Have you been given anything for the pain?" she asked.

In response, he spat at her. His spittle, tinged with blood, made a pink stain on her uniform. Part of her knew she should be angry. How dare he spit at her when she had only come to help? Yet her anger blew out like a flame deprived of oxygen. He and the others had been hurt on behalf of every American, including her, whether he wanted to acknowledge that or not.

"If you change your mind, please let Nurse Hale know. He'll

be happy to help you." She gestured toward Mak, who appeared anything but happy. Returning to stand beside him, Kay watched her nurses bow their heads as if ashamed.

"Coming here was a bad idea," said Mak.

"I won't be sorry we came," said Kay. "Our country was attacked, and we need to do what we can."

"We can only treat patients who allow us to do our job," said Amai.

As Kay looked at the barely suppressed rage in the patients surrounding them, she couldn't disagree. Not only did she wonder how they would treat patients, she wondered how she would keep her nurses safe.

THIRTEEN

Major Lance stared at Annie as if he hadn't heard her correctly. "You never told me your plan included bringing Japanese nurses to this hospital!"

"I brought Japanese *American* nurses."

"What in the name of God were you thinking?"

"I was thinking about the men who might live if we had more help."

"You honestly believe that men who watched their buddies die… The men who've been shot at, burned, and blown up by the Japanese military, would let Japanese nurses—"

"They were born in this country."

"That makes no goddamned difference! Did it not occur to you that the last thing these men need is to look at their nurse and see the face of the enemy?"

"They won't. Not if the nurses work in the recovery ward or the OR."

"Where our patients are unconscious. They would consider that a betrayal."

"Why? The nurses are only here to help save lives. Unless you really believe that every Japanese American on this island was in on the attack."

"I'm not paranoid, Lieutenant. And neither are the men and women who managed to survive despite all the bombs and bullets that rained down on us this morning. They deserve to be safe while under our care, but they won't feel safe if they see a Japanese face. It doesn't matter where they were born or what country they're loyal to. If our men see the enemy, they'll strike out if they can. Putting everything else aside, I can't promise those nurses will be safe."

"I'll make sure our patients never see their faces. But I won't send them away. My nurses are overwhelmed. They can't begin to take care of all the casualties we have now, never mind what might happen when it gets dark. It's just not possible."

"I know. And I appreciate your intentions." He sighed. "Just do your best to make sure they stay in the recovery ward. If any of them have experience in an OR, I'll work with them. I'm not sure about Metcalfe or Doyle, but I'll check. If you ask, they're likely to say no out of hand."

"I imagine they would, although I'm not sure what I've done to offend either one, other than not agreeing with everything they say because, of course, they're doctors and are always right." She waited for a reprimand. Instead, he laughed. It was brief, but it made her feel a little less hopeless and gave her the courage to ask, "Do you think they'll be back?"

"If I were them, I'd take advantage of my enemy's weakness and finish the job," he said without hesitation. No doubt he'd been thinking about it. "There are rumors that during the attack, Japanese soldiers parachuted into the mountains to prepare for a final assault."

"Are there enough men left to defend the base if we're attacked on the ground?"

"I'm not sure," he said. "I have no idea what the death toll is at Pearl Harbor. I don't even know what the death toll will be here when all is said and done. But I do know that every able-bodied man we have left will be armed. And most will have a hair trigger."

"You don't think they'd shoot a nurse."

"After what they saw today, I honestly don't know."

"But these women aren't a threat."

"Whether the president has officially declared it yet or not, we're at war with Japan. These men will react accordingly when they see the face of the enemy. They won't take the time to ask them where they were born. So keep those nurses away from any soldier who isn't unconscious. Understood, Lieutenant?"

"Understood."

"Once you've got them squared away, get yourself up to the operating theatre for triage."

"Yes, sir." She turned to leave.

"Annie…"

He'd never called her by her first name. For a second, she thought she'd imagined it. But she turned to him anyway.

"I'm glad you're back," he said.

"Me too." His smile looked like a crescent moon. Like his laugh, barely there, but shining enough light so that her world no longer seemed completely dark.

Annie had asked Monica to tell the others about the new nurses, who would all be assigned to the recovery ward for now. After that was done, Monica could take a half-hour break, after which she would relieve Irene, who would take a break, and then Kathy, Sara, and Winnie in turn. Knowing her nurses would get a bit of rest was a huge relief, and Annie couldn't feel anything but pleased about her decision to bring the new nurses to Hickam.

Too tired to react to the news that she would actually get some relief, Monica knelt by a badly burned soldier and prepared a syringe of morphine. Annie watched for a moment to make sure she was still able to perform her duties. It had been several hours since the attack, and adrenaline only took you so far. During the Great War, Annie had found that once the adrenaline wore off, it left her more exhausted, more spent.

Monica lifted the patient's arm to insert the hypodermic needle. His eyes shut before all the morphine entered his vein, so he didn't see Monica pull her hand away from his forearm, unknowingly taking the burnt skin that had sloughed off with her.

Monica held the needle in one hand and her patient's skin in the other. She looked at Annie, and the tears she'd been holding back all morning began to fall.

Taking Monica gently by the arm, Annie steered her toward a small two-stall ladies' room—the only room in the entire hospital where there were no patients. Annie took the patient's skin and placed it in the trash bucket. "Cool water," she said, gesturing to the sink. "If there's any left in the pipes. The water main broke."

Monica turned on the faucet and quickly washed her hands and flushed her face before the water slowed to a drip.

"Better?" asked Annie, handing her a towel.

Monica nodded. "Sorry."

"For what? Doing a great job while I was gone?"

"You know what I mean, Chief."

"I know you need to rest and get something to eat."

"Where?" asked Monica with a half smile.

"I'll be right back," said Annie. Five minutes later, she was back with a pillow and blanket that she laid on the floor. "Now, have a rest. I'll give the others the update, and I'll ask Irene to come trade places with you in twenty minutes. After which, take ten more minutes to go to the kitchen and grab a sandwich or a piece of fruit."

Monica's eyes filled again, but she smiled. "Thanks, Chief."

"No need," said Annie, knowing thirty minutes was not going to give her nurse much relief.

Annie was halfway out the door when Monica called to her. "Chief, when will you take a break?"

"I was off base getting supplies. That was break enough." She had decided not to tell her nurses what had happened to Honolulu. Let them think the insanity of the day was confined to military installations. Let them believe, for now, that safety was just outside the gates.

Kay looked over scores of bodies laid out like an obscene puzzle in the backyard, searching for Mak, who looked even taller as the only man standing. Annie had told Kay she'd assigned Mak to the back porch. He was their last sentinel, checking to make sure each person was dead before the body was laid to rest in their ever-growing morgue in the backyard. He was also strong enough to move a man back inside if he was still hanging on to life. Kay had gotten the distinct impression that Mak would remain in the "morgue" while she would stay in the recovery ward. She'd come to let him know that she and the others were safe; all their patients were unconscious. It would appear that Mak was also safe, at least from the wrath of dead men.

As she precariously made her way over and around the bodies, she saw Mak checking for signs of life and knew he felt no satisfaction in seeing the defeat of his island's conquerors. There were no signs of triumph in his face, only sorrow and that ever-simmering anger that was perhaps focused on a different enemy. She remembered thinking that might be a problem when they first met.

When the new Japanese American Community Center opened its door, Mak had been sent by those in his own community to explain how things would work best for everyone concerned. His proposal had been simple: each side—Hawaiians and Japanese Americans— would keep to themselves. After making his pronouncement, he'd obviously believed Kay was in agreement because he'd turned to leave. Kay, however, told him it was customary to eat and drink at the end of a business negotiation. He'd hesitated but had stayed for tea and rice cakes. Two hours later, he was helping her with a patient and, before he left, had promised to come back to "help out." He'd been helping out for four years.

She watched as Mak bent down and put his cheek to a young man's face, the skin so smooth and pale he appeared barely old enough to shave. Straightening, he put his finger under the man's nose and smiled.

"Is he alive?" asked Kay as she walked closer to him.

"Did she assign you here too?" asked Mak, gazing up at her.

"No, I just came to let you know about—"

"Ice cream!" the man shouted, his eyes snapping open.

Kay and Mak both jumped, then knelt on either side of their new patient, who was peering up at the sky as if they weren't there.

"Ice cream?" Kay looked at Mak, who shrugged. They quickly surveyed the man's wounds and found cuts and abrasions but none that were life-threatening. Except for the gash in his lower right abdomen. Gauze was still packed around some kind of metal. Kay could see the tip of something embedded under the flesh. Shrapnel. Or a piece of an airplane or ship. Apparently too big to excise without fatal blood loss.

"USS *Conyngham* moored as before." The patient's tone was clipped and efficient, as if he was giving a report. "0630."

"He's a sailor," said Kay.

"Received the following provisions for use in general mess," the patient continued, "inspected to quantity by Lieutenant J. R. Hansen, USN, and as to quality by Parcheski, P. C., from Dairyman's Association: ice cream—six gallons."

Kay turned to Mak with an expression that clearly said, *Say something.* "Report…received," said Mak.

"Japanese planes commenced bombing Pearl Harbor area at 0755," continued the patient. "Held general quarters, manned all guns, commenced breaking out powder. Commenced emergency repairs on main engines to get underway. Captain on the bridge."

"Understood," said Mak.

"At 0808, opened fire with five-inch guns at Japanese planes over Ford Island and all machine guns on attacking planes as they flew low past the nest heading northward from Ford Island."

Ford Island was an islet in the center of Pearl Harbor. The Navy used it to repair battleships and submarines. Kay assumed Ford Island had been hit, along with other military targets on the island: Wheeler Field, Schofield Barracks, and Fort Shafter.

"At 0813, attacking plane shot down by combined fire of nest and crashed in the vicinity of USS *Curtiss*." Their patient took a deep breath that sounded like a broken car muffler.

Kay had heard the "death rattle" several times, but always from elderly patients, as if they were opening a creaky door to whatever comes next.

"At 0818, opened fire with five-inch guns at horizontal bombers passing overhead in direction of Schofield Barracks. At 0825, opened fire with forward five-inch and machine guns at planes strafing nest from direction of Pearl City. At 0826, planes crossing low ahead of nest to northeast were taken under fire. One burst into flames and crashed in a clump of trees in Aiea Heights and exploded."

"Aiea Heights is cursed," whispered Mak.

Kay didn't believe in curses, but she'd heard the story. Aiea was once ruled by a Hawaiian chief before being taken over by sugarcane and the Honolulu Plantation Company. Five months ago, a commander from the USS *Dobbin* had vanished while walking in the hills above Aiea. The Navy searched and searched, but he was never found. Native Hawaiians suspected the commander had been taken by the spirit of the Hawaiian chief in recompense.

"At 0830, plane diving toward… At 0855, opened fire at planes strafing ahead and astern. At 0908, plane attacking starboard bow… shot down… At 0920, opened fired on…" The patient reached up with his right hand and grabbed Mak's shirt. "Must open fire."

Kay saw the young man's panic push through the dullness of death. He'd finished his final report, and it was time to—

"Open fire!" cried the young man as pink foam formed around his pale lips.

Reaching into his waistband, Mak pulled out the gun hidden by his shirt.

"What the hell are you doing?" said Kay.

"We're at war." Mak quickly unloaded every bullet, put his gun in the sailor's hand, and said, "Open fire."

Raising the gun toward the sky, the sailor pulled the trigger. Not appearing to notice that there were no bullets, he kept pulling the trigger until he could no longer hold up the gun.

"You got them," said Mak. "They're gone. Listen to the silence."

Kay watched the young man's panic recede and he lowered his arm. A moment later, his eyes closed, and the gun fell from his hand.

Annie's ward had been turned into a place for only those patients recovering from surgery. So far, they had about two dozen patients. Those in the worst shape had beds, and those in better shape were lying on mattresses on the floor. Every patient had some part of his body bandaged, and some injuries were still seeping blood.

Kay had returned from checking in with Mak and stood in a huddle with her nurses. Annie realized how difficult it must be for them—to be nursing in the shadows, afraid patients would see their faces. She just hoped they realized how important they were to keeping these men alive and would choose to stay, at least until things were somewhat under control. Annie wasn't sure how she would continue to cover this ward without Kay and her nurses.

Even Rita and her girls, not one with any experience in nursing, were making critical contributions.

Glancing at Rita, Annie noticed how pale she looked, especially against the white surgical gown she wore over her low-cut dress.

"Feeling okay?" asked Annie.

"Yeah, swell. They gave me OJ."

"Good, then you'll be one of the smiling faces our boys see when they wake up. After what they've been through, it's important they believe everything will be fine. If they ask about their condition, tell them you weren't in the OR, but you'll ask the chief nurse to speak to them. If they ask about the attack, just tell them it's over."

"If I say it's over, they'll think it's actually *over*. And we can't know for sure."

"They'll believe what they see. If you look like everything's going to be fine, then that's what they'll believe. It's what they need to believe, Rita." Demonstrating, Annie forced a smile and spoke with complete confidence. "You're in recovery, just like Pearl Harbor and Hickam Field. Everything's going to be okay."

"I don't believe you." She reached into her pocket and pulled out a tube of Victory Red lipstick. "But I might if I had a little morphine." Applying it perfectly without benefit of a mirror, she smiled with confidence and strode toward a patient.

Annie approached Kay and her nurses. When she was close enough to hear, the only words she caught were, "Don't let the patients see your face." But as she got closer, they grew silent.

"How can we help?" asked Kay, facing her.

"While the patients are unconscious, I need you to monitor

their vitals and any seepage. If the bleeding is more than you'd expect post-op, let me know. And when a patient begins to regain consciousness, if I'm not close, call for Rita"—she pointed her out—"or Nurse Entrikin." She pointed at Sara, who was across the ward checking on a patient. "If no one's available, please remember to turn away from your patient before he opens his eyes and can focus. I'm very sorry it has to be this way. I know you've left your own people to be here."

"These patients are our people," said Kay.

"Of course, my apologies," said Annie. "One more thing. Please don't leave the recovery ward."

"And while we're here," added Kay, "speak English because we don't know what our patients can hear while they're unconscious."

"I suspect they hear more than we might think," said Annie. "I had a patient in the Philippines with a very high fever from malaria. He was unconscious and we believed close to death, so another nurse and I thought nothing of complaining about our Army-issued brassieres. Two days later, his fever lifted. When he woke, he observed my chest and told me I was right to complain about my bra because it did absolutely nothing to flatter me. And that I still had a fine figure. Despite my age."

Some of the nurses giggled, and Kay smiled. But Amai did not appear amused.

Standing over her patient, Kay read his chart without looking for his name. For the first time since becoming a nurse, she could make no personal connection to her patient. It didn't matter if she could address him by name because she couldn't talk to him long enough to say anything of substance. The only thing she could say to him as he was regaining consciousness was that someone else would be with him shortly.

Yet these men were still *her* patients, even if they didn't know it. She would pretend she was working on a coma ward. Her job wasn't to soothe their concerns, because they didn't have any, at least not consciously. Her only job was to make sure they kept breathing.

Her first patient was a twenty-four-year-old man. He'd suffered from a penetrating wound to his back, and Dr. Doyle had removed a piece of the bomb that had hit Hangar 7, where the patient had been working that morning. The shrapnel had caused spinal damage that would cause some paralysis, but the degree of paralysis was unknown until the patient woke and they could run tests.

If he had been one of Kay's regular patients, she would be on the phone trying to figure out his best way forward. She would contact relatives and prepare them for visitation, helping them find a middle ground between being overly optimistic and despondent. She would look for places where he could get physical rehabilitation. Even if there was little hope in the prognosis, she found that patients rarely wanted to give up. Most importantly, she would give him permission to feel outrage at being paralyzed, and she would allow him to wallow in depression. But not for long. Her rule was to let patients give in to self-pity for no longer than twenty-four hours, after which she was afraid it would take root.

Yet Kay could do none of these things. All she could do was check his vitals and hang a new bag of saline. She couldn't remember ever feeling so useless.

★

Rita mopped the floor with such a vengeance that the bucket full of bloody water slopped right over Annie's shoes. "Sorry," said Rita without much regret. "Believe it or not, I'm not used to mopping floors."

"I wish you didn't have to, but our orderlies are moving patients, bodies, and mattresses." Ignoring her shoes and reaching for a blood pressure cuff from a tabletop, Annie saw her hand tremble and remembered that she'd never eaten her ham and cheese sandwich.

"They're coming back, aren't they?" said Rita. "To put the final nails in the coffin."

Apparently, she had seen Annie's hand shake and assumed the worst. "Those are just rumors, Rita."

"Sometime rumors are true. A woman hears that her husband might be seeing me or one of my girls, because nine times out of ten, he is."

Annie moved closer to Rita and spoke softly. "If the island is invaded, they'll target what's left of our military first. You and your girls would likely be safer on Hotel Street. If you want to leave, I can arrange an escort to get you through security checkpoints."

Rita surveyed the recovery ward, considering the offer. Annie followed her gaze from one patient to the next. All were unconscious and pale, many so young they looked like they'd just graduated from high school. If she checked their charts, Annie was sure half of her patients weren't old enough to drink yet.

"I can't speak for my girls," said Rita, "but I'll stay and perfect my mopping skills. Who knows? When I get to be your age, it might come in handy."

Sincerely hoping Rita would have another retirement plan by then, Annie suggested an alternative. "If you'd like to pick up another skill, I need someone to help me with pre-op checks. I can teach you how to help recognize the difference between someone in distress who needs to be in the operating room right away and someone who can wait."

"No thanks. I'm not into the whole blood-and-guts thing. But Carole is. I've caught her giving roadkill a closer look because she wanted to see what's inside a chicken. I told her she'd eaten plenty of chickens, but she said it's not the same. By the time she sees the chicken, everything interesting has been taken out." Rita rolled her eyes at the thought.

"Sounds like she's the one I need. Thanks." Annie left her to continue mopping, grateful that Rita hadn't taken the out she'd been offered.

As Rita had predicted, Carole was keen to help and told Annie she wasn't the least bit squeamish. In fact, she said she'd already seen the inside of a stomach. "Correction," said Carole, "it was the small intestine."

"How did you see someone's small intestine?" asked Annie, leading Carole down the stairwell toward the operating theatre.

"My nanna couldn't go to the bathroom. Number two," whispered Carole, though no one was in the stairwell but them. "The doctor said she had an…"

"Obstruction?"

Carole nodded. "He told her she needed to go to the hospital, but she wouldn't. My grandpa had died in the same hospital. Anyway, the pain got so bad, she begged the doctor to open her up and get rid of whatever was causing the pain. I swear she thought it was as easy as snaking a clogged drain."

"He operated at home?" Annie knew that most women gave birth at home, and she'd seen her father perform more than a few tonsillectomies outside a hospital. However, he would never have attempted a small bowel resection unless the patient was in a hospital operating room.

"He did the operation on the kitchen table. I was his assistant. I boiled instruments and helped him put my nanna to sleep before he picked up the scalpel, but I'm not too sure he was glad I was there. I kept asking him questions, especially when I could see what was inside. Not that I could see that much. There was a lot of blood. He finally told me to shut up and promised to give me one of his anatomy books. I still have it."

"*Gray's Anatomy?*" asked Annie, wondering if it was as dog-eared as her own.

"Yes!" Carol looked like she found a long-lost twin, and for the remainder of the journey in the stairwell, she gave Annie a quick run-down of her greatest discoveries. Top of the list was finding out the heart was only slightly left of center. "All those years in school, I'd been putting my hand in the wrong place when I said the Pledge of Allegiance."

"At least you weren't the only one," said Annie. "May I ask how your grandmother withstood the surgery?"

"She got through it but passed two days later. The doctor had found a tumor. He couldn't take it out because it was too big and she would've bled to death. He stitched her back up and let her say her goodbyes. And he gave me enough morphine to…"

"I understand." Annie realized the doctor must have given Carole enough morphine to ease her grandmother into a permanent sleep when she was ready to go. On occasion, Annie had wished she had the ability to do the same.

As they stood near the pre-op line, Annie told Carole about surgery-related risks, very relieved that she didn't have to also explain basic anatomy. "Our most important task is making sure everyone in line absolutely needs to have surgery, which is always a risk no matter how skilled the surgeon. We'll also be looking for anyone who appears to be in serious distress," said Annie. "For instance, let me know right away if you notice anyone having trouble breathing."

Carole nodded, gazing down a hallway lined with gurneys.

"Look for bleeding too. If you see a lot of blood and the patient is unresponsive—doesn't seem to see or hear you and has trouble talking—tell me. Another thing to watch for is something called aphasia, which means the patient can't speak properly. The words they use might not make sense, or they might sound like a strange language you've never heard before. Aphasia is usually caused by a brain injury that might not be visible. So if a patient is speaking gibberish tell me, even if you don't see an injury."

"I will," said Carole, appearing somewhat bewildered.

"I've given you a lot of information," said Annie apologetically. "Do you have any questions, Carole?"

Carole shook her head. "I've always had a good memory. When we got back from church, my nanna used to have me tell her every bit of gossip I'd heard. She'd make cracklin' bread and give me as much as I wanted as long as I kept giving her the gossip."

"Well, all that cracklin' bread doesn't look like it hurt you any," said Annie.

"Nanna passed when I was ten. Haven't had good cracklin' bread since. I tried to make it just like she did because I remember every step. But it was never the same."

Annie tried to imagine ten-year-old Carole handing her grandmother's doctor a scalpel.

FOURTEEN

Kay had seen Annie leave for the pre-op patients with Carole—the prostitute who had hidden Mak's gun. On occasion, she had wondered what kind of woman he would fall in love with and marry. Once, when she was making umpteen dumplings for a celebration at the community center, she'd let her mind wander and had conjured up the perfect wife for him. She would be intelligent, witty, kind, and pretty. She would be independent and have her own interests. And she should be strong-willed because Mak could only respect a woman who wasn't afraid of speaking her mind.

Carole did not fit this profile. How could she? Her job was to please men. Sexually. By doing whatever they asked and, as far as Kay could tell, by playing a role. Having always liked Carole Lombard because her movies made her laugh—and because she'd had the good taste to marry Clark Gable—it was difficult for Kay to dislike a woman who looked so much like her. Perhaps dislike was too strong. Or maybe it wasn't strong enough, because she could barely look at the woman. Fortunately, Annie had taken her elsewhere, which was another point of contention. Or competition, if she was being honest.

But why should they be allowed to tend to wounded soldiers rather than actual nurses? Carole "the impostor" Lombard should not be in pre-op. Kay should be the one checking for seeping wounds or spiking temperatures. Her skills were wasted in the recovery ward.

She'd made up her mind to talk to Annie about the situation when someone grabbed her arm. A man whose grip was fairly strong considering the fact that he'd been under anesthesia a short time ago, which indicated that he was upset. Or angry.

Kay was almost afraid to turn around. What if he screamed at her? Or struck out? She tried to pull away, but he held on.

"Please," said the patient. "Tell me what's happened."

Kay had no choice but to face him. She turned, hoping her smile would ease the shock. But there was no need. The man's eyes were wrapped in bandages.

"What's happened?" he asked again.

"You were injured," she said softly as he released her arm. "You're at Hickam Hospital. You've had surgery, and you're in the recovery room. You're just coming out of the anesthesia, so it may take a little while before you can think clearly."

"I remember…a hissin' sound. Like a steak got thrown on the grill only…louder. I heard a commotion from the mess hall. Sounded like chairs bein' overturned. I left the kitchen to go see what the hell was goin' on. After that, I don't remember nothin'."

"Pearl Harbor and Hickam Air Field were attacked. By the Japanese."

"Well, fuck me," he said, quickly followed by, "Sorry."

"It's all right," said Kay. "If there was ever a time…"

"Why can't I see?" He put his hands up to feel the bandages.

"Better not to touch." Kay gently pulled his hands away from the wounds. "Give me just a moment to check the doctor's notes, and I'll give you more information." She reached for his chart and scanned Dr. Lance's notes, appreciating the fact that his penmanship was fairly easy to read. "You had foreign objects in both eyes. Dr. Lance removed a sliver of wood from your right eye and smaller pieces of metal from your left eye. He's recommending that you see a specialist for additional surgery in a few weeks, in case there's damage to your retina or the vitreous—"

"Regular people words, please."

"Sorry. The vitreous is like jelly. It sits behind your eye and helps it to stay round. The retina is a layer of tissue that lines the back of your eye. They both help your eyes do their job."

"What if they can't fix 'em? Could I be blind?"

Kay was a firm believer in being honest with her patients. She didn't believe in sugarcoating or giving false hope, but she also didn't believe in borrowing trouble. "With any serious eye injury, there's a possibility of vision loss. However, I don't think Dr. Lance would recommend further surgery unless he thought there was a good chance that you'll be able to see."

"Hope so," he said. "While I might be able to feel my way around a kitchen to cook for myself, I sure as hell couldn't cook blind for my boys."

"You have sons?" she asked.

"Hundreds and hundreds. They come in every day—morning, noon, and night."

"Oh," she said, reminding herself where she was. "Your soldiers." Glancing at his chart again, she noted his name. "I only cook for three, Sergeant McCray. I can't imagine making three meals a day for hundreds of hungry men."

"It's a challenge," he said, smiling as if he loved nothing more. "The amount of food it takes to feed these guys on a daily basis… I'm talkin' a ton of meat, half a ton of potatoes, eight hundred pounds of bread, fifteen cases of eggs, one hundred pounds of butter, and about four hundred pies. I've got two hundred men workin' in shifts around the clock, and half the time, I still have to help out on the grill."

Kay knew she should move on to another patient; he was clearly stable. But he was the only one she could talk to, so she lingered. "Do you enjoy cooking?"

He shrugged. "It's all I've ever done. I started workin' at Magee's Diner when I was fourteen."

"I imagine feeding so many soldiers is very different from that diner."

"Yes, ma'am. At first, I was intimidated—until I checked out the competition."

"Pearl Harbor?"

"Not exactly," he said. "I went to the Black Cat Café, because that's where off-duty soldiers and sailors go."

Kay had never been to the café because it was across the street from the Army and Navy YMCA on Hotel Street. She did know a couple of women who had been there, but not for the food. The women's husbands were best friends and had made a habit of having dinner once a week at the Black Cat, followed by a few beers at a nearby bar. At least that was what they told their wives, who'd believed them until one found the proverbial lipstick. Not on her husband's collar but on his white briefs. She'd told her friend, who agreed that if one was up to no good, so was the other. Hence, they sat at the Black Cat Café sipping coffee while they surveyed every woman who sauntered by the Army and Navy YMCA. After seeing the competition for themselves, they put an end to their husbands' weekly "get-together."

"What did you think of the competition?" she asked.

"They make a decent porterhouse for a buck. And you can get a pretty good roast turkey dinner for fifty cents. But what they get on Hotel Street… Let's just say it ain't on my menu."

She saw his cheeks flush and helped him off the hook. "Like the Waikiki Theatre. Don't you love the big indoor palm trees? I think they nearly reach the ceiling."

"They do," he said. "We got nothin' like that where I'm from."

There was a moan from a patient in a nearby bed, and Kay watched Amai hurry to check on him. Amai turned away before her patient opened his eyes and motioned for Nurse Entrikin.

"How bad is it?" asked the sergeant. "How many did we lose?"

Kay followed the same rule she used when giving patients the truth about their medical situation. "Many were killed, and many were injured."

"Ballpark?"

"I'm not certain. If I had to guess…hundreds. Maybe thousands."

He was quiet for a moment. When he spoke, his voice shook with fury. "Did we get any of the slanty-eyed bastards?"

Feeling pure revulsion, Kay took a step back from her patient. She hadn't heard that particular slur since high school. It took her a moment to respond without conveying the anger she felt. "I heard several Japanese planes were shot down."

"They comin' back?"

"No one seems to know," said Kay. "Not for sure."

"Do me a favor?" he asked.

"If I can." Though she was less inclined to do so than she'd been a few moments ago.

"If they come back, tell them I can fight. All they need to do is put a gun in my hand and tell me which direction to shoot. I won't go out flat on my back."

She understood. There was nothing worse than feeling helpless to defend yourself.

FIFTEEN

Kay had done all she could to not let herself be seen as she made her way to the ladies' room. Still in stealth mode, she entered quietly and flattened herself against the wall when she heard voices. What if the women were patients? She began to inch back out.

"Before you go back to the OR," asked one woman, "what do you think of the hookers?"

Kay stayed put. She would introduce herself when they finished discussing Carole and the others. Hardly objective, Kay would keep her opinion about those women to herself.

"Don't call them hookers," said another woman.

"All right, which do you prefer—prostitutes or ladies of the night?"

"Honestly, Winnie. Have you even met them yet?"

"Haven't had the pleasure," the woman named Winnie said with sarcasm. "They were giving blood. Then a few went to the recovery ward. I'd rather meet the new male nurse. But he's on backyard duty, and I can't bring myself to go out there. I wonder if the chief put him there because he's not a very good nurse."

Kay wanted to tell them Mak was a wonderful nurse and they were lucky to have him. She started to come into view when she heard the next topic of conversation.

"Most of us will take a turn in the backyard," said the other nurse. "And it's got nothing to do with our nursing skills."

"Speaking of which, have you seen the new nurses?" asked Winnie. "The Japs?"

"They're Americans, Winnie," said the other nurse. "The chief said they were all born here."

"Okay then, Kathy. What do you think about the new *American* nurses?" asked Winnie.

"I think they were brave to come," said Kathy. "Not sure I would've. I mean, part of me is glad I'm here and wouldn't want to be anywhere else. But part of me is terrified and expects to be blown to bits any minute. And the surgeries…one after the other. I check the patient's chart every ten minutes to remind myself who we're working on and what's wrong with him and what if any allergies he has. I just hope I haven't made any mistakes. What if one of my patients doesn't wake up and it's my fault because I gave him too much ether?"

"If that happens, you'll know you're capable of making a mistake even when you're trying very hard not to," said Kay, coming into view. "We've all done it." She turned to the nurse whose face was flushed and said, "My name is Kay. I prefer it to Jap."

"I'm sorry," said Winnie. "I didn't know—"

"Any better?" offered Kay. "Or you didn't know I was here? Neither is a good defense."

Winnie glanced at Kathy, who stepped away as if to say, "You made your bed. I'm not jumping in there with you."

★

With Carole in tow, Annie nearly passed by the woman on the gurney without a second look. The open fracture in her lower arm appeared to be properly splinted, and blood barely seeped out of the dressing. But something made her doubt the original assessment and she backed up. Glancing at Carole, she saw the same doubt as they both began to scan the patient.

"There," said Carole, pointing to seemingly insignificant blood spots creeping out from under the blanket that covered the woman's legs.

"Your name, Sailor?" asked Annie, smiling at the patient.

She blinked her eyes, finally focusing, barely, on Annie. "Betty Donnelly," she said weakly. "Telegrapher Third Class, ma'am."

"I'm going to check your injuries, Betty, because we sure could use you back at work if we're going to communicate with the mainland any time soon." Lifting the blanket, Annie and Carole both saw blood pooled under the patient's skirt but no apparent wound. Leaning down, Annie whispered, "Any chance you're pregnant, Betty?"

Betty's eyes filled.

"How many periods have you missed?" asked Annie.

It took a few moments before Betty whispered back, "Three."

Rising, Annie spoke softly to Carole. "Please go tell Sara we've got one who needs to move to the front of the line or as close as she can get her. Tell Sara the patient is at least three months pregnant."

Carole hurried off to find Sara, who was moving patients into and out of the OR like the hostess at a popular restaurant on New Year's Eve.

Leaning back down, Annie again whispered to her patient.

"Doctors and nurses aren't allowed to discuss your medical condition without your permission. When you're well, no one will know unless you decide to tell them."

Betty nodded in acknowledgment, too weak to do anything more.

Pulling Betty's gurney out a few inches so it would be easy to find, Annie continued down the line, quickly assessing each patient. She had no time to ask their name or hold their hand or give them the least bit of comfort or reassurance. She had no time to do the part of her job that she'd always felt was most important—letting them know they weren't alone.

Since the first time she'd accompanied her father on a house call to her training to her twenty-plus years as a nurse, the thing that bothered her more than the worst injury or the most unforgiving disease was seeing a patient go through the experience alone. Before she was old enough to work with her father as his "apprentice," she'd naively assumed that everyone had someone, be it a parent, sibling, spouse, or good friend. Later she learned there were people who were alone by fate or design. Some seemed to manage illness or injury on their own, but others were unable. It was when she could provide help for those people that Annie had been the most satisfied with her career choice.

"Nurse Fox!" Carole called out.

The patient Carole had flagged was bandaged around his ribs, each breath coming with a high-pitched whistle. Still a teenager, he didn't appear as panicked as Annie expected, and she thought she knew why.

"His name is Andrew," said Carole. "He told me he has a few broken ribs. They were going to check for shrapnel in his lungs."

Using her stethoscope, Annie listened to his heart and lungs, confirming her suspicion. "Do you have asthma, Andrew?"

He stared at her, his eyes wide with fear.

"You need to tell me the truth. That's an order, Private. Do you get asthma attacks?"

Reluctantly, he nodded.

"Adrenaline," said Annie as she pulled a vial and syringe out of the medical bag. Carole watched closely as she prepared the injection and gave it to Andrew. "Your heart is going to feel like it's beating out of your chest, but you'll be able to breathe."

"I've had it before," he said with a southern accent. "Doctor used to come to the house to give me shots when I was a kid. Haven't needed one in a long time."

"Stress can induce an attack, and everyone's had plenty of that today." Annie listened to his lungs again. "Your breathing is improved. No surgery for you today, Andrew." She picked up his chart to make a note.

"Don't say I have asthma. Please, ma'am. They'll send me home."

Annie saw Carole stare at the patient as if she misheard. How could he not want to go home after what had happened? But Annie understood. She'd seen the same thing during the Great War—men she'd treated who had more than enough reason for an honorable discharge yet did everything they could to stay in the fight. It took her a while to figure out why, but she finally determined that it was usually because the soldier didn't want to leave his buddies, especially if they'd trained together. If it wasn't that, it was often because their sense of patriotism—country first—was stronger than their sense of self-preservation. But once in a while, it was revenge for the death of a friend. Many friends had been lost today.

"Where are you from?" asked Carole.

"Tallulah Falls, Georgia."

"Sounds pretty."

"Sure is," he said, smiling. "Tallulah Gorge is something to see. Lotsa waterfalls."

"You got a girl back home?" asked Carole.

He nodded with pride. "Miss Tallulah Falls, 1940."

"I bet she misses you."

"Guess so. She writes twice a week."

"She'd be so excited to know you were coming home."

He shook his head. "She'll think I'm a coward."

"You're a hero," said Carole. "That's what she'll think. That's what everyone will think about the boys...the men who were at Hickam when Japan attacked. I'd probably be wearing a kimono by now if you and the others hadn't put up a good fight."

Andrew blushed behind a modest smile, and Annie wrote *acute asthma attack, chronic condition* on his chart. *Recommend medical discharge.* If nothing else, she would save one life.

Kay was hanging an IV for an unconscious patient when Rita came for her, pulling her toward another patient. "I put a bedpan underneath to catch the blood. I just finished mopping this floor," said Rita.

If not for the concern in Rita's eyes, Kay would've thought the only thing she was concerned about was keeping a mop out of her hands. Kay bent down and saw the blood that had soaked through the thin mattress and was dripping into the pan. Picking up his chart, she saw that the surgeon had left one of three bullets inside because the patient would've bled out in the OR had they tried to remove it, though the patient was certain to die anyway.

"I'm afraid there's nothing we can do," said Kay softly, knowing that hearing was the last sense dying people lost. "And he's been given as much morphine as we dare."

"You're sure?" asked Rita.

"Just be with him. That's the most important thing you can do now."

"You mean, be with him when…he dies?" It was clear Rita had never been with someone when they passed away. "Isn't there a priest?"

"Nurse Entrikin told me there are four chaplains on base. Three have been outside the hospital giving last rites. The chaplain assigned to the hospital…his wife got killed during the attack. He's making sure his children are being taken care of before he comes back. I just don't know if he'll return in time for your patient."

"*My* patient?"

"For all intents and purposes," said Kay.

"But I'm not a nurse."

"You don't have to be. All you need to do is offer him the same care and compassion you would for anyone who was dying."

"I had a girl who got roughed up. Thought she was going to die before the doctor got there. She was passed out cold. I told her about a movie I saw. She'd wanted to come see it with me and some of the other girls, but it was her turn to…see this one customer."

Kay saw a flicker of guilt on Rita's face and assumed the one customer was the one who'd inflicted the damage. "Maybe you could tell"—she glanced back at the chart—"Ben about the latest movie you saw."

"I just saw Rita's new movie—*You'll Never Get Rich*. I have to watch them all in case a customer asks me about them. Sometimes they like to pretend I'm really her."

"And that's all this will be," said Kay. "Pretend. All you're doing is telling Ben about a movie you think he'd like."

Pulling up a stool, Rita sat by her patient, held his hand in hers, and began. "Ben, I'm going to tell you about a movie you're going to go see when you get better. Rita Hayworth plays a dancer named Sheila, and Fred Astaire plays Robert, her manager, only he's really working for this jerk who wants to cheat on his wife, who already knows what her husband is up to. I know, it sounds confusing, but it'll all make sense eventually."

As Kay left to check on another patient, she heard the drip, drip, drip under the bed punctuating Rita's story and hoped she'd get to the end before it was too late.

The thing that most struck Kay about the back stairwell was that there was no blood. The steps were clean and, most importantly, deserted. Annie had given her a half-hour break, and Kay was using the back stairs again to navigate the hospital. Mak was the only one of her nurses who wasn't in the post-op recovery ward, and she wanted to see how he was coping after several hours of morgue duty. If she were being honest, the main reason she wanted to see him was because she needed to feel safe, even if it was only for a few minutes. The closer it came to nighttime, the more anxious everyone was becoming. Kay didn't think there was a conscious person on base who didn't expect another attack when the sun set.

Sitting on the second-floor landing, Kay knew she'd be tempted to do one of two things: cry on his shoulder and let herself fall apart—or talk to him about her husband. Neither was a good idea. She couldn't fall apart. What kind of example would that set for her nurses? And talking to him about Daiji would only lead to the conclusion Kay had already come to—her husband had known about the attack before it happened. Why else would he have insisted she and the children get off the island? No one could ever know about that note. She would burn them all when she got home.

It was so difficult to accept the fact that her husband had committed treason, but there was no other explanation. No matter how he'd learned about the attack, he hadn't sent a warning to Pearl Harbor or Hickam Field or the mayor of Honolulu. He'd let people be taken unawares. He'd let people die. How could she have cared for someone like him? How could she not have seen the part of him that was capable of such disregard for human suffering?

Kay knew she would have to live with what the father of her children had done, but she would make sure they never knew the truth about him. However, eventually she would need to tell them why he was never coming home. But what if Japan took ownership of Hawaii, and he tried to retake ownership of his family? With the Pacific Fleet and Hickam's planes hobbled, they might all be at the mercy of the Japanese Emperor by morning.

She wondered what part her husband had played in the day's horror. Had he gone to Japan to join the military? As an intelligence officer perhaps? Daiji had always believed he was too smart for manual labor. He'd married her, in part, because she was smart too. He'd told her he never wanted to be bored at home, so he'd married a woman he could talk to about important things. This hadn't meant he didn't want a subservient wife, just an obedient one who was also intelligent. Daiji had never understood the paradox of that requirement.

It was almost dark, but none of the peace that should come with it was felt by anyone. If anything, the apprehension was more intense. Blankets had been nailed over the windows, and nurses used flashlights with their beams covered in blue cellophane to check on patients.

During the day, they had lost as many patients as they'd saved. Night seemed to bring a certain stasis. Many of the patients who couldn't be helped at Hickam Hospital had been transferred to the Army's Tripler General or the civilian Queen's Hospital. Pearl Harbor had also transferred patients to Tripler and Queen's. In addition, they had the *Solace*—a hospital ship that had been unharmed during the attack—and a mobile base hospital in addition to a field hospital that had been set up in the officers' club of the Navy yard. And the Marine Corps air station at Ewa, which was about seven miles west of Pearl Harbor, was taking patients. All day, ambulances and local drivers using every available vehicle had transported patients.

The only patients Annie had not ordered for transport were those who would recover just as well without being moved and those who were too critical to move. Most of their critical patients were in the recovery ward, where Annie had stayed for the past few hours. Then she'd received word that the hospital kitchen was serving supper and had been sending her nurses to get hot food in shifts. She had waited to go herself because she wanted to accompany Kay and her nurses in case there was any trouble. She was hoping most soldiers would have eaten and gone by the time they got there.

Annie approached Kay, who was taking an unconscious patient's blood pressure. "Time for supper. Hot food will do everyone a world of good."

"I can't leave," said Kay. "His BP's falling fast."

"Could be the anesthesia or shock from blood loss." Annie picked up the patient's chart. "Bullet hit the pancreas…" Her eyes went from the chart to the face of Corporal Jeremy Tig. How had she forgotten about him? She'd promised to take care of him.

She pulled back the blanket to see the bloody dressing across his abdomen. "He's still bleeding from somewhere." Looking for help, she spotted Sara and spoke loudly but calmly despite the increase in her own pulse. "Nurse Entrikin! Go tell Dr. Lance we have a post-op patient who needs to get back in stat."

Instead of doing as she was told, Sara came to Annie and spoke in a low tone so none of the patients would overhear. "I just spoke to Winnie. Dr. Lance said they can't take any more patients. If there's a problem in post-op, he said…you're to use your best judgment." Sara took a vial of morphine out of her pocket.

Annie didn't need Jeremy to tell her to keep the morphine to herself. She knew he'd want her to keep trying. She'd seen the strength of his courage that morning. Waving the vial away, she turned to Kay. "Will you assist?" she asked with a mix of dread and determination.

"I'll do my best," said Kay without hesitation.

"Sara, we'll need everything you can get."

"Right away, Chief." Sara rushed toward their shrinking hoard of supplies as Annie leaned down and whispered in Jeremy's ear. "You'll be dancing again soon, soldier."

Just nine minutes later, Sara stood by with a tray of surgical instruments, gauze, needles, and thread. She and Kay watching as Annie carefully searched Jeremy's open abdomen, gently lifting organs with her fingers. "How's he doing?" she asked, glancing at Kay, who was monitoring his blood pressure.

"BP's still dropping. You don't have long."

"I just need to find out why his blood's pooling around the small intestine. Sara, more gauze." Sara handed Annie more gauze to soak up the blood, and Kay surveyed the area.

"There," said Kay, "the celiac artery."

"Good eye, Kay," said Annie with relief. "Sara, needle and thread, please."

"Nurse Entrikin!" called Amai from across the room.

Sara handed Annie a needle and thread. "Do you need me to stay, Chief?"

Annie stayed focused on her work, steady fingers stitching the hole in Jeremy's artery.

"Nurse!" called Amai again.

"Chief?" asked Sara.

"How are we doing, Kay?" Annie asked, tying off the sutures.

Kay checked his blood pressure. "BP's beginning to stabilize."

"You can go, Sara. We've got this." Annie glanced at Kay, saw her eyes smile, and wondered if she'd ever dreamed of becoming a surgeon. Annie had thought about it more than once, but many medical schools wouldn't accept women when Annie was younger, and some still refused. Now she felt it was a dream too late to pursue.

And for the first time, Annie was grateful she hadn't. Having had Jeremy's life literally in her hands, with no time to spare, was enough. She wondered how the major would deal with the patients he hadn't had time to save.

Carole rose from the blanket on the floor of the ladies' room and, eyes only half-open, headed out as Annie and Kay entered. The water carts had come by the hospital several times that day, and Annie had asked them to fill the sink whenever they did a water delivery and to set a few buckets on the floor near the toilets, keeping those refilled as well. Kay filled the sink with clean water and washed. "Your patient should recover."

Annie, who stood nearby waiting her turn at the sink, barely nodded.

"You need a break," said Kay.

"Not yet," said Annie.

"You've been saying that since we got here." Kay leaned up against the wall while Annie splashed her face with cool water. "Afraid to stop?"

Annie dried her face and hands. "I feel like an old car with an unreliable starter. Turn me off, and I'm not sure you'll be able to turn me back on." Too tired to laugh, she and Kay exchanged a half smile. "Why don't you rest a bit before we go to the kitchen?" She gestured to the pillow and blanket on the floor.

"No thanks," said Kay. "If I'm working, I'm not thinking about whether we'll hear sirens again or whether my kids are safe or how Mr. Taketa will cope without his wife."

"I'd almost forgotten this." Annie took a small envelope out of her pocket. "Before I left, Mr. Taketa asked me to give this to you." She held it out to Kay, who hesitated. When she finally reached for it, her hand trembled. "He said it was a secret," said Annie.

Like a wounded ship, Kay slowly sank to the floor, the envelope unopened in her hand.

"If you need some privacy…"

"Mrs. Taketa introduced me to my husband, Daiji. He wanted to marry and trusted her to choose for him. And I trusted her to choose for me."

Annie sat on the floor beside her. "Someone else chooses who you marry?"

"It's more like matchmaking. A man and woman are introduced, and then they each make their own decision."

"Daiji must've been a good match. You have two beautiful children."

"He's very smart. He graduated from Kyoto University with a degree in engineering. Top of his class."

"He came from Japan to find a wife?"

"He came to find a job. Finding a wife was secondary. Daiji believed his prospective employers would hear the potential behind his accent. But they didn't. Not in Los Angeles. Not in San Francisco. Not here. We married because it had been two years, and people were expecting it. And we had come to love each other."

"And then he found a job?"

Kay nodded. "On a sugarcane plantation. For almost ten years, he never missed a day of work." Kay stared at the unopened envelope and spoke slowly, the words like ice cracking under a heavy boot. "And then he went to Japan, where he believes he will be valued for his true talents. He wants us to join him there, but that's not possible now." She gazed at a new fracture in the wall across from where they were sitting. "I should get back to work." She stood slowly.

Rising, Annie recognized the guilty torment in Kay's eyes. "Your husband didn't drop those bombs."

"Does it make a difference?"

Annie couldn't think of an answer as Kay tucked the note into her pocket and headed out the door. Briefly eyeing the blanket and pillow with the most intense need to lie down, Annie followed. Her nurses needed to eat. And then, maybe, she would take a break.

SIXTEEN

Annie's nurses had eaten and were back on duty. Monica and Irene had taken over the recovery ward, while Winnie continued to carefully dole out morphine, and Sara had taken over for Mak in making the "final" final check before a soldier was placed in the backyard morgue. Kathy was back in the OR, but Annie had promised she would take over for her as soon as she'd eaten. Having given the sandwich in her pocket to one of the orderlies hours ago, Annie's body was letting her know she had to eat or deal with the consequences. Light-headed, she'd waited as long as she could to allow the crowd in the dining room to thin out.

Using a flashlight covered in blue cellophane, she led Kay and her nurses down the back stairs toward the mess hall on the first floor.

"Annie, are you sure we should go in?" asked Kay.

"I'm sure you all need to eat," said Annie.

"Others might not think so," said Kay. "At least they might not think we should be eating with them."

Annie looked at Kay's uniform. The white was smeared with different shades of blood—from brown to rust to pink to crimson, depending on how fresh it was. How could anyone look at the remnants of the day they all wore and deny them food? "I think they'll appreciate what you've done."

Less than convinced, Kay turned to her nurses. "If things get out of hand, don't respond in any way. Don't speak. Don't run. Just walk out and go back to the recovery ward."

"I can't do this," said Amai. "I'm too tired." She started back up the stairs.

Kay turned to the others. "Anyone who wants to follow Amai back to the ward is free to do so. But I don't know when you'll have another chance to sit down to a hot meal."

No one else went up the stairs after Amai.

Kay and her nurses quietly followed Annie inside. Taking one step at a time, they lingered at the back of the room, in shadow, and silently took the tenor of the room.

Hickam Hospital's dining area had been turned into a mess hall with additional folding chairs and tables. Word had gotten out that Hickam was serving hot food, so the people kept coming. Per the blackout order, blankets covered the windows, while oil lamps set on a few tables provided dim light. With a capacity of about three hundred, the makeshift mess hall was on its third dinner service and still crowded with enlisted men, bandaged soldiers well enough to walk, and military families, including children who'd been evacuated from damaged homes. Military wives, most in jeans and sweatshirts, served stew with hopeful smiles.

At first the mood was somber, and the only sounds were the scraping of pans and plates and children crying. But eventually people felt the need to speak. Despite the hope that daylight would find nothing worse than it already was—and maybe, somehow, a little better—rumors bounced from one table to the next like a pinball looking for a hole to fall into.

The topic of rumors ranged from how many Americans had been killed to how many ships had been sunk and planes destroyed to how and when the Japanese were coming back. Most people knew four battleships had been sunk. Beyond that, no one was sure of the damage, but they did know it was extensive. Most people also knew Hickam Field had lost nearly two hundred planes and nearly that many had been damaged. It wasn't so much a matter of estimating how many had been demolished but how many could still fly. As for knowing with any certainty how many servicemen and women had died, the consensus was too many to count. Yet the horrific job of counting and identifying the dead had already begun.

At tables where children were not present, the most prevalent topic of conversation was another attack. When, how, and by which method—air, land, or sea—had been debated since the mess hall opened two hours ago. The most popular scenario had the Japanese attacking by land. Most thought they were hiding in the mountains, waiting until everyone was asleep to come in and set off more bombs, slitting throats just for the pleasure of seeing more American blood spill. Others believed there would be another air attack, while others argued that too many antiaircraft nests had been set up for that to be effective. The element of surprise was gone. As for an attack by sea, they weren't defenseless, not completely. The battleship USS *Nevada* had been able to pull away from Pearl Harbor during the attack, and there were several undamaged destroyers.

Annie motioned Kay and her nurses to follow when the front door opened and Mak led Rita, Carole, and the rest of the girls from Hotel Street into the dining hall. Having taken off their nursing aprons, they wore their street clothes as they took their places at the back of a long line. The women's low-cut dresses in addition to reapplied lipstick in various shades of red left no doubt that the rumor about the women who'd been helping with the wounded was true.

Kay was relieved that Annie had decided to wait until the others took their seats because it would take her a moment to come to grips with seeing Mak standing near Carole, obviously in the role of protector.

Kay watched as the women moved up in line and got the attention of the nearest table full of enlisted men. Many appeared dazed, eating mechanically. But one of the younger men looked up and grinned at Rita. The young man nudged the man next to him, who nudged the man next to him. Soon all the men at that table and the next were staring at the women, some with telltale recognition. A man whose right arm was in a sling tried to raise his hand in a wave as he called, "Hey, Miss Lombard!"

The military wife in charge, who wore her husband's pajama top over her jeans, looked up from ladling stew. She glanced at Carole, who awkwardly waved back at the soldier. Using the ladle, the military wife banged on the side of the pot until she had everyone's attention. "These ladies have been a tremendous help today! Please show them your appreciation and respect and let them eat in peace. They've earned it."

The men in the room applauded, some standing in appreciation for more than just what the women had done that day. The other military wives joined, but their applause was subdued.

Kay continued to watch Carole, who appeared both surprised and embarrassed by the attention. But not Rita, who waved to her adoring fans like she was ready to sign autographs. Obviously not a fan of the attention, Mak hurried the women through the line and then to a table near the back of the room. The table next to theirs was the only empty one available.

Heads down and turned away from the tables, Kay and her nurses followed Annie toward the food line, which, thankfully, had dwindled. As they silently made their way, Kay noticed the uniforms first. When she saw patients in the recovery room, they wore white hospital gowns and didn't speak. Here, their uniforms were mosaics of blood, oil, and smoke, and their constant chatter focused on what had happened and what would happen next.

"I heard the Japanese who live on the island guided the pilots here usin' signals," said a sailor whose white uniform was still fairly white on top but black below his waist, as if half of him had been dipped in crude oil.

"I heard Jap paratroopers landed in the mountains while they were bombing us this morning. And the bastards who live here are helping them get ready to finish us off," said a sailor whose face looked as if it had been painted in charcoal, his eyes the only white.

"If they'd just give each of us a fucking machine gun and let us go find 'em," said the sailor who appeared to have been dipped in oil, "we'd be better off than sittin' here waiting for who knows what." Pushing his seat back, he bumped into one of Kay's nurses and then spotted the others. Grabbing the oil lamp from his table, he held it near their faces like he was inspecting an unexpected and wholly unwanted delivery. "Japs!"

The dining hall erupted. Women screamed, which made their children scream. Men jumped out of their chairs, eyes darting around the room for the enemy, many picking up knives they'd used to butter their biscuits.

"We're Americans!" shouted Kay, stepping in front of her nurses, arms spread. "Just like you." She felt the same panic she had that morning when she'd watched the planes fly over Pearl Harbor and Hickam Field. Only she couldn't hide under her kitchen table. She and her nurses were at the mercy of these men, especially the one who stood only a few feet away—a revolver in his hand.

"These nurses cared for your brothers today," said Annie, standing beside Kay. "They came here to help."

"Bullshit! They came here to kill us!" The man with the gun started to raise it.

"Drop the weapon," said Mak, holding his own gun to the soldier's back. "Everyone needs to calm down, starting with you, Private. That's an order."

Mak had spoken with such authority that the man dropped his weapon. Before the soldier could turn and see that Mak wasn't military, Annie took his gun.

Then gunfire broke out. Kay expected she was about to find out what it was like to be shot. Her first and only thought was her children. What would happen to them if she was killed?

But then Kay realized the gunfire wasn't coming from inside but outside. Were they under attack again? Was this the final assault everyone had been predicting all day? For the second time in the last few minutes, Kay expected she was about to die.

People hurried to the windows and pulled down the blankets. Kay and her nurses followed Annie to the window farthest from the others. Mak pulled down the blanket and stood behind Kay to watch.

At first, all anyone could see was the rain. Seconds later, a search-light from Hickam revealed something over the ocean. Six planes flew in formation, riding lights pointing toward Pearl Harbor and Hickam Field.

This was it then. Kay felt Mak's hands on her shoulders, gently tugging her to move behind him. But what was the point? Besides, all she could think about were her children. Were more planes headed for Honolulu? How many antiaircraft guns had they been able to set up around the city? She was desperately trying to remember what Ivy had told her about the governor's plans when Hickam's landing lights suddenly went out.

The darkness was followed by an explosion of antiaircraft gunfire arcing tracers into the night sky. There was so much firepower, the night sky lit up like it was midday. One after the other, the planes' riding lights spiraled into the ocean or suddenly disappeared.

Spontaneous cheers erupted from everyone in the mess hall. And Kay joined in because if they could stop the planes from attacking Hickam, then Honolulu and her children had a chance. Her face filled with happy relief, Kay turned to see the man who'd been point-ing the gun at her.

He was not the only one who looked at her and her nurses, still gleeful at the apparent downing of the enemy planes, in puzzlement as he and his buddies also cheered.

When the cheering subsided and all the blankets were back up, several military wives brought hot food to Kay's table. The military wife in charge, her husband's pajama top spotted with stew, set down slices of gingerbread at their table. "Thank you for coming here today," she said. "We know it wasn't easy."

"Like everyone else," Kay said loudly enough for all at the nearby tables to hear, "we came because our country was attacked. And because we'll do all we can to make sure our men are well enough to fight back."

"We appreciate it," said the military wife, wiping away a stray tear with a shaky hand.

"Have you eaten?" asked Annie.

"No, ma'am," she said.

"Would you please join us?" asked Kay.

"I can't." Noting the hurt that floated over Kay's features, she moved closer to her and Annie and whispered, "My husband was working in Hangar 11 this morning. His body is pinned under the wreckage."

"I'm so sorry," said Kay.

"Is there anything we can do?" asked Annie.

The woman shook her head. "Being here is the only thing I can do for my husband now."

"I'm sure he'd be very proud of you," said Annie.

"Thank you, ma'am. Now please eat. I know you've been working hard to help the men who have a chance. I'm so grateful for the blessing of each and every soldier who survived."

Kay and Annie watched her return to the food line, doling out stew and biscuits. In silence, both reached for a glass of milk first because they needed to soothe the lump of grief in their throats before they could swallow solids. When they could speak, they wanted to talk of nothing that had anything to do with that day.

"Have you ever been ice skating?" asked Annie.

"In Hawaii?" Mak smiled like he needed to.

"There used to be a skating rink," said Kay. "But it closed when I was young."

"A rink wouldn't be the same," said Annie. "Have you ever been ice skating on a pond or a lake?"

"Again, Hawaii," said Mak.

"What's it like?" asked Kay.

"Flying," said Annie. "If you don't have to think about what your feet are doing or whether the ice is thick enough. If you can stop thinking about everything and just glide. No tricks. No spins. Nothing special. Except that everything is special. The air is so crisp that everything seems brighter. The sky is bluer, and the snow is white enough to hurt your eyes, so you close them and listen. I can hear my blades gliding along the ice. The birds making all kinds of sounds I'd never noticed before. And my grandfather humming a tune I can almost remember. Even when the ice was a foot thick, he wouldn't let me skate alone."

Kay had never known her grandfathers, one of whom still lived in Japan, and they had nothing to do with one of her favorite memories. "Have you ever sung on a radio talent show?" asked Kay.

Speechless, Mak's eyes widened as her nurses' mouths dropped open, gingerbread notwithstanding.

"Did you actually sing on the radio?" asked Annie.

Kay nodded. "I was seventeen. KGU-AM was a new station,

and they thought featuring some local talent was a good way to get new listeners. They invited singers and storytellers. My best friend Millie had a wonderful singing voice, but she was too shy to sing on the radio, at least by herself. She told me if I went first, she could do it. I didn't care if I won the talent contest or not, so I thought it was no big deal. My family didn't own a radio because they were too expensive. I didn't know anyone who did except for Millie's dad, who only got one because President Harding had gotten a radio for the White House. Anyway, the day of the talent show finally came, and I thought it would be easy. Until I looked at the microphone. It was nearly as big as my face. I started to think about how many people might be listening. I asked the station manager, and he told me hundreds of people would hear me sing. Only they didn't hear me sing because all that came out was a squeak. Like a mouse. A very scared mouse."

"What about Millie?" asked Annie, laughing. "Did she squeak or run?"

"She felt so badly for me that she forgot her own nervousness. She sang beautifully and came in second in the talent show."

"Then your sacrifice was worth it," said Mak.

"Yes, other than the fact that Millie's dad had invited my parents to listen to the talent show at his house. And from that day forward, my dad only called me mouse. As if he'd never chosen the name—"

"Kaya Kimura!" boomed a voice from the doorway.

Everyone at the table turned to see Major Lance, in his uniform, with four other men, two standing on either side of him.

"Stay here," said Annie. "I'll find out what's going on."

"What if something's happened to my children?" Rising, Kay

hurried toward Major Lance, wondering if other planes had made it to Honolulu. Eyes on the major, she didn't notice that the four men standing behind him wore military police uniforms.

Annie had been waiting more than an hour. To keep her mind off whatever was going on inside the major's office with Kay and the military police, she'd been helping Winnie with patients still waiting for transport to Tripler General or Queen's Hospital. There were only half a dozen patients left in the first-floor offices, thanks to all the locals who'd been using every kind of truck to help out with transport.

When she was finally allowed inside, she saw that the windows in Major Lance's office were also covered. The room was lit by only one oil lamp on the desk. Kay stood in the shadows by three military policemen, who appeared more than ready to escort her off the base.

Annie didn't wait for a question. "I know this woman. She's one of the best and most caring nurses I've ever worked with."

"With all due respect, ma'am," said the senior ranking MP, Sergeant Miller, "I don't care if she sprouts a halo in the next five minutes. Our orders are to bring in every community leader, even if it's a woman."

"Why?"

"Because they're suspected of treason," said Major Lance.

"That's ridiculous! She's been tending to our wounded all day."

"Lieutenant Fox is right," said Major Lance. "Mrs. Kimura and her nurses have gone above and beyond the call of duty. They didn't have to come here."

"She didn't answer the call of duty because she's not military," said the sergeant.

"You're wrong, Sergeant," said Annie. "She and her nurses only volunteered out of a sense of duty to their country."

"How do you know that for sure, Lieutenant? How do you know she didn't come here to gather information? Maybe she came here to find out how bad Hickam Field got hit. Maybe she came here to find out how many soldiers are still alive to fight back when they strike again."

Kay came forward. "I did not—"

"Step back, Mrs. Kimura," said the sergeant sternly. "You'll have your chance to speak in your own defense later."

Kay hesitated until one of the MPs pulled her back by the arm.

"Who ordered you to take her into custody?" asked Annie.

"My orders come from the top."

"How high?" asked the major.

"General Short," said the sergeant.

Annie looked at Major Lance, who shook his head. There was no point in arguing an order that came from the U.S. commander in charge of every military installation in Hawaii. Not when he was dealing with everything that had happened that day in addition to preparing for another attack. He was too busy to concern himself with one civilian nurse. Annie also understood why they wanted to talk to community leaders. They had to follow up on every rumor. They couldn't afford to be blindsided, not again.

As they moved Kay toward the door, Annie saw how frightened she was and wanted to reassure her that everything would be all right. Despite knowing it was a waste of time to bring Kay in for questioning, Annie still had faith in military justice and believed Kay would be back home within a few hours. As they were about to leave, Annie embraced her. "I'm so sorry, Kay. This is all just a big misunderstanding. You'll be home soon."

"Please ask Mak to watch over my children until I get back," said Kay with what sounded like a sudden calm. "And please explain the situation to my mother. She'll be very upset when she learns I've been taken."

"Of course." Reluctantly, Annie let go of her, watching as the MPs escorted her away, leaving her alone with the major. "Where are they taking her?"

"I have no idea." Major Lance reached into his bottom drawer, took out a bottle of whiskey and two shot glasses, and poured, holding one out to Annie. "All I know is that the MPs will turn her over to the FBI. And she's not the only one. They're going to question every Japanese community or religious leader. If any of them had anything to do with the attack in any way, they'll find out."

She took a long swallow of whiskey before she spoke. "Kay had nothing to do with it. I'm as sure of that as I am my own name. How can we help her?"

"I don't know that we can."

"We have to. I have to. It's my fault she's here."

"They would've found her wherever she was, and it was a good thing they found her here. It might just save her."

"From what?"

Ignoring the question, he put his whiskey bottle back in the drawer. "I'll talk to General Short in the morning."

"You think they'll keep her in custody all night?"

"If they're taking in every community leader, I doubt they'll have time to question them all before morning. Besides, it's not a good time to ask General Short for any favors. He's dealing with the fallout from shooting our own damn planes down."

"*Our* planes? The planes we just watched get shot down?"

He nodded. "Six Wildcats. They came from the *Enterprise*, part of their fighter squadron on an air search looking for the Japanese fleet. It was getting dark, and they were running low on fuel. They were going to land on Ford Island when our guys on the ground starting shooting because they thought it was another attack. Three pilots were killed."

"Jesus Christ." She watched him sip his whiskey, fatigue making the creases around his eyes appear deeper. "What about the other three?"

"One headed to Wheeler Field, where his plane was hit and he crashed. They got him out, but his head injuries are serious. Another pilot crashed on the Ford Island golf course—uninjured. He picked up his parachute and walked to the seaplane base at the other end of the island. Got there just in time to stop them from killing the other pilot. Not that you could blame them. It was just…"

"A tragic ending to a tragic day."

"Day's not over yet."

Annie swallowed the rest of her whiskey and put her glass on his desk. "I need to find Kay's nurses and tell them what's happened."

"If they want to leave, I'll arrange an escort. But I'm honestly not sure any place on the island is safe tonight."

Annie wondered when and if they would ever feel safe again and suddenly felt the need to check in with her own nurses. She was in no hurry to see Kay's nurses, especially Mak, and tell them Kay had been taken away to be turned over to the FBI for questioning.

Annie hadn't met with all her nurses since right after the attack had begun, but she'd asked Monica to round them up and meet her in the ladies' room. It was still their only private space. Before she met with them, Annie was determined to deliver what she prayed would be some good news and set about finding any injured sailors from the *Pennsylvania*.

Half an hour later, Annie walked into the ladies' room. Her nurses were all there, each one looking weary, anxious, and terribly sad. She wanted to embrace them, but it was Sara she approached. "I have news about your sister, Helen."

Sara leaned against the wall as if bracing herself for the worst.

"I found a sailor from the *Pennsylvania*. He said their ship was damaged, but not the sick bay. He saw Helen before they sent him here for surgery."

"You're sure, Chief?" asked Sara, eyes full of hope.

"I'm sure," said Annie. "Helen told him to ask for you when he got here, but he couldn't remember your name. All he could remember was that he was supposed to tell someone her twin sister Helen is fine and she'll see you soon."

Sobbing with relief, Sara sank to the floor. Annie sat beside her and pulled her close, and with her free hand, she motioned the others to join them. Everyone had tears of joy in their eyes.

"We don't have long," said Annie, "but I want to know how you're all doing."

"Better than our patients," said Winnie with a crooked smile.

"I know you've all reached your limit, but for the next day or two or even longer, we'll need to get by on too little sleep and too much caffeine."

"Do you think we'll get more casualties?" asked Kathy, who was picking dried blood out from under her fingernails.

"I hope not," said Annie. "But we can't be sure there won't be another attack. In the meantime, is there anything you need?"

"I need to know what to say," said Irene. "When someone is dying."

Monica nodded. "So many call out for their moms. I've been lying and telling them their mother is on her way. It seems to help."

"If it helps them at the end, then a fib is fine," said Annie. "But I think the most important thing any of us can do is hold their hand and let them know they're not alone."

"What if they don't have any hands left to hold?" asked Winnie. "What if there's no place left on your patient that you can touch without inflicting more pain?"

"Then talk to them. But keep it simple. Food. Movies. Books. Sports. The weather. The important thing is that they hear a soothing voice. And give them as much reassurance as you can. Tell them the Japanese won't be back. And tell them they're going to be all right."

"We should lie about that too?" asked Irene.

"We never know for sure who will or won't make it," said Annie. "I've seen men with terrible injuries recover, and I've seen men with nothing more than a scratch succumb to an infection. The will to live can make all the difference, and they have to believe they have a chance. Even if it's a small one."

They all nodded.

"Now tell me what *you* need." Annie understood it was going to be the little things in life that kept them going.

"Other than a long, hot bath followed by a very stiff drink and two days in bed," said Monica, "I could use a rubber band. I need to put my hair in a ponytail. My curl's gone, and it keeps falling into my eyes."

Annie pulled her notepad and pen out of her pocket and wrote down *rubber band*. "One rubber band on the list. Next?"

"My uniform," said Sara, who was still wearing her pajamas under the nurse's apron. "And some stockings, please."

"A clean pair of stockings for me too," said Irene, whose white stockings were spattered with various bodily fluids.

Annie wrote down their requests and looked at Winnie.

"I'd like my perfume," she said.

"I know you're always in the mood to flirt," said Monica. "But now isn't exactly the right time for it, Winnie."

"I don't want it for flirting," explained Winnie. "I've had a few men want me to lean in so they can smell me. I think it's because all they can smell is burning oil and blood and death. Before I left, my mother gave me a bottle of Shalimar for special occasions. It's in my locker behind my magazines."

"I'll get it," said Annie, writing it down on her list. "Might be a good idea to give everyone a spritz." She lifted her arm and smelled herself. "Including me."

They all laughed for the first time that day. When they stopped, they were quiet for a while as if listening to the laughter's echo and not wanting to let go of it—or each other.

SEVENTEEN

Kay might as well have been blindfolded. There were no streetlights, and the blue cellophane used to cover flashlights at the hospital also covered the car headlights. Not to mention the fact that theirs was the only car on the road; martial law had been declared and curfew strictly enforced.

Sitting between Sergeant Miller and another MP in the back seat, she'd asked where they were taking her as soon as they'd begun driving away from Hickam Field. No one had answered. No one had said a word in the past eighteen minutes. The only thing she could do was check her watch. It was almost nine miles from Hickam to Honolulu, and it normally took about twenty to twenty-five minutes to drive that distance. Of course, that was with traffic. Without traffic, if they stopped soon, she would be fairly certain they were in the city, where she assumed they would deliver her to the FBI.

Kay had a feeling that Sergeant Miller would like to do the questioning himself. He reminded her of her high school principal, Mr. Jeffries. Whenever he was called to an "incident," as he referred to them, no matter how trivial, he would take the "culprits" to his office where he would conduct his "investigation." Kay had only been called to the principal's office once, but she would never forget it.

It had been her senior year, and she planned to attend the University of Hawaii in the fall to begin her nursing education. This had been her singular goal for four years. Many of her friends were taking a different path. Most planned to marry their high school sweethearts, including Lucinda—Lucy—Lehman. She and Teddy Ryker had been dating since their freshman year. Until their senior year when Teddy decided to see if the grass was greener in Greta Thompson's backyard. Apparently, it wasn't, and he'd been begging Lucy to take him back. Even during chemistry class.

Kay sat between Teddy and Lucy and had been passing notes between them, but Lucy refused to read them. Trying to follow what the teacher was doing on the blackboard, Kay simply gave Teddy a shrug—there was nothing she could do to make Lucy read his notes. Teddy persisted. He wrote another note and handed it to Kay, who got caught with it in her hand.

Shortly after, Kay sat in the principal's office across from Mr. Jeffries. He put on his glasses, unfolded the note, and read aloud. "Please take me back. I love you. I never stopped. We can still get married." He took off his glasses, refolded the note, and placed it on his desk. "I thought you were planning to attend the university this fall, Miss Kimura."

"I am." Kay wondered why he would think this had changed. She assumed that he, like everyone else, knew Teddy and Lucy were a couple.

"You don't think that will be even more difficult if you're married?"

"Married?" Kay suddenly wondered if he thought she was the "other woman."

"Unless you don't intend to take him back?"

"I'm not taking anyone back. I never—"

"Many young women decide to get married after high school rather than furthering their education. Personally, I see nothing wrong with choosing to be a homemaker. It's a worthy ambition for a young lady. But for you…"

Kay assumed he was going to talk about her excellent academic record. Or the fact that she'd never missed a day of school.

"Marrying a white boy would present some…unique challenges."

For some reason, she felt much more insulted by him than she had been when her mother had warned her about dating white boys. Kay had quickly put an end to the conversation by telling her that she had no intention of dating until after high school. Maybe if she shared her resolve with the principal, it would help clear up this misunderstanding. "Mr. Jeffries, I don't plan on getting married. At least not until after college. The note—"

"Sounds desperate. Some boys feel that dating a Japanese girl is exotic. However, I have rarely seen a white boy actually marry a Japanese girl. My advice is that you forget about him and date boys who you have more in common with."

Never in her life had Kay wanted to hit someone, and the sudden urge to slap the condescension off his face made her heart pound.

"That aside," he continued, "I'm sure I don't have to explain the disruption you caused in passing notes. And I'm sure I don't have to tell you how inappropriate it is to discuss things of such a personal nature while in school."

"I didn't discuss anything of a personal nature." If Kay was going to be blamed, then at least Mr. Jeffries could get his facts right about something. "Teddy Ryker wrote the note."

"I can see you still have some hard feelings toward the boy. I'm glad. It may help you keep your distance from him."

"Yes, sir," said Kay, accepting the fact that Mr. Jeffries would not change his mind.

"Good. Then I won't put a letter in your file. But I will speak to your father."

"My father?"

"I want to make sure he understands what's at stake for you so he can help you make the best decisions going forward."

She didn't hear what else Mr. Jeffries said because all she could think about was how to explain this to her father, who would never believe the principal called him about something that had never happened. Still, she would have to try. Her father would be more upset if he thought she'd been dating a white boy. Especially without his permission, which he would never have given.

Kay's father had brought his wife to Hawaii so their children could live a free life, but that hadn't meant he wanted them to stop being Japanese. While he'd told Kay more than once to embrace being an American, with all the freedoms that bestowed, he'd also asked her to hold on to the Japanese culture and traditions that her ancestors had held so dear. This would include marrying a good Japanese boy who was also an American. She thought she'd fulfilled her father's wish by marrying Daiji.

Now, feeling the car slow, Kay gazed out the window and saw that they were close to the water, though it was difficult to distinguish land from sea in the darkness. She glanced at the sergeant and knew he already had his own story about her in his head. As with Mr. Jeffries, she doubted that anything she could say would change that story. The note was all the evidence the principal had needed. Would it be the same with the FBI?

The car came to a stop. Sergeant Miller got out and held the door open for her, but she had to figure out how to get out of the back seat without using her hands. Looking down at her handcuffs, she nearly panicked when she remembered playing cops and robbers with Tommy. Beth had refused to play because she didn't want to be a robber, so Kay had volunteered. Tommy had chased Kay through the apartment, finally cornering her behind the couch, where he pointed his gun and told her she was under arrest for robbing the bank.

He'd handed the gun to Beth, his deputy, and she held it on Kay while Tommy put his toy handcuffs on her wrists. She was then escorted to the jail—the pantry—where she would await trial. A merciful judge, Beth had sentenced her mother to one night without dessert, which she then revoked when she learned the defendant was making chocolate cake. She couldn't let her mother miss out on her favorite dessert.

As Kay maneuvered herself across the back seat, she pretended the handcuffs would break if she pulled hard enough. She pretended these men were just boys playing at cops and robbers. She pretended she would go home soon and make a chocolate cake, and she would let Beth and Tommy stay up late. They would eat until their stomachs ached.

Then she got out of the car and saw the dim blue light coming from the top of a police patrol boat. Why was she getting on a boat? Where the hell were they taking her?

Trying to get her bearings, she looked to her right and left for some kind of landmark. She kept searching for something the least bit familiar as the sergeant and the other MP took her by each arm and wordlessly pulled her toward the boat.

EIGHTEEN

Annie had gone back to find Winnie's perfume and had found something—rather, someone—she'd never expected to see in the nurses' quarters: Chaplain Elmer Tiedt.

He sat on the floor leaning against Kathy's bed, head down, hands folded, though he didn't seem to be praying. None of the beds had a mattress; they'd all been moved to the hospital. Annie wished she'd bought those sleeping bags she'd teased the major about. "Chaplain Tiedt?" she said.

"I'm sorry," he said, peering up at her. "This was the only place I could think of where no one would look for me. I just needed a minute."

"It's all right." Annie sat on the floor across from him, leaning against Monica's bed. "My nurses and I have been finding respite in the ladies' room. Not that you should go there."

He tried to smile but couldn't manage it. No wonder. Annie had heard his wife had been killed. She couldn't imagine what he was feeling. "I'm very sorry about your wife."

"Thank you."

"Feel free to stay as long as you like. I just came in to get a few things for my nurses." Annie started to rise.

"I hesitated," he said, looking at her.

She lowered herself back down and waited because he had a look she'd seen before, mainly in men who needed to confess something to someone before they died. Only he wasn't hurt, not physically.

"When the bombing started," he began, "I went to the dispensary. One of my clerks had been setting up the service, dressing the altar. He was struck by a strafing bullet. There was nothing I could do but pray for him."

"Many have died today without even that." Annie knew she would be haunted forever by the thought of so many dying without a prayer or a hand to hold.

Bowing his head again, the chaplain spoke into his folded hands. "I left him to get to the hospital. I started to cross the parade ground but had to wait because it was being strafed. When the plane passed, I was about to cross when I saw an airman come from the PX. He was holding a case of beer and a carton of cigarettes, and I thought, God have mercy on his soul for choosing that moment to steal. I was going to ask him to put everything back and pray for forgiveness when another plane came. It was so loud. The airman must've heard it, but he still started across the parade ground. I shouted for him to stop, but I'm not sure he heard me. And then he got hit. More than once. He fell, and the beer cans scattered and packs of cigarettes flew everywhere."

"Dear God," said Annie, feeling nothing but sorry for the man who'd picked up a case of beer and a carton of cigarettes rather than a gun to shoot at the enemy. She sincerely hoped his family would never know the dishonor he'd died with.

"I was so angry. Not at the pilot or the gunner who'd shot him. I was angry at the thief." He looked up at her, eyes full of shame. "I couldn't bring myself to go to him, because I knew I couldn't pray in earnest. For the first time, I couldn't fulfill my obligation to another human being. Or to God. Maybe that's why…my wife was killed."

"God didn't take your wife. The enemy did. Along with thousands of others."

"How can you know that for sure?"

"What I know for sure is that you were in shock. You'd just left your clerk, and we were under attack. No one, including God, could blame you for not reacting as you normally would."

"But that soldier deserved absolution."

"Then pray for him now." Annie had never been very religious, but she folded her hands and bowed her head. A few moments later, Chaplain Tiedt began to pray. For all who had died that day, including the thief.

Major Lance had told Annie he was calling a halt to all surgeries. Even with several oil lamps and flashlights, there wasn't sufficient light to see well enough to avoid doing more harm than good. He and the other surgeons were also physically and mentally drained. Not one of them was performing at the best of their ability. The other thing that had played a part in his decision was knowing the most serious cases had been dealt with earlier or had been transferred to Tripler General or Queen's Hospital. He also told her that if anyone took a turn for the worse overnight, they would be transferred. He'd given his surgeons a supper break, and then his senior staff was to meet in his office for an update.

When Annie entered, the first thing she noticed was how spent Drs. Metcalfe and Doyle appeared to be. Yet Dr. Doyle rose and brought Annie a chair as Dr. Metcalfe said, "You and your nurses did fine work today, Lieutenant Fox."

"Thank you," said Annie, who couldn't hide her surprise at the compliment.

"You've all done amazing work today," said the major, "under extremely difficult conditions, which may or may not improve."

"Did you get word from General Short?" asked Dr. Metcalfe.

"Not yet," said the major. "I'm still waiting for my liaison to return."

"Did you ask whether he expects another attack?" asked Dr. Doyle.

"Yes. I also asked about antiaircraft guns. The last time I met with him—"

"You mean the last time you kicked his ass on the back nine?" asked Dr. Metcalfe.

The major ignored the praise. "As a matter of fact, we were on the golf course just two weeks ago when he expressed his concern about a short supply of antiaircraft guns and ammunition. Not just at Hickam, but Army-wide."

Annie understood what this implied. If there was another attack and they didn't have enough weapons, Japanese forces might be able to take the island.

"Jesus Christ," said Dr. Metcalfe. "How the hell does the U.S. Army run short on guns and bullets? And don't get me started on the stupidity of lifting the full alert yesterday!"

"I'm sure there will be a review of what was done and what wasn't done before and during the attack," said the major, "but that's not under our purview."

"I wish to hell it was," said Dr. Metcalfe. "General Short would follow Kimmel out the door and into retirement."

"Placing blame on our own won't help," said Annie.

"I agree," said the major. "It does us no good to second-guess leadership, especially when we don't have all the facts. Let's just focus on getting through the next few days."

"How about the next few hours?" said Dr. Doyle. "I'm not sure I could operate any better than Annie could if we get more casualties tonight."

Annie was tempted to tell him about the successful surgery she'd performed on Jeremy when there was a knock on the door. The major's liaison with General Short entered and took a note from his satchel. "Should I wait for a reply, Major Lance?" he asked.

"No, go get some rest."

The liaison saluted and left.

Major Lance opened the note, read it quickly, and then read aloud. "Emperor Hirohito has undertaken a surprise offensive extending throughout the Pacific. They've attacked Malaya in addition to Hong Kong, Guam, the Philippines, and Wake Island. As for the antiaircraft gun shortage, it's still an issue. More so because 'nervous Nellies' keep shooting at shadows and wasting ammunition."

Annie watched him continue reading for a few moments before putting the note on his desk and laying his hands over it. She got the distinct impression that there was something he wasn't telling them.

"The Emperor wants Southeast Asia," said Dr. Metcalfe, "and we were in his way."

"We're still in his way," said the major. "And our job is to make sure the soldiers who are still able to pick up a weapon stay that way."

"What about the wounded who want to fight?" Annie had lost count of how many patients had asked her for a gun in case the enemy infiltrated the base. "Do we change how we assess patients for medical release?"

"No," he said without hesitation. "I won't risk a patient relapsing. Not unless the enemy is on our doorstep. If that happens, any soldier can fight if he so chooses."

"If he or she so chooses?" Annie had treated more than one woman who also wanted to be armed.

"Of course," said the major, turning to his doctors. "Get some sleep. One of the admin offices that was holding transports to Tripler has been cleared. If it stays quiet, I won't let anyone disturb you for at least four hours."

"What about post-op checks?" asked Dr. Doyle.

"Nurse Fox and I will handle those."

Annie wasn't sure how much more she could handle, but doctors, especially surgeons, were more valuable in war, and the major had prioritized correctly. As soon as Drs. Doyle and Metcalfe closed the door behind them, heading for desperately needed rest, Annie asked, "What didn't you tell them?"

"I didn't tell them about the FBI."

"You have news about Kay?" Annie leaned forward in her chair.

"All he wrote was that the order to round up potential subversives wasn't his call. It came from above his pay grade."

"The president?"

"I assume so. General Short also said they've been escorted to a secure location for questioning. Any further information will be given on a need-to-know basis."

"Meaning he won't tell you."

"And I can't push him. Not now. He's got enough to deal with."

"I know, but Kay is dealing with God knows what because people's fears and suspicions have gotten out of control."

"For good reason," said the major. "If the strongest Navy fleet in the world lost the battle this morning, then why not Navy bases in San Diego or Norfolk? And if Hickam Field could be destroyed, then why not Langley Field or Fort Benning, for that matter?"

"We were taken by surprise. Japan couldn't get away with this again."

"Maybe not," said the major. "But I can't fault the president for using the FBI to find out if any other attacks are planned."

He might not be able to fault the president, but Annie could.

Annie surveyed the outside morgue. The rain had washed away some of the blood, so when the rain stopped and the moon peeked out from behind clouds, many of the men appeared to be sleeping. If she didn't look too closely, the dark camouflaged the individual carnage.

Preferring to think of them as asleep, she wanted the sound of gunfire to stop before it disturbed them. Antiartillery weapons had been going off periodically since the downing of the six planes. However, so far, there was nothing to shoot at but rumors. Listening to pregnant raindrops dripping from palm trees as well as crickets and katydids, who went about their business as if it was just another night, she made her way to Mak.

He had bent down to retrieve a cowboy hat that had slid off Billy Lardner's face in the rain. Despite how the man had treated Mak and every other Hawaiian plantation worker, she watched him gently place the hat back over Billy's face.

"Wherever he is, I'm sure he appreciated that," said Annie softly.

"Where's Kay?" asked Mak, straightening to face her.

"The military police took her somewhere to be questioned by the FBI. They have orders to question every community leader."

"You mean every Japanese American community leader."

"Yes." Annie held up a note. "Mr. Taketa gave this to me, and I gave it to Kay as he asked. I slipped it out of her pocket just before they took her away. I thought the FBI might misinterpret what her husband had written, at least from Kay's perspective."

"Have you read it?"

"No. But I know her husband's loyalty to the Emperor of Japan is dangerous to his family. It's important that Kay isn't associated with whatever he's involved in." She held the note out to Mak.

"Thank you," he said with sincerity.

"I'm the one who should be thanking you, Mak. You've watched over our fallen men and women without complaint."

"Then show me your appreciation by getting me to Honolulu."

"In the morning—"

"I have to leave now." He moved closer and whispered as though the dead could hear. "There are more notes and letters from her husband. I need to get rid of them before the military police or the FBI searches Kay's apartment."

"Why would they go that far? Kay might even be home by now."

"Do you really believe they'll let her go? Or is it more likely they'll keep her and anyone else they've taken until they know whether the enemy is coming back?"

Annie couldn't be sure, and she wouldn't take the chance. "I'll ask Major Lance to provide an escort. You can't drive yourself, not with martial law in effect."

"You think he'll give me one?"

"I do. After I tell him Kay asked you to watch over her children until she gets home. He'll want to make sure they're safe." Under normal circumstances, Annie wouldn't dream about taking advantage of the major, but nothing about this day had been normal. She couldn't even imagine what "normal" would look like in a month, never mind a day.

"Kay asked that I take care of her kids?"

Annie nodded. "I don't know why you sound surprised. Kay thinks the world of you. I doubt there's anyone she trusts more."

"She's trusting you too," he said, gesturing toward the pocket that held the note.

"Don't worry, Mak. I won't betray her."

"You already did," he said, "by lying to us about who you are and what you were really doing at the center."

What he said stung, but she couldn't fault him for stating the truth. "I'm sorry." She hoped he heard the sincerity in her voice. "The only way I can think to make it up to Kay—and to you—is to help her in any way I can."

Annie went back inside the hospital to find the major, knowing she would have to bend the truth to get Mak on his way back to Honolulu as quickly as possible.

The day from hell was officially over. It was a little past midnight when Annie finished helping Kathy clean the three operating rooms and then reviewed patient charts in the recovery ward. She spent a little more time reviewing Jeremy's chart, noting with relief that his vitals were still stable and the infection site was clean. On the other hand, the pain for him and the rest of their patients would increase tomorrow and the next day, as was normal following surgery. They would need more morphine from the other hospitals on the island if they had any to spare. If not, they would need to send for morphine from the military hospital at the Presidio in San Francisco. She would talk to the major about getting on that right away.

When she got to the first floor, she checked in with Monica and Winnie, who were both keeping watch over patients who hadn't been transferred to Tripler General. Those patients were thought to be stable, but you could never be sure there wasn't something that had been missed. They worried most about undiagnosed internal bleeding on a slow but steady drip or a head injury that would produce a delayed brain bleed.

"We need more morphine," said Annie as she walked into the major's office. He'd given her permission to request an escort to take Mak home once she'd mentioned the children, who she let him think were alone. She pushed the guilt she felt about that little lie by omission aside as she told him about her new request. "With the phones out, we'll need to send someone to all the hospitals on the island. If they don't have any to spare, we should send a plane to the Presidio. Getting clearance for a medical supply transport might be tricky, and God knows I don't want another plane shot down by our own, but we don't have a choice. We can't tell these men to grin and bear it, not after what they've been through." Not realizing she'd been pacing back and forth, she stopped because her legs felt wobbly. Everything she'd ignored all day—from physical to mental exhaustion—suddenly caught up with her.

Major Lance noticed and cleared several soiled operating gowns from the small couch in his office. "Lie down, Lieutenant."

"I don't need to lie down, sir." She would never admit to feeling that weak.

"Then sit. That's an order."

Sitting on the couch, she felt her legs tremble in earnest. "Low blood sugar," she said quietly, as if ashamed.

"Delayed shock is more likely."

"I'm not suffering from shock." Except she heard her voice tremble in sync with the rest of her. There wasn't a part of her body that wasn't shaking.

"So you're immune?"

"Yes," said Annie. "I've already been through one war. I know what men look like after their flesh and bones have been decimated by a bullet or a bomb." She rubbed her eyes, trying her best to recover from the images.

"Maybe that's why you were able to stay so cool under fire today."

"I was just doing my job." She would not say another word because her teeth were chattering, and she didn't have time to fall apart.

"I don't know what we would've done without you."

She shook her head because everyone had risen to the occasion. Her nurses. Kay's nurses and the women who had donated blood. The sailors and soldiers who'd risked their lives to fight back and save as many lives as they could. The civilians who'd driven their vehicles to Hickam and Pearl Harbor to transport the injured to Tripler. The military wives who stayed in harm's way to feed people. Even the orderlies had gone above and beyond without a single complaint. Everyone had done all they could. Had it all happened in just one day? Images came at her like sleet—cold and penetrating.

The Japanese pilot who'd waved to her from his plane before strafing the parade ground.

The men who ran out of their barracks raising pistols to a sky already filling with smoke.

The sailor whose fingers were sticks of charcoal.

The bottomless crater left by the bomb in the front yard.

The men in the burned-out car with a Thompson submachine gun.

Mrs. Taketa with a ragged hole in her temple, bent over her breakfast.

A half-eaten sundae on the drugstore counter.

The little girl in the morgue at Tripler General, still holding the handle of a jump rope.

Billy Lardner slumped over the steering wheel of his truck turned ambulance.

The small patch of pale skin near Private Sam Baker's hip.

Every wound and grotesque disfigurement she'd seen over the past eighteen hours.

Every brief and inadequate goodbye she'd taken down in her notepad.

She watched the major go to the closet and take out a lap blanket. Putting it over her shoulders, he sat and put his arm around her, squeezing just hard enough to feel his warmth. If she closed her eyes, she would fall asleep, and all those images would disappear. But she couldn't give in to exhaustion and the safety she felt in his arms. Not yet.

"I'm worried about Kay," she said.

"She'll be all right. Between you and me, I think General Short is just trying to cover his own ass. He made a few mistakes leading up to the attack."

"What kind of mistakes?"

"He created three alert levels for the kind of attack we anticipated. But today, we were still on Alert One—the sabotage alert."

"Because he thought we'd be attacked by the Japanese already living here?" She felt him nod, his chin touching the top of her head.

"Alert One required that all ammunition not needed for immediate training be boxed and stored, including most of our antiaircraft ammunition. He also ordered the planes to be parked wingtip to wingtip to make them easier to guard and harder to sabotage, which only made them burn faster after they were hit."

"One could argue the general was the one who sabotaged us."

"He did order full-scale exercises last week," he said. "Antiaircraft stations were set up all over the island. But then it was right back to Alert One status."

"Do you think he's arresting people to prove he was right? About the sabotage?"

"Even if he finds saboteurs, the fact remains that if he'd only raised us to Alert Two, fighter aircraft would've been put on alert, antiaircraft units would've been deployed, and long-range reconnaissance would've been launched. We would've stood a chance."

"But we didn't because he was too focused on a nonexistent threat."

"We don't know that it's nonexistent. Many on the island have strong ties with Japan. I can't fault the general for being suspicious."

"You think they were right to take Kay?"

"I think we can't be too careful."

Despite realizing that most on the base likely felt as he did, Annie pulled away. "I'm okay now." Her own voice sounded so distant she wasn't sure if she believed it.

"You will be," he said. "After you get some rest."

"I can't. My nurses—"

"Have had breaks throughout the day. You haven't."

"Neither have you."

"I'll make you a deal. You rest for one hour while I go make rounds. Then I'll come back, and you can order me to lie down."

She almost smiled.

"It's a one-time deal, Lieutenant. What do you say?"

"I suppose I can't pass up such a good offer." Sighing in surrender, she lay down and was asleep almost before her head hit the cushion. But she still felt him remove her shoes and cover her with the blanket. As she slipped further into sleep, she desperately wanted to ask him to stay. But he was needed elsewhere.

NINETEEN

Sand Island. It had to be where they'd taken Kay because she hadn't been on the boat long, and Sand Island was at the entrance to Honolulu Harbor.

Sergeant Miller and an MP had escorted her from the car to the front door of a one-story, L-shaped building with a double door. They'd waited outside the door for nearly ten minutes. When it finally opened, a man in a black suit motioned Kay to follow him. Sergeant Miller started after them, but the man in the suit shook his head and shut the door. Kay took some small satisfaction in seeing the sergeant's disappointment as he turned back toward his car.

They proceeded down a long corridor past doors with numbers but no names, finally stopping at a door with the number fourteen. The man in the suit knocked. When the door opened, he motioned her inside. As soon as she'd stepped into the room, he left her.

The lights were bright, and it took Kay a moment for her eyes to adjust before she could see who and what was in the room. File cabinets lined a back wall. On the opposite wall was a wide mirror that made the room feel slightly less claustrophobic. And in the center of the room there was a small, rectangular wooden table with one wooden chair on either side. In the center of the table was a yellow legal pad. On the right side of the pad were three sharpened pencils; on the left side was a manila folder.

"Please take a seat, Mrs. Kimura."

Tall, stocky, and wearing a brown suit, the only other person in the room walked toward the table. She'd never seen anyone wearing a brown suit in Hawaii before and wondered if he was from the mainland. Someplace where it got cold in December.

"Can I get you anything? Water? Coffee?" He placed a glass ashtray on the table and waited for her to sit before taking his own seat.

"Water, please." Her throat felt as if she'd been screaming for an hour, even though she'd been perfectly quiet in the car. "And could you please remove the handcuffs?"

As if debating the wisdom of it, he hesitated before taking a key out of his suit jacket and unlocking the handcuffs. Kay rubbed her wrists, trying to appear nonchalant as she slid her hand inside her pocket to look for the note Annie had given her. It was more difficult to appear unfazed when all she found was the *omamori* her mother had given her for good luck. What could have happened to the final note from Daiji? Then she remembered Annie's embrace before they placed her in custody; she must have taken it. This gave Kay hope that she would get back to her children. Unless they found the other notes and letters at her apartment. She just had to remain calm and have faith that Mak would get there first and was so glad she'd showed him the shoebox. He would know how important it was to destroy it.

The FBI agent took a pair of reading glasses out of his suit pocket, opened the folder in front of him, and took out a sheet of paper. Lighting a cigarette, he read silently.

Kay studied the man, noticing that his straw-colored hair had begun to thin. She would've guessed him to be her age because his complexion was so smooth, but now she suspected that was only because he rarely saw the sun. His pale skin told her he preferred the indoors or was very dedicated to his work and didn't get outside much.

"Please tell me who currently resides in your apartment." He picked up one of three sharpened pencils and pulled the yellow legal pad closer.

She noticed a slight Southern drawl. But people in the South typically don't wear brown suits in the winter. "You're not from here."

Ignoring her observation, he asked, "Who lives with you, Mrs. Kimura?"

"Are we on Sand Island?"

"Our current location isn't relevant to this interview."

"Don't you mean interrogation?"

"We just have a few questions."

"We...meaning the FBI?"

"If we never begin, we can't come to an end."

"At least tell me your name," said Kay.

"You may call me Agent Harris."

"How long will I be here, Agent Harris?"

"That depends on you. If you're forthcoming, our time here might be brief."

"I'd like to call my mother and let her know where I am. She's watching my children."

"As you might guess, most of the phones are out on the island."

"Are you telling me the FBI doesn't have a way to communicate with—?"

"There are a few things I should tell you, Mrs. Kimura. The most important is that misleading the FBI by telling half-truths or flat-out falsehoods could result in very serious consequences for you. You should also be aware that Mr. Hoover has made the investigation of sabotage, espionage, and subversion a top priority."

"Is that what you suspect me of?" asked Kay. "Or do you just suspect everyone who looks like me?"

"Why don't we get started." His finely sharpened pencil hovered over the legal pad. "Please tell me who resides in your apartment with you."

"My children."

"Their names?"

"Beth and Tommy."

"Full names, please."

"Elizabeth Emika Kimura and Thomas Kaito Kimura." She watched him write her children's names down and almost wished she'd taken them to Japan before the attack. Would they forever be included in an FBI file? Always linked to a mother suspected of sabotage?

"Their ages?"

"Beth is nine years old, and Tommy is six."

"Your husband's name?"

"Daiji Kenji Kimura. But he doesn't live with us."

"Where does he live?"

"I'm not sure." This wasn't a lie. There had never been a return address on anything she'd received from him, and she'd never asked the Taketas where he was living.

"Are you divorced?"

"No."

"Remember what I told you about half-truths, Mrs. Kimura."

"He's in Japan. But I don't know exactly where."

"Does he have family there?"

"His parents live in Osaka."

"Why did he move to Japan?"

"To find work."

"He couldn't find work here?"

"He had a job on a sugar plantation. But Daiji has a degree in engineering and wanted to do something more."

"Like what?"

"He wanted to teach. At the university."

"A university in Japan?"

"Yes. He'd thought about becoming an engineer, but he prefers teaching." The man she'd married wanted to teach. She just wasn't sure if that was what he still wanted to do.

"But he trained to be an engineer?"

"Yes."

"Was he ever involved in politics?"

"Never." This was also the truth. He'd never been interested in either local or national politics. At least not when he was living with her.

"I'm assuming you've heard from your husband since he went to Japan?"

"Yes."

"He writes to you?"

Kay wished she knew if the FBI had gotten to her apartment before Mak, if he'd even been able to get from Hickam to Honolulu in time. What if Agent Harris had already read the letters and notes and was simply testing her? She couldn't risk lying to him about it. "Yes, he's written to me and the children."

"How often did he write letters to you and your children?"

"Every two weeks. At first."

"At first?"

"He stopped writing letters about two months ago." Also the truth. If Agent Harris didn't specifically ask about the notes, she wasn't obligated to tell him.

"The last time you heard from him was two months ago?"

"The last time I received a letter from him was two months ago."

"Let's not play word games, Mrs. Kimura. When was the last time you had any correspondence from your husband?"

In a matter of seconds, she weighed the consequences of lying. If Agent Harris already knew the truth and she lied about the notes, he'd never believe another thing she told him. But if he didn't know and she lied, he might let her go. She might be able to go home and destroy every letter and note, and they would have nothing to find, nothing to be suspicious of. And yet he looked at her with such an assured self-righteousness that she doubted he would believe anything that didn't feed into the truth he was looking to shape—Japanese Americans were all spies or saboteurs for Japan. If the FBI could contain that threat, Japan would lose its advantage. At least in the short term.

"The last time I heard from my husband was a few weeks ago." Kay would play her half of this invented spy game fairly. It was the only way she would be able to explain it to her children. It was the only way to move forward in their own country.

"Did he ask you to join him? In Japan."

"Yes."

"When?"

"When?" Kay was still worried about how much to say. She couldn't be sure they hadn't already been to her apartment. She couldn't be sure of anything.

"When did he ask you to join him in Japan?"

"I'm not sure if he…" She did what she'd told every patient she'd ever treated who was struggling with anxiety—take a deep breath. "I never discussed a specific date with him." True. He'd told her to leave before December 7, and she hadn't responded.

"Had you made plans to leave the country?"

"No."

"Why not?"

"Because my home is here. My children and I were all born here."

"But the rest of your family," he began, flipping through his files, "your parents and their parents and—"

"My parents left Japan more than thirty years ago." She wondered if he knew why they'd left but didn't think it was possible. Her father had died and her mother, Shizuko, never talked about it, not even with her closest friends. She'd only spoken to Kay about it once, so she would understand why she would grow up without grandparents, aunts and uncles, and cousins. Her mother also wanted her to know why no one from Japan ever wrote to them or sent gifts.

Before Kay was born, Shizuko and her husband were living in Japan. Like many young couples, they coped with low wages, long work hours, and cramped housing. Unlike most couples, Shizuko and her husband began to complain. Not just to their friends in the privacy of their own home but in public. Subsequently, Kay's parents were put on a watch list. They were surveilled day and night to see if they were meeting any other "subversives." They weren't, but it made no difference. Family and friends discovered they were under surveillance and kept their distance; soon after, Shizuko and her husband were entirely isolated. Fearing they would be imprisoned—and learning that Shizuko was pregnant—they used their savings to book passage on a freighter ship from Tokyo to the United States. For nearly a month, they shared a small space with two other families and crates packed with canned fish. All to make sure their child would grow up in a country that treasured freedom of speech.

Agent Harris laid his cigarette butt in the glass ashtray with care, as if he were afraid it would break, and lit another cigarette. "Mrs. Kimura, please tell me about the letters you received from your husband."

"There isn't much to tell. He wrote about missing his family. He wrote about looking for a job. Sometimes he wrote about the weather. They weren't very long."

"Did you keep his correspondence?"

How should she answer? Had Mak been able to get to her apartment in time? Would he have thought to destroy the letters? "I kept the letters. At first," said Kay. "But after it became clear that he planned to stay in Japan for much longer than we'd agreed, I threw them out."

"Did you throw them all away?"

"Yes."

"My mother still has the letters my father wrote to her during the Great War. It's been my experience that most women are sentimental when it comes to letters."

"I'm a nurse," said Kay. "My job demands that I be more practical."

"Surely that doesn't apply to your personal life," he said.

Oklahoma. That was where her interrogator was from.

A woman had wandered into the community center for help one day. She'd come to the island with her husband. He'd gotten work in one of the pineapple fields, but she couldn't get a job because she was seven months pregnant. She'd come in because she was cramping. Kay had examined her and found nothing wrong with her or the baby. She'd hydrated the woman and had her lie down for a few hours. When the woman woke, the cramps were gone. Kay gave her a sandwich, and while she ate, she'd talked about leaving Oklahoma after a particularly brutal winter. She said her goal was to have her children grow up in a warm place where they wouldn't have an Okie accent. Agent Harris's Okie accent wasn't as pronounced, but it was there.

"Are you actually telling me you didn't save any of the letters from your husband?"

"I'm not sentimental." Kay wondered how long she could answer him without really answering. Glancing at the two sharpened pencils in waiting, she thought he must have many more questions, most of which were likely about her husband. But even if Daiji couldn't be arrested, it felt like a betrayal. And if he was branded a traitor or saboteur, what would that mean for their children?

"Did you tell your husband you wouldn't be joining him in Japan?"

"Not yet."

"Why not?"

"Because I knew it would hurt him."

"You care about him?"

"He's the father of my children."

"Yet," said Agent Harris, raising a doubtful brow, "you don't know where he's living?"

"I assumed he was staying with family."

"Does his family support the Emperor?"

"I don't know. We never discussed politics."

"Tell me what you do know about them."

"I've never met most of them. I haven't even seen my in-laws since they came to our wedding. It's a long way to come."

"Did they ever write to you?"

"No."

"What about their grandchildren?"

"They send gifts. Occasionally."

"Did they write to their son when he was still living with you?"

"Not very often."

"Did he keep those letters?"

"No," said Kay.

"Your husband's not sentimental either?"

"He doesn't like clutter." This was true. Daiji liked everything in its place. But the reason he didn't keep the letters was because they always said the same thing—*Bring your wife and children to Japan. You all belong here.*

"There seems to be very little you can tell me about your husband or his family. I'd hoped you'd be more forthcoming, Mrs. Kimura."

Suddenly, Kay felt more anger than intimidation. Why should she tell him anything about her personal life? She'd done nothing to deserve being handcuffed and brought to the FBI like a dangerous criminal. "I'd like that glass of water now, Agent Harris." She'd decided she wouldn't say another word until he started to treat her like a citizen of the United States.

TWENTY

Having slept in the major's office for a generous two hours, Annie returned to the recovery ward, where she stayed until dawn. She grabbed a coffee and doughnut (bless the locals who brought them) and was using her next break to see what had happened to the base for herself. She was as weary of rumors as she was of telling her patients that everything would be fine. Whether President Roosevelt had made it official yet or not, they were at war with Japan, and the Hawaiian Islands were dangerously vulnerable.

She crossed the parade ground with her eyes down, dodging twisted metal and pulverized wood, avoiding bloodstains turning the color of rust.

She passed the enlisted men's barracks—the largest one anywhere in the Army Air Forces—and could barely look at the edifice, which had been repeatedly strafed and bombed. They had pulled thirty-five bodies out of the mess hall where the men had been eating breakfast. Part of the building was still smoldering, smoke rising like it was exhaling its own grief. The nearby Snake Ranch beer garden, where Sara had spent such a wonderful evening, had been demolished. All that was left was half of a handmade sign that read *Snake Ranch* and had somehow landed atop the rubble.

She followed Hangar Avenue to the Hawaiian Air Depot building. Last night, Annie had treated several men for smoke inhalation; most had been trying to control the fire that had raged through the depot and was still smoldering. As soon as the fire was out, men had pulled tools and equipment that could be salvaged from the building and were already servicing planes and working on turret guns, their faces grim yet determined.

The post exchange, chapel, schoolhouse, and fire station had all been hit but not the gasoline storage tanks. Small mercies. Knowing many of the dead and injured had come from the hangars, she was almost afraid to take a visual inventory but kept walking. Hangar 7 had been shattered by bombs—so much for the lucky number. Hangar 11 looked like a large black skeleton; nearly all the Eleventh Bombardment Group's technicians had died. However, Hangars 9 and 17 were only slightly damaged, and Hangars 3 and 5 were intact.

At the flight line, Annie saw that the Zero fighters had concentrated their firepower on the B-17 bombers; of the fifty-one planes that had been on the ground, nearly half had been destroyed or badly damaged. Like the ships in Pearl Harbor, the planes had lost their spit and polish and looked like gray husks with faces of white ash.

Nearby was an improvised machine-gun nest made from a burned plane engine, sandbags, a table, and various debris. She'd seen several gun nests and wondered how many of the incredibly brave men who'd attempted to down an enemy plane had survived.

Having traversed the base, Annie reached the water tower and couldn't believe it was still standing. She looked up in wonder at the tallest target at Hickam Field, which had been ignored, maybe because Japanese pilots had used it as a reference point. If Private Baker had only stayed there working on the radios instead of trying to learn about radar, he'd still be alive. But he hadn't been the type to wait things out in relative safety. He was the type who had kept shooting at the enemy after being shot himself—and burned alive. It was the kind of self-sacrifice that was difficult to comprehend. She hoped Private Baker's name would be put forward for a Purple Heart.

Turning back toward the hospital, she gazed at the thousands of tree seedlings and shrubs that were planted around the tower to beautify the base, all still green and flourishing despite the dirty smoke that clung stubbornly to the breeze. Annie had thought it silly to have so many seedlings and shrubs on an Army air base and couldn't remember ever being so wrong.

Kay had been sitting in the wooden chair for what felt like days. It had become difficult to think, never mind coming up with counter-arguments for the conspiracy theories Agent Harris seemed to conjure every time he took a coffee break. "I can only tell you you're wrong," she said.

Agent Harris sipped his coffee and lit another cigarette. While he wouldn't tolerate a dull pencil—he would sharpen them during his bathroom breaks—he appeared to have no problem with an overflowing ashtray. "What am I wrong about exactly?"

Unsure she could say anything coherently, Kay said, "Everything." She'd been exhausted by what had happened yesterday and had had no sleep since.

"Then your husband isn't in Japan?"

They'd been over this a hundred times. Kay wouldn't respond.

"And he isn't a member of the Imperial Japanese Army?"

"I've told you Daiji was never in the military—*any* military."

For the first time in all those hours, Agent Harris opened the folder. Not fully, just enough to slide out a photograph that he pushed toward Kay. There were half a dozen Japanese soldiers in the photograph. Her husband, the taller, lanky one, stood to one side.

"I don't understand."

"I agree. It is confusing." He pointed to the insignia on his cap. "See the two stars? That means he's a first lieutenant."

For a moment, Kay wondered if she'd been knocked unconscious during the attack and the past twenty-four hours were all in her imagination. There was no other explanation.

"I served in the Marine Corps, and I can tell you no one got promoted from second lieutenant to first lieutenant without serving at least eighteen months. But your husband hasn't even been in Japan for a year, so how do you explain—"

"I can't explain. I didn't even know he was in the Army."

"In all those letters, your husband never mentioned that he'd joined the Imperial Japanese Army?"

"No." Though he had written about his increasing dedication to the Emperor, she just never thought he would join the Army. He'd never expressed any interest in a military career. Why begin at the age of thirty-seven?

"I find that difficult to believe, Mrs. Kimura. It's easier to believe your husband, who expected you and his children to join him in Japan, had told you about joining the Army and about his promotion.

I'm sure he was proud and, like any man, wanted to share the news with his wife and kids. It would also explain why your friend burned your husband's letters."

Kay's heart skipped a beat. Had Mak been able to burn everything? Had he been caught? Was he in trouble? She didn't trust herself to speak. Instead, she took a sip of water.

"I can imagine how desperate you must've been," said Agent Harris, "to get rid of such damning evidence."

"I don't know what you're talking about," said Kay.

"So you didn't ask Makani Hale to burn your husband's letters?"

"No," said Kay, wishing she'd never shown him that shoebox.

"Then why did my agents find him with a trash bin full of ashes in your apartment?"

"Did you bring Mak here too?" asked Kay, hoping that all they'd found were ashes.

Lighting another cigarette, he studied her but gave no answer. "How would you like to take a walk outside? Do you think it would help clear your head?"

"Yes, it would help," said Kay, who had never longed for fresh air so much in her life.

"Okay then," he said. "But first, tell me what kinds of information you were giving to you husband through the Taketas."

"I don't know what you mean."

"This is a tit-for-tat situation, Mrs. Kimura. I've asked you many questions, and you've given me very few answers. So let's make a deal. You answer one question for me, and I'll answer one for you. Answer one more after that, and we'll take a walk outside. Sound fair?"

"That depends on your questions."

"I'll make it easy." He took a long drag on his cigarette. "Are you having an affair with Makani Hale?"

"No."

"I believe you."

"My turn," said Kay. "Do you have Mak in custody? Or is he with my children?"

"Technically, that's two questions, but I'll let it go. We do not have him in custody. And yes, he's with your children." He checked a note in his folder. "As is Shizuko Kimura."

"Thank you." Kay sighed in relief. Her children were safe, as were Mak and her mother.

"Next question—for a walk in the fresh air," he said. "When did your husband begin spying for the Emperor? Did he start when he first arrived in Oahu thirteen years ago?"

"My husband has never been a spy for Japan." Kay hoped this was true.

"Mrs. Kimura, I'd really like to help you because you helped our soldiers. Going to Hickam Field took courage. However, when my supervisor asks me how it's going, I'll need to be honest and tell him you've been less than forthcoming. And he'll be left with no alternative but to suspect that you volunteered to go to Hickam so you could observe the state of our defenses and feed that information to your husband. Under U.S. Code Title 18, Section 2381, the penalty for treason is death."

"*Treason?*"

"Your husband has been in the Imperial Japanese Army for seven months. As a member of the Japanese Army, he's an enemy of the people of the United States. If you gave aid and comfort to the enemy, that makes you a traitor."

Kay felt nauseous, and then her vision began to darken like a stormy sky. She'd never fainted before, but she would welcome oblivion even if it was short-lived.

Annie jogged toward the parking area to catch up with Rita. She wanted to thank her again for all they had done. Taking turns sleeping in the ladies' room last night, Rita's girls had continued to do everything they could to help without complaint. A few had even given a second pint of blood early that morning, and Annie had made sure they all ate a good breakfast.

"Thank you for everything you did," said Annie, catching up to Rita. "You and your employees were a tremendous help."

"We'd be outta business if it weren't for the military," said Rita. "Although I'm not sure what the hell's going to happen now. I heard everyone on the island, except for little kids, needs to get fingerprinted and have ID papers at all times. Anonymous sex won't be so anonymous if the police start asking for my customers' ID papers every time they walk down Hotel Street. Between that and the curfew, business may slow down for a while. I just hope martial law won't last too long."

"Me too," said Annie as they both turned toward the sound of water spraying from a fire truck into one of the still-smoldering hangars. Annie and Rita continued walking. Rita gracefully circumvented unrecognizable debris in heels, while Annie kept pace in her sensible but homely shoes. "I don't know how you managed to get through the last twenty-four hours in those high heels. Don't your feet hurt?" asked Annie, who was genuinely curious.

"My feet are used to them. My legs are nearly as good as the real McCoy, so I have to show them off before they get covered in little blue veins like my mother's."

"You mean varicose veins?" asked Annie.

Rita nodded. "She got 'em when she was about fifty. If I'm lucky, my legs will hold out until then, along with the rest of what I've got to offer." She glanced at her legs as if to make sure they were still in fine form and frowned at the blood spatter on her heels. "Rita Hayworth wore these same blue high heels in the poster for *You'll Never Get Rich*. I spent a small fortune on these."

"White vinegar usually takes the bloodstains off my shoes," said Annie.

"Thanks," said Rita. "I'll give it a try."

At last, they reached the cars where Rita's employees were waiting as they smoked cigarettes or reapplied lipstick.

"If you need us again, Lieutenant, you know where to find us," said Rita.

"I'll actually be seeing you soon. I promised Carole I'd drop off some pamphlets."

"Don't tell me she's joining the Army." Laughing, Rita glanced at Carole, who didn't seem to think it was a joke. "Are you?"

"I might try to become a nurse," said Carole, her chin lifted in defiance. "Annie said the Army's going to be looking for lots of nurses."

"If you join," said Rita, "they can do whatever they want with you, Carole. And more than likely, a man will still be telling you what to do."

"The Army will give her the education and training she needs to get a good job when she gets out," said Annie defensively. "She'll be able to work in a hospital."

"If she survives the war," said Rita.

"I won't be on the front lines." Carole glanced at Annie for confirmation.

"I was sent to the front lines on my first tour." Annie couldn't lie about the potential dangers of nursing. No nurses died in the Great War from bullet wounds, but nearly three hundred had died of diseases. However, she didn't think it would do any good to tell Rita that Carole should be more fearful of catching tuberculosis or pneumonia than a bullet. Besides, syphilis could be just as deadly in the long run.

"I only want you to be safe," said Rita.

"I've never been safe in my entire life," said Carole matter-of-factly.

"You've got a point," said Rita. "Okay, if you want to be a nurse, who am I to stop you?"

"Thanks." Carole grinned.

"You can thank me by helping me find another Carole Lombard."

"What about a Lana Turner?" asked Carole. "There's a new waitress at the Black Cat Café who I swear could be her spitting image with the right makeup and a wardrobe change."

Annie watched Rita and Carole discuss the waitress's potential as they loaded up their respective cars and drove away. Turning back toward the hospital, Annie couldn't help but notice the bullet holes that had scarred the concrete, which were accentuated by the giant hole in the front yard left by the five-hundred-pound bomb. Maybe Carole would be safer on Hotel Street.

Annie, Drs. Doyle and Metcalfe, and Major Lance sat in his office around the radio listening to President Roosevelt's address to Congress and the nation.

"I believe that I interpret the will of the Congress and of the people when I assert that we will not only defend ourselves to the uttermost but will make it very certain that this form of treachery shall never again endanger us. Hostilities exist. There is no blinking at the fact that our people, our territory, and our interests are in grave danger. With confidence in our armed forces, with the unbounding determination of our people, we will gain the inevitable triumph, so help us God. I ask that the Congress declare that since the unprovoked and dastardly attack by Japan on Sunday, December 7, 1941, a state of war has existed between the United States and the Japanese Empire."

Annie knew that President Roosevelt's words would change everyone's life. Even before the speech, they'd heard that young men, boys really, were flocking to recruitment centers to join up: Army, Navy, Marines—it didn't matter. Everyone was filled with patriotic fury and wanted to get in the fight. FDR's speech would only rally more to the cause. Annie also expected a significant jump in women joining the U.S. Army Nurse Corps.

"So it begins," said Major Lance as he turned off the radio.

"Due respect, sir," said Annie, "I think it began yesterday." They all glanced at the clock on the wall, still stopped at 7:55 a.m.

"Do they think the initial assault is over?" asked Captain Doyle.

The major shook his head. "Wake Island is still under attack. It may fall to the Japanese."

"How many on the island?" asked Annie.

The major glanced down at a sheet of paper on his desk. "Four hundred and fifty Marines, sixty-eight Navy personnel, and twelve hundred civilians. Most of the civilians work for Pan Am. Wake is a major refueling stop for their planes."

"What about Guam?" asked Captain Metcalfe. "My brother-in-law's stationed there."

The major looked glum. "I'm sorry, Carl. Guam will likely fall by tomorrow. The island was just too big for less than six hundred Marines and sailors to defend."

"The Philippines?" asked Annie, wondering how Lieutenant Colonel Horan was holding up under the pressure. His temper was like brown grass in August; it didn't take much to ignite. Would he be able to keep his temper in check and lead the soldiers she'd left behind?

"Let's just say I'm glad you're not there. Apparently, Japan sees the Philippines as a major part of their new empire. They're hitting it hard."

"But they've got General MacArthur," said Captain Doyle.

"Japan hit Clark Field north of Manila and Iba Airfield in Luzon as hard as they hit us."

"Jesus Christ," said Annie. "They attacked everything we've got in the South Pacific."

"The bottom line is that Wake Island, Guam, and the Philippines won't be available to help us. In fact," continued the major, "they'll be looking to us for help."

"Are we able?" asked Annie.

"Pearl lost the *Arizona* and the *Oklahoma*. Several other ships were sunk, and they lost one hundred and forty planes. We lost about two-thirds of our bombers."

"How many people did we lose?" asked Annie.

"Still counting," said the major. "For Pearl, the number will likely be in the thousands. For us, it'll be in the hundreds."

"Do you have any good news?" asked Dr. Doyle.

"The good news is that the Emperor of Japan thinks he's broken us," said the major. "He thinks we'll be too afraid to stop him from taking complete control of the western Pacific and Southeast Asia."

"Underestimating us would be a huge mistake," said Annie.

"It sure as hell would be," said Dr. Metcalfe.

"Unless they come back today," said Dr. Doyle. "Or tomorrow."

They all glanced outside, where every single person on base who was able-bodied held a tool and was working to clear debris. Everyone had a gun tucked into their waistband. No one would be caught off guard again. Even Annie had requested a gun of her own.

Despite the weapons and high-alert status, if the Zeros came back before they were actually ready to engage, Annie wasn't sure Hawaii wouldn't fall to the enemy.

TWENTY-ONE

December 15, 1941

Annie got in the major's Jeep and started the engine, thankful she would have enough gas to take her to see General Short. Initially, Major Lance hadn't wanted her to go. He'd said that he would call the general about Mrs. Kimura's whereabouts soon but that both he and the general had more important priorities at the moment.

Other than her patients and getting the hospital back in shape, Annie's priority was making sure Kay was reunited with her children. As she had done every day since Kay was taken a week ago, she'd called the Japanese American Community Center again this morning to see if Kay was back. Each time she called, Amai or Mak had answered the phone and given her yes or no answers. "Has she come home?" No. "Have you heard from her?" No. "Has anyone heard from her?" No. "Has anyone called to tell you where she is?" No. "Are the children all right?" Yes. This morning, she had gotten the same answers.

She understood why they were frustrated. She also understood that they wouldn't be able to get access to anyone with information. That was something only Annie could do.

Annie sat across from Lieutenant General Walter Short, waiting for him to finish his paperwork. She didn't know much about him, only that he'd risen in the ranks quickly and had the confidence that came with such a rise. However, hindsight being twenty-twenty, he was being greatly criticized for not doing more to protect and defend the island's military installations. Rumor was that both he and Rear Admiral Husband Kimmel, commander in chief of the U.S. Fleet and Pacific Fleet, would be removed from their posts any day. Annie felt somewhat sorry for them. She knew what it was like to be forced to consider retirement before you were ready to go. At least it wouldn't come as a surprise to them. They had to realize someone needed to fall on his sword, and they had been in charge that day.

"Thank you for seeing me," said Annie when he finally looked up from his desk.

"I assume you're here about the hospital, Lieutenant Fox. I know you're short-staffed and running low on supplies, and I'm doing what I can to make sure you get what you need as soon as possible."

"I appreciate that, sir. But I'm actually here about one of our nurses."

"Major Lance didn't tell me one of your nurses had been hurt. If it's a Purple Heart you're here to discuss, we've never given one to a woman before."

"No, sir. I'm talking about one of the civilian nurses who helped us."

"Ah, yes. Major Lance mentioned something about a Japanese nurse being taken in for questioning by the FBI."

"Japanese American, sir. She was born on the island."

"Point being that she's a civilian nurse, not Army."

"But the MPs took her into custody after she'd spent all day tending to *our* wounded."

"I'm sure they had their reasons."

"She's not a subversive, sir."

"And you know this how? Because she told you so?"

"I watched her nurse our men with as much compassion as any Army nurse I've ever worked with. I'd stake my career on her innocence."

"You're that certain?"

"Yes, sir. All I'm asking is that you find out when she's coming home so I can tell her family. The FBI couldn't object to letting her children know when their mother will be home."

"How about the children of the men and women who died here and at Pearl Harbor? What do we tell them?"

"With all due respect, General Short, it's not the same thing. Kay isn't a soldier; she's a nurse. She didn't sign up for this, and she certainly never signed her children up for it."

"If she's nothing more than what you say, she'll be home soon enough." General Short picked up his pen and peered down at his paperwork.

"Soon doesn't mean a thing to children. If you could just—"

"You're dismissed, Lieutenant," he said without looking up.

Realizing there was nothing more she could say that would make any difference to him, Annie saluted, turned, and left. Already planning what she would tell the person who took his place, she would make a nuisance of herself until Kay was home.

When President Roosevelt declared war against Japan, he also directed that "all measures be taken for our defense." One of those measures had brought Annie her newest patient—Private Lyle Lavoie, who was lying on one of the ten extra beds that had been recently added to Hickam's ward.

Annie put several pillows under his leg to keep it elevated and to get a better look at the zigzag cuts on his right calf. "How did this happen, Private?"

"Barbed wire."

"Barbed wire?"

"Yes, ma'am. We're puttin' it up everywhere to keep the enemy out—along the beaches and highways, even around the schools. Only I hadn't been working on it, which was the whole problem. My sergeant assigned me to show civilians how to dig zigzag trenches."

"You're digging zigzag trenches?"

"Yes, ma'am. We dig them that way because—"

"I'm familiar with the concept, Private Lavoie." Annie had seen zigzag trenches used in the Great War. The belief was that if the enemy couldn't shoot down a straight line, they wouldn't be able to kill as many soldiers. It had been effective. "I just didn't realize they were building trenches in the city."

"Yes, ma'am, 'specially near the schools. They want the kids to practice walkin' through the trenches, which might get confusin' given the zigzag of it all. Anyways, I backed up to show some civilian volunteers how to angle the shovel and stepped into this coil of barbed wire somebody had left out for who knows what reason. The more I tried to get untangled, the more it tore at my legs."

She glanced at the latticework of cuts on his legs. "First, we're going to clean up those cuts. Then I'll apply some ointment as well as a dressing. And you may need a tetanus shot."

"A shot?" he asked apprehensively.

"It'll feel like nothing more than a mosquito bite compared to barbed wire. I'll be right back, Private." Annie left him to gather what she needed, wondering how her patients still managed to surprise her by what they could and could not endure.

"Hi, Annie."

Turning, she saw her favorite patient, though she would never admit it to him, nor would she remind him to address her as Lieutenant. He'd endured two surgeries in one day with no complaints. Of course, he had been unconscious most of the time. "How are you feeling, Jeremy?"

"Like I could spin you around a dance floor. In a week or two."

"I'll look forward to it. In the meantime, is there anything I can get you?"

"Tapioca pudding would be—"

"Chief," said Winnie, hurrying toward Annie. "The major wants to see you."

"Would you tell him that I'll be there in about twenty minutes?"

"He said I should take over for you, Chief."

"Fine," said Annie, hoping the urgency wasn't related to another threat. They'd received several warnings about possible attacks over the past few days. Thankfully, nothing had happened. Yet. "Take care of Private Lavoie." Annie gestured toward his bed. "Cuts from barbed wire on his lower legs. And check his records to see if he needs a tetanus shot. Then please get my favorite patient some tapioca pudding." She winked at Jeremy and walked away.

Since Kay was taken, Annie had wanted nothing more than to speak to the FBI. She'd been working past exhaustion since the attack but still had trouble sleeping at night. As she literally tossed and turned, she'd thought up one speech after another, all beginning with the words, "How dare you take a mother away from her children for no good reason?" For a moment, she wasn't sure whether she'd actually said those words to Agent Harris while sitting across from the major.

"Agent Harris is just doing his job, Lieutenant Fox," said the major. "And you should do yours by answering his questions."

"Yes, sir," said Annie. "I'm sorry. What was the question?"

"Agent Harris asked if you'd ever met Mrs. Kimura's husband," said Major Lance.

"No," said Annie, who could see sweat beading across the major's forehead. She'd only ever seen him sweat after his morning run. He didn't like the questioning any more than she did.

"Did she talk to you about her husband?" asked Agent Harris, his sharp pencil poised over a notepad.

Annie had never lied to anyone in a position of authority, but she would not help this man keep Kay away from her family. "Mrs. Kimura is a very private person."

"Did you know she and her husband were separated?"

"I knew he didn't live with her and the children."

"You never asked why not?"

"It was none of my business. We haven't known each other that long."

"Lieutenant Fox was only transferred here last month," confirmed the major.

Agent Harris didn't bother acknowledging him and went on with his next question. "Have you spoken to a man named Makani Hale recently?"

"Not really."

"What does that mean?" asked Agent Harris.

"It means I call the community center every day to see if Kay has returned. Sometimes, Mak answers the phone. But the calls are always very brief."

"Can you describe the relationship between Mr. Hale and Mrs. Kimura?"

"They're colleagues," said Annie.

"Are they also friends?"

"I suppose you could call them work friends." She was certainly not going to tell this unctuous man that she suspected Kay and Mak were in love with each other.

"They didn't see each other outside work?"

"If you're asking whether they were seeing each other romantically," said Annie, "they were not. Not to my knowledge."

"And you can verify that there was nothing romantic between them when you all spent the evening at a bar in Honolulu?"

"Were you watching Kay before—"

"Answer the question, please."

"We had a few drinks while we discussed work issues." She sincerely hoped the major had not told him that she was trying to find out if Kay was involved in sabotage. Glancing at the major, she saw him nod subtly, like he would in the OR when she'd handed him the right instrument before he asked for it.

Agent Harris jotted down a few notes and, without looking up from his notepad, asked, "Are you familiar with a Mr. and Mrs. Taketa?"

"Yes. Mr. Taketa is a patient at the community center. He suffers from gout."

"Did you know Mrs. Taketa was killed in the attack?"

Annie nodded. "She died from a head wound." She saw the major try to hide his surprise. She'd never told him about Mrs. Taketa or what she'd seen in the morgue at Queen's Hospital.

"After you saw that his wife was beyond help, you left Mr. Taketa at his home?"

"Yes," answered Annie. "How did you know I was there?"

"Again, you're here to answer my questions, Lieutenant Fox. Perhaps that would sink in if we continued at my office."

"Not necessary," said the major. "I can't afford to lose my chief nurse, even for a few hours. Continue with your questions, Agent Harris."

Annie was glad Major Lance had insisted on staying. He'd almost demanded that they wait for a JAG officer to be present, but most of the military lawyers on the island were tied up with issues regarding martial law. Besides, Annie hadn't wanted to wait. She'd always been in favor of getting something unpleasant over with quickly.

"How did you come to be at the Taketa home on the day of the attack?"

"That was unintentional," she said. "I was on my way to Queen's Hospital for supplies, and I saw Mr. Taketa sitting outside on the curb. He was disoriented but brought me to his wife. Mrs. Taketa was in their dining room, slumped over her breakfast. She was dead."

"Cause of death?" asked Agent Harris.

"As I said, she died from a head wound."

"What kind of wound?"

"I can't be sure. You should contact the coroner."

"As you can imagine, he's quite busy. You're a nurse who's seen combat wounds. In your professional opinion, how did she die?"

"There was a hole in the window near the body. My best guess is that she was hit by antiaircraft fire that day."

"Could someone have shot her at close range?" asked Agent Harris, casually sipping the coffee the major had given him before Annie arrived.

"Are you asking me if her husband—"

"All I'm asking is whether, in your professional opinion, you think she might have been shot in the head at close range?"

"Do you have Mr. Taketa in custody?"

"No one has seen him since his wife's body was recovered."

"Lots of people seem to be disappearing." Annie heard that the FBI had detained hundreds of community leaders, not just Kay. "Are you sure you don't have him somewhere?"

Agent Harris put his slightly dull pencil down and took a sharper one out of his briefcase.

"Is Mrs. Kimura still in your custody?" asked Annie.

"You seem quite concerned about a civilian *work* friend, Lieutenant."

"She has children, who miss their mother."

"Mothers should take their children into consideration when they get involved in...questionable activities."

"Since when is nursing a questionable activity?" asked Annie, wanting to smack the smirk off the agent's face.

"Lieutenant Fox needs to get back to her duties, Agent Harris." The major stood. "If you'd like to ask her anything else, you'll do so with a JAG officer present."

"And please give me more notice next time," said Annie. "JAG officers are difficult to get these days. But I'm sure we could arrange something in a month or two. Does that timeline sound about right, Major Lance?"

"Yes. A few months sounds about right, Lieutenant."

"Until then, can you at least tell me when Kay will be released?" asked Annie.

Ignoring her, Agent Harris rose from his seat as he addressed the major. "Put your JAG officer on notice. I'll be back."

"Of course." The major kept a polite smile in place until Agent Harris left the office, shutting the door behind him.

"What a son of a bitch," said Annie.

"I agree. Now tell me what the hell's going on. And before you answer, consider the fact that I can't help you unless I know the truth. Neither can a JAG officer."

Annie sat, wondering how much she should tell him. If he knew the truth, could he help her find Kay? Or would his involvement only make matters worse?

He sat in the chair across from her rather than behind his desk. "It's clear to me that the FBI had Kay and the Taketas under surveillance before the attack. Does that have something to do with her husband?"

"I think so. But he's in Japan, and Kay chose to stay here because she's loyal to her country. And because…I think she's fallen out of love with her husband."

"They won't care. All that matters is the fact that she's a community leader with a husband in Japan. A husband who wanted her to join him there. That's enough to arouse suspicion. But I don't understand how the Taketas were involved in all this."

He was looking at Annie as if he knew she could provide an answer to the mystery. But she couldn't tell him about the notes. If he knew, he'd be obligated to tell the JAG officer, who might be obligated to tell the FBI agent. And what good would it do now? Mrs. Taketa was dead, and Mr. Taketa was who knew where. "I don't know exactly how Mr. Taketa is involved, but his wife was the matchmaker between Kay and her husband."

"The FBI could care less about a matchmaker," said the major. "Obviously, there's something more going on."

"If there is, I wasn't privy to it." Annie knew she sounded defensive.

"I understand your wanting to protect your friend. But a JAG officer may not be able to help you if you're withholding useful information from the FBI."

"Telling him anything about Kay won't be useful, because she's done nothing wrong."

He waited a moment, looking into her eyes as if she would tell him more. She nearly did.

"I want you to stay on base for the next few weeks. You can't be seen anywhere near the community center."

"I was going to leave for a few hours tomorrow to check on Kay's children."

"You can't. I'm sure the FBI is watching her home."

"If they ask why I'm there, I can tell the truth—I'm checking on the children."

"That's not your job. Your job is here."

"Yes, but—"

"You'll stay on base for the next few weeks. That's an order, Lieutenant."

"It sounds more like a punishment, Major."

He shrugged. "There's usually a price to pay for poor decisions."

"Like not telling you everything you want to know?"

"You're dismissed, Lieutenant."

And there it was. No matter what was between them, he had the authority to dismiss her. "Yes, sir." She saluted and left.

Annie stood on the steps and surveyed the backyard. More than one hundred and twenty bodies had been transferred to an indoor morgue, but the grass remained depressed and had faded to yellow after just more than a day without sunlight. She was very lucky none of her nurses had made one of those faded yellow depressions. She just prayed they would survive the war, however long it might last.

She had hopes that the United States would defeat Japan quickly, especially given that their men were so anxious to fight. But Germany had just declared war on the United States and vice versa. President Roosevelt also declared war on Italy. The chances of defeating three countries in a few months were slim to none. It would likely be a long war.

"Penny for your thoughts, Chief?" said Monica as she lit a cigarette.

"Believe me, they're not worth that much." Annie smiled at Monica and Irene, who still used the backyard for their breaks, despite the fact that the orderlies were certain it was haunted.

"I'm glad the bodies are gone," said Irene.

"Some might even be home by now and buried with family. May they rest in peace." Monica crossed herself.

"Do you think that's possible?" asked Irene. "I mean, if you die so suddenly and in such a violent way. I wonder if a soul can find peace."

"Once you enter heaven, you're granted peace," said Monica with conviction. "You don't have to look for it because it's part of what God gives you when you enter his kingdom."

"I hope you're right," said Annie.

"Chaplain Tiedt seemed sure of it at his service on Sunday," said Monica. "I think he's even more filled with the spirit since they told him his wife was alive."

"I still can't believe they told the poor man she was dead!" said Irene.

"There was a lot of confusion that day." Annie couldn't help but feel bad for whoever had made that mistake. But she'd been very happy for the chaplain, who'd seemed so full of despair when she'd spoken to him in her barracks.

"Too bad you missed service. Again." Monica gave Irene a slightly reproachful glance.

"I've told you many times, Monica." Irene took a drag on her cigarette, blowing the smoke skyward. "Surfing is how I pray."

"The ocean doesn't have an altar," said Monica.

"An altar doesn't change colors as the sun rises," said Irene. "A porpoise isn't going to jump out of one either. The ocean reminds me that wonders exist. It reminds me that there are things that are so amazing they can't be accidents. The ocean reassures me that God exists."

"Evidence of God's work is everywhere," said Monica. "Especially in a church."

"I've known many people who find peace on the ocean," said Annie, remembering all the fisherman in her village in Nova Scotia. All getting up early to take their boats out, sometimes even on Sundays. "Or on a mountaintop. Or in a church. It doesn't matter where you find it, only that you do. Over these next few months"— she wouldn't say years—"take the time to find solace where you can. Every day. Even if it's only for a few minutes."

"Like we did in the ladies' room," said Irene. "Knowing I would have time to lie down, even on the floor, and talk to another nurse got me through that horrible day," said Irene, "and the two days from hell that followed."

"Me too," said Monica.

"I'm glad," said Annie, who left them to their break. They still needed solace, and she was grateful they could give that to each other.

More than a week passed and still the major refused to give Annie permission to leave the base. But she could leave the hospital, and on Christmas Eve, she finally had a full day off. She left the women's barracks and was nearly off hospital grounds when she saw Jeremy standing near the front lawn. She hadn't seen him since he'd been discharged the week before.

"How are you feeling?" she asked, walking up to him.

"Almost good as new." He grinned. "Like your front yard."

She looked at what he'd come to see. Over the past week, volunteers had been working to fill the huge crater left by the bomb. They'd wanted it covered by Christmas, and they were nearly done. Only one small hole remained—large enough to plant the tree a group of men were huddled around. "What are they planting?"

"A banyan tree," said Jeremy. "I heard them say it'll be about one hundred feet tall."

"Then it'll be here for a very long time." Just like the bullet holes they had decided not to fill. They wanted them to remain as a testament to what had happened at Hickam Hospital that day, both the good and bad.

"Day off?" he asked, giving her trousers and blouse an approving glance.

"First one since the attack."

"I'll walk you to your car."

"There's no need."

"I could use the exercise," said Jeremy, patting a nearly imperceptible belly pouch. "Too much tapioca pudding."

"Then I'd enjoy the company."

They walked in companionable silence across the parade ground that still carried the echoes of the Sunday morning that had changed so much. She saw Jeremy glance at the spot where he'd fallen after being shot in the back, but his eyes didn't linger.

They continued past new construction, hammers and saws so loud they didn't bother to yell over the noise. The smell of new lumber wafted through the air as they walked by the theatre, chapel, and schoolhouse—all under repair. The entire base was being patched up and restored, including barracks and hangars. Some had thought they should wait, because what if the enemy struck again? Others thought the best way for the base to recover was to get on with it. Keep calm and carry on, as their British "cousins" would say. Besides, it wasn't like any enemy would catch them with their pants down again. Most men slept in their clothes these days with a pistol nearby, just in case.

"I heard they offered you a medical discharge," said Annie as they entered the parking lot. When the major had told her, she'd hoped Jeremy would take it. Yet she knew they would need every able-bodied soldier they could get. And his body had recovered despite the enemy's best efforts.

"They did," he said. "I called my dad and talked to him about it. He told me I'd already done enough for my country."

"He's right, Jeremy."

"He also said that if I came home, I'd listen to every radio report and read every newspaper I could get my hands on about the war. And I'd feel like…"

"You were missing out on something important?"

Jeremy shook his head. "He told me I'd feel like I was letting my buddies down. My dad said I'd spend every day worrying about the friends I've made here. And if something happened to any of them, I would always wonder if I could've made a difference. He said it was hard enough worrying about one person, because he worries about me every day. It would be a lot harder to worry about half a dozen men or more. He also reminded me that I have ants in my pants, and if I came home, I'd be bored every minute of every day."

"All true?"

Jeremy nodded. "My dad knows me pretty well. It's only been me and him since my mom died when I was five. By the time the influenza turned into pneumonia, she was too weak to fight anymore."

"I'm sorry about your mom," said Annie. "And for what it's worth, I think your dad's right. But I also believe you've more than earned your ticket home."

Jeremy shook his head. "You can't get rid of me that easy. There's a New Year's Eve dance coming up, and my name is the first one on your dance card, Annie Fox."

Smiling, Annie stopped at the Jeep.

"Yours?" asked Jeremy.

"It belongs to Major Lance. He lets me use it."

Jeremy smiled and raised a brow.

"What?" asked Annie.

"Nothing. I just didn't know you and he were…you know."

"We're not."

"Nobody lets a girl drive his car unless she's *his* girl."

"I'm too old to be anyone's girl. He's just letting me borrow his car because I have some errands to run off base. And because I'm a very good driver."

"If you say so, Annie."

"I do say so, *Corporal.*"

"Yes, ma'am." Jeremy saluted through his grin.

Feeling herself blush, Annie got in the Jeep and found that first gear was stickier than usual. She would need to baby the transmission. And when she got back, she would ask for the major's forgiveness for taking his car—and for going off base—without his permission. It was Christmas Eve; he would have to forgive her.

TWENTY-TWO

December 24, 1941

After weeks of interrogation, Kay was unsure of everything she had been so sure of before the attack. She'd gotten to the point where she questioned everything except her love for her children. But she knew a few things for certain, which was what was keeping her sane.

At first, she'd been very sure of who she was—a mother, nurse, and community leader—and what she stood for, especially as it related to her community center. Even though she'd established the center to serve the Japanese American community, she'd never turned away anyone who'd come there for help. Because that was what her country stood for—welcoming people of different ethnicities and religions. She'd believed in that with her whole heart.

Now, she only believed in a few facts.

She was in a hotel in San Francisco. The hotel was run by the Justice Department's Immigration and Naturalization Service. When Agent Harris told her she'd be held for an undetermined amount of time—until they'd come to a satisfactory conclusion about her case—he'd explained how President Roosevelt had signed a proclamation invoking the Alien Enemy Act of 1798. The Act stated that in times of war, "all natives, citizens, denizens, or subjects of an enemy nation shall be liable to be apprehended, restrained, secured, and removed as alien enemies." Agent Harris had told her that her place of birth had made a difference in that she could have been held in jail. Evidently, the INS had run out of room in their detention centers and was housing detainees in jails and hotels. Because she was in a hotel, he'd told her she was one of the lucky ones.

She would have a hearing. Agent Harris had explained that at some point—he didn't specify when—she would go before a hearing board made up of civilians who would decide whether Kay would be released, paroled, or interned. She'd asked Agent Harris if a defense attorney would be provided. He'd said no. Because it would be a "nonlegal" hearing, Kay would not be allowed counsel and could present no witnesses in her own defense. The case against her would be based on evidence from the FBI. Judging by the questions he'd asked her hour after hour, day after day, week after week, she assumed the case would focus on proving she had colluded with her husband, who'd received another promotion within the Imperial Japanese Army following their success in the Pacific. The hearing board would be told he had received that promotion because he'd helped make the attack a success, thanks to his wife. At this point, Kay wondered if it were true. Had she helped Japan's cause by not turning Daiji's correspondence over to the authorities? If so, maybe she deserved to be there.

Kay also knew it was Wednesday—and Christmas Eve. She knew

because she'd heard the maids talking, even though they weren't allowed to enter the rooms. Detainees would put their trash bins outside the door every day, and once a week, they could also place soiled towels or sheets outside their door. Every day, one maid took one side of the hallway while the other took the opposite side, and they would chat along the way. Kay kept her door open just a crack so she could listen. One maid still had to buy a Christmas tree but had waited until the last minute so she could get one cheap enough to afford. The other maid seemed more concerned that her favorite butcher shop was closed, and Wednesday was when he put out pork shoulders, which she would make last until the following Wednesday. They'd also mentioned in passing that U.S. forces on Wake Island had surrendered to the Japanese. For a moment, Kay wondered if that was her fault too. Logically, she knew it made no sense, but after spending weeks with Agent Harris, it was easier to believe that the war would never have broken out if not for her ignoring the warning signs that must have been part of her marriage from the start.

The last thing Kay knew for certain was that the only power she had left was the power of prayer. Lately, she had spent a lot of time praying that there would be a few mothers on the hearing board. Even if there was only one, she would understand how difficult it was to be separated from your children, particularly in a time of war. Nearly every night, Kay dreamed about Japanese planes flying over Honolulu. And sometimes, the pilot was her husband.

TWENTY-THREE

Driving into Honolulu, she saw the same rebuilding that was going on at Hickam. She could also see they were preparing for another attack. Men were digging trenches outside Central Union Church; civilians, including children, wore gas masks as they participated in a poison-gas drill; and there was a ten-foot barbed wire fence that ran the length of Waikiki beach, along with every other beach on the island. People sat in beach chairs on one side watching swimmers on the other side, as if it had always been that way. Annie, however, refused to accept these changes as anything but temporary.

Honolulu would recover, just like this street. The last time Annie had driven here, everything had been in shambles—an assortment of goods littering the ground, from mattresses to Christmas cards to the Pinocchio lunch box she kept in her locker. Today, the sidewalk was clean. The drugstore had reopened; its windows sparkled in the sun as shoppers hurried to do what they could before curfew and Christmas.

Annie also had a lot to do before the sun went down, and her first stop was the owner of the drugstore. She'd brought an envelope full of petty cash with which to reimburse him for what she'd taken the day of the attack. She'd spoken to the major about it, and he'd agreed. If he found out she'd gone into the city, she'd tell him she wanted to reimburse the store owner before Christmas.

The owner of the shop appeared frightened when Annie told him who she was and took out the envelope. He was probably afraid he would be suspected of being a sympathizer, as was every other person of Japanese descent on the island.

"No, no," he insisted. "I don't need money."

"Please let us repay you for the things I took," said Annie.

"It was for a good cause," he said, shaking his head at the envelope. "Just tell the Army I'm a good patriot."

She took fifty dollars out of the envelope and held it out to him. "You're a very good citizen. Please accept this small token of the Army's appreciation for your help to us."

Reluctantly, he took the money.

"Thank you, sir. I'll let the Army know how gracious you were." She smiled, and he finally smiled back. "And now if you could help me find a few Christmas presents. I need a Captain America comic book and a jump rope."

Having wrapped the presents for Beth and Tommy in the Jeep, she wasn't as pleased as she could be with the presentation. She loved wrapping presents. Never having had a lot of money to spend, she'd always taken her time in making sure her gifts were wrapped in pretty paper with as many strings and bows as she could tastefully manage. These presents weren't wrapped with her typical flair; however, she had been able to buy the latest issue of Captain America and the best jump rope the drugstore had to offer. It didn't have red, white, and blue handles, but she'd found one with navy-blue handles and white trim that looked quite grown-up. Beth seemed like a girl who would appreciate something smart.

Annie parked the Jeep behind Kay's car, wishing this was a sign that she was home. However, she'd been calling the community center every day, speaking to either Mak or Amai, and neither had heard from Kay since she'd been taken to the FBI.

As she walked toward her apartment, Annie was surprised by how important Kay had become to her. Annie hadn't had a best friend since she'd left Nova Scotia. Theadora Turner and she had been friends since they were six years old. They were always together. Thick as thieves, her father used to say. Until Thea married at the age of eighteen and had her first child at nineteen. By the time Thea was twenty-five, she had three children and nothing in common with her best friend but their childhood friendship. Thea started spending more and more time with other young mothers, while Annie spent more time thinking about what she could do with her life when she left Pubnico, Nova Scotia.

Since she'd left, Annie had occasionally felt the absence of a best friend, mainly in not having someone she trusted completely who she could talk to about all things female. The problem was that she rarely wanted to talk about all things female. It had been different with Kay. They shared the same passion—taking care of their patients. Annie felt that Kay would not judge her for choosing the Army over having a family, which Annie had to admit was what she'd done. And most of the time, she was content with that choice.

One of the first things Annie wanted to tell Kay was that Corporal Jeremy Tig was alive and doing well because of the surgery they had performed as a team. She knew Kay would be nearly as thrilled as she was about his recovery. Of course, she would also like to talk to her about her feelings for the major, though there wasn't that much to talk about. She was a few years older than him and couldn't offer him children. It was too late for that, at least as far as Annie was concerned. However, she knew Kay would understand that as well.

Hoping they would get a Christmas miracle, Annie knocked on the door of Kay's apartment, gifts in hand. When an older woman opened the door with an expression of fixed worry, Annie knew it was pointless to ask but did anyway. "Is Kay home?"

"Who's asking?"

"Annie Fox. I worked with Kay at the community center." She held out her hand.

"I'm Shizuko, Kay's mother." She shook Annie's hand firmly. "You're the one who took my daughter to Hickam Field."

Annie nodded. She let go of Shizuko's hand and cringed inwardly. She deserved whatever was coming, especially from Kay's mother.

"Come in, please." Shizuko smiled as she swung the door open.

Annie followed her into the living room. The apartment was quiet. Too quiet.

"Is Kay out with the children?" asked Annie. A last hope.

"Mak took the children for ice cream. He's been by every day since Kay…left."

"She hasn't come home?"

"No."

"Have you heard from her?"

Shizuko shook her head. "Have you?"

"I'm afraid not."

"Do you know where my daughter is?"

"No," said Annie with a huge amount of guilt.

"They didn't tell you where they were taking her?"

Annie shook her head. "I only know that the military police took her to the FBI. Since then, I've spoken to an FBI agent, but he won't say where they're keeping her."

"You can't order him to tell you?"

"No. The FBI is a separate part of the government."

"What does the government want with Kay?"

"They're questioning hundreds of community leaders. I'm sure they'll let her go soon."

Shizuko appeared less than convinced of her daughter's safety. "You need to tell them what a fine patriot she is," she said. "As a dutiful daughter, Kaya has kept many of our traditions, but she's an American. She would never betray her country. More important, she would not do anything to put her children at risk."

"How are Beth and Tommy?"

"They're fine," said Shizuko. "They think their mother is still helping take care of injured soldiers. How do I tell them she was arrested?"

"Perhaps you could wait a little longer. I'm still asking questions." Annie had asked questions all the way to the top and gotten nowhere. General Short had been called back to Washington, DC; maybe his replacement would be more forthcoming. "People usually feel more generous at Christmas, so maybe they'll share something soon." Forcing a smile, she placed the Christmas presents on the coffee table. "This is just a little something for Tommy and Beth. I hope it's all right. I didn't know if you celebrated Christmas."

"It's fine," said Shizuko. "Thank you."

"Other than finding out where your daughter is, is there anything else I can do?"

"There is nothing you can do for me, because I am Issei. But the children are Nisei, and they can be protected."

"I'm sorry. I don't know what you mean."

"I'm Issei because I was born in Japan and cannot become a U.S. citizen. The children are Nisei because they were born here. People have heard that the Issei will be taken away, but I don't know where to."

"I haven't heard that rumor," said Annie, "and I would have if it were to be taken seriously."

"You don't think they'll come for me?"

"Why on earth would they? You've done nothing wrong."

"Neither did my daughter. What if they take me, and there's no one here for the children? I don't want to leave them with Makani unless I have to. He's a good man, but he's a man—not a mother or grandmother. But if you could find out when they're coming for the Issei, then I'll make sure Makani is with the children."

"I'll see what I can find out." Annie took her notepad and pen out of her purse. Since the attack, she'd kept it with her always. She wrote her name and the phone number for Major Lance's office along with his name on the paper and handed it to Shizuko. "This is my contact information. If anyone comes for you, please give this to them and say that I will be responsible for making sure the children are taken care of. Tell them I'll come for them—day or night."

"Thank you, Miss Fox." Shizuko took the note. "I just hope they listen to me."

Annie hoped for the same. The hint of euphoria she'd felt when she came here had been replaced by a sense of foreboding and utter frustration.

Parking on Hotel Street was tricky. Annie had assumed that men didn't indulge themselves on Christmas Eve because…well, it was Christmas Eve. However, if the number of cars on the street was any indication, men were giving themselves an early Christmas present.

Her gifts in hand—a big box of bonbons for Rita and her girls and the nursing pamphlets she'd promised Carole—Annie knocked on the door.

Carole opened the door, red lipstick perfectly applied, and could not have looked more surprised. "What the hell…"

"Does that mean you're happy to see me?" asked Annie.

"Yes! Come in."

Annie followed her inside. The room was larger than she'd imagined and nearly hospital clean, which pleased her almost as much as the bowl full of condoms on the end table.

"Please, have a seat." Carole pointed to an overstuffed chair by the window, which was crisscrossed with masking tape like most windows in the city. "Can I get you a cup of coffee?"

"No, thank you, Carole. I can't stay," said Annie with genuine regret. "I need to get back before the sun goes down, and I have another stop. I'm sorry it's taken me so long to come, but this is the first time I've been off base since the attack." She reached into her purse and pulled out several U.S. Army Nurse Corps pamphlets. "As promised. All you need to know about how to apply and what to expect."

Carole took the pamphlets like they were a Christmas gift. "Isn't that"—she pointed to the face on the pamphlets—"one of your nurses?"

"Yes, she's one of mine," said Annie with pride. "Second Lieutenant Monica Conter. If you join the Corps, you'll go through the same training she did."

"What if…they don't want me?" asked Carole. "Because of what I do."

"Why do they have to know?"

"Won't somebody tell them?"

"I won't. And neither will Major Lance. The only thing we'll tell them is that you donated blood that was desperately needed. And that you volunteered to help with the wounded and kept your composure during the most difficult day this country has ever seen. That's what's most relevant to becoming an Army nurse during wartime."

"You're sure they don't need to know about what I do for a living now?"

"I'm sure. Just keep using those condoms so you don't get anything that might affect your physical exam."

"Rita always keeps our bowls full."

"Good for her," said Annie with a smile. "How is she?"

"She's fine. She's spending the day in her parlor. It's a really pretty room, and no customers are allowed inside. She won't even let her girls in there without an express invitation."

"We all need a place of our own," said Annie, though she had no idea where that place was for herself. "These are for Rita and everyone who helped that day." She put the bonbons on a small table by the bed.

"Thank you, Annie."

"It's nothing." Annie wished it could've been more. "Now, when you get ready to apply to the Corps, use my name as a reference. And make sure you tell them my duty station is Hickam Hospital so they know how to reach me."

"Thank you," said Carole, her eyes full of gratitude.

"No need. The Army will be lucky to have you. We were lucky to have all of you that day. You made a big difference." Annie turned to leave.

"Annie…"

Turning, Annie saw the worry in Carole's face and thought she might have to spend a little more time convincing her she could be a nurse. "What is it, Carole?"

"I need to tell you something. About Kay."

"Kay?"

Walking around Annie, Carole closed the door to her room and lowered her voice. "I know what happened to her."

"What do you mean?"

"A customer told me. He didn't know he was telling me. He was just talking. Some of them talk more than what they come here for. Anyway, this customer's in the Army. I think he's more of a boss because he complains about decisions he has to make instead of what other people tell him to do."

"Did he mention Kay by name?"

"No. But I think it was her. I mean, I think she was part of the decision he was complaining about."

"What kind of decision?"

"Where to send the woman—the subversive—who has little kids."

It was nearly dark by the time Annie arrived at the community center. Everyone had already left, not wanting to take the chance of being out after curfew. Annie had counted on the fact that Mak would be the last one to leave. Even when things were normal, when Kay was still there, he'd been the last one to go home. Annie had suspected it was because Mak had no one to go home to. Not unlike herself.

When she walked into the center, Mak was checking the floor for anything that might have been dropped during the day—from pacifiers to needles. Annie had done the end-of-day check herself a few times. Picking up a white button, Mak tossed it into the lost and found box, where it joined a pink barrette, a quarter, half a roll of Life Savers, and a pair of sunglasses.

"Those sunglasses have been in there since the last time I was here," said Annie. "You could probably claim them at this point."

Mak looked up at her.

"Merry Christmas, Mak."

"I don't celebrate Christmas. I celebrate the winter solstice."

"Then happy winter solstice," said Annie, who held out a bottle of okolehao, which she had gotten from the tiki bar. She, Kay, and Mak had all had such a good time there—before Annie had revealed who she really was.

"Thanks," said Mak, taking the bottle. "Will I need this after you tell me whatever it is you haven't said yet?"

If Annie didn't have to get back to the base before the major figured out she was gone, she would help him drink the entire bottle. "I saw Carole, who has a customer who's a high-ranking official. He told her that in a few weeks, they're going to transport hundreds of Japanese community and religious leaders to prison camps."

"That doesn't mean Kay's going to a prison camp."

"Carole's customer told her there was a mother among the prisoners, and he felt guilty about taking her from her children."

Mak opened the bottle and took a long swig. "Where are these prison camps?"

"Montana, New Mexico, and North Dakota."

"I'll find her. Once I get to the West Coast, I'll start looking in New Mexico."

"Mak, how would you ever find her without more information?"

He took another swig of okolehao. "The prison camps will be new. The locals would notice. They might even have been hired to help. I'll find someone who knows something."

"And then what? You break her out of a federal prison camp?"

"She shouldn't be there!"

"I know, Mak. But even if you find her, she'll be under guard. You can't just walk in, take her by the hand, and walk out. They'd shoot you—and her." She watched Mak's eyes fill with defeat. She needed to remind him of his purpose. "Kay asked that you watch over her children. If you leave—"

"They have their grandmother," he snapped.

"Yes, but she's not a young woman. And what if they take her? What happens to Beth and Tommy if you're nowhere to be found? Kay would never forgive you." She watched a tear roll down his cheek as he must have realized he could not rescue the woman he loved, but he could be there for her children. "I know how hard this is for you. All I can do is promise that I won't give up trying to find out exactly where she is. And if there's anything I can do to bring her home, I will."

After returning to base, Annie went to operating room one to wrap presents for her nurses. It was empty and quiet, and it was where she was most comfortable. When she worked next to the major, everything seemed right. Not just because he rarely lost a patient on the table but because they needed few words to communicate. She almost always knew what he wanted before he asked for it. She also never had to worry about him losing his temper or indulging a god complex, because he didn't have one, which was rare in such a good surgeon. The bottle of whiskey she'd gotten him for Christmas wasn't the best one she could buy, but only because there was an ethical limit on what you could spend on gifts for your superior.

Humming Christmas songs, she almost felt happy as she spread the wrapping paper over the operating table. But then she thought about Kay, and her humming sounded off-key. Now that she knew Kay was going to be transferred to a prison camp, she would make an appointment to see the new general and make a strong case for her immediate release. Once he understood what a serious mistake had been made, he would take steps to free her. Why wouldn't he? After all, they couldn't have any evidence against her, including that last note from her husband.

Annie had never told anyone what was in that note—the one she'd given to Mak, who had destroyed it. When Kay eventually returned, Annie wasn't even sure she would tell her. What good would it do her or the children? He'd promised her an "important life." They would be a couple with influence. In the last line, he'd written, "All those years in the fields paid off because I always paid attention to what the Americans were doing." Annie hadn't known exactly what he was talking about, but she was very glad she'd destroyed those words.

Hands full of gifts, Annie almost felt like Santa Claus as she tried to open the door to the women's barracks without dropping anything. When she finally got the door open, it was pitch-dark. Immediately, she regretted stopping in the kitchen for a sandwich. She'd taken too long; her nurses were asleep. No matter. She would set each gift on the small table by their beds, and they could open them in the morning. She was on the a.m. shift, so she wouldn't see them all open their gifts, but they were small so—

"Merry Christmas, Chief!" they all shouted as the lights went on.

The first thing Annie saw was the surfboard held on one side by Irene and on the other by Winnie. Polished to a gleaming shine, CHIEF was painted in blue down the center. But it still took her a moment to realize the surfboard was for her. "I...don't know what to say."

"That's a first," said Winnie.

They all laughed, including Annie.

"Well, who's going to teach me how to surf?" asked Annie, placing the gifts she'd wrapped on top of her own bed.

"That would be my honor," said Irene.

"Thank you all, very much. It's the best Christmas present I've ever gotten." Wiping a tear away, Annie gestured them all to her bed. "Time to open your gifts, though none is as wonderful as mine."

Irene and Winnie set the surfboard carefully against the wall near Annie's bed. In their pajamas, their curls held in place by bobby pins or rags, all her nurses gathered around.

"These are just tokens of my affection and admiration for each of you," said Annie. "I'm very grateful I had you all with me that day—and all the days after. None of which have been easy. I honestly don't know what I would've done without you." Clearing her throat, she passed out the gifts.

Winnie didn't wait and ripped open her box of Shalimar perfume. "My favorite!"

"You got us through quite a few days without showers. You deserved a new bottle."

Irene went next and opened her smaller box to reveal a new wristwatch.

"It's water-resistant for when you go surfing," said Annie.

"Thank you, Chief. It's just what I need." Smiling, Irene took off the watch she was wearing with the bloodstains on the leather band and replaced it with her new watch.

Monica opened her box next. "Oh, my!" Inside were two hair combs—one tortoiseshell and one mother-of-pearl. She held them up to show the others. "Aren't they beautiful?"

"Your hair is much too pretty for rubber bands," said Annie.

"I love them!"

"So will Barney." Sara winked as she opened her box, and then her eyes filled as she pulled out all that was left of the sign for the Snake Ranch beer garden, where she'd spent the one night she wanted to relive. The only part of the handmade sign that had survived read "Snake Ranch." The wood had been cleaned and varnished. "How did you…?"

"I saw it after the attack. I waited a few days to see if anyone would take it. When no one did, I claimed it. One of the mechanics in Hangar 5 who we'd treated brought the wood back to a shine."

"He did a great job. It's good as new." Sara smiled and wiped her tears away.

"There's a lipstick in there too. Nothing too bright, but a pretty shade of pink. You can wear it to the next Snake Ranch beer garden you find."

Sara managed to squeak out, "Thank you, Chief."

"You're more than welcome." Annie handed the last box to Kathy. "Last but not least."

Kathy held the box and smiled. "It smells good."

"Like Shalimar?" asked Winnie.

Kathy shook her head. "Like chocolate and…" She opened the box and carefully lifted out a chocolate cake topped with maraschino cherries.

"It won't be nearly as good as the cake you made with your grandmother, and the cherries are the kind you get on sundaes. But I thought it might remind you of home."

Kathy plucked a cherry from the top, dipped it in the chocolate icing, and put it on her tongue as if she were tasting a fine wine. After a moment, she chewed and swallowed. "It's absolutely delicious. I think we should all have a piece!"

"Shall we take it to the kitchen?" asked Annie.

A collective "Yes!" and Annie followed her happy group of nurses to the Hickam kitchen, where just a few weeks ago, they'd listened to the whine of airplanes as they were hit by antiaircraft fire. Tonight would be different.

It was difficult to fall asleep after so much chocolate cake. While her nurses had finally managed it, Annie was wide awake. Since the major had Christmas Day off, she decided to go to his office and leave her gift there so he would see it when he came back from wherever he was going. He hadn't mentioned a trip to her, but she knew he would be gone for two days.

Still wearing her civilian clothes, Annie swung a stethoscope around her neck and brought her flashlight—the beam still covered with blue cellophane—to check on her patients on the way to his office. Her ward was still full and then some. The shuffling and transporting of patients had taken many days. The Naval hospital at Pearl Harbor, the *Solace*, and Tripler General had taken the most serious cases, unless the patient was too critical to move. Some of those men had died from their injuries, but several others were in the process of a recovery that would take a few weeks longer. Annie was dedicated to all her patients, but she wanted to make sure the sailors they were treating would never have a reason to say the care they received from the Army was less than Navy care.

After dispensing aspirin, emptying a bedpan, and pouring fresh water for three separate patients, she finally got to the major's office. She had brought her key, expecting the door to be locked, but it wasn't. Inside, she used her flashlight to make her way to his desk and placed the wrapped whiskey at its center with a small thud. Which was followed by a snore that made her jump. Turning the flashlight toward the sound, she saw the major asleep on the couch, still in his uniform, tie loosened, shoes off.

She took the lap blanket from the closet, shook it out, and laid it over him. Resisting the urge to tuck him in, she stepped back and watched him sleep for a few minutes. His brow was furrowed, just enough to make it look as if he were solving some problem in the

OR even while he slept. She bent down by the couch and whispered, "Patient's in the clear." This was what she said to him whenever they were in surgery together and they'd passed the point when there would normally be trouble. It was like rounding third base or running the last lap around a racetrack. She waited to see if it would work and smiled when his brow relaxed. Now he could sleep peacefully.

She headed back to the women's barracks, exhausted, though she would admit that to no one else. There were still many letters to write on behalf of the soldiers and sailors who had spoken their last words to her. Tonight, she would write to Sam Baker's father and emphasize the fact that he hadn't been in pain when he passed. Annie would find a way to tell him about his son's extraordinary bravery and his excitement about working with radar technology without telling him he'd been shot at while being burned alive.

TWENTY-FOUR

February 20, 1942

Soon after the attack on Pearl Harbor, Admiral Husband Kimmel had been relieved of his command of the Pacific Fleet. He had requested an early retirement as opposed to a court-martial. Those who preferred the latter thought he deserved it because he'd been given a war warning, which he had ignored. However, he wasn't the only one who hadn't believed Japan would be so bold as to attack Pearl Harbor—the U.S. high command hadn't believed it either. The majority thought Kimmel was being scapegoated, though no one was saying this out loud, and should be allowed to retire.

General Short had also opted for retirement but, unlike Admiral Kimmel, seemed committed to fighting for as long as it took to preserve his pre–Hickam Field reputation. Nonetheless, ten days after the attack, Short was replaced by Lieutenant General Delos Emmons, who became the military governor of Hawaii. Annie had heard him referred to as a "desk" general, which meant he was there to preserve order on the island rather than to participate in the war effort. Despite that directive, he'd ordered more bombers be sent to Hickam.

Like a good soldier, Lieutenant General Emmons also worked toward the directive he'd been given and was overseeing the replacement of U.S. dollars on the island with new ones that were overprinted with the word HAWAII. If the island was captured by the enemy, any money they collected from banks and businesses would be worthless on the mainland or anywhere else. In the spirit of Hawaiian harmony, he'd also promised the Japanese American community they would be treated fairly as long as they remained loyal to the United States. This had given Annie hope that he would be sympathetic to her cause in fighting for Kay's release.

Something else had also given her hope. When talk about relocating Japanese Americans to internment camps first reached him, Emmons countered by pointing out the logistical difficulties. Nearly 160,000 Japanese people lived in Hawaii, making up more than one-third of the population. In addition to the logistical nightmare of transporting that many people off the island, how would they compensate for their sudden disappearance from Hawaii's economy? Every island business—small or large—would suffer. But despite common sense and moral arguments, relocation talks had persisted in earnest.

It had taken Annie almost two months to get an appointment with the new military governor of Hawaii. By the second week in February, both Emmons's secretary and his assistant had received so many calls from Annie that they no longer had to ask her name. They recognized her voice and the tenor of her mood. Every time she called, Annie also managed to give them one more piece of Kay's story.

Emmons's office staff knew the names and ages of Kay's children. They knew she was a nurse who'd run a community center and had helped in Hickam's darkest hours. And they knew she had been taken by the FBI and hadn't been seen or heard from since.

"My secretary practically begged me to give you five minutes." Lieutenant General Emmons sat behind his desk with an expression that was a mix of amusement and irritation. "Use thirty seconds of it to tell me what you said that upset her."

"I believe it was something about a jump rope, sir," said Annie, seeing his irritation overshadow his amusement. "I think she was moved by the plight of my friend, Kay Kimura, a local nurse and mother who was arrested after nursing our men at Hickam Hospital. She's been held for two months, but her family doesn't know where or why."

"Was she a community leader?"

"She ran the Japanese American Community Center in Honolulu, but it was hardly a hotbed of political activity. I volunteered at the center, and all Kay ever did was take care of her patients—hers and ours, sir."

"Since you're chief nurse at Hickam Hospital, I take it you weren't at the community center day and night. There could have been more going on there than you were aware of."

"Yes, but I knew Kay outside the center. We were—are—friends. I've rarely met anyone more loyal to her country."

"Maybe she was loyal. Or maybe she just wanted you to think she would never betray us. You can't know for sure."

"Why assume the worst? She was born in Hawaii. She had no reason to—"

"Except for her husband."

Annie couldn't mask her surprise.

"I do my homework." He took a folder from the top of a neat pile on his desk and opened it. "Daiji Kimura. Left Hawaii for Japan more than a year ago. Ostensibly for employment. He had a degree in engineering from Kyoto University, but he'd been working on a sugarcane plantation. And now he's a rather high-ranking member of the Imperial Japanese Army."

Annie couldn't hide her surprise.

"You didn't know?"

"No, sir."

"I take it your argument is that Mrs. Kimura shouldn't be punished because her husband is our enemy?"

"Yes, sir." The discussion was not going as she'd planned. However, sometimes, especially with men in positions of authority, it was best to let them lead. As long as this one kept going in the direction she intended.

"Well, the FBI disagrees. And they haven't finished their investigation, so my hands are tied. Is there anything else I can do for you, Lieutenant?"

"Could you tell me where she is? Her family is very worried. I'm worried."

"I'm sorry. I cannot divulge her location."

"Could you arrange a phone call? Her mother could come to your office. The FBI could set the rules. I think everyone would be very relieved to hear her voice."

"If I arrange a call for your friend, I'd be obliged to do it for hundreds of others."

"But she deserves special consideration. She went to Hickam and—"

"I wish things were different, Lieutenant. But until she's been cleared of all charges, she'll remain in custody under the same rules and regulations as everyone else."

"Can you tell me what the charges are against her?"

He gazed down at the file. "Sedition. And conspiracy to sabotage."

"With all due respect, those charges are ridiculous."

"If you're right, she'll be free soon enough."

"Not soon enough for her children, sir. She's already been detained for more than two months."

"I imagine this is very difficult for them. But all I can do is keep an eye on her case and let you know if any red flags come up."

"I would very much appreciate it, sir." Annie knew it made a big difference if someone was paying attention, particularly someone like him. They might have hobbled his authority as far as the war effort, but he was still the military governor of Hawaii.

Major Lance had sent an orderly for Annie. Mags, who had greatly appreciated the ten dollars Annie had put in his Christmas card, told her the major had said to take his time. In Mags's opinion, it was because he had bad news and didn't want to tell her. Thus, Annie steeled herself before she entered his office, but the news still rendered her speechless. For a few moments.

"You spoke to a JAG officer about me?" asked Annie, gripping the arms of her chair.

"I needed to find out how serious the situation is—for your own good," he said.

"I'm quite capable of doing that myself, sir."

"I'm well aware. However, there's a new executive order, and I needed to know how the order would affect you, because your status affects my hospital."

"My status?" Was he going to make her retire? Was that what the new executive order was about? Out with the old, in with the new because of the war? She thought she'd proved her worth, but maybe it wasn't enough. "What is my status, Major?"

"You're my chief nurse."

"Then what are you talking about?"

"Executive Order 9066 was passed yesterday. To be perfectly honest, it was so convoluted, I wasn't sure what it meant, which is why I called a JAG officer I know. Basically, it gives the secretary of war and military commanders broad authority to relocate people living in certain areas. Meaning it gives them the right to relocate Japanese Americans to a place where they could pose no threat."

"You're telling me we're going to round up Japanese Americans who live here and transport them to the mainland?"

The major nodded. "The relocation begins in the next few days."

"But where will they go?"

"They've been building camps." Even though they were alone, the major leaned in and lowered his voice. "Some people are calling them concentration camps, but I'm sure they're not like the one Hitler built." He paused before asking, "Did I ever thank you for the whiskey?"

She'd barely heard his question; she was still stuck on the words "concentration camps."

"If I didn't thank you, I really did appreciate the gift. And I'm really glad I still have some." He opened his desk drawer, took out the whiskey and two glasses, and handed her a glass with just enough whiskey to take the edge off the news without impairing her judgment for the hour left on her shift.

"They can't do it. Can they?" she asked. "Send all those people away?"

"Yes, they can. According to the JAG officer."

"But that doesn't mean they will."

"The president doesn't issue an executive order unless he expects it to be carried out."

"Every Japanese American on the island—on the entire West Coast—will be devastated."

"And outraged. Which is why I'd like you to stay on base for a while. I know you planned on going back to the community center soon, but they'll notify the public about this any day, and at least one-third of the island's population won't take it well."

"How could anyone take it well? How could anyone stand for it?"

"Lieutenant—"

"Explain to me how it's different. Explain to me how putting our own people in concentration camps is any different from what Hitler's doing."

"It's very different," he said. "First of all, a concentration camp is just an unfortunate term for housing. They won't be mistreated."

"Relocating people is already mistreating—"

"Keeping them separate will protect them from people who see them as the enemy, no matter how unjustified that might be. As the war goes on and casualties mount, people may focus their fear and anger on Japanese Americans. Until the war is won, their safety might depend on being out of sight."

"Out of sight, out of mind? Hiding them away like they don't exist?"

"I won't pretend to know why President Roosevelt gave the order, but I'm sure he had his reasons. I'll also remind you that he's our commander in chief and doesn't owe us an explanation. We carry out his orders. We don't question them."

"But if the orders are unjust—"

"Not your call, Lieutenant. And until you can come to terms with this, you'll stay on base. We don't need members of the military adding to the outrage on civilian streets."

He watched Annie swallow whatever she was going to say along with the rest of her whiskey. Then she put the glass on his desk and stood. It took every ounce of her willpower to salute before she turned to leave.

Annie knew she couldn't speak to the major again yet, at least not about the executive order, so she'd asked Monica to personally deliver a request for a day pass to him and asked her to wait until he'd handed the pass to her. In the request, she'd told him she'd reluctantly come to terms with what they'd discussed, in that she would abide by the chain of command and her duty to country, no matter her own personal feelings.

Monica returned with her pass—for the following week. The major obviously thought Annie needed more time to cool off, which may have been her own fault. They'd had a follow-up surgery that morning for one of the soldiers hurt on December 7—his third—and she hadn't said a word to the major beyond what was necessary in regard to their patient.

In the envelope with the day pass was also a note, which read, *Please don't do anything you'll regret. But if you do, call me. Day or night. For you, I'm always on call.*

Annie folded the note and tucked it in her pocket. Despite her outrage at the situation and irritation with the major, she knew she would keep his note. Always.

TWENTY-FIVE

February 26, 1942

They had put her on a train to Bismarck, North Dakota. There were hundreds of detainees who were being transferred to prison camps, but she had not seen any other women. When Kay arrived in Bismarck, she and the others were herded toward a caravan of trucks where, again, she saw no women.

Sitting in the back of the truck, she couldn't see where they were going because there were no windows. She wished she could at least time how long it would take them to drive from the train station to their destination—wherever it was—but they had taken her watch. She had nothing left that was her own, not even her clothes.

They'd given her trousers, a flannel shirt, boots, and a coat. She'd never worn trousers or flannel shirts before. When she'd disembarked from the train, she realized they'd only been preparing her for the cold. Even in the sun, she doubted it was more than twenty degrees. It was painful to breathe the frigid air, and the snow was so bright it hurt her eyes to look at it. On the way to the trucks, she'd bent down to pick up a handful of snow to see what it was like but had dropped it almost immediately because it was so cold it felt like it was burning her palm.

She guessed they'd been driving for only about fifteen minutes when the truck came to a stop. They waited for what felt like hours before an armed guard opened the back of the truck and told them to form a single line; they were to be counted and identified before they entered the camp.

She glanced at the line of trucks in back of them, waiting their turn, and was grateful she'd been in one of the trucks near the front of the line. After being cooped up in the hotel for a few months, standing out in the fresh air was a relief despite the icy wind. Kay turned her face up to the sun, which seemed to radiate no warmth, and saw a curved iron sign that read *Fort Lincoln* over the front gate. She'd not heard of it before but assumed this was a military post. Then she spotted the guard towers and the ten-foot double fence topped by barbed wire. Apparently, the post had been turned into a prison for them.

That was exactly what she felt like—a prisoner—since the FBI had escorted her from Hickam. And now it was official, despite the fact that there had been no trial. Her nonlegal hearing had gone exactly as she feared it would. As soon as she'd seen the six stern-faced white men who would decide her fate, she'd known they wouldn't release her. They had believed every word Agent Harris said, coming to the conclusion that she was complicit in her husband's scheme. They still had no idea what the scheme had entailed, but that hadn't made any difference. She was married to the enemy; therefore, she was the enemy.

After their identities were checked and doubled-checked, the prisoners were led toward the Japanese side of the internment camp. The other side was occupied by German nationals who had been deemed dangerous to national security. Every Japanese and German internee at Fort Lincoln had been on a custodial detention list that used an A-B-C classification system to evaluate their individual degree of threat, which had been used to predesignate those who would be interned if the United States went to war. During her weeks with the FBI, Kay had learned that she'd been watched for months. As soon as Daiji began making inquiries about the possibility of leaving for Japan, he was under surveillance, and so was Kay. Her association with Annie had only heightened the military's interest.

As Kay and the others were led past the mess hall, the armed guard at the front told them it was divided into two wings with separate kitchens: one prepared food that would be agreeable to Germans, while the other prepared food for the Japanese. He turned to smile at them as if he were the concierge at a five-star resort. A young Japanese man near the front thanked him for his thoughtfulness. Kay couldn't tell if he was being sarcastic or was simply trying to get along with his captors.

They passed wooden buildings used as barracks as the new prisoners were led toward three two-story redbrick buildings. Stopping at the first building, two of the guards split off to escort the Issei men inside. Those designated as Issei had emigrated from Japan and weren't eligible to be U.S. citizens. The Issei were slightly older than those known as Nisei men, who, like Kay, had been born in the United States. Three guards escorted the Nisei men into the second brick building. This left only Kay.

An armed guard pointed Kay toward the last brick building. Inside, she found that she was one of less than half a dozen women at the camp. Two of the women appeared to be somewhere in their midthirties, like Kay. The youngest woman couldn't have been more than twenty-two or three, and the eldest was likely in her early sixties. All wore trousers and flannel shirts. Kay thought Annie would be pleased by their commonsense attire and almost smiled thinking of her friend, wondering, not for the first time, if she was still at Hickam Hospital. Or had the attack made her want to retire? For what Kay considered selfish reasons, she hoped Annie would still be there when she returned home. Whenever that would be.

The older woman approached Kay. "Welcome," she said, holding out her hand. "My name is Yoshi."

"My name is Kaya, but everyone calls me Kay." She took Yoshi's hand in hers, so glad to be able to talk to another woman. "How long have you been here?"

"We arrived about two weeks ago."

Yoshi reminded Kay of Mrs. Taketa; she spoke with a similar accent and had the same soft creases around kind eyes. "It looks like a prison, at least from the outside," said Kay.

The other women retreated toward steel cots lined against the far wall while Yoshi motioned Kay closer to the woodstove at the center of the room. Near the stove, there was a wooden table where the women had been playing cards before Kay arrived. Gin rummy by the looks of what was left on the table.

"Are you from Honolulu?" asked Kay after they sat across from each other.

Yoshi shook her head. "I live…lived in Kona."

"I've never been to the big island," said Kay. "Were you a community leader? Is that why they detained you?"

"I was arrested," Yoshi said without rancor, "because I taught a class on Japanese culture so our people could carry on our traditions in America."

"I'm sorry." Kay lowered her voice. "And the others?"

"The youngest, Iris, taught English to those who wanted to feel more American. She was living in Hilo. Kyoko and Inari"—Yoshi gestured toward the two women who were Kay's age—"worked at a Japanese-language newspaper. Both had written articles about the increasing hostility toward Japanese Americans in Hawaii. They also criticized the police for not doing more to protect Japanese-owned businesses."

Kay shook her head. "I never would have imagined this could happen."

"My husband and I came to the United States because we believed it couldn't happen here," said Yoshi. "Why did they take you?"

"I ran a community center where we offered medical care and a place for those in the community to air their grievances. I never thought it would lead to this." And she wasn't sure that it had. Over the last few months, Kay had grown more resentful of her husband, blaming him for being taken, because her interrogators always circled back to Daiji. However, she had no intention of discussing her husband with any of the prisoners, because it would make her look guilty by association, and she was tired of being alone. Until she'd arrived at Fort Lincoln, she'd not seen another woman since the initial days of her captivity. There had been no one to talk to who would understand her biggest fear. "Do any of the women have children?"

Yoshi shook her head. "Iris is engaged. Kyoko and Inari both refused matches. They're committed to being journalists."

"They'll have quite a story to tell when they let us go."

"By then, I'm not sure they'll want to write about anything more controversial than who wasn't invited to join the local garden club."

"By then? Do you know how long they plan to keep us?"

Yoshi shook her head. "Do you have children?"

Kay nodded. "Beth is nine and Tommy…he's seven now. His birthday was last month. My children are with my mother—and a friend." The one thing that had been getting Kay through each day was knowing her children were under her mother's care and Mak's protection. "I just wish I could let them know where I am."

"They told Iris they would let her fiancé know she was well, but I doubt they told him where she's being held. Kyoko and Inari asked that their editor be told about what's happened to them, but their request was denied."

"And you?" asked Kay.

"My husband died three years ago. My daughter gave birth to my second grandchild in early November. I went to Seattle for several weeks to help with the children. I'd been back home for less than a day when they came for me. My daughter must know I'm missing, but I don't want her looking for me. I don't want her to draw attention to herself."

"But didn't you say she's in Seattle?"

"Under the new law, that might not make any difference."

"What new law?" asked Kay.

"Have you not seen a recent newspaper?"

Kay shook her head. "They only gave them to the men at the hotel."

"The men get them first here too," said Yoshi. "By the time we get one, it's in pretty bad shape and the news is a few days old. We throw them in the woodstove when we're done. We all took some pleasure in burning the newspaper about Executive Order 9066."

"What does it do?"

"It authorizes the removal of every person living on the West Coast who they believe is a threat to national security."

"Removal?" Kay's heart began to pound. "What does that mean?"

Before Yoshi could answer, Kyoko and Inari came out of the shadows near the steel cots. "They've divided the West Coast into military zones," said Inari, whose calm delivery made her sound like a radio news broadcaster. "The executive order gives military commanders the right to move civilians from designated military areas to relocation centers."

"But…" Kay could barely think. "They can't just take everyone."

"They're not taking everyone," said Kyoko, whose voice nearly shook with anger. "They're only taking people who look like us."

"They can't believe all of us are working against our own country," said Kay.

"People are still afraid Japan will invade the West Coast," said Kyoko, "and that anyone with a drop of Japanese blood will help them."

If they took Kay's mother, the children would still have Mak. They wouldn't be alone. Unless… "They're not taking children, are they? No one could think of them as a threat."

"They'll take the children too," said Iris, who was sitting on the bed with what looked like a well-read issue of *Reader's Digest* on her lap. "I heard the guards talking. One of them said he was going to stop complaining about being cold all the time, because freezing his balls off was better than babysitting"—Iris spat the next two words out like rotten fish—"Jap brats."

Kay felt as if she couldn't breathe. How would she find her children if they were taken? Mak wouldn't be allowed to go with them because he wasn't Japanese. Would her mother be taken too? Would Beth and Tommy be separated? Where the hell were these relocation centers?

She felt herself hyperventilating and cupped her hands over her nose and mouth, trying to breathe slowly, trying to focus. Mak would do what he could to find out where they were taking her family. And Annie would help him. But what if Annie was sent to Europe or someplace in the South Pacific? They'd sent her there before. What if Mak couldn't find out where they took her children? What if she never found them?

Tears ran down her cheeks.

Yoshi reached across the table for her hand as Inari, Kyoko, and Iris joined them. They all reached over the scattered deck of cards toward the center, hands extended toward their uncertain fate.

TWENTY-SIX

March 21, 1942

Annie had made several trips into Honolulu over the past few weeks. She'd been given permission to volunteer at the center again and sometimes stayed to have dinner with Shizuko and the children. With Shizuko's patient instruction, Annie was even getting good at using chopsticks. When Shizuko cooked, which was every night unless Annie brought takeout, forks were forbidden.

During those dinners, the children would tell her about school and focused mainly on gas mask and trench drills. Beth had become adept at putting on her gas mask so quickly that she could assist the teacher in helping other children. Tommy was better at navigating the trench that now took up a big part of the playground. They would all try to make light of these drills, but the children knew it was deadly serious. Two children from their school had died in the attack.

Neither Beth nor Tommy ever mentioned their father, at least not while Annie was there. She wasn't sure if this was due to one of their grandmother's rules or not, and she wasn't sure how she felt about it.

Their father was an enemy of their country; on the other hand, he had been a good father. Kay had told her that was one of the reasons she'd loved him. The children were encouraged to talk about their mother though. Shizuko would say things like, "When your mother gets home, she'll want to hear you recite the poem you learned in school today." It was as though Kay had just gone out to the store and would be back in a few minutes.

After Annie had learned about Executive Order 9066, she'd spent the week the major had confined her to the base trying to learn who might be affected. She'd read the order several times and had met with the JAG officer, who explained that anyone of Japanese heritage might be relocated. She'd asked him if there was any way she could protect Kay's mother and children from being relocated. He'd told her that even if she adopted the children, they would still be subject to relocation. The War Relocation Authority planned to deport Japanese Americans to internment camps in any of seven states. Only two of these camps would be located in California, close enough that Annie might be able to visit. As a member of the U.S. Army, she hoped she would at least be granted that permission.

Shizuko and the children never discussed the executive order. Annie had a feeling that it would be like discussing their absent father in that it would do no one any good. They had no control over what he did or didn't do, and they had no control over what would happen once the relocation process began. All they could do was wait and see.

On Monday, March 16, 1942, Major Lance had told Annie he'd heard from the JAG officer—the relocation process would begin the following weekend. Annie had been on pins and needles all week and left Hickam Field early on Saturday morning.

Even though she wasn't on duty, Annie had worn her uniform for two reasons. It gave her license to drive like she was on official business, and no one would stop her to ask for identification papers. She had no time for it. As soon as she'd driven into Honolulu, she'd seen Japanese Americans walking with suitcases toward different bus stops where they would board and begin their relocation journey. She had to get to Kay's apartment.

Jumping out of the Army Jeep, she ran to Kay's front door to find it locked. She banged on the door until her hand was red. A neighbor finally came out to tell her that Shizuko and the children had left more than an hour ago. People had been leaving the apartment building for two days. He was fearful he'd be the last one left or be ordered to a bus too. The older man clearly needed comforting, but Annie had no time to offer kind words.

She drove and drove and drove. It seemed like every neighborhood had a bus where Japanese Americans stood in line, waiting to board, suitcases and small boxes on the sidewalk beside them. Annie would park and search their faces for Shizuko or the smaller figures of a brother and sister. Over a few hours, she saw many older women, eyes full of trepidation, and she saw many children. Younger ones played, clearly oblivious to what was happening, while the older children appeared forlorn and confused.

Stopping at a red light, she wondered if she'd been at the same stop before when she heard a baby cry. Turning toward the cry, she saw a row of buses. More Japanese American men, women, and children stood in a line waiting to board. Scanning their faces, she stopped on a familiar one—Chie stood next to her husband, trying to calm her baby. And a few feet behind them stood Shizuko with Tommy and Beth.

The light changed, and Annie turned toward the buses. Driving an Army vehicle was like driving a police car; she could park wherever she liked. Once parked, she ran toward the line. By the time she got to Shizuko, she was breathless, more from indignation on their behalf than from physical exertion.

"I don't think they'll let you on the bus, Miss Fox," said Shizuko with a half smile.

"Did they tell you where you're going?" asked Annie.

Shizuko shook her head. "Have you found out where my daughter is?"

This was the same question Shizuko had asked whenever Annie had come for supper. And Annie had the same answer. "Not yet."

Annie glanced at Beth and Tommy, who knew their mother had been taken away but weren't aware of the details. They'd also been told she'd done nothing wrong and it was all a big misunderstanding, which would be cleared up. One day.

"How will Mom know we've been taken too?" asked Tommy.

"I'll tell her," said Annie. "As soon as she comes home." Annie had come to believe Kay wouldn't come back until the war was over. But how soon could they defeat Japan while also fighting Germany? She looked away from the children to focus on what she might be able to make right. Breaking away from the line, she approached one of the soldiers guarding the line. "Private!"

He turned to her; the anger flushing through his cheeks stalled as he saw the bars on her uniform. "Yes, ma'am?"

"Where are you taking these people?"

"Not sure, ma'am. My order was only to load them on the buses."

"They're not cattle, Private. Where's your commanding officer?"

"On base, ma'am."

"Who's in charge here?"

"Sergeant Knapp."

"Take me to him."

He hesitated as Annie watched Shizuko and the children move closer to the bus.

"Now, Private!"

"Follow me, ma'am."

She followed him to Sergeant Knapp, who was directing a bus out of the parking lot, yelling at the young soldier driving the bus. "Move it! We don't have all goddamned day!"

"Sergeant Knapp…"

The sergeant turned to the private but only saw Annie and the bars on her uniform. "Lieutenant." He saluted.

She returned his salute with a snap of her wrist. "Are all these buses heading for the same destination, Sergeant?"

"No, ma'am." And then to the soldier who'd brought her to him, he said, "Go back to what you were doing, Private."

"Yes, sir." He saluted and left, looking relieved that he was leaving Annie's proximity.

"Tell me where that bus is going," said Annie like it was an order, pointing to the bus that Shizuko and the children were waiting to board.

"Can't do that, ma'am."

"Yes, you can, Sergeant. If it's a direct order from a superior."

"Sorry, Lieutenant, but my captain's order supersedes yours. And he told me the final destination of potential spies and saboteurs is classified."

"Do they look like spies and saboteurs?" She pointed to Shizuko and the children, but he didn't move his eyes from her.

"I have my orders, ma'am. From someone who outranks you. I'm sure you understand."

"I do," she said with more sorrow than she'd thought would ever be possible. She returned his salute and hurried back to the bus where Beth and Tommy were climbing on board. The Captain America comic book she'd given Tommy poked out of his back pocket, and Beth held the jump rope she'd given her. Shizuko was right behind them.

"Wait!" Annie stepped ahead of Shizuko and told the driver. "I need a minute, soldier."

The young soldier nodded.

"I couldn't find out where they're taking you," she told Shizuko, but not softly enough.

"They're taking us to jail," said Tommy. "That's where they take all the bad guys."

"No," said Annie. "You've done nothing wrong, Tommy. Neither has anyone else in this line. We talked about this, remember? They're just taking you to a new place to live until the war's over because Oahu is too dangerous." This was what she and Shizuko had agreed to tell the children when it was time to discuss the executive order.

"But they have guns," said Beth.

"Yes, but only to protect you," said Annie, trying very hard to smile her assurance before turning to their grandmother. "I'm sorry I couldn't do more."

"I'll write if they let me," said Shizuko. "So you can tell Kay where we are."

"When this is over, I'll make sure she finds you."

"Thank you, Nurse Fox," said Shizuko politely but without a shred of belief.

Climbing the bus steps, Annie addressed the driver and the two armed guards at the front of the bus. "This is Shizuko Kimura. Her daughter took care of our wounded soldiers and sailors at Hickam Field after the attack. Make sure you take care of her family with as much compassion as she showed your brothers and sisters in arms. And when you get to your destination, wherever that may be, tell whoever's in charge the same thing. Understood?"

They replied with a collective "Yes, ma'am."

As if someone were physically pulling her off the bus, Annie stepped down.

She stayed in her Jeep watching the bus until it pulled away, tears streaming down her eyes for the family she felt like she was losing.

For the first time, Annie arrived at the community center in her Army uniform, which literally made Mak take a step back when she came through the door. He was alone, which wasn't surprising. People not on their way to a bus were lying low inside their homes, hoping no one would notice they were still there.

"Why are you here?" asked Mak.

"They're gone," said Annie, taking a seat at one of the tables. "I tried to find out where Shizuko and the children were being taken, but they wouldn't tell me."

"What a surprise."

"I was surprised."

"Why? You still haven't been able to find out where Kay is."

"That was different. She was taken into custody."

"And you think everyone else isn't in custody?"

"They're being relocated for their own safety."

"Believe whatever helps you sleep at night."

"Stop being such an asshole."

"I'm the asshole?"

"Yes. Because since I've known you, you've done nothing but complain about this country. *Your* country. It's easy to bitch from the sidelines. It's a lot harder to work with people you might not like to make things different."

"I do make things different. I come here every day to—"

"See Kay. And since she's been gone, you come to keep this place going—for her. Am I wrong, Mak?"

"She's not why I became a nurse."

"I know," said Annie. "I saw you with the soldiers."

"Dead soldiers for the most part."

"The respect you showed them told me all I need to know about you. And if you'll let me, I'd like to keep coming here to help. Kay will need this place when she gets back."

"And if I decide to go look for Kay," said Mak, "would you help Amai with the center?"

"Of course," said Annie. "But please give me a little more time. Let me try to get Kay released under the law. For her sake and for yours."

"Okay," said Mak. "But not too long."

"Thank you." Annie held out her hand. Hesitating, Mak shook it.

Annie took a long walk around the base that night. It made her feel better to see the progress being made and to know they were no longer sitting ducks. In addition to Guam, Wake Island, and the Philippines, Japan was making progress in Hong Kong, Singapore, Southeast Asia, the Dutch East Indies, and parts of China. The next big battle was rumored to be in the Midway Islands, which were halfway between California and East Asia—and more than one thousand miles north of Hawaii. If that battle happened, Pearl Harbor and Hickam Field would need to be ready to defend their part of the Pacific.

Annie stopped at the base of the tower. She'd been coming here once a week to set a small bouquet of plumerias in memory of Private Sam Baker. The private's father had sent her a letter saying how much he appreciated her telling him about his son's bravery. He kept her letter with him at all times as a reminder of why his son died—to help save his brothers in arms.

"Thought I'd find you here."

Annie turned to see the major, who wasn't in his running clothes. "Is something wrong?"

"It's a beautiful night. Let's walk."

Walking beside him, she almost felt as if they were a couple. A real couple. She had never had that experience before. She had dated her fair share of men when she was younger, but those relationships never lasted very long. When her father was still alive, he'd asked how would she ever find a man who could meet her high standards. She'd responded by asking him why she should lower her standards for the person she was expected to spend the rest of her life with. It wasn't as though she weren't willing to accept flaws. Everyone had them, including herself. And she was willing to accept the fact that the major's biggest flaw was in agreeing with the president's decision to imprison innocent Japanese Americans.

Annie kept her arms at her sides, relaxing her right hand so he could feel free to take it. However, after walking for several minutes in silence, her hand still dangled.

"I'm being transferred," he said.

She stopped, sure she'd misheard him.

"They've activated the United States Armed Forces in the British Isles. The chief surgeon asked that I help with the medical planning because of my experience with evacuating the wounded and—"

"I'll go with you," said Annie.

"No."

"But I have more experience than you do operating under conditions of war."

"I'm aware."

"Do you think I'm too old? Because I'm pretty sure I kept up when—"

"Of course I don't think you're too old. I just don't want you in England where bombs are dropping every day. I won't allow it."

"You won't allow it?" She wanted to scream. "I'll go over your head."

"Won't matter. The only way you can go is if I specifically request your transfer."

"Then make the damn request."

"Not under any circumstances. Even if you despise me for the rest of your life."

Devastated, she took a step back.

"I leave at dawn. Captain Metcalfe will assume command of the hospital. I know he's not your favorite person, but he's an excellent surgeon."

"Is that why you came to find me?" Annie crossed her arms. "To inform me of the new chain of command?"

"Partly. But I also wanted you to know you're the best nurse I've ever worked with."

"Then let me come with you," she said, her voice strangled by the unacceptable notion of never seeing him again.

"You need to stay here, Annie. Find your friend and finish your tour of duty. Hawaii is a beautiful place when it's not being bombed." He gave her his signature sardonic smile.

This was going to happen. He was leaving. "Promise me you'll come back to this beautiful place."

"No one can make promises in wartime, Annie. Everything's too unpredictable." He took her face in his hands. "But I can promise that I will miss you every minute of every day." He kissed her on the forehead. "Goodbye, Annie."

"See you on the other side of the war…David." She watched him walk away until there was nothing left to watch.

TWENTY-SEVEN

October 23, 1942

Since Captain Metcalfe had taken over for Major Lance—and been promoted to major himself—Annie and her nurses had met frequently in the supply closet. It was a good place for her nurses to rant about Major Metcalfe's autocratic management style. Annie would always let them feel heard and promise to be more of a buffer when possible. However, being said buffer had caused some strain between Annie and Metcalfe, so she was more than surprised when he informed her that she'd been recommended for a Purple Heart—until he clarified that it had been Major Lance who'd made the recommendation before he left for England. Annie had felt deeply moved, but she knew no other woman in the U.S. Army had ever received the award and quickly put it out of her mind, believing it would never come to fruition. However, a few weeks later, Metcalfe told her that her presence would be required at the official award ceremony.

It took a few days for the reality to sink in. Partly because, after a fairly decent job of congratulating her, Metcalfe had said, "I suppose performing surgery, saving who knows how many lives, is valued less than organizing the flow of patients into my operating room." Annie had been grateful she was already speechless.

Annie gave her nurses the news in the supply closet, followed quickly by a qualifier. "This honor isn't just mine. It belongs to all of us." She looked at Monica, Irene, Sara, Winnie, and Kathy, grateful they would all be allowed to attend the ceremony. "I could not have succeeded in carrying out my duties that day without all of you. I couldn't be prouder of your courage, your professionalism, and the compassion you showed our patients."

Monica and Kathy applauded her award, while Winnie, Irene, and Sara wept.

Three days later, all Annie's nurses had tears in their eyes as the new commander at Hickam Field read from her Purple Heart citation. "During the attack, Lieutenant Fox, in an exemplary manner, performed her duties as head nurse of the station hospital. She worked ceaselessly with coolness and efficiency, and her fine example of calmness, courage, and leadership was of great benefit to the morale of all with whom she came in contact." Pausing, the commander spoke to Annie's nurses. "Your chief is the first woman to receive the oldest U.S. military award. Our founding father, General George Washington, first awarded the Purple Heart to three soldiers who fought with distinction in the Continental Army during the American Revolution. Back then, it was a cloth badge—purple and heart-shaped—that the soldier wore over his left breast." He held up the new Purple Heart—a heart-shaped cameo of George Washington that hung from a wide purple ribbon. "I present this to First Lieutenant Annie Gayton Fox for valorous service in the U.S. Army during the worst attack on our soil by a foreign nation."

Annie's nurses applauded her for the second time in a week, and she thought how perfect the moment would be if only Kay and her major had also been there to share it.

It had taken several months for Annie to feel comfortable enough to surf without Irene, who had been a very patient teacher. Not that Annie was completely alone. Other surfers who chose sunrise as their favorite time of day to surf had carried their boards beyond the barbed wire fencing to the beach, which wasn't home to anyone but surfers at this time of the morning.

Some came early, not just because the waves were better but because they wanted to keep watch for Japanese Zeros. They didn't trust the military to warn them in time. Not after what had happened on December 7. Others came early because they thought the Japanese would attack at sunset so as not to repeat themselves. Almost all the surfers Annie had spoken to—none of whom knew she was Army—still believed the Japanese would be back. And if surfing a good wave was the last thing they did, then so be it.

However, today was different. Today the surfers hadn't done as much surveilling of their surroundings because they knew the enemy was busy licking their wounds. Thanks to the work of American code breakers, the U.S. Navy was able to successfully carry out a surprise attack on the larger Japanese fleet. The enemy had lost the Battle of Midway in June and, with it, their claim to dominance in the Pacific. Many thought the victory had turned the tide of the war.

Paddling out, Annie stopped and looked to her right. In the distance, she could see Pearl Harbor. Despite an army of engineers, welders, carpenters, pipe fitters, and divers who had been dispatched to the harbor, the crippled ships were still visible. It would take many more months to fix them all. Yet even the damaged ships appeared peaceful in the stillness of the water that reflected a pearl-pink sky. Perhaps the dead who rested beneath that still water were somehow aware of the Midway victory—and smaller ones that had followed—that could not have been fought by their brothers and sisters without some thoughts of atonement.

As she always did when waiting for the right wave, Annie thought of David. Now that he was no longer her commanding officer, she could imagine the major as more. She had received several letters from him, telling her about their work to open a six-hundred-bed emergency medical services hospital in Bristol, England. They were working to open more medical installations in several other English towns to serve the steady stream of U.S. troops in the European theatre.

As soon as she received a letter, Annie would write back. She told him the hospital was running well under Metcalfe's leadership, though she could have written that it was running well *despite* his leadership. In fact, he was much better in the operating room than in the office, where Annie had assumed many of his administrative duties. She also kept David apprised of her search for Kay as well as her children.

Thanks to Kay's neighbor Ivy and her connection to the governor's office, Annie had been able to find out that after spending three months at an "assembly center" in Portland, Oregon, which Ivy had called a makeshift concentration camp, Kay's mother and children had recently been relocated to an internment camp in Heart Mountain, Wyoming. All she knew about that camp so far was that the military was trying to recruit young Japanese American men there. To the military's surprise, many said they'd rather stay than risk their lives for the country that had put them in the camp.

Ivy had also promised to find out what she could about Kay and had been able to tell Annie that she was being held at Fort Lincoln in Bismarck, North Dakota. However, they were planning to transfer them later that fall. Ivy promised to keep Annie posted. As soon as she had an address, Annie would write to Kay and tell her about the children. But Ivy warned that her letters would likely be read by people from the Immigration and Naturalization Service so to be very careful about what she wrote, for Kay's sake as well as her own.

Mak had been relieved to find out exactly where Kay was being held, and Annie had to talk him out of going to North Dakota. There was no point. He couldn't break her out of Fort Lincoln, nor would the Army let a civilian visit her in the camp, and the community center Kay had created would collapse without him. There were still some Japanese Americans on the island, and they would only go to the center for their healthcare needs. Now more than ever, they believed white hospitals could not be trusted.

Annie turned her board so she could catch the next wave that looked challenging without being death-defying. She would write to Kay about her new hobby and promise to teach her how to surf when she came home. When the war was over, they would all come home. Kay and her children. And David, who Annie missed with every breath she took.

Paddling fast, Annie rose and spread her arms. She felt like she was flying. She felt as if no one could catch her. Yet she kept her eyes on the horizon, searching for planes. Whenever she saw one come close, she would watch until she was sure it didn't have a rising sun on its wings. She'd come to accept the fact that she would watch for that harbinger of death and destruction until the day she died.

EPILOGUE

February 3, 1946

Annie couldn't believe that almost two years had passed since she'd last heard from him. The last letter from Lieutenant Colonel David Lance had arrived on June 14, 1944. For the rest of her life, Annie would feel bereft every June 14, even when she was too old to remember what David had looked like when she'd last seen him.

The letter was four pages long, but Annie had only skimmed everything beyond the first paragraph. She kept the letter in a locked box with her passport and other important papers and thought that one day, when she could stand it, she would read it more carefully. For now, it wasn't necessary. She understood the basic premise: David was getting married. Her name was Madeleine. At least it wasn't Peggy.

As soon as Annie read the letter, she told Major Metcalfe she was ill, which was no lie, and drove to Honolulu. She waited until the community center closed and then told Mak he needed to take her to their favorite tiki bar, where she consumed enough okolehao to anesthetize her for major surgery. Before she got to the point where she was too inebriated to speak, she told Mak what she could remember from his letter.

David had written that his younger brother, Michael, had been badly wounded at the Battle of Normandy. He'd been part of the 101st U.S. Airborne that had landed near Utah Beach. David had gone to France to oversee his care. He was at his bedside day and night, along with Michael's nurse, Madeleine. When his brother succumbed to his injuries, she'd helped David through his grief. Annie told Mak she didn't remember the rest of the letter. It was something about realizing he wanted children, which Madeleine could provide. They would be married soon, and she would go with him to England so he could resume work on creating more medical stations with their allies.

When Annie woke up in Mak's bed the next morning—he'd slept on his couch—she'd apologized more than once for making him deal with her emotional wreckage as if she were a teenage girl. He'd waved away her apology. She'd listened to him go on and on about missing Kay more times than he could count. It was then, her head pounding from hangover hell, that Annie realized how close she and Mak had become.

The bond they had formed with every shared hour they'd spent at the community center or talking about Kay only strengthened after Annie's retirement in December 1945, when she officially became a full-time nurse at the center. That was also the day she'd moved into Kay's apartment. As soon as Shizuko and the children were taken, she and Mak had joined forces to pay Kay's rent while she was gone. Occasionally, Annie had stayed there on the weekends if she worked at the center.

When she officially moved off the Army base and into Kay's apartment, she stayed in Beth's room and kept everything the way she'd left it, down to school papers Beth had left on her small desk. Not that Beth would need to learn fourth-grade multiplication tables by the time she returned. It was accepted by all, though not discussed, that the Japanese Americans who had been relocated would not return until the war was over.

But the war had ended in September, and no one who had left four years ago on those buses had come home yet. Still, Annie held out hope that she would see her friend soon and that Kay would reunite with her children and mother.

Annie was in an exam room at the center stitching up a finger accidently sliced by a cutting knife when she heard Mak shout something indecipherable. She quickly finished with her patient and ran to the kitchen to find Mak sitting on a stool, head in his hands, weeping.

"Mak, what is it?" she asked, putting her arm around him. She wondered if his mother, who'd been struggling with a heart condition since the day of the attack, had died.

He looked up at her and said, "Kay... She's coming home."

It was the news she'd been praying for so long, yet Annie couldn't quite believe it. Only when Mak embraced her did it sink in, and her tears of joy joined his.

Six days later, they picked Kay up at the airport. Annie stood back, letting Mak embrace her first. For a moment, she let herself imagine what it would feel like to embrace the major after so long apart. She no longer thought of him as David, because that was who he was to his wife, or Lieutenant Colonel, because that was who he was when she was still in the Army. But Annie's time with her major had been hers, and she would never forget it.

When Kay finally let go of Mak and turned to Annie and they put their arms around each other, they both began to cry. For lost time and lasting friendship.

On the day Kay's children were expected home, Annie had dropped Kay off at the bus station and left, wanting Kay to have this reunion all to herself.

As she waited, Kay wondered, not for the first time over the past four years, about how her children might have changed. Tommy had only been six years old when she'd last seen him. At six, she could get away with calling him her baby because he still had that faint baby smell at the back of his neck. He'd liked to cuddle and didn't complain when she kissed him. His biggest concern in life was when the next issue of the Captain America comic book was coming out. Beth, on the other hand, was thirteen and entering puberty. Getting her period was one of the biggest events in a girl's life, and Kay might have missed it. Shizuko had never told her daughter what to expect, though maybe it was because she hadn't expected Kay to have her first period at the age of eleven. Kay had planned to explain everything to Beth on her tenth birthday. All she could hope was that her own mother had learned her lesson and explained things to Beth in time.

The bus pulled into the lot, and Kay wanted to push past

everyone blocking her way, but they had also been anxiously waiting for the return of loved ones, so she stood her ground, watching as people embraced the lives that had been stolen from them.

Finally, Kay saw her family disembark, Beth in the lead.

Beth was thirteen and no longer a young girl. Not only was she nearly as tall as her mother, she was beginning to look like the lovely young woman she would become. Tommy stepped off the bus right behind his sister. At the age of ten, the cuteness that had defined his face had been replaced by features that would define him as a man. He had his father's straight nose and held himself like his father had—tall and without apology.

Kay wondered when she would tell them about their father. Two years ago, Kay had received notification that her husband had been killed in action. The where and when had been redacted from the official letter, so she would never be able to tell her children exactly how he'd died, other than the fact that he had been fighting for Japan. She really didn't want to know if he'd been an active part of that awful Sunday in December. Either way, she would wait another few days before telling her children. When she did, Kay would mourn the loss with them. Daiji had been a good father—until he'd decided to join the Emperor's crusade for world domination. He'd also been a decent husband. It hadn't entirely been his fault that Kay had fallen in love with someone else.

All the months Kay had spent away had given her perspective on what was important moving forward. Beth and Tommy would always come first, and she loved her mother dearly. She also loved the community center she'd created and the man who'd helped her build it. Kay could not imagine a future without Mak in it. After the children had had time to cope with the death of their father and Kay's return, she would talk to them about her feelings for Mak.

Tommy held his hand out for Shizuko, who slowly got off the bus, and both he and Beth let their grandmother walk ahead of them. Embracing her, Kay felt the bones under her mother's skin and thought how frail she'd become over the past four years. "Thank you for taking such good care of my children," she whispered.

"You don't need to thank me," said Shizuko. "They're my grandchildren."

Kay kissed her mother's cheek, tasting a salty tear, and then reached out with both arms for her children. They stood there, arms wrapped around each other, like they were making sure the moment was real. Keeping hold of each child's hand, Kay said, "Let's go home."

"Kaya, we have no home," said Shizuko.

Kay herded them into the waiting taxi, ignoring every question about where they were going until the taxi pulled up to the apartment building they'd left four years ago. She paid the driver and ignored her mother, who kept whispering that this wouldn't be good for the children. It would only remind them of what they had lost.

When they got to the door of their apartment, Shizuko stopped. Music could be heard from inside. "Someone's home," she said. "We shouldn't disturb them."

"I thought we'd just ask if they kept any of our things." Kay looked at the children.

"I don't need my old stuff," said Beth unconvincingly. "It was for kids."

"Yeah," said Tommy. "Let's go."

"Well, there's a necklace I'd like to have back, and I'm going to see if it's still there." Kay watched her family cringe collectively as she knocked.

A few moments later, the door opened, and Kay pulled her family inside. She grinned as they all stared open-mouthed at their old apartment, which looked as if they'd just left to take in a movie. Except for the balloons. And the cake on the kitchen table. And Mak, who grinned back at Kay from where he stood next to Annie, who couldn't stop her tears of joy.

At last, they were all back where they belonged.

NOTES

The courage of women

Annie Gayton Fox was born on August 4, 1893, in Pubnico, Nova Scotia, to Charles James Fox, MD, and Deidamia (Annie) Gayton Fox. She joined the U.S. Army Nurse Corps in 1918 and served during the last year of World War I. After serving in various posts for more than twenty years as an Army nurse, she was promoted to first lieutenant and was transferred to Hickam Field in November 1941—one month before the devastating attack, during which she served as chief nurse for the only functioning medical facility between Pearl Harbor and Hickam Field. On that day, she oversaw the care of hundreds of wounded servicemen and women, leading her small team of nurses through the darkest day of their lives with strength, grace, and compassion. She organized all those who tended to the wounded and dying, including military wives and civilian volunteers. In addition to administering anesthesia during surgeries, she took care of the wounded, along with her nurses.

On October 26, 1942, Lieutenant Annie Fox became the first

woman to receive the Purple Heart for her courage under fire during the attack on Pearl Harbor and Hickam Field, which began World War II.

Later, the criteria for a Purple Heart changed so that only those who were injured in action were given the award. In 1944, her Purple Heart was rescinded and replaced with a Bronze Star, with the same citation.

Promoted to the rank of major, Annie retired from active duty after the war ended, on December 31, 1945, and eventually settled in San Diego, California. Annie never married. She died in 1987 at the age of ninety-three.

Monica Conter reported for duty at 7:00 a.m. on December 7, 1941, and served heroically. After the war, she left nursing to raise three children. Monica passed away at the age of ninety-seven and is buried beside her husband, U.S. Army Ranger Lieutenant Colonel Bernard (Barney) Benning—a Pearl Harbor survivor—in Arlington Cemetery.

Sara Entrikin transferred to Hickam Hospital so she could be closer to her twin sister, Helen, who was stationed at Pearl Harbor. Sara and Helen both survived the attack and made careers of the military, retiring as a major and lieutenant commander, respectively.

Irene Boyd, Kathy Coberly, and **Winnie Mallett** were also Army nurses at Hickam Hospital and never left their patients or their posts during a bombardment that lasted for more than an hour. They cared for their patients through the day and night and the tense days that followed, never knowing if they would need to survive another nightmare scenario.

The **U.S. Army Nurse Corps** had fewer than 1,000 nurses on December 7, 1941. Eighty-two Army nurses were stationed in Hawaii, serving at three Army medical facilities that day. By the end of World War II, more than 59,000 American nurses had served in the Army Nurse Corps. They received 1,619 medals, citations, and commendations during the war, including sixteen medals that were awarded posthumously to women who died from enemy fire. Lieutenant Fox and her thousands of fellow nurses exemplified the courage and dedication of all who served.

More Hickam Hospital heroes

Three Filipino orderlies—Maguleno Jucor, Torihio Kendica, and Cosme Echanis—literally ran through gunfire to get to Hickam Hospital and do their jobs. Their help that day was invaluable.

The generous women on Hotel Street

After the attack on Pearl Harbor, Hickam Field, and other military installations on the island of Oahu, the sex workers on Hotel Street donated gallons of blood, assisted nurses, and turned one of the brothels into a makeshift medical ward.

A moral left when we should have turned right

Just hours after the attack on Pearl Harbor and Hickam Field, the FBI began arresting nearly 1,300 Japanese American community and religious leaders. Those who were arrested were transferred to prison camps in Montana, New Mexico, and North Dakota. Like the fictional Kaya Kimura, many of the real people (mostly men) who were arrested were held for the duration of the war and were unable to contact their families. With the exception of a German immigrant who was convicted of espionage, not a single one of the internees or detainees was found guilty of covert acts against U.S. laws. Moreover, not one was investigated for sabotage, and only a few were suspected of espionage.

After the attack on Pearl Harbor, nearly 130,000 Japanese Americans—anyone who was at least one-sixteenth Japanese— including 17,000 children under the age of ten, were gathered and taken to internment camps. Open from 1942 to 1946, the camps, called "relocation centers," were surrounded by armed guards and barbed wire. These centers were referred to in many government documents as "concentration camps."

Even for those who were not detained in camps, martial law was imposed for everyone on the island of Oahu and lasted for nearly three years—from December 7, 1941, until October 24, 1944. Civil liberties were substantially limited, food was rationed, liquor was strictly controlled, and a curfew and blackout were put in place. Additional restrictions were placed on enemy aliens, mainly the Japanese, who were restricted from traveling or changing residences without permission and could not meet in groups of more than ten. They were also ordered to turn in all firearms, flashlights, portable radios, cameras, and other items. Japanese fishermen were even forbidden to go to sea lest they commit espionage.

Violations of martial law as well as other crimes were tried before military courts, which had replaced the civil courts. It was common for an individual to be arrested, tried, and sentenced in the same day. In all, the military courts collected more than $1 million in fines during the war and imprisoned hundreds of civilians.

In 1976, Executive Order 9066 was formally rescinded and in 1988, the Civil Liberties Act was passed, awarding $20,000 each to more than eighty thousand Japanese Americans, along with a formal presidential apology. In offering a "sincere apology" to those whose lives had been forever changed by the order, President George H. W. Bush stated that their fellow Americans had "renewed their commitment to the ideals of freedom, equality, and justice."

Hickam Field and Pearl Harbor

The attack on U.S. military installations on the island of Oahu resulted in the loss of 2,403 Sailors, Airmen, Marines, Soldiers, and civilians, including seven children and two infants. In addition, more than 1,100 were injured. Battleships still lie at the bottom of Pearl Harbor, while the ruins of U.S. airpower were scattered over Oahu's airfields—the majority at Hickam Field.

Due to the incredible tenacity of the military and civilian workforce, of the twenty-one ships that had been damaged or sunk on December 7, all but three were salvaged and helped the United States fight their way to victory in 1945. At Hickam Field, the base recovered and served as the hub of the Pacific aerial network.

Between 1948 and 2010, the Air Force operated the renamed Hickam Air Force Base as the primary U.S. mobility hub in the Pacific, supporting U.S. operations by servicing transient aircraft and facilitating the deployment, return, and supply of service members in Korea, Vietnam, the Middle East, and those on humanitarian missions.

On October 1, 2010, Pearl Harbor joined with Hickam Air Force Base to become Joint Base Pearl Harbor-Hickam (JBPHH), combining the two historic bases into a single joint installation to support both Air Force and Navy missions in the Pacific.

READING GROUP GUIDE

1. War brings out the worst in people, but it can also bring out the best. Discuss the ways in which both of these sentiments are true throughout the book.

2. How do you think Annie's experience in World War I and her inherently cool demeanor help her in her role? Do they hurt her in any way?

3. Should Annie have told Kay what she saw written on her son's back?

4. Do you think Kay's and Mak's reluctance to trust Annie after they found out she was Army was warranted?

5. Had you ever heard of Hickam Field before? If not, do you think this fact is a disservice to those who served there?

6. Another part of U.S. history that is largely ignored is the

government's usurping of Hawaii in order to set up a strong military installation to help defend against potential enemies in that part of the world. What are your feelings on this?

7. When Daiji pushed Kay to bring their children to Japan, why do you think Kay was adamant they stay in the United States?

8. What do you think the Japanese American nurses' willingness to help the American soldiers at Hickam despite the soldiers' objections says about them?

9. In what ways do Annie's leadership abilities stand out?

10. The detention of thousands of Japanese Americans in concentration camps in the United States following the bombing of Pearl Harbor and Hickam Field is not a well-known part of American history. Did you learn about this in school? Should it be taught today?

11. In his defense of the concentration camps, Major Lance says that "keeping them [Japanese] separate will protect them from people who see them as the enemy." Do you think this is a legitimate reason for the U.S. government's actions?

12. Annie's age is relevant to the story in that she thinks she was sent to Hickam Field as a step toward retirement. Is ageism still a factor in a woman's career path today?

A CONVERSATION WITH
THE AUTHOR

**How did you first encounter Annie's story? What made you decide
to write about her?**

I first saw Annie's name while at work. I'm a medical writer for the
VA Boston Healthcare System, and I was writing an article about a new
telemental health app called Annie—a messaging service that allows
veterans to take a more active role in their care. Messages you receive
from the Annie app include tips for reducing stress and how to prepare
for appointments. In writing the article, I found out it was named after
U.S. Army Lieutenant Annie Fox, the first woman to be awarded a
Purple Heart. On the other hand (or gender), the first man to receive
the modern-day Purple Heart was General Douglas MacArthur, who's
been portrayed by actors that include Gregory Peck, Tommy Lee Jones,
and Liam Neeson.

There are several reasons I wanted to write this story. First, Annie
was a nurse. Like teachers, it's an often thankless but essential job,
especially during a war—or a pandemic. Second, I'd never heard of
Hickam Field, and no one I knew had either. And third, my father

served in World War II as a pharmacist's mate on an aircraft carrier in the South Pacific. He'd spoken to me about his service only once. At the age of nine, I'd broken my arm badly, and as a distraction on the way to the hospital, he told me about the kamikazes that had hit his ship. He never spoke of it again, but I knew it had to have had a profound effect on him.

Tell us about your research process when writing this book.

For me, research means getting on an internet search engine where one discovery leads to another. When I first began writing—back in the dark ages when writers used libraries—the process was much slower and therefore not as comprehensive. Now, if you hone your detective/computer skills, it can be fast and full of intriguing surprises. It certainly was during my search for information about Hickam Field. U.S. government records and reports with firsthand accounts of the day of the attack were particularly helpful.

Real life is often much stranger than fiction, which is why I enjoy the research part of writing. For example, I discovered that a Japanese banker "hosted" the dance at the officers' club the night before the attack and that the waitresses wore kimonos. I nearly didn't include it in the novel because I thought those details were too ironic. The scene in which I describe the morgue at Queen's Hospital—when Annie sees the civilian casualties—came from actual descriptions I'd read. Samuel Baker is also based on a real soldier who sacrificed himself in the most heroic but tragic way, and Chaplain Elmer Tiedt really was told that his wife had died and later found out she was alive. I stayed as close to true events as I could, because it does give historical fiction a necessary degree of authenticity.

What was the most surprising thing you learned about Annie while doing research for this book?

The most surprising thing was that there wasn't much to find. From the paucity of information about her service on December 7, 1941, other than her award citation and a few mentions of her in accounts of that day, I can only assume that Annie didn't think she'd done anything extraordinary. I think she was military to her core and thought she was simply doing her duty, as anyone else in her position would have done.

The other thing I found surprising was that Annie was born in Canada, yet she chose to leave her country and become a U.S. Army nurse. This was an amazingly bold move for a young woman in the early twentieth century. Annie left her family, home, and country to serve in World War I—for the United States—and continued to serve in World War II. She also chose to lead an unconventional life for a woman in her time in that she served in the Army until she retired and never married or had children. I think she considered herself married to the Army, and the nurses under her command were like her children. On December 7, when her nurses were in danger, she did everything she could to keep them safe while still allowing them to do their duty. I'd call that first-rate parenting.

What was your path to becoming a writer? Did you always know you wanted to be a novelist?

My mother told me that the first thing I wrote about—at the age of eight—was a cat. I don't remember the story, but I was allergic to cats and had asthma as a child, so my guess is that I wrote about a cat after an unfortunate encounter that resulted in me getting a shot of adrenaline. The poor cat was likely the villain of my story. Point being that I've always wanted to be a writer. I went to Roger Williams University in Bristol, Rhode Island, and graduated with a BFA in creative writing. My first short story was published shortly after graduation, which gave me a bit of confidence that I was on the right path.

I earned my master's degree in professional writing and publishing at Emerson College, where I fell in love with screenwriting. Living on the East Coast was and still is a disadvantage; however, over the years, I had a few successes along with many, many rejections. Nevertheless, I learned how to take notes from producers, how to manage expectations (keep them low, because screenplays rarely get produced), and how to tell a story that will keep an audience engaged. I also learned that it's very much a collaboration. So I left room on the pages for the director, actors, set designers, cinematographers, etc., to add their own voices. But when I write a novel, the only voices I need to make room for are those of the characters in my story. There's a wonderful freedom in that but also more responsibility. And many more blank pages to fill.

What does your writing process look like? Do you outline before you write? Or do you let the story progress organically?

The most important part of the writing process is choosing what to write about. A writing professor once told me not to write unless I have something important to say. I try to follow that advice. I also look for something that will hold my interest for several months. If I get tired of reading my story, so will everyone else.

As far as the writing process itself, I use a somewhat unconventional outline that also leaves room to write organically. *The Woman with a Purple Heart* is based on a screenplay I wrote titled *Hickam*. The screenplay is about 120 pages in length and provided a good outline of where my story and characters were going. Then I got to color in the lines. This part of the process is more organic, and it's when the magic can happen. It's when you don't feel like you're writing but rather like you're taking dictation. All you need to do is listen—and type.

I'm fortunate in that I have several screenplays that I've written over the years that I can use as outlines for novels. However, I wouldn't recommend learning to write a screenplay just to have a detailed outline. Too much work. Seriously.

What books are you reading these days?

I always have a stack of books on my bedside table. I literally get anxious if I don't have at least three books in my queue. I'm currently reading *Demon Copperhead* by Barbara Kingsolver. Next up are *Shutter* by Ramona Emerson, *The School for Good Mothers* by Jessamine Chan, and *The Ship of Brides* by Jojo Moyes.

I also keep a stack of nonfiction books. I just finished *The Choice* by Edith Eva Eger, an openhearted and honest memoir. Next up is *Quiet: The Power of Introverts in a World That Can't Stop Talking* by Susan Cain, and *The Facemaker: One Surgeon's Battle to Mend the Disfigured Soldiers of World War I* by Lindsey Fitzharris.

BIBLIOGRAPHY

Arakaki, Leatrice R., and John R. Kuborn. *7 December 1941: An Air Force Story*. Hickam Air Force Base, Hawaii: Pacific Air Forces, Office of History, 1991. https://media.defense.gov/2010/Sep/17/2001329818/-1/-1/0/AFD-100917–040.pdf.

Arakaki, Leatrice R., and John R. Kuborn. "Medical Memories from December 7, 1941: Attack on Pearl Harbor." Air Force Medical Service. December 7, 2017. https://www.airforcemedicine.af.mil/News/Display/Article/1390929/medical-memories-from-dec-7–1941-attack-on-pearl-harbor/.

"At Pearl Harbor, Japanese Americans Were Victims of the Attack—and Their Own Government." The World. December 9, 2016. https://theworld.org/stories/2016-12-09/pearl-harbor-japanese-americans-were-victims-attack-and-their-own-government.

Borgquist, Daryl S. "Advance Warning? The Red Cross Connection." *Naval History Magazine* 13, no. 3 (June 1999). https://www.usni.org/magazines/naval-history-magazine/1999/june/advance-warning-red-cross-connection.

"The Bravery of Army Nurse Annie G. Fox at Pearl Harbor." National Women's History Museum. December 5, 2016. https://www.womenshistory.org/articles/bravery-army-nurse-annie-g-fox-pearl-harbor.

Cannon, Lou. "Debunking Myths About the Attack." *Washington Post.* December 7, 1991. https://www.washingtonpost.com/archive /politics/1991/12/07/debunking-myths-about-the-attack/88509 bae-94be-48bd-a2fe-a251a52385c8/.

"Eye Witness Accounts of Bombing of Hickam AFB." Hawaii Aviation. Accessed January 22, 2023. https://aviation.hawaii.gov/world-war-ii /december-7–1941/eye-witness-accounts-of-bombing- of-hickam-afb/.

"History and Culture." Hono'uli'uli National Historic Site. January 4, 2017. https://www.nps.gov/hono/learn/historyculture/index.htm.

"Immigration and Relocation in U.S. History: Japanese: Behind the Wire." Library of Congress. Accessed January 22, 2023. https://www.loc.gov /classroom-materials/immigration/japanese/behind-the-wire/.

"Japanese-American Incarceration During World War II." Educator Resources, National Archives. Accessed January 22, 2023. https:// www.archives.gov/education/lessons/japanese-relocation#background.

Kaye, Harold. "Hickam Field, 7 December 1941—The First U.S. Army Air Corps Flying Fortress (B-17D) Combat Mission in World War II." *Aerospace Historian* 33, no. 4 (December 1986).

Matthews, Lopez, Zachary Dabbs, and Eliza Mbughuni. "Remembering Pearl Harbor…70 Years Later." *Prologue Magazine* 43, no. 4 (Winter 2011). https://www.archives.gov/publications/prologue/2011/winter /ph-decklogs.html.

Niiya, Brian. "Fort Lincoln (Bismarck) (detention facility)." Densho Encyclopedia. June 7, 2021. https://encyclopedia.densho.org /Fort_Lincoln_(Bismarck)_(detention_facility)/.

"Pearl Harbor Navy Medical Activities." In *The United States Navy Medical Department at War, 1941–1945*, 1:1–31. Washington, DC: Administrative History Section, Administrative Division, Bureau of

Medicine and Surgery, 1946. https://www.ibiblio.org/hyperwar/USN /rep/Pearl/Medical.html.

"Personal Narrative: Monica Benning Collection." Veterans History Project, American Folklife Center, Library of Congress. Accessed January 22, 2023. https://www.loc.gov/item/afc2001001.74157/.

Scheiber, Jane, and Harry Scheiber. "Martial Law in Hawaii." Densho Encyclopedia. July 22, 2020. https://encyclopedia.densho.org /Martial_law_in_Hawaii/.

ACKNOWLEDGMENTS

I have loved spending time with Annie and her nurses, Kay, Mak, and Major Lance. And I'm so grateful to have learned about the many real-life heroes of Hickam Field.

I would never have known about Lieutenant Annie Fox or Hickam Field if not for my "day" job as a medical writer. As part of VA's Health Services Research & Development Service for more than twenty years, I have come to know many VA doctors and nurses—clinicians and/or researchers—all dedicated to improving the health and care of veterans. The VA health care system has come a long way since *Born on the Fourth of July*. I think Annie would be proud to work in a VA hospital today.

I want to thank my first writing teachers: Martha Christina, Geoffrey Clark, and Bob McRoberts. Part of the creative writing program at Roger Williams University when I was a student in the late 1980s, they gave me confidence that I was on the right path. I think they'd be happy to know I'd returned to writing novels. I owe them a collective "You were right."

I also want to thank my kindred spirits in writing: Gail Mackenzie-Smith and Mike McGeever. Over the last seventeen years, we have seen each other through the ups and downs of writing and of life in general. If I'd been an Army nurse at Hickam Hospital on December 7, 1941, there's no one else I'd rather have served with than Gail and Mike, two of the bravest and kindest people I know.

I've also very grateful to my agent, Mark Gottlieb at Trident Media Group in New York City. I will always follow his lead because he led me to Sourcebooks and Erin McClary, editor extraordinaire. Many thanks to Erin for her wise counsel, especially in regard to giving Kay more pages of her own.

Last but never least, I want to thank my husband, Rich, for never, ever losing faith. He bought me my first typewriter (back in the dark ages)—and my first computer—despite having trouble paying the rent. He also helped me deliver the three best people I know into the world. My daughter, April, an amazing teacher and writer and my first reader/editor. My son Rich, a multitalented designer and, more importantly, an exceptional father to Violet and Julian. And my son Pete, whose songs can lift my spirits no matter how far into the proverbial abyss I've fallen. He is a true artist.

ABOUT THE AUTHOR

© James P. Jones

Diane Hanks has a BFA in Creative Writing from Roger Williams University and an MA in Professional Writing & Publishing from Emerson College in Boston, Massachusetts. A medical writer by day, she has written numerous screenplays and recently returned to her first love—writing novels. Diane also is a mentor for the Writers Guild Initiative, which makes the art of storytelling accessible to underserved populations.